TEXAS FORSAKEN

LONE STAR REDEMPTION

BOOK ONE

SHERRY SHINDELAR

WILD HEART
BOOKS

Unless otherwise indicated, all Scripture quotations are taken from the Holy Bible, Kings James Version.

Cover design by: Carpe Librum Book Design

ISBN:

PRAISE FOR SHERRY SHINDELAR

In *Texas Forsaken* Sherry Shindelar captures the physical conflicts and moral conundrums of war, on the windswept Texas plains, the eastern battlefields of the Civil War, and the contested ground between two hearts. Fans of captivity narratives will find this sympathetically rendered callback to the true stories come down to us through history a heart-tugger, with its vibrant leads and redemptive themes of love and duty, guilt and forgiveness.

— LORI BENTON, CHRISTY-AWARD WINNING AUTHOR OF *BURNING SKY* AND OTHER HISTORICAL NOVELS

This book is dedicated to my husband for his unwavering support.
And to my mother who has always believed in me.

CHAPTER 1

September 1860
Pease River, Texas

Eyes-Like-Sky's arms ached. She had spent the morning beneath a gnarled hackberry cleaning the buffalo hide. Granular bits of dirt and gristle bored into her bare knees below the bottom of her bunched skirt. Better her knees take the brunt of the filth than her buckskin garment.

No whimpers or babble from Little Star today to keep her company. Owl Woman, her husband's mother, had volunteered to watch the baby for the morning. The infant would enjoy a chance to escape the cradleboard and wiggle her tiny limbs.

Blushes of red and yellow wove their tapestry across the patches of oaks and cottonwoods, turning their leaves into brightly colored jewels. Autumn—despite the sprigs of new growth poking up amongst the withered grasses. There was much to be done before winter swooped south from the northern plains. A buffalo robe and new moccasins to finish, not to mention a season's supply of pemmican to preserve—

A shout cut the air. A distant war whoop crackled on the

breeze billowing across the narrow valley. Tomopuikatukatu, Eyes-Like-Sky, froze in mid-scrape, her fingers curled around the pumice stone. From within the Comanche camp, more cries rang out, bouncing off the rust-colored canyon walls. The raiding party had been sighted. She pushed up off the half-treated hide. Her husband, Dancing Eagle, would be with them. Her heart galloped.

Grease coated her arms and clothing. She grimaced. It didn't matter that Dancing Eagle would understand. She knelt and rubbed her hands against the grass, wiping away the minced basswood bark and buffalo brains she used for softening the hides. The warriors would stop to deck themselves in full regalia and paint before entering camp. Even their horses would be decorated for the victorious entry. Time enough for her to get clean.

With a change of clothes laid on the bank, she stepped over the sprawling roots of a cottonwood tree and into the creek. The cool water pricked her skin as she plunged to the center and scrubbed with the sponge Dancing Eagle had gifted her from his raid into Mexico last spring. He never mentioned how many Mexicans had died. He wouldn't discuss it this time either. Except this time, it might be Texans. She would see the horses and the cattle. The whole village would celebrate with a dance. And she'd celebrate too. That he'd come back alive. That maybe they'd instilled enough fear that their village would be left in peace. And that no one recalled she'd once been Texan too.

Yelps echoed through the stand of scrub oak behind her. Wringing the water out of her waist-length hair, she slushed to the bank and slipped her finest dress, doeskin as soft as a baby's cheek, over her head. She smoothed her hand over the turquoise beads, then buckled the silver belt above her waist. Fringes swayed against her arms as she tugged on her leggings.

Eyes-Like-Sky hummed as she stood. A tune from long ago,

the words forgotten. A chill shivered through her. She rubbed the thin scar on her wrist and touched another milky-white mark, wider, whiter on her forearm. Two of the seventeen scars that marked her body from her early days with the tribe. Her life before Dancing Eagle paid three ponies for her and took her to his lodge to be his wife.

But no, the song on her lips was older than that, further back in the fog of her mind than the years she'd spent as Old Wolf's slave. Before the Comanche captured her. Her head throbbed with the thought, as it did every time she tried to push aside the curtain of blackness that separated her from the before. With a sharp inhale, she pinched the flesh of her palm, digging her nails in deep, until the pain overshadowed the blurred memory.

More whoops and female voices chanted the songs of victory welcoming the warriors home. A hawk sprang from an overhead branch, pumping its wings in flight.

Eyes-Like-Sky scurried up the bank and wove her way toward the center square. Her heart thumped as loud as any drum. What if Dancing Eagle wasn't with them? She wouldn't even think it. He'd be here in minutes, safe and well. He'd take her in his arms...

Naked children toddled by her. Where was her own precious baby? Women young and old, along with the braves who hadn't gone out with the raiding party, flowed toward the edge of the hundred-lodge camp. The smells of bear grease, horse, and buffalo tallow assaulted her nose.

Scanning the crowd for Owl Woman, she dug a walnut-size jar out of the small pouch which swung from her belt, dipped her fingers into the vermillion, and smeared a streak across each cheekbone and then another line beneath each eyebrow. She wanted to look her finest for her husband. A heel mashed the toe of her moccasin as a brave elbowed forward. She stepped to the side as she scraped her painted finger over the edge of the jar and returned it to the pouch.

"Yeeeeee!" Charms-His-Horse galloped down the lane, leading the war party in full regalia. A bone breastplate covered his upper chest, and a gold medallion swung down the middle, clinking against the rows of cylinder-shaped bones and shells. The crowd roared as he reined in his pony. Three tepee-pole lengths from the center square, he raised his scalp pole high.

Eyes-Like-Sky's stomach shifted. Dancing Eagle would have his own pole, and he'd place it in their lodge. *Namatunetsu, fear is a weapon,* he'd told her. *We must create a taste so bitter in the mouths of our enemies and make their knees knock together at the very thought of the Comanche so they crawl back off our prairies and leave us be.* Peace and security...the longing of her heart. To have her husband near and raise their child without threat. How many lives would it cost?

Horse hooves pounded. An uncontainable smile spread across Eyes-Like-Sky's face. Dancing Eagle cantered down the lane on the back of a fine black stallion, in the honored second place. Her husband. Safe. Home. She stretched up on her toes. Blue swirls decorated the horse, matching the blue and black paint of Dancing Eagle's face, chest, and arms. His long, dark hair fell loose well past his shoulders. Two eagle feathers dangled from his scalp lock. His muscular body unmarred from battle, he wore nothing but a breechclout and red leggings. Handsome, free, and proud. Warmth flooded her cheeks as people cheered. How had she ever won the favor of the finest warrior of the band?

Other warriors followed, leading a small cluster of disheveled captives. Clothes torn and dirty from head to toe, the three Mexicans, one a girl on the threshold of womanhood, and two white children cowered as they were yanked off their horses. They'd be roped to the poles tonight, the center of the festivities. Only the children would be spared the humiliation and beatings. She winced and turned away. Not quick enough. A flash of memory. Bloodied rawhide digging into her wrists and ankles. Her whole body quivering beneath the lashes. Jeers pounding in her head. She had wished for death...

Eyes-Like-Sky shivered. A lifetime ago.

The crowd parted. Dancing Eagle reined his horse to a halt and extended his hand.

Her gasp spilled into a laugh as Comanche rolled off her tongue. "You cannot—"

His hand clasped hers and hauled her up. His left arm encircled her back and pulled her into his lap facing him. Blue and black paint smeared from Dancing Eagle's chest to her blouse.

"Who says I cannot?" he whispered against her hair.

"The chief. Tradition." But her arms slipped around him as the crowd cheered. Sweat and man and horse filled her nostrils. The nearness of him, the safety of his arms, melted the tension that had bound her neck and back ever since his departure.

His gaze roamed over her. "And where is our beautiful Little Star? I fear I've been gone so long she must be walking and talking by now."

"She wouldn't dare think of doing such a thing without you here to see her first step." She beamed. "Besides, she decided it'd be best to master sitting and standing first."

He chuckled.

Other warriors whooped past. Dancing Eagle shifted off the main lane, nudging his horse through a cluster of women.

He cupped his hand around her cheek. "I have missed you, Eyes-Like-Sky." His lips brushed hers, feather light at first, before his mouth overtook hers in hunger.

A few young warriors hooted and cheered.

Scratches and cuts, unseen from the ground, scraped her palms as she swept her hands over his arms and back.

"Tonight, after the dance..." He breathed in her ear and drew back a few inches.

She kissed his palm. "We could forget the festivities?" And the prisoners.

"My warriors would come looking for us. Besides, I couldn't bear to miss seeing my wife dance." His brown eyes shone.

Words of protest died in her throat. Dancing Eagle wouldn't understand how the thought of seeing the captives strung from the poles cinched her stomach into a knot.

Wood poked her legs.

Cane in hand and cradleboard on her back, Owl Woman stood by the horse. "Go say your welcomes elsewhere, my doves." She shuffled onto a patch of grass. Gray-streaked hair framed her kind face. "The baby's sleeping. I'll bring her to you by and by."

"If you say so, Mother." Dancing Eagle gathered his reins. "I'll take my bride to our lodge where she belongs." His smile widened as he turned his stallion through the outskirts of the crowd and down a worn path, sidestepping a drying rack filled with strips of meat.

Eyes-Like-Sky's foot bumped a burlap sack that swung from his saddle.

"I almost forgot. I brought you something." He reached into the burlap and dug a book out. "Your holy book." A battered Bible, the weathered edges of the pages crumbled and stained. "This time not for my shield."

A tremulous smile crept to her lips. The warriors stole every scrap of paper they could find to stuff between the two buffalo-hide sides of their shields for added protection. The cracked leather stung her hand as she accepted the Bible. Her head throbbed. The lettering blurred. The stain on the margins... blood? Surely not.

Did she think no one ever died on these raids?

Her hold loosened. She'd have dropped the book to the

ground if he hadn't been sitting there waiting for her approval of the gift.

He pulled her to him again, the book pressed between them. "I want nothing to do with the white man's God, and you are white no more. But if the Great Spirit speaks to you through these lines on the pages, then so be it."

Did the Great Spirit say anything to her heart at all anymore? Had He ever?

CHAPTER 2

October 1860
Pease River, TX

Captain Garret Ramsey crouched atop the sandstone bluff, his rifle clutched in his hands, thighs stiff from eighteen hours in the saddle. A norther pelted his face and field glasses with sand, blurring his vision and lifting the edges of the neckerchief which covered his nose and mouth. Grit coated his lips and his nostrils.

Forty or more tipis lay spread out along a narrow creek, less than a mile away. Too small to be the whole Comanche village. Probably a large hunting party. No one stirred, except for a stray mutt. Curls of wind-whipped smoke bent south from the tipi tops. Their sentries were likely hunkered down beneath the brush and rocks.

An encampment this size would include women and children, not just warriors. The strip of buffalo jerky he'd eaten an hour ago threatened to return to his throat. He'd had one of those dreams last night, the woman dead on the ground, his bullet through her. Drenched in sweat, he'd woken with his hands shaking.

Two years had passed since Wichita Village. His first battle. Still the nightmares persisted. He'd attended West Point to get away from his father and learn cartography, not to become more savage than those they called savage. The academy hadn't prepared him for a commander like Van Dorn who'd ordered him to fire into tipis.

Not about to obey such a command, Garret had kept his revolver's aim outside of the lodges. But in the heat of battle when a moment's hesitation could cost a man his life, how much time did a soldier have to discern if the buffalo-robed enemy was male or female?

Garret lowered the field glasses. Would this time be any different? He'd seen the Johnson homestead. Five family members dead. Two of the women raped before their demise. Twenty-one settlers in all hadn't survived the latest raid, one of many this year.

The Comanche would pay. Captain Rick Jamison of the Texas Rangers would see to that. Jamison was in command here, not him. Governor Sam Houston had requested U.S. Cavalry as support, not as the lead, for the contingent force of Rangers, volunteers, and scouts. Some hotheaded newspaper editor back in Fort Worth had called Jamison an Indian-lover. Tell that to the scores who'd felt his bullets.

Garret blew out an uneasy breath. The company needed to strike before they were spotted. On his hands and knees, he backed away from the edge of the sandstone bluff. Then, notching the toes of his boots into crevices and scraping the palms of his gauntlets against limestone, he worked his way down the backside to the men waiting below. Pebbles and white dust clung to his blue wool uniform, no worse than the sand which covered every inch of him in a fine, coarse layer.

In the protective shadow of a copper-colored overhang,

Captain Jamison spit out a chaw of tobacco and nodded as Garret finished his report. "Get your troops mounted and ready to ride, Captain Ramsey. Tell your men to put a bullet in every warrior they lay eyes on."

Garret's stomach soured as he saluted.

A chain of whispers spread through the men as Jamison's Ranger lieutenant signaled the same orders to the rest of the posse who waited by their mounts.

At his horse's side, Garret swallowed a swig from his almost-empty canteen. His cracked lips smarted as he pressed them to the metal rim. It'd be a day's ride before they reached a watering hole decent enough to refill the canteen. Had to live through the morning first. His face stiff, he stuck his extra Colt revolver in his belt.

Clothed only in buckskin leggings and brightly colored calico shirts, the Apache scouts at the front of the line turned their backs to the wind and smeared war paint across their faces.

Cavalry Lieutenant Charlie Fuller stepped up alongside of Garret. "There'll be no holding them back once the fighting starts." Thick blond hair, two shades lighter than his thin beard, poked out from beneath his Hardee hat.

"You pass along my orders to our men? No shooting at the women unless they shoot first."

"Yes, sir. Threatened them with the stockade just like you said." Charlie tightened his cartridge belt and brushed his hand across his usually spotless uniform, soiled from a week on the trail. "But a couple of the greenhorns are so worried about being taken alive by the enemy they're liable to think a tree's a man. Plan to save a bullet for themselves."

Garret grabbed his saddle horn, slipped his left foot in the stirrup, and mounted. "Split up the new fellows. Have each ride between the more seasoned troops. That'll settle them down."

Up and down the line, horses shifted and snorted as riders

swung into their saddles. Most of the men tugged neckerchiefs over the lower half of their faces and tipped their hats low. Once they left the protection of the canyon walls, the wind would scour every inch of bare skin.

Revolvers and carbines in hand, the posse nudged their horses along at a quiet walk around outcroppings of rugged rock. Hooves crunched on hard soil. The first riders neared the clearing that led into the open valley. Garret shifted his Sharps carbine across his lap and mumbled a prayer.

A quick bugle blast. Captain Jamison lifted his rifle and jabbed it forward. Spurs dug into horse flesh. The Rangers and Apaches broke into a full gallop toward the middle of the encampment. The Texas volunteers swung to the left and splashed through the shallow river. They'd circle around the far mesa and cut off any enemy retreat.

Unearthly howls trilled through the air as warriors sprang from their tipis. Their mangy mutts picked up the chorus.

Reins gripped tight, Garret charged to the right between the village and the creviced bluffs with his cavalry troopers as ordered, tromping over racks of drying meat and hides, unloading the fury of their weapons into the braves who dashed to rescue their horses.

Arrows flew like a swarm of hornets, joined by sporadic bullets from the Comanches' one-shooters.

"Aim and fire, stay low on the horse," Garret hollered to his men as he led them into the choking mixture of sand and dust.

Spooked mustangs from the native herd reared and whinnied. A hundred or more pushed and shoved against each other, some tethered, some not, moments away from an all-out stampede. A few warriors slipped onto horseback, smooth as water onto rocks, their bodies pressed flat to their mounts. Others latched onto the horses' manes to hold the animals steady as they fired from behind them.

"Shoot the horses," Garret bellowed, his throat raw. Once a

Comanche on horseback got into the open, they were almost unstoppable.

Two riders bundled in buffalo robes broke from the fray. Garret goaded his mount after them, skirting around scrub oak and cedars. Private Kern followed. Lower legs clamped tight to his horse's flanks, Garret reloaded and fired his Colt revolver once, twice.

One of the bullets struck the rider on the right. His body jerked, and he fell against the mustang's neck, his fur-matted buffalo robe slipping from his neck and shoulders. A cradleboard showed above the hide. *Dear God.* Garret lowered his gun. Had he shot a baby? And a woman, not a man? He shuddered. The rider tumbled from the saddle onto a scruffy cedar tree before hitting the dirt on her side. Her long hair splayed behind her.

The rider on the left yanked his pinto around and yelled. An arrow pinged from his bow, then another. Garret raised his revolver. His own horse reared beneath the onslaught. He shot and missed, threw his weight forward, and fired his Colt again as he struggled to stay in the saddle.

An arrow whizzed by his ear. Gunfire from behind. Private Kern? The Indian's pinto stumbled and crashed to the ground. The man launched himself free of the animal and rolled. Another arrow zipped from his bow before he scrambled to his knees.

Kern crumpled in the saddle.

Garret's next bullet struck the warrior in the left shoulder as he gained his feet. Two arrows, each shot as fast as a breath, flew toward Garret. Pain seared through his upper arm as one pierced his flesh. Beneath him, his horse swayed, wounded as well. A shaft jutted from its neck.

Garret fired.

The warrior rocked backward. Red seeped onto his bare, blue-painted chest.

A scream rent the air. The female rider who'd been thrown was alive. She clambered to her feet.

Garret's horse toppled. He jerked his foot from the stirrup and sprang from the saddle, barely saving his leg from the animal's crushing weight. He crashed against a gnarled root. Fire shot through him as the impact drove the embedded arrow farther into his left arm. He winced and groaned. His gaze skimmed the pebbled dirt and cedar sprigs for his revolver. Nothing.

There.

He saw it. A second before the woman snatched it from the ground between them.

He clenched his jaw and rolled to his knees.

Tears streamed down her grime-covered face as she strangled the grip of the Colt in her right hand and cocked the hammer with her thumb.

His mouth went dry.

The gun shook. She curled her finger over the trigger, one-handed. Maybe she'd miss. Her left hand cradled a doeskin bundle secured to her chest.

"Please. *Haamee.*" He scraped for every trace of Comanche in his brain as he rose from his knees, lifting his hands.

"*Kee.*" No. She growled at him and aimed at his chest. Her eyes narrowed even as her lips trembled.

Dear God. She was going to fire. Dive left or right?

A howl broke the air—a baby's cry. The woman shuddered. Her finger slipped from the trigger.

Horse hooves pounded the limestone. More troopers. They'd shoot her. He lunged at the woman, knocked the gun from her grasp, and carried her with him to the rough ground, hitting hard on their sides as a soldier's bullet skimmed across his thigh.

Her startled blue eyes stared wide at him out of a face that would have charmed him in a parlor. Blue eyes. At a baby's whimper and movement against his chest, he gasped. Blue eyes and a living, breathing baby, not dead in the cradleboard on her back.

"She's a captive," he hollered at the shooter. "White."

She cried out in Comanche and shoved the heel of her palm against his wounded arm. Pain seared up his neck and down his spine. His hold loosened, and she wrenched free.

Out of his reach, she tugged at the doeskin pouch strapped to her front. A little head with thick, dark hair moved above the hide. The mother's voice lifted in a cry that resonated relief, no matter the language.

He'd almost killed that baby and its mother.

Clutching the small life, she stumbled toward the downed warrior and dropped to her knees at his side. "Kee." She screeched and clasped the man's face in her hands.

A low chant, more of a moan, crept from the warrior's lips.

Garret hobbled over and picked up his revolver. A handful of his men rode up. Smoke from the village stung his nose. Fire.

"You all right?" Charlie drawled, shoving cartridges into the breach of his carbine. "I'll have Brown take you and Kern—"

"No." Garret grimaced. Kern lay face down on a rock a few yards away, too still for life. His horse was nowhere in sight. "Get on after the others. Leave me two men."

"Yes, sir." Charlie motioned for two privates to remain and rode off with the rest toward the last traces of resistance at the end of the canyon. Dust flew behind them.

The woman's voice, gentle, rushed, pleading softer than a lullaby, poured over the warrior as she pulled him into her lap. Blood seeped across his chest and onto her doeskin dress. The splintered cradleboard teetered at the base of her neck against a circle of stretched buffalo hide—a warrior's shield strapped to her back beneath the cradle. It'd saved her life.

Scattered gunfire and whoops echoed in the distance.

Garret straightened. His men might need him. "Brown, give me your horse. You and Taylor stay here. Guard her."

The hefty private squirmed his way out of the saddle.

Garret stepped forward. The world spun. He wavered. His soaked sleeve clung to his arm. He had to tie off his wound.

A whinny broke through his haze. His horse struggled to lift its head. Its leg curved at an unnatural angle. Large, wide eyes begged him for help. His heart sank. Poor girl. He swallowed hard and aimed his revolver. His finger wavered on the trigger. He squeezed and ended the mare's misery.

Nearby, the baby whimpered. More hushed words from the woman as she caressed the man's cheek. A gasp. The man stilled. She wrapped her arms around him and shrieked.

Her cry shivered through Garret as he took the reins from Brown and struggled into the saddle. "Don't let anyone touch her."

Thank God, his bullet had missed. He didn't need anyone else to haunt his dreams. The way she wept over that Indian, as though she loved him, as though she'd been his of her own free will. Even though she surely must have been a captive.

What would it be like to be loved like that?

He shuddered and nudged Brown's gray mare forward. It was not a time of love. The acrid smell of death clung to his nostrils.

CHAPTER 3

The gunfire, the screams, the assault of the wind-driven sand, all of it faded as Eyes-Like-Sky smoothed her palm over her dead husband's fine, midnight-colored hair. With her fingertips, she memorized his high cheekbones, jawline, and lips, the warmth already fading from his sunbaked skin. Gone. Her mind clawed for his last words, seeking to lock them in. *Love you. Take care... of Little Star. Pray to your God for me.* She bit her lips, but a wail burst through and filled her ears.

Never again would Dancing Eagle's eyes light up at the sight of her. Nor would she hear his laugh or see his smile. Never again would he embrace her, shutting out the world and wrapping her in the cocoon of his protection.

Dancing Eagle had given her his shield, insisted she wear it, and refused to take no for an answer. Why? God of heaven, why? He should have worn it. Not her. He could have still been alive. And that dog of a soldier dead. She clenched her hands and screamed within the hollow of her heart.

She could not bear this. She could not—

Little Star's high-pitched wails pierced through the quicksand of despair. Little Star. How long had the darling been crying? Eyes-Like-Sky tugged at the fur-lined doeskin. Her scraped, bloodied fingers fumbled with the ties.

"Hush, darling. Momma's here," she cooed, her voice cracking on every other word. "Momma will take care of Little Star."

Face scrunched, the child sucked a breath and let out another cry, puffy baby cheeks below a swollen nose and red-rimmed eyes. But a bruise darkened the side of her face, and a bump rose beneath her hair. The fall from the horse. Dear Lord. Poor baby could have been killed. Eyes-Like-Sky shuddered. Had the Creator protected her? He hadn't saved Dancing Eagle.

"Come here." Eyes-Like-Sky slipped her hands into the half-opened pouch and wrangled the seven-moon-old girl free of her wrappings. "Baby girl." She moaned and tightened her arms around the child, pressing the babe against her chest and rubbing her jaw against the small, silky head.

The shrill cries settled down to a wounded whimper as Little Star rubbed her eyes and nuzzled her cheek against mother's shoulder. The baby turned her head and opened her mouth, working her upper body down to the milk, hungry in the midst of destruction.

Fresh tears streamed down Eyes-Like-Sky's cheeks as she lowered the child and worked herself free of the cradleboard, shield, and front pouch. "Dada loves you. Momma loves you. Precious baby girl." Her broken voice struggled to find the melody of the song that was their own.

Little Star sniffled and rolled toward Eyes-Like-Sky's belly, oblivious to the sticky dark red. Her little rear rested against her father's shoulder.

Eyes-Like-Sky pulled at the lacings that bound her blouse to her skirt. No robe, only the doeskin pouch to cover herself with. Let those two worthless guards gawk if they pleased. They meant less to her than the dirt on her moccasins. Raising the shirt, she lifted the child to her breast.

The three of them together, father, mother, and child. Never to be again. She trembled.

Horses clomped. Rough voices. Rangers, Apache scouts, and a few scattered soldiers dismounted and moved across the field. Scalping the dead, male and female. Her people.

Arrogant men, to think they had so little to fear that they had time to riffle through the bodies. Let them wait, fatten themselves with stolen buffalo meat around a warm fire, give her people time to reach the next band and return with more warriors than these pitiful excuses for men could count.

She gritted her teeth and snuggled Little Star closer. With the baby's body blocking the guards' view of her free hand, she drew her blade from the sheath at her waist and hid it beneath her leg.

Riders came near. She lowered her gaze. Bits of words came through the string of garble. *Horse, dead, warrior, white, woman, baby, soldier*. English, shelved away years ago, lay dusty in her brain.

A man in rough trousers and oiled leather boots speckled with sand tromped over to her. "Whoareyou?" He repeated it slowly, a breath between each word. "Who are you?"

If only she could slay him with a glare. "Tomopuikatukatu." Eyes-Like-Sky.

"Your white name?"

"Tomopuikatukatu. Numunuu Comanche." *Get away from me. I want nothing to do with you and your kind.*

He rattled off a string of sentences to a man in a plumed hat atop a gray mare.

They called a young Mexican over. Neckerchief hanging below his chin, he squatted and spoke to her in Spanish, the language of trade across the vast Comanche domain known as Comancheria, stretching to the Rio Grande, Sante Fe, and north of the Cimerron River and beyond. "You're a white captive? Captain Jamison and his men won't harm you. They just want to know your name and where you're from."

"Not harm me?" She dug her nails into her palms. "They killed my husband. I don't have an English name. I'm Comanche." *Maggie.* The word throbbed in her head. She would never be Maggie again.

The Mexican frowned and conveyed her message.

"Comanche trash." The man with the oiled boots latched onto Dancing Eagle's arm. His fingers snagged on a golden band.

"Kee. No." She screeched at him. Her hand closed around the hilt of her knife. But if she attacked, they might kill her. Little Star would have no one. Her grip loosened, and she threw herself across Dancing Eagle's body. "Please." She grasped for the Spanish words. "Don't scalp my husband. Let me bury him. Leave us be. You have done enough."

Squished, Little Star whimpered and pushed her feet against Eyes-Like-Sky's belly. Eyes-Like-Sky shifted back and repeated her plea.

The Mexican translated, but the grubby man raised his voice and tightened his grip. The man with the plumed hat, Jamison, issued crisp orders. Two men closed in behind her.

She braced herself. "Arrogant hogs."

A rough hand clamped onto her arm.

"Wait." Another rider hobbled over on his horse.

Eyes-Like-Sky looked up. The soldier who'd taken Dancing Eagle's life. Bare-headed and face uncovered, he leaned in the saddle as if he might topple over at any minute, his face pale between his short beard and dark-brown hair which dipped onto his forehead. He cradled his blood-soaked arm limp against his body. The broken shaft of an arrow jutted out from a hole in his sleeve. His eyes were red, tortured. Maybe Dancing Eagle's arrow would claim another victim, after all.

He addressed the one in charge. A jumble of sentences exploded between the two. The man let go of her arm.

Glare fixed on the dog of a soldier, she repeated her plea. Was the man trying to help her, or was he simply arguing over his right to the spoils?

Another battle of sentences, then Jamison nodded, and the soldier saluted.

With a wince, he shifted in his saddle. His gaze locked onto her. "My men..." Spanish first, then English. "Bury him. Take you...and the baby."

The grubby man muttered a curse and stood. His reaction signaled more than any words or gaze that the soldier meant what he said.

She raised up, fighting against the spark of gratitude which threatened to ignite, and sat the blinking Little Star beside her, holding the pouch over her breast until she tugged her shirt down. "I take what's mine." She slipped the knife from beneath her leg and cut off a lock of her beloved's braid, tucked it in her pouch, then proceeded to slice through her own hair despite the protests of the men around her. The blade ripped through the dark-brown waves just like her heart had been torn in two. Her beauty fluttered to the ground, leaving a circle of chin-length, jagged edges around her head.

Someone grabbed the knife.

From atop his horse, the wounded soldier gaped at her. Dog or warrior? Enemy. There was nothing on this earth he could do to make things right. She turned away from his prying eyes, scooped the baby onto her lap, and cuddled her close, but Little Star's warmth couldn't abate the core-deep trembling which cascaded through her.

The white world held nothing for her. Nothing and no one.

She would comply. Go with them for now. Maybe they wouldn't tie her. The chance for her and Little Star to escape would come.

CHAPTER 4

Eyes closed, Garret drifted into consciousness. The lush green fields of his family's estate and his father's angry voice disappeared in the vapor of his dream. He lay listening among the buzz of camp, muffled voices, a harmonica, the scraping of tin against tin as someone finished their meal. Wood smoke scented the air. Dinner time? His tongue scraped like sandpaper against the roof of his mouth. How long had he been asleep? He shifted beneath his blankets. A mistake. The dull throb of his wound crescendoed into a pounding.

Garret moaned.

Illuminated by the flicker of a dim fire, Charlie leaned over, his shell jacket collar crumpled against his unshaven jawline. "You awake?"

Last Garret recalled, he'd been atop a horse, tied to the saddle. He blinked. "Where are we?"

"Two days shy of Fort Belknap and a decent bed." Charlie held an open canteen. "You want a drink?"

Garret nodded and pursed his cracked lips around the metal opening, savoring the bitter water. In this country, a man was thankful for anything short of mud. "How's the girl and the baby?"

Charlie blew out a breath. "Tried to run away again. Third time in five days."

"Third time?" Garret groaned as he sagged back onto the saddlebags which served as a stiff pillow. Why did she keep putting herself and the baby at risk like that?

"She tried it again last night. Crept past two guards. Jamison's not taking any more chances. He's keeping her tied up all night. Figures it's for her own good and the baby's." Charlie held out a tin pan of beans. "Up to eating anything?"

Garret shook his head. His stomach felt clamped shut. "How's she supposed to take care of the baby if her hands are bound?"

"I reckon one of the men will help if the baby cries loud enough."

"Not good enough."

"I can check on her later."

"No." Garret lay there a moment gathering his strength. His sweat-dampened shirt clung to his back. "Any clue yet of who she is?"

"Not a word from her. Other than her Comanche name, Tomopuikatukatu. Eyes-Like-Sky." Charlie scooped a spoonful of beans into his mouth. "Jamison figures she's been driven insane by whatever those savages did to her. Some of the other fellows believe she's done turned Indian, that there's no hope of bringing her back to her senses. Maybe she was taken as a young child. Doesn't know anything but being with the Comanche."

Maybe. She'd cried over that warrior as though her heart was broken. But the way she concentrated on every syllable of English she heard? English wasn't new to her.

Charlie reached for a tin cup. "I had the cook boil you some bone broth. Do you good."

"Later." Garret rolled onto his good side, careful to keep his bound arm tight against his blood-stained jacket, and pushed himself up to his knees. Pain shot down to his fingers and up to his neck, as if someone had twisted a blade in his wound. He groaned.

"What do you think you're doing?" Charlie clamped his hand on Garret's good shoulder.

"Going to see her."

"You're in no shape to do any such thing." The pressure from Charlie's hand increased. "I'll make sure she's okay. You just settle back—"

"I'm going, Lieutenant." Garret sucked in a steadying breath.

"Well, sir, if you fall flat on your face, don't call me to come pick you up." Charlie frowned, then slapped his knees and stood. "Wear yourself out too much, and you'll be lying, not sitting, on your horse again tomorrow." He reached down and helped Garret to his feet.

The world spun. Garret closed his eyes and held onto Charlie's arm for a moment. "Kindly point me in the right direction."

"The right direction is at your feet. Your bedroll. But if you insist upon seeing her, I'll walk you there."

Blanket draped over his shoulders, Garret trudged through the camp beside Charlie. A few fellows shot him curious glances, but most went about their jawing, his own men giving a salute or a nod. Some had already stretched out, boots toward the hot coals, slouch hats over their eyes, resting for the morrow's ride. Captain Jamison must have finally given in and let them light a couple fires. A luxury according to the captain's Ranger code.

Charlie turned back when they came within sight of the girl. Girl or woman? A mother, but beneath the hard-tanning of sun and wind, she was young, early twenties, at the most. She lay on a pile of animal hides beyond the warmth of the fire. The waning harvest moon bathed her in its orange glow.

Hands tied behind her back, she struggled up on one elbow as Garret approached. The jagged edges of her hair fell across her cheek. Sullen eyes shone like sapphires in the moonlight. A cougar in her den.

He'd killed her husband, and she knew it. Almost killed her and the baby too. A wave of nausea washed over him. Thank God, he had not.

What in the world would he say to her? His knowledge of Spanish was only tolerable, the sum of what he'd gathered from two years of talking with the scouts and an occasional trader from the Rio Grande. He turned and waved Miguel over from where he sat sharpening his knife.

Garret's glance fell to the hides. Head and broken cradleboard poking out from beneath a buffalo robe, the baby sputtered, working itself up to a cry. Little arms erupted from the bundle, hands reaching for its momma.

Eyes-Like-Sky ignored the child.

"The child's hungry?" Garret braced himself on a rock and lowered himself down on a patch of withered sawgrass. He repeated the question in his rough Spanish.

Miguel swiped his coat sleeve across his nose and squatted a couple feet from Garret. "She hasn't spoken in two days. Except to tell the fellows they were no better than dirt when they caught her trying to escape."

The baby whimpered. Eyes-Like-Sky's glare bored into him as if to say he was to blame.

He nodded to Miguel. "Untie her hands."

Miguel cocked his eyebrows. "But, sir, Captain Jamison said—"

"I'll take responsibility. Untie her while I'm here."

The woman jerked up to a full sit as Miguel approached.

Her eyes widened when he stepped behind her and knelt to undo the knots.

Miguel tromped back over to him. Leather strips dangled from his callused hands.

Eyes-Like-Sky's fingers scrambled over the lacings of the cradleboard with it's splintered top and squirmed the sniffling baby free of the contraption. "*Tatsinuupi u Tutaatu.*" Her voice lilted as she snuggled the child close, nuzzling her cheek against the babe's dark hair.

"Comanche for 'Little Star.'" Miguel hitched his trousers up and sat cross-legged near a bristly sagebrush.

"Little Star." Garret repeated the name in Spanish. "*Estrellita.*"

Eyes-Like-Sky lifted her chin. Uneven, dark waves of hair fell away from her face.

Thank goodness they'd gotten the knife away from her before she cut more than her hair. He'd heard stories of Comanche women in mourning slicing their arms, palms, even breasts.

The cracked surface of the rock bit into his sore ribs. "I'm thankful Estrellita is okay." His tongue tripped over the Spanish like a schoolboy fumbling through a recitation. "I'd never shoot at a woman or a child on purpose."

She scowled and shot out a string of Spanish his feverish brain couldn't decipher.

"Miguel, translate for us word for word."

The Mexican shifted his chaw of tobacco to his other cheek. "She said that's why the bodies of women littered the ruins of her village."

"Not by my hand or my men." Not this time. Pausing for each sentence to be translated before going on to the next, Garret slipped his free arm beneath his sling as support. "Try to understand. Some of the volunteers, scouts, even Rangers have lost family at the hands of the Comanche. And even with the best intentions, in the heat of battle, mistakes can be made."

"*Error*?" She spit on the ground.

Miguel communicated the rest of her message. "'You might as well have put a bullet in me. You stole my husband's life. My child will never know her father.'"

Garret flinched. The word *sorry* stuck in his throat. He was. Sorry for her loss but not for killing a man who would have killed him given another moment or two, a man who'd likely slaughtered a score of settlers. He searched for words of comfort. "Your husband was a brave man. He died a warrior."

Her eyes narrowed as Miguel repeated.

The baby burst out in a gurgle of one-syllable *coos*, then grabbed at her mother's shirt and nuzzled.

Eyes-Like-Sky gritted her teeth as she shifted the robe and covered her chest along with the child. She spoke again. Tears slid down her smudged cheeks.

Miguel repeated. "'My husband was a man of honor.'"

Honor? A rebuttal scratched Garret's throat, but it died on his tongue. He rubbed his throbbing arm.

"You are the savages. Not him." Eyes-Like-Sky sniffled and shuddered. Her tone made it clear he was lower than the dirt on her moccasins even before Miguel had turned the words into English. "I want no part of your settlements and civilization."

Miguel leaned toward Garret and muttered under his breath in English. "Done turned savage herself."

Garret glowered at him. "Has anyone checked to see if she was injured from falling off her horse?"

"It's hard enough to tie her up without her kicking up a fuss."

Garret's jaw tightened. "Has she eaten today?"

"I reckon. She was offered something." He nudged his sombrero farther back on his head. Thick hair poked beneath its brim. "More than they gave me when I was held captive by the Comanche."

"Punish her for what some tribe did to you? Fetch the lady a cup of soup from Lieutenant Fuller."

Eyes-Like-Sky's gaze followed Miguel as he shuffled off. How much of their English had she understood? Her motions stiff, she propped her shoulder against the coarse bark of a gnarled mesquite tree. Sore from her tumble during the battle?

A breeze ruffled his hair and sent a chill down his spine.

Alone, with nothing, and a babe to care for. What was going to become of her and the child? Her attitude wouldn't win her friends.

"*Como te llamas en ingles*?" *Tell me your English name.*

She didn't even bother to look over at him. A slight hum slipped from her lips, a lullaby tune, the words Comanche, as she cradled Little Star in her arms. Was it days-old blood or mud which stained her buckskin sleeves?

Garret scraped together more Spanish. "We'll help find your family. You must have kin from before your capture."

Her fingers curled into a fist against her daughter's blanket. "*Me llamo Tomopuikatukatu*. I am Comanche." She jutted her hand toward him and stuck with Spanish. "Give me a horse. Let me and my daughter go. Trouble you no more."

A hundred miles of prairie and canyons between here and where they'd found her. No place for a woman and child on their own, no matter how many years she'd lived in the wild. His brow furrowed. "I can't do that."

Her lip curled. "Dog of a soldier."

He blew out a breath and kicked at a small lizard that slunk through the shadows near his boot. The movement unsettled his arm. A lightning bolt of pain shot up his shoulder and into his neck. He winced.

Shadowed eyes followed his every twitch. "My husband's arrow?" A hardened smile hovered on her lips.

He snugged his robe tighter. “Tore into my muscle. Hit bone. I’ll live.”

“Probably. If you don’t take fever.”

“I’ll live.” Yet he didn’t know how his legs were going to carry him back across camp.

Eyes-Like-Sky dropped her gaze and smoothed her palm over Little Star’s head. “Her father will not.”

A coyote howled in the distance, his lonesome call unanswered. A couple of whinnies drifted up from the horses staked by the creek.

Garret swiped a hand over his sweaty brow. Tomopuikatukatu, Eyes-Like-Sky. Little Star. They had no one, not until he could find their kin. It didn’t matter what Jamison or Colonel Thorson said or did. He was responsible. “Listen to me, Tomopuikatukatu.” His tongue trudged through the Spanish. “When we reach the fort, news will spread. Folks will come from the settlements to see if you’re their lost kin. They’ll gawk. Ask questions, convinced you’re their loved one. Demand to take you with them. Is that what you want?”

Her brow furrowed. “I have a choice?” She shifted her bound feet from beneath the robe. Leather strips knotted around her ankles.

He sighed. His trouser leg chafed against his thigh where a bullet had grazed him. “I don’t know. Colonel Thorson is in charge of Camp Cooper, but the return of a white captive is bigger than that. The governor might get involved.”

Wide eyes focused on him, shimmering pools of murky blue. “Don’t send me back to what I don't know.” A tremor laced her voice, penetrating his meager defenses. “My life before the Comanche is nothing. A forgotten dream.”

His breath caught in his throat as he lost himself in her gaze. What was she afraid of? The memory of the past, or the loss of the present?

Miguel's tromp broke the spell. "Bone soup. The lieutenant sent one for you, one for her."

She scooted her feet away as Miguel's boots crunched against the pebbled ground.

Garret accepted a tin cup from the man's scabbed fingers. Eyes-Like-Sky ignored Miguel's outstretched hand, waiting until he'd set it on the robe before she snatched it up. Turning her back to them, she gulped the broth. Hungry. Determined.

The Mexican settled down a few feet away and dug out his tobacco pouch. "So you want me to translate?"

Garret shook his head. *Don't send me back.* Her words shivered through him. He couldn't let her run off. But the plea in those eyes drew him like the southern pole of a compass needle finding north.

CHAPTER 5

Nine days since her capture, the morning was bright and warm, but dark clouds swallowed the sun by noon. Dusk fell early, and a bitter wind snatched up sand and scraped it against every exposed inch of flesh.

Eyes-Like-Sky huddled beneath the buffalo robe, driving her pony onward. Bits of sleet stung her hands as she clasped the reins. Beneath the robe, Little Star squirmed, bound to her mother's chest, her tiny nose and mouth peeking out from her nest of fur.

Up ahead, the soldier called Garret Ramsey swayed in his saddle.

Stubborn man. He could have stayed with the Rangers at the first fort they came to, a scattering of stone buildings close to the northern bend of the Brazos River. Instead, he'd headed out this morning with the rest of his cavalry troops bound for Camp Cooper, scruffy prairie still miles west of the line of settlement. Couldn't even make it into his saddle on his first attempt. It'd taken a step and hand from that lieutenant friend of his to boost him atop his horse.

Ramsey and that Ranger Captain Jamison had argued last

night. The words had flown too fast for her to discern, but it'd been about her. Jamison had wanted her to stay at the fort. Ramsey had wanted her to come with him and the cavalry.

Thank goodness, Ramsey had won. Every man in that fort had gawked at her, and the women hadn't been any better. Jamison had set her and Little Star on a wagon seat above the crowd and made some speech, as though she was a show and he was some hero. The crowd had clapped and hooted. If that wagon had been teamed with a couple of horses, she'd have grabbed the reins and run over anyone who didn't have sense enough to jump out of the way.

No guarantee Camp Cooper would be any better.

The lieutenant shouted to Captain Ramsey, his voice barely discernable above the whine of the wind. The troopers around her closed up ranks, their hats turned down, only their noses and beards visible above their upturned collars. One fellow's ears poked out from his short-cropped hair and lopsided cap, the lobes bright red.

Would they notice if she slowed? Maybe they'd keep right on going bound for camp, their sights set on a warm fire and supper, like hunting dogs locked onto prey. She could fall behind. Find a crevice in some rock or cave.

And risk freezing to death?

Little Star whimpered. Eyes-Like-Sky shivered beneath the heavy, sodden robe and kneed her pony forward. She would not endanger the child.

A bugle blared. In the distance, beyond twisted patches of hackberry and mesquite, dull squares of civilization littered a bare scrap of land. The men beside her picked up speed. The lieutenant yelled and raised his gloved hand. Ramsey hunched forward, his cradled arm tight against his side.

Her stomach knotted at the sight of the mud-walled and shingle-roofed hovels, nothing like the majestic tipis of her adopted people. No wide stream and grasses in a protected canyon. Just hard ground and a stretch of a creek. This would not, could not be her home.

Sand scratched at her exposed ankles and seeped into her cracked fingers. The last time a norther had blown through, she'd been safe in her tipi, the floor covered with skins and hides. Gale-force winds had whipped down the smoke hole, almost extinguishing the fire. But the coals had prevailed, and she'd snuggled close to Dancing Eagle as they'd shared roasted venison with Owl Woman. Little Star had lain nearby on a patch of buffalo wool, waving her tiny arms at two small moccasins strung on a pole overhead. Their home. Their little family.

No more.

Eyes-Like-Sky raised her head, loosening her face from the protection of the matted fur. Sleet pelted her cheeks. She closed her eyes against the onslaught. Her hair whipped across her face and into her mouth. Her grip on the reins loosened. If not for the bundle on her chest, she'd let go. Let the storm and the horse do their worst. In Dancing Eagle's last words to her, he'd asked her to pray to her God for him. Would her God even care?

Thump. Something banged into her foot. She jerked alert. Hollowed-eyed beneath his wide-brim hat, Ramsey had dropped back and now rode at her side. His stirrup inches from hers, he kicked her moccasin again and nodded toward her hood.

She scowled and tugged it over her head.

Seemingly satisfied, he shifted forward in the saddle, teetering with the effort. Let him fall. Her husband lay in a shallow grave by the Pease River. Did this man deserve any better?

Two troopers in blue rode toward them, three small stone buildings on the right and a corral of horses, with no shelter aside from spiny mesquite trees. Two long, mud-walled structures dotted with windows lay in front, perpendicular to a row of rough board sheds and a couple stone cabins. A handful of wind-battered tents filled in the other side. No wooden-staked palisade to keep intruders out or prisoners in. *Camp* was the right word for it. The prairie could swallow it whole.

Wood smoke stung her nostrils. Hope of warmth. If only she and Little Star could crawl into a hovel by themselves.

Ramsey slumped forward across his horse's neck. His hat brim crumpled against the mane. A bump, then Ramsey slid to the ground. Eyes-Like-Sky jerked on her reins as the man thudded on his side, unmoving beneath the pelting ice.

If Captain Garret Ramsey died, she had no one to protect her. The thought ricocheted through her. Since her capture, he was the only one who'd looked her in the eyes. The only one who hadn't treated her like a savage or a madwoman.

Someone called out. The lieutenant turned. Not about to wait, Eyes-Like-Sky swung out of the saddle and dropped to her knees in the gritty mud. Nauseated at his nearness, she rolled Ramsey onto his back. He groaned at the touch of her hand to his wounded arm. His head landed at the edge of her lap. She swallowed back a scream. Too much like Dancing Eagle lying in her arms. Her nails dug into her palms. She could not do this. But his bloodless face called to her. A muscle contracted in his jaw, but his eyes didn't open. Unconscious. In need of protection from the weather.

Flinching, she opened her robe, covering him with her body and the buffalo hide sealing in every dry bit of warmth she could sequester, praying the rest of them would have sense to bring blankets and a stretcher.

Across the wide oak desk filled with paperwork, Colonel Thorson steepled his fingers. Polished brass buttons decorated his coat, and a stiff collar jutted into his chin. This man wore his authority like a string of eagle feathers. "We need your name...remember... find your family. We want to help you, miss."

Eyes-Like-Sky shifted on the hard wooden chair and wiped a trail of drool from Little Star's chin. She and the baby had spent the first two days huddled in a tent weathering the storm before the colonel had seen fit to demand their presence is his office. How long had it been since she'd been inside adobe walls? Sunlight streamed in through the open window, along with a morning breeze, a thread of relief in the midst of unfamiliar smells and hard stone that loomed too close, hemming her in like a stockade.

"Miss, did you hear me?" A lock of sandy-colored hair with a trace of gray slipped onto the colonel's wide, ruddy brow as he leaned forward. "Do you speak English?"

Little Star unleashed a round of baby chatter.

Eyes-Like-Sky bit her lip and met his gaze. "*No hablo ingles.*" No reason to tell him that with each day, more and more of the words crystalized in her understanding, multiplying like rabbits giving birth.

A frown dimpled his whiskered jowls, and he waved his fingers to the orderly.

Eyes-Like-Sky tensed, but the man reappeared, followed by the colonel's servant.

The woman's long black braid swung down her back as her leather shoes, visible beneath her ankle-length skirt, pattered across the plank floor. Middle-aged and plump, the woman paused at the corner of the desk and clasped her hands, ready to work. "*Si, Señor*?"

"Interpret for us, Angelina."

"Yes, sir."

Face unmoving, Eyes-Like-Sky bounced the fussy Little Star on her knees. She listened without listening as Thorson, through Angelina, assured her of his and the state of Texas's regret for all that she must have endured at the hands of the savages. Now that his men had rescued her, they'd work to find her kin.

Savages? Rescued? The truth trembled on Eyes-Like-Sky's tongue. She dug her fingers into her palms. Prudence dictated silence, but she would not keep silent while this man dishonored Dancing Eagle.

"Rescued?" She answered in Spanish. "Your men killed my husband. Took me prisoner." She lifted her chin. "If you want to help, send me back to my people, the Comanche."

Thorson's eyebrows dug a furrow in his brow above his nose. He took to coughing and required two swallows of water before he shook his head and continued, with Angelina speeding into action. "It's obvious, miss, you're not in your right mind at the present. Too many years of ill-treatment and abuse."

Eyes-Like-Sky leaned forward, missing a word here and there, as the man continued.

"I'm going to have my wife and the other women folk look after you for now. You'll think differently after you've been around civilized folks for a few weeks. We'll find your family, or someone to take you in. You'll thank us some day."

She clutched Little Star to her chest and glared at him. "Never."

Bubbles foamed to the brim of the large metal washtub. Eyes-Like-Sky hugged her arms to her chest and edged her moccasins off her feet as Angelina emptied the last bucket of hot water. A flash of memory, another tub, in a room with painted wood walls and carpet, not rough stone and a rag rug like this one. Warm and safe. A lifetime ago.

Her auburn hair sporting a touch of gray, Mrs. Thorson's face shone as she rocked Little Star in her arms. Angelina translated between them. "You'll feel so much better after a good bath. Like a new person."

Eyes-Like-Sky glared at the water. She had no objection to a bath in her own tent, in her own time. How had she let them drag her here? They'd been relentless ever since her interview with the colonel. She'd told them no, three days in a row. Then, today when she'd been in the yard scrubbing the diapering rags they'd given her in place of grasses, the sergeant's wife, Mrs. Clark, bustled over. She'd scooped Little Star off the blanket before Eyes-Like-Sky was able to get her hands out of the dirty wash water and stop her. Then the chatty woman had jabbered something over her shoulder in that fake cheery tone of hers as she skedaddled across the parade grounds to the colonel's house.

The door had closed behind Eyes-Like-Sky the moment she'd entered the stone cabin to retrieve her child. A trick. The nerve of that woman. The three conspirators, Mrs. Thorson, Mrs. Clark, and Angelina, had wasted no time in sequestering her in the back room.

Sweat dampened her palms. Too many people. Too many walls. Enough to suffocate a person amongst the foreign world of frills. A yellow ruffled cover and bed curtains decorated a bed so high, a person would need a footstool to climb into it. Then there was the engraved chest of drawers and a washstand. Nothing crafted on this prairie. A silver-plated mirror and brush lay on top of a lace cloth, alongside a curved oil lamp and two miniature portraits, fancy and dust free in a sand-swept land. Didn't Mrs. Thorson have anything to do with her time besides fret over trinkets?

Strands of her mouse-brown hair clinging to her forehead, Mrs. Clark hummed as she laid out white underthings. *Petticoat*, was that the word? And a chemise? Followed by a soft green dress with a skirt so long, it was no wonder these women couldn't run.

They had another thought coming if they expected her to wear such garments.

Mrs. Thorson hefted the cooing baby to her shoulder and lapped a towel over the chair by the tub.

Untranslated chatter between the two women buzzed around Eyes-Like-Sky. Fragments of English touched her. "Poor girl," "savages," "make her look decent," "smells." Mrs. Thorson's fingers cradled Little Star's dark head. That woman had better not get comfortable holding her daughter.

More fragments. "Tomopuikatukatu...needs an English name."

Eyes-Like-Sky gritted her teeth. Her name wasn't theirs to change. And neither was her daughter's.

Mrs. Thorson sashayed over, with Angelina in tow to translate. "Why don't you hop in? Nothing to be afraid of, dear. Just water. Angelina will have those filthy rags off of you and have you clean and sweet-smelling in no time."

"I don't need help." Eyes-Like-Sky lifted her chin and touched her shirt. "And these aren't rags. My husband shot the doe last fall, gave her to me. Finest hide I've ever tanned."

Mrs. Thorson smiled and nodded as she listened to the translation, her pale, delicate features barely flinching as her gaze flickered over the blood- and mud-splattered doeskin. "Whatever you say, dear. Hurry into the tub before the water gets cold."

Little Star blew a bubble of drool and reached out her little hands. Mrs. Thorson swung her away. "We'll clear out of here. Angelina will stay for your dirty clothes. Then she can come back later and give your hair a good wash."

My daughter. Eyes-Like-Sky narrowed her eyes at the woman's retreating back. "My baby stays with me."

Angelina's brow creased as she finished the translation.

Mrs. Thorson's shoulders arched to her ears. She turned. "Surely, you don't want her in the tub with you. Mrs. Clark and I can entertain her."

"I'll put her on a blanket on the floor." Eyes-Like-Sky marched over and snagged the startled Little Star from Mrs. Thorson's clinging arms.

"That hard floor? Poor baby. You leave her with us." Mrs. Clark's fingertips grazed the baby's doeskin gown.

"She stays with me." Eyes-Like-Sky locked her arms around the child.

Mrs. Thorson blew out a breath. "Have it your way, dear. We were only trying to give you a few minutes' peace."

Angelina tugged a quilt off the bed and spread it on the floor as the women strode out the door.

Little Star babbled and waved her fists as Eyes-Like-Sky kissed her silken dark hair and laid her down.

"Don't you worry." Angelina pulled an empty spool from her apron pocket. "I'll give the little señorita something to play with." She also retrieved a beaded necklace from around her neck and laid it across the baby's belly.

"Thank you." Eyes-Like-Sky tugged off her leggings, then her shirt and skirt, leaving herself bare except for the small pouch which swung on a narrow strip of leather around her neck. Nothing was separating her from the lock of Dancing Eagle's hair cut from him at his death.

Angelina chucked Little Star under the chin, then extended her hand for the garments. "Never mind those ladies. They're just trying to help. Mrs. Thorson's missing her own children back home in Virginia. You hop in and enjoy the water a bit while I take these out to the wash."

The door closed. Alone again at last. Her and her darling.

"Good baby girl." Eyes-Like-Sky lowered her foot into the stinging heat. Every cut and scratch prickled. She sucked in a breath and stepped in with the other foot. Muscles tense, she eased her body into the bubbles. Suds sloshed onto the bare wood floor. Thankfully, not as far as the quilt.

Little Star babbled, then jammed the spool to her mouth for a good gnawing.

Eyes-Like-Sky closed her eyes and leaned back, careful not to bang her bruised ribs against the side of the tub. The fall from her horse had taken its toll. Steamy warmth seeped into her sore body, leaching out the stiffness. Luxury.

Fourteen days since the battle, and she still carried most of the filth. She'd had nothing more than a quick wash in a stream on the trail and a few splashes from a washbasin in the tent the army had assigned her.

Dancing Eagle and she used to bathe in Mule Creek after nightfall, around a bend from camp, at a shaded spot with a patch of scrub cedar and oak close by the water. Her swallow stuck in her throat. She would never be in Dancing Eagle's arms again. Never again would he smile into her face or smooth his hand over her hair. Not on this earth.

She crumpled. A torrential downpour of tears shook her body. Her chin skimmed the water as she clutched the pouch in her palm and wept into her hands, pressing the heels of her palms to her mouth to muffle the sound.

If only she could slip beneath the bubbles and never rise. *Dear Lord, help me! Creator of the universe, almighty God, help me! Help me to go on.* She drew her knees up, thighs to elbows, and poured out her grief.

Little Star whimpered.

Eyes-Like-Sky sucked in a breath and fought for control. "Mommy is fine, baby girl." Averting her tear-streaked face from Little Star's view, she reached out of the tub, snagged the necklace, and dragged it across the floorboards by the child's head. *Bumpity, bump, bump.*

Little Star squealed at the noise and rolled over in pursuit of the new object with her chubby hands.

Eyes-Like-Sky dropped it just out of reach. Let the little girl scoot and push with her elbows and toes. Maybe she'd squirm enough to reach the treasure.

The water had begun to cool. Exhausted, nose streaming, Eyes-Like-Sky splashed water on her face. Her daughter. Her reason. She would protect her, look after her. Raise her to be a fine young woman. A young woman who'd honor her father for the good man he was. Just as sobs threatened to overtake her once more, a tap rattled the door.

"You all right? Ready to get your head washed, señora?"

"Not yet." Eyes-Like-Sky wiped her nose and grabbed the scrub brush, determined to scour every trace of blood, mud, and sand from her skin. If only she could do the same with the pain in her heart.

Half an hour later, Angelina, with her blouse sleeves rolled to her elbows, handed her a towel. "After you dress, I'll bring in a bucket of warm water to bath the baby."

"Thank you." Dripping, Eyes-like-Sky stood, wrapped the thick cotton around herself, and stepped out of the tub. "Where are my clothes?"

Angelina lifted the fidgety Little Star from the quilt. "On the chair, señora. Pretty green dress. I'll help you with the pantaloons—"

"No. You don't understand." Eyes-Like-Sky ran her fingers through her wet hair. "I mean *my* clothes. The leggings, skirt, and shirt you washed."

Brow creased, Angelina frowned and shifted Little Star to the crook of her arm. Little hands patted the red floral pattern of the woman's blouse. "Sorry, señora."

"What do you mean? I don't mind if they're still damp."

"Mrs. Thorson—she decided your things were too dirty."

"Too dirty for what? That's why you were going to wash them."

"Mrs. Thorson—" Angelina wrung her hands and heaved a breath. "She threw them in the fire."

Eyes-Like-Sky gaped. A shiver ran through her. "Don't you mean the kettle? Not the actual fire?"

"Not the kettle, señora. Sorry. But the green dress is yours—"

Eyes-Like-Sky screeched, half dropped the towel, then snatched it up again.

Little Star startled and let out a cry.

"How dare they?" Her Comanche clothes. Eyes-Like-Sky started for the door, turned back for the baby, and ended up tripping on the rug. She caught herself on the washstand and gritted her teeth. Those vultures. Trying to change her name. Taking her clothes. They'd take her whole past if they could. Turn her into some pale-face city girl who'd never seen a Comanche.

"Señora, let me help you." Angelina grabbed the pantaloons. "You can't go out there with nothing on."

Eyes-Like-Sky snatched them from her and jabbed in one foot, then the other. "They had no right." She shimmied the chemise over her head, then scooped Little Star into her arms, shoving the puke-green dress to the floor.

Mrs. Clark jumped away from the door as Eyes-Like-Sky slammed through. Eyes wide, Mrs. Thorson dropped her sewing and hopped out of her cushioned rocking chair.

"What did you do to my clothes?" Eyes-Like-Sky gripped her daughter to her hip, the words spilling out in Comanche first, then Spanish.

Red-faced, the women gawked at her.

Angelina hurried forth to translate.

Eyes-Like-Sky cut her off mid-sentence in English. "Where

—are—my—clothes?" Her glare scoured the room and landed on the cool, empty hearth.

"She speaks English." Mrs. Thorson fluttered.

"Where's the fire?" Back to Spanish, Eyes-Like-Sky turned to Angelina. "You said they burned them."

Angelina hung her head.

Mrs. Thorson bent and picked up her sewing, a small, silky gown. "Your things were filthy—"

"You'll thank us later." Mrs. Clark crossed her arms. Her double chin wiggled. "We're trying to help you to look civilized."

"It's none of your concern what I look like. You had no right to do away with my things." Comanche, Spanish, and English all jumbled together, she thumped a hand to her chest. "Where—" The fireplace. Of course it was empty. The wash kettle would be outside.

Dangling Little Star's upper body over her forearm, she headed for the door.

"No." Three voices screamed behind her.

She spun toward them, Little Star's feet thumping against her hip.

Mouth agape, Mrs. Thorson pointed at her. "You can't go out there like that."

Eyes-Like-Sky glanced down at the whisper-thin chemise, which clung to her chest and brushed against her knees. Air hissed through her teeth as she stomped over to the wall and yanked down the multi-colored hanging which covered the barren boards. Ignoring their gasps, she clutched it around herself and barged out, Little Star in tow.

Maybe by some miracle, she'd be able to salvage something of hers from the fire. Her throat tightened. Civilized? These women didn't know the first thing about being civilized. They could take their grubby fingers off of her life.

Shoulders against the stone wall, Garret soaked in the warmth of the midday sun as he sat outside the assistant surgeon's quarters. He closed his eyes and lifted his face toward the light. Five days in a hospital bed. His fever had broken last night. This morning, he'd kept down soup and toast.

Any trace of sleet from the storm had evaporated days ago. Blades of green poked up through the dirt and gravel, struggling to taste life. Temporary at best, before winter hurried back.

A light breeze carried neighing and clapping from the corral on the west side of camp. A couple of new mustangs were being broken, or so he'd heard. Wood smoke and the scent of fresh bread wafted his way from the kitchen. His mouth watering, he closed his eyes and imagined the meal he'd eat tonight.

Footsteps.

He opened his eyes.

Uniform brushed and buttons shined, Charlie sauntered up and sat down on the bench beside Garret. He dug a cigar out of his shell jacket pocket. "Waiting to catch a glimpse of Miss Tomopuikatukatu all cleaned up?"

Garret rolled his eyes. "Clearly, the men at this post don't have enough to do if the highlight of the day is a rescued captive taking a bath."

Charlie grinned. "Two hundred and twenty-five men. Less than a dozen women? Every man not assigned to fatigue or forage duty is interested in the goings-on at the colonel's cabin this afternoon."

"With all of that attention, I'm surprised the poor girl doesn't just hide in her tent."

"Exactly what she's been doing. The first couple of days, the colonel assigned guards outside her tent. Then, he decided she seemed tame enough and just told everyone to watch out for escape attempts." Charlie broke a match off from its miniature picket row of thin red-tipped sticks and struck it. "And of course, the whole camp has heard about how she tried to protect you from the rain. Or maybe she was really trying to scalp you." Charlie chuckled.

The way she'd looked at him the night he'd tried to find out her name, he wouldn't put it past her. But no. She'd hopped off her horse and swooped down into the mud to help him. Why? The question had been going round and round in his head ever since he'd heard about her actions. Too bad he hadn't been conscious. "Still hasn't told anyone her name?"

"No. But she spoke right up when the colonel interviewed her. Complained about us killing her husband. Said she wants nothing to do with being white." Charlie sucked on the cigar and blew a ring of smoke. "A few of the men figure we should have left her to fend for herself."

Garret rubbed the fingers of his left hand. The sling was a bother. Kept his elbow bent too tight. "The woman's grieving. Comanche or not, the man was her husband."

"That may be, but there's a family coming from Fort Worth in three or four days. Hoping she might be their kin, and a reporter's riding shotgun with them. If Miss Tomopuikatukatu spouts off about loving the Comanche, and it gets in the paper, some of those fine folks along the frontier might be ready to—"

A faint screech echoed across the grounds.

"What do you suppose that's all about?" Charlie ran his fingers through his wavy blond hair.

"Don't know." Garret's glance traveled to the limestone cottage across the parade grounds. Its oak shutters closed tight, no smoke crept out of the chimney. In the yard, a kettle swung over a low-burning fire next to the lone myrtle tree.

The door flew open, and Eyes-Like-Sky stormed out.

Draped in what? A blanket? A tablecloth? Little Star hung over her forearm. Eyes-Like-Sky stopped at the kettle, crouched, and grabbed a stick. After a couple of jabs into the flickering flames, she flung out a wisp of black material that fragmented as it fluttered to the ground.

A couple of whistles reverberated from the enlisted men's barracks.

"What the devil is she doing?" Charlie leaned forward. "It doesn't look like she has a dress on under that rug thing."

Not a rug. Red with diamond shapes of blue, yellow, and green. Garret had seen it before. "It's Thorson's tapestry. The one he got during the Mexican War."

"Thorson will have a fit."

Eyes-Like-Sky flung the stick. The tapestry slipped to reveal white ruffled sleeves. A chemise? She snatched the tapestry over her shoulders and stood, turning one way and then the other until her gaze locked on to Garret. Like an arrow shot from a bow and marked for a target, she tromped across the sandy ground barefoot, with nothing covering her lower legs but white lacy pantaloons.

Charlie whistled under his breath.

A hoot rang out, then another. Troopers poured out of the barracks and from the corral. Grins spread across the soldiers' faces as they elbowed each other and gaped.

"I'm guessing it's your fault, Captain," Charlie whispered.

"I don't even know what's wrong." Garret struggled to his feet.

"Maybe she heard you have her dead husband's armbands."

"His what? I have no idea what you're—"

"The gold armbands that warrior had on. Some Ranger tried to abscond with them. I retrieved them for you. It was your kill, after all."

"Shut up." Garret tugged down his half-buttoned jacket. Probably looked as if he'd just crawled out of bed.

Charlie smothered a snicker and stood as Eyes-Like-Sky crested the porch. "Afternoon, Miss Tomopuikatukatu."

Lip curled, she waved her hand at the lieutenant as if she shooed away a stray dog and stopped dead-center in front of Garret. Wet ringlets of dark hair slipped across her face. She shoved them behind her ears, exposing a slender scar above her left cheek.

Sapphire-blue eyes blazed into his. "Did you tell them to do this?"

Garret's breath caught in his throat. A whiff of perfumed soap drifted his way. "I have no idea what they've done, señora. Or even who *they* are."

"Those women are snakes. Vultures. Took my clothes. Want to make me white." She hissed out a spat of Spanish, then sputtered in English. "I am Comanche. Not white. Not settler. Comanche." She thumped her fist against her chest while Little Star dangled off the other arm and chewed her fists, leaking drool. "My husband...gave me deer. I not wear the green dress, No."

English? He stuttered. "Maybe they washed your clothes. Hung them out—"

"See that?" She jabbed a finger toward the kettle, letting go of her makeshift shawl. "They burnt them."

"Your clothes?"

"Burnt. Gone. Didn't ask me. Had no right."

The ashes she'd stirred up. He scrubbed a hand over his unshaven jaw. "I'm sorry."

The baby's lips puckered into an extended whimper. Eyes-Like-Sky shifted the child to her shoulder. The tapestry slipped open, revealing a couple of inches of thin white linen.

As she snatched the covering back across the chemise, Garret averted his gaze.

"You promised." Tears trickled past her lashes as she patted Little Star's back. "You promised."

What had he promised? When? Had there been mistranslation?

Brow furrowed, she shivered before him. From cold or anger?

His gaze drifted into hers. The depths of murky blue engulfed him. "I'll find you more clothes, Eyes-Like-Sky. Indian clothes." He said it in English and Spanish.

Lips pressed tight, her chin wobbled.

"You could put on a dress until then?"

"No. I put on that dress, they win." Her fist knotted around the fold of red mixed with diamonds. "I wait. For Comanche clothes."

His glance skipped down to her ankles and quickly back to her face, as he tried not to consider how much she didn't have on beneath the tapestry. His cheeks warmed. "I'll get you clothes."

Eyes narrowed, she studied him for a moment, then swiped the back of her hand to her cheeks. "I wait in my tent. No dress. Comanche clothes. I see green dress, I burn it."

Chin lifted, she pivoted, her dust-covered feet thudding on the bare boards as she descended.

Charlie blew out a breath. "What in the devil did you promise her?"

Garret sank onto the bench, knees wobbly, his sight full of Eyes-Like-Sky as she marched across the parade ground through a gauntlet of gawks and whistles. Little Star's head bobbled over her shoulder, looking back at him.

CHAPTER 6

Garret pulled a horn comb through his hair, which was still damp from a basin-washing. His left arm throbbed. It'd been a long day, and what he really needed was to rest the sling on a good pillow. But that could wait.

He glanced at the sack on top of his trunk. Charlie had managed to scrounge up buckskin clothing with the money Garret had provided. A skirt, leggings, and a poncho-style shirt from the wife of one of the Apache scouts. No moccasins to be had, at least none that'd fit a lady's foot. What were the chances Eyes-Like-Sky would be reasonable and wear a pair of slippers provided by one of the ladies of the fort?

He stepped across the rice-sack carpet, picked up the bag, and headed into the outer room of his "temporary" quarters. Two years in a picket-sided, canvas-topped cabin of sorts felt too permanent for his liking, but he and Charlie had done their best to make their place dry, tight, and comfortable. Originally a wall tent, the sides had been strengthened by shoulder-high picket boards on the outside, and even though they didn't have a single window, the canvas let in a decent amount of light.

Plus, most days and nights, they kept the flaps open wide, hungry for any bit of breeze they could catch, suffering through the flies and mosquitos that followed.

Boot heels on the desk top and head resting on the back of his chair, Charlie lowered his newspaper. "Fresh from Ft. Worth. Only a month old. You're welcome to it when I'm finished."

Garret set the bundle down on their small dining table and lifted his jacket from a hook on an inner pole. "Tomorrow. I'm doing good to still be standing today. When I get back, I'm going to crawl into bed and take my supper there."

Charlie folded the paper. "You should have let me drop those clothes off at her tent when I got them. Save you a trip. Let you rest up as Doc ordered." He leaned forward and picked his cigar up from the ashtray. "But I reckon Doc wasn't aware of your interest in our Indian maiden."

Garret scowled. "I have no interest in a woman whose husband I killed twelve days ago. I'm just trying to show her some decency." He tossed his shell jacket onto a straight-back chair at the table. Too much of a struggle to work his injured arm into the sleeve for a walk across the parade grounds.

"I see." Charlie clunked his feet to the floor and drew on his cigar. "Guilt. Not that you have any business feeling that way. The man was a murdering savage who'd have been more than happy to take your life if you hadn't shot him first."

"Not guilt." Garret leaned against a supporting post, tempted to settle into the chair. "Decency. She's alone with a baby to care for. No telling what she's been through. Maybe she doesn't even remember her family."

"If she'd show a trace of gratitude for being rescued, one of the ladies might take her in rather than leave her out there in the tent."

"I don't think the word *gratitude* is in her vocabulary, in any language." Garret straightened. "Wish me luck."

"If you don't get that tapestry away from her, the colonel will be sending in two men to take it, ready or not."

A couple of men saluted as Garret made his way across the grounds. Pebbles, sand, a blade of grass here and there. Not much could survive the constant barrage of weather, boots, and hooves. Sagebrush and chaparral dotted the more sheltered areas next to the buildings.

Outside the commissary, a man sat on a porch strumming a banjo. Boisterous voices echoed from the mess hall.

Garret had dreamed about the battle again last night. A cradleboard and blood. But not at Pease River. No, he'd been back at Wichita Falls. Troopers firing into tents. Him shooting at a warrior running for his horse. Trying to stop his finger from pulling the trigger. Because he knew. The warrior fell. Not a warrior, a woman and beside her the cradleboard. He'd been afraid to turn it over and look.

He'd woken in a sweat and had to shake himself. Tell himself he'd never killed a baby. He'd never killed a baby. It was only a dream.

A dream. He sucked in a breath and braced himself as he neared Eyes-Like-Sky's tent, a Sibley that sat beyond the quartermaster's office and the commissary storehouse, tall and round, wide enough to sleep ten men with their feet turned to the middle like wagon spokes, plenty big enough for one woman and a baby. The flap was closed knee-height and up. She'd managed to tie it off so that only the lower portion opened to allow fresh air, and anyone with prying eyes would have to kneel down if they wanted a peek of the goings-on inside.

He tapped the canvas. "Señora? Captain Ramsey here. I've got clothes for you."

"Leave them under the door." In Spanish, voice tight.

"No, ma'am." He wasn't some errand boy. "I need to speak with you face to face."

A rustling, then the canvas snapped and drooped. The musky scent of animal hide and wood smoke drifted out. Wasn't she going to step out?

Lifting the fold, he tied the flap to the side, ducked his head, and stepped in. The room spun for a moment. He steadied himself with a hand to the tent wall. The fever had taken its toll.

"Far enough." Eyes-Like-Sky gripped the tapestry tight across her chest and retreated past the center pole. Clean and dry, her hair crinkled in slight waves around her face.

Early-evening shadows stretched across the bare dirt. A buffalo robe had been spread out for bedding, and a couple of crates sat nearby. Close to the cone-shaped Sibley stove, Little Star lay on her belly. Her forearms braced on a worn blanket, she looked up at him wide-eyed.

"Sorry to interrupt your dinner." He glanced at the tin plate on the second crate which still held a half-eaten buffalo strip and bread.

"Please. The clothes. You leave." English.

He gazed into those blue eyes under her frowning brow. "Your name first. I'm serious about finding your family."

"I told you. Tomopuikatukatu. Eyes-Like-Sky." She held out her hand. "Clothes."

He switched to Spanish. "Your English name." His gaze snagged on the pinkish scar which cut across her cheekbone, close to her hairline. Courtesy of her Comanche friends, no doubt. "Listen. There's some folks coming here in the next few days. Want to see if you're their kin. There will be more. Many more. Tell me your name." He lifted the sack and held it out to her.

She crossed her arms. A two-inch scar shimmered amid the tan skin on the back of her hand. "I tell you my name, you make them leave?"

"I can't stop the ones on their way. But I can stop others.

We'll send word to Fort. Worth, Austin, San Antonio, all along the frontier."

Her gaze lingered on the sack. "Let me see."

The corner of his mouth edged upward as he set the sack on an empty hardtack crate and worked open the strap one-handed. He tugged a corner of the skirt out through the opening, smoothing his thumb over the yellow beads and fringe. "Buckskin. As I promised." Wrong word. What in the devil had he really promised back there on the trail without even knowing it?

She bit her lip. "Apache. Worse than dogs for showing pony soldiers my village. But I make do."

Thank goodness. "Skirt, blouse, and leggings. Couldn't find any moccasins yet. Maybe you could wear—"

"I go barefoot."

He cocked his eyebrows. "It's the middle of October."

"I go barefoot." She shuffled a step closer.

"Stubborn."

"I know that word." She pointed at him.

Did she mean he was stubborn too?

Little Star grunted and rolled over to her back, letting out a gurgle before waving her hands in the space over her head. Her feet and legs were bare, as she was dressed in nothing but a doeskin gown of sorts.

"The sooner we find your family, the sooner you can take your baby home."

"Home?" Eyes-Like-Sky's voice scratched. "You stole me from my home, Pease River. Palo Duro Canyon. Other places you don't know." Her glare sparked at him through newly formed tears.

"I'm sorry." Sorry for her pain. Not sorry they'd rescued her.

"I don't need your pity." Her fist clenched. "I need to be left alone. Have my things left alone. You want my name? Maggie."

"Maggie?"

She marched over and snatched the sack from the crate. Close enough for him to get a whiff of that perfumed soap again and something else. Milk? "Maggie Logan. You keep that family away."

"The family on their way here, yes. Not your family." She did understand, didn't she? "Miss Logan, I'll be sending out—"

"No. Eyes-Like-Sky to you. And everyone here. You not make me white." She hugged the sack to her chest, as if it were a child. "And no 'miss.' Mrs. Wife of Dancing Eagle." She jutted her finger toward the door. "Make them leave me alone."

He nodded, but his feet wouldn't quite move. Better get out of here before he did something really stupid. Like promise to loan her a horse. "The colonel needs his tapestry back. I'll wait outside the door."

Eyes-Like-Sky tossed the colonel's rug through the tent opening onto the pebbled ground and tied the flap shut. Well, almost shut. Hugging the bundle of clothes, she peeked through a slit in the doorway.

Bare-headed, no jacket, Captain Ramsey trudged across the parade field, the colored rug weighing down his good arm with slow, deliberate steps, as if he'd been climbing a mountain and had almost crested the peak. His wound and recovery had taken a toll. Yet he'd found clothes for her and delivered them himself. As he'd promised. Why?

Then she'd had practically asked for him to protect her.

How stupid of her to ask so much of him. Or of any man. So unwise. He was sick now, but he'd get stronger. What would he expect of her? He'd be on the receiving end of her knife if he asked too much. She'd been touched against her will in the past. Far too many times. She shivered.

And she'd let Ramsey set foot in her tent. He'd better not

get comfortable with that. Maybe he felt guilty for killing her husband. Felt he owed her. Maybe not.

Little Star whimpered. Poor baby. Hungry, no doubt. Eyes-Like-Sky's milk wet her chemise. She secured the last tie on the flap and turned to her child, scrunching the sack and digging out the buckskin. Apache. But she could take the beading off and add more fringes. Make it Comanche.

Minutes later, with Little Star nestled to her breast, Eyes-Like-Sky pressed the blouse to her nose and inhaled. Animal hide, sweet smell of leather, home. This tent almost felt like a tipi. But it wasn't. Never would be home. Nothing would ever be the same again. She touched the small pouch that swung from her necklace.

A shudder rippled through her. Oh, dear God, why couldn't Dancing Eagle be here? If only she could lie in his arms, his lips to her hair and her fingertips tracing the scars of his muscular chest, scars she knew so well. Safe and loved. Would she ever be again?

CHAPTER 7

Horse hooves pounded in the distance, then dropped into silence at the blaring of a bugle.

Spared from drill, Garret leaned back from his writing desk and crumpled the letter in his fist. Why couldn't his father leave him be? Years ago, he'd given up on receiving praise from his father. What he couldn't abide was the man's generous disapproval. His drive to shape his only living son into his image.

And now, in the matter of a month, he'd see the man face to face. Grand way to spoil his first furlough.

He tossed the wadded epistle on the floor and ran his hand over his hair, lingering over the rope-tight muscles at the back of his neck. If it wasn't for his mother, Garret would never have agreed to the visit. She wrote him every month—encouragement, anecdotes from their daily lives. Not the social backbiting of upper-class Pittsburgh. She spared him that. Instead, she wanted to hear about his life on the frontier, the people, even the plants, and his sketches. For her sake, he'd meet them in St. Louis.

Them. Lily would be joining them, according to his father's missive. Blonde, hazel-eyed, slim-waisted, and sugar-tongued.

His hand moved to his jaw as he exhaled. He hadn't counted on her making the train trip with his parents. Two and a half years since he'd seen her. In between graduation from West Point and his assignment to the Texas frontier, he'd had two months with her and his family. She had dazzled him, and he'd welcomed her company for a season. Dinners, dances, strolls, enough parties to make him eager to reach the prairies. Everyone had expected an engagement. His father would be bound and determined to set the matter right in St. Louis.

Garret's throat constricted, as if a fetter had been clamped around his neck.

Enough of this. He snatched up the crumpled letter and stood. His left elbow banged against the chair back. A needle-sharp ache pierced his upper arm. With a mutter, he strode to the stove and shoved the paper into the cool grate.

Drawing would clear his thoughts.

He shuffled into the back room and retrieved his sketchbook and kit from his trunk. Pausing for a moment before shutting the lid, he plunged his hand beneath the linens and wools and dug out a clump of metal wrapped in a neckerchief. He unfolded the cotton to reveal two golden armbands, two inches wide and engraved with images of eagles. Taken from the arms of Eyes-Like-Sky's husband. Someday, he would give these to her.

Swallowing the bitter memory of the battle, he shoved them back into the linen. Sketchbook in hand, he headed out the half-closed flap onto his makeshift porch, which encompassed a straight-backed chair, a few worn boards, and a couple of shrubs to keep out the wind and give a glimmer of privacy. A canvas awning was the real blessing, protection from the too-often scorching heat.

He squished a beetle beneath his boot, then swiped his hand over the layer of dust coating the wicker-bottom chair.

The seat creaked as he settled in. His left ankle crossed over his right knee, he created a support for his sketchbook.

Yet his pencil languished between his forefinger and thumb.

The sergeant's barking cadence at the drilling company faded in the distance. Thank goodness. White puffs of clouds scrolled across a blue-bonnet sky. Gray clouds lurked on the horizon, promising another storm tonight or tomorrow.

For now, the warmth of the sun buffered the chilled breeze. A couple of hawks circled above the north end of camp, after scraps, no doubt, from a steer the cook had butchered earlier in the day.

The ammonia odor of horse manure along with an occasional whinny carried from the corral. He could sketch a wild pony brought in this last week. But his gaze drifted to the sliver of the Sibley tent visible beyond his shrub barrier. The flap was open.

Yes. He knew what he wanted to draw, and he couldn't see it from here. Today, with his arm throbbing and the bitter taste of his father's letter souring his stomach, he'd allow himself the luxury. Sketchbook tucked between the sling and his side, he picked up the chair with his good hand and moved it beyond the small grove into full view of the parade ground and Tomopuikatukatu's tent.

A smile edged across his lips. A couple feet outside the Sibley, Eyes-Like-Sky sat crossed-legged on the bare ground, her back to the men's barracks, Little Star nowhere in sight. Dressed in buckskin, she sat with her upturned palms resting on her knees, her back as straight as a rifle barrel. The ends of her too-short hair fluttered with the wind. Eyes closed?

That's the way he'd found her yesterday when he'd dropped off a pair of well-worn men's moccasins. He'd left them at her door, figuring she could work them down to size. A better option than going barefoot, and sturdier than the chemise linen he'd heard she'd ripped up to use as slippers.

Yesterday, she hadn't stirred at the sound of his footfall, so he'd left without a word. Should he risk going over there today? He could sketch her portrait. Give it to the reporter when he arrived. The fellow could publish it in his paper. Maybe someone would recognize her, provided she hadn't been with the Comanche too many years.

As if she'd agree to any such thing. Best to keep his mouth shut and not venture too close. He set his chair down a couple of feet from the stone front of the assistant surgeon's office, in full view of Eyes-Like-Sky's back and a partial view of her profile. Slender nose, firm chin, full cheeks. Now if everyone would leave him alone...

Face upturned to the sky, was she praying, or just shutting them all out?

His pencil scratched across the parchment, outlining her form before narrowing the focus to capture the details and rub in the shadows. Thoughts of his father's letter receded as he lost himself in the charcoal.

As he finished the last smudge an hour later, voices, clanks, and stomps advanced around the other side of the surgeon's office. Shovels in tow, a handful of infantrymen appeared—trousers and boots filthy with dirt, only half of them in their uniform coats, grime-bedecked from head to toe. The digging party sent out to find a new well.

A bearded private swiped his brow. "There's our Indian princess."

"Miss Logan?" Another swaggered along, wiping his nose with his handkerchief. "Hah. Indian-lover pining after her brave."

"No decent man would have her as a wife."

A chuckle. "Bet she could earn a pretty penny at the trading post warming beds."

Garret knocked his chair back as he jumped to his feet, sketchbook in hand. "Corporal." His pencil and charcoal fell to his boots.

The men halted. A couple of them gaped at him as if they hadn't noticed him sitting there. A shovel blade clunked to the ground.

"Yes, sir?" The red-nosed corporal managed a salute that knocked his forage cap sideways.

"What in the devil are you doing, Corporal? Dragging these men through the grounds like drunken miners? Get them back out to the pit and march them through the front of the camp like the soldiers they are."

"All the way back to the pit, sir?"

Garret strode up close enough to smell the stink of the man's sweat-stained shirt. A faint sniff of whisky tainted the air. "You got a problem with that, Corporal?"

"No, sir." He saluted, then pivoted on his heel and bellowed. "Attention. About face. Forward, march."

Garret blew out a breath. He couldn't control the men's thoughts, but he could give them enough work so they wouldn't have time to jabber like that. Didn't matter that they were Captain Williston's company, not his. Williston would be happy to oblige with an extra work detail or two.

He turned.

Across the way, Eyes-Like-Sky stood staring at him, arms at her side, hands clenching and unclenching.

Had the men's words carried to her hearing? No telling how much English she could understand. But their tone had likely been too clear.

Her glare moved to the retreating men, then back to him. Her frown deepened.

He should speak. But no words came. He stood immobile as his gaze met hers, the wind whipping dark locks across her face.

A baby's cry erupted from her tent. She pivoted on her moccasin-clad feet and entered, snapping the flap shut behind her.

His grip on his sketchbook tightened. The sooner they found her family and got her out of the fort, the better. He'd sent three riders out to the settlements and Fort Worth with word to be passed all the way down to Austin and Houston. Surely, someone would recognize her name and claim her. Give her a real home, a new start.

He knelt and picked up his pencil and sand-speckled charcoal. As he stood, he glanced at the Sibley. The flap fluttered, closing a slit. So...he wasn't the only one who could watch and observe.

CHAPTER 8

People in her tent, sitting on her crates. Not one had bothered to ask Eyes-Like-Sky's permission. As if she had no say so over any little inch of her life.

Teeth gritted, she hugged her arms around her waist as Mr. and Mrs. Berger rattled on about their Mandy. Blonde and blue-eyed, stolen by the Comanche at age ten. Eight years ago.

Mrs. Berger sniffled and wiped her sallow cheeks with her handkerchief, her fingers fumbling over the scar which ran along her jawline, courtesy of the Comanche.

Bleary-eyed, Mr. Berger wadded his hat in his hands as he spoke. His unkempt mustache twitched with each word.

Angelina squatted on a stool nearby, translating the painful details.

Devils, savages, murderers. Mr. Berger's words swirled in Eyes-Like-Sky's brain. She had given her name to Captain Ramsey so this wouldn't happen, but this morning, she'd been dragged off to meet with a newspaper man. He'd talked. She'd said nothing. Tried to make her sit still so he could flash a light at her from behind a black-curtained box. Then, this afternoon, two soldiers had traipsed these people into her abode without a word of apology. Colonel's orders, Angelina had explained. The folks wanted to see if she'd heard or seen anything of their lost daughter. They could have sent a messenger, or at least allowed her to meet them out in the open.

"No, I haven't seen her. Never heard of her." Maybe if she repeated it enough, they'd finally listen and leave. She dropped her hand to the cradleboard which leaned against the crate and smoothed her palm over Little Star's silken hair.

"That's an Indian baby." Mr. Berger dropped into silence.

Eyes-Like-Sky stiffened.

"You poor dear." Mrs. Berger's voice trembled.

Sweat broke out along Eyes-Like-Sky's brow and beneath the back of her hair. "My husband was Comanche."

Angelina's voice wavered as she translated.

"Husband?" Mr. Berger jumped to his feet. "Those devils butchered my brother and our oldest daughter. Only, they didn't kill her right away. Strung her up to a tree—"

"Arthur!" Mrs. Berger gasped.

"And my poor wife—"

"Shut your mouth!" Mrs. Berger sprang up and latched onto his arm.

Little Star wailed. Her face scrunched up at the scary man.

Eyes-Like-Sky's head pounded. "I don't know where your daughter is." She grabbed the cradleboard and headed for the door, sliding her arms through the leather straps of the board as she plowed through the loose tent flap.

Tripping on a stake, she caught herself. She had to get out of here. Her lungs constricted. She needed fresh air. Open space. Not this prison of a camp with its grimy soldiers and pitiful hovels. She marched straight for the entrance.

Screams echoed in her head. A wagon in flames. Vice-like fingers wrenched in her hair, dragging her across the hard dirt. A warrior throwing her on the back of a horse. Her poor mother—

Eyes-Like-Sky pinched the soft underside of her wrist with all of her might until the memory faded beneath the immediate pain.

At the forge, the blacksmith pinged his hammer against his anvil. She looked away and hurried past.

Her foot came down hard on a rock, and the moccasins slipped on her heels as she plunged past the corral. Men hung on the rails and cheered as an unbroken horse flipped a soldier on his back like a rag doll.

Hoots and hollers rang out, but not at her. Good. Maybe they wouldn't even notice. The entrance lay ahead. Guards. She would head out the side of the camp instead.

A bearded trooper ran up alongside her—the one who'd paraded people into her world against her wishes. "Where are you going?"

The sentries perked up. One charged over and blocked her path, gripping his rifle at an angle across his chest. Freckles covered his face. "Halt. End av camp." His thick accent distorted his words.

She darted around him. He wouldn't touch her.

"Miss Logan." Another guard, broad-chested and gruff, possessed a voice that descended like a hammer as he stomped into her path. "Your tent. You go there." He jutted his finger.

She sidestepped.

The freckled soldier grabbed her arm. "Miss Logan, please."

"My name is Tomopuikatukatu." She shook free of his touch, but her feet stopped. Three of them, foul-breathed and dirty, and there would be more.

A hiss wet her lips. Her spit flew onto the boots of the one who pointed toward her tent.

He muttered a curse and raised his hand.

Arms pressed to her sides, she pivoted out of his reach and retreated toward the main part of camp.

Her tent loomed ahead. Couldn't even go there. Invaded.

Nothing of her own except the child on her back. And those screams in her head. Her mouth went dry. She'd go to the sinks out back, the women's privy beyond the kitchen and storehouses. Let them follow if they liked.

She tromped across the parade ground and beyond. Past the stone and picket buildings and along the well-worn path, until she swung the door open to the last women's shanty.

The two guards halted at the corner of the mess hall.

The door banged behind her. Fully clothed, she lowered herself on the seat. Sunlight peeked in through cracks and the gap between the roof and the warped side-boards. Better not to see. On her back, Little Star whimpered. The stink oozed around them, filling her nostrils, but still she sat. Those dogs wouldn't dare come in here, and if she waited here long enough—

A burning sensation crept into her throat. She threw up. From the odor or from the shadows of memories?

By the time she moved again, her legs were stiff. With a nudge to the door, she peeked out. One guard remained. Handkerchief in hand, he removed his hat and dabbed his forehead, his gaze toward the mess hall. Her chance.

She edged the door open and slipped around the far side of the outhouse. Out of sight, she dropped to her hands and knees and crawled away from the building at an angle across hardened clay until she reached the sawgrass. There, she covered Little Star's face with the loose end of fur from her bundlings and wove her way through the shoulder-high, needle-toothed leaves that snagged and sliced at unprotected skin.

She wouldn't get away. Some sentry would locate her, and they'd come. Besides, she'd need a horse and supplies to make any real attempt at escape. Something like that had to be planned.

But for now, clean air uninhibited by walls and prying eyes would have to be enough.

Hands and neck scathed, she emerged from the swath a few feet shy of the river's edge. Water bugs skittered across the murky surface. Clear Fork, the soldiers called it. Nothing clear about it today. Heart-weary, she slid the cradleboard off her back and settled in the shade of a gray-barked hackberry tree. Her tongue stuck to the roof of her mouth. What she wouldn't give for a drink of clean, cool water. What she wouldn't give to be a hundred miles away from here. With Dancing Eagle. She clutched the small pouch which swung from her neck, a small token of what once was.

Little Star sucked in a couple of breaths, working up to a full cry. No. They'd hear it. Eyes-Like-Sky scooped her daughter out of her trappings. The baby rubbed her eyes with tiny fists, her world so small.

Eyes-Like-Sky tugged at the lacings that tied her blouse to her skirt. The sweat-soaked buckskin clung to her upper back and underarms as she lifted Little Star to her breast and nursed her until the baby slept and the trembling within her own limbs had subsided.

The screams, a distant murmur between her ears, returned. She pressed the heel of her palm hard against the sharp edge of a rock at her side. Eyes clenched against the past, she willed herself back to the spring on the Arkansas River where she and Dancing Eagle had fallen in love. Tears slipped down her cheeks.

"Tomopuikatukatu?" Someone touched her arm.

She started, eyes wide. A chill shivered down her spine.

Ramsey withdrew his hand and rocked back on his heels. Broken snags of leaves clung to his jacket and trousers. He'd come through the sawgrass, as well. In the week, the stamp of illness had receded. His arm still swung in the sling, but his coloring had improved, and his cheeks had started to fill out. "We've been looking for you." Spanish.

How had he managed to sneak up on her like that? "I

couldn't breathe." She yanked her blouse down against Little Star's cheek. "People in my tent. No place to call my own."

His brow furrowed above his deep brown eyes. "I'm sorry." A lock of sun-streaked brown hair dipped beneath his hat brim. "But you can't go running off from camp. It's not safe."

She struggled to her feet. "Not safe? From what?"

He hopped up and reached out to steady her. "Snakes. Or an Apache with a grudge."

She jerked her elbow away and pointed at the three soldiers farther up the bank. "Only snakes I see."

He swatted at a fly. "The trouble is the snakes you don't see."

"I saw people in my tent. You promised I tell you my old name, you keep them away."

Little Star stirred and stretched, raising her small fists above her head.

Ramsey exhaled and tipped his blue felt hat back a notch. "They begged the colonel. Hoped you might know something about their daughter. I didn't hear about it till after."

Their daughter. Mr. Berger's scowl at Little Star. *Savages. Murderers.* Her stomach lurched. "Never mind." She pushed past Ramsey, dropped down to her knees at the river's edge, and splashed her face. Swallowing back the panic, she scooped a handful of water.

"I have a canteen. You're welcome to it. Fresh from the well."

She swiped her forearm across her mouth and glared up at him. "No. Not from man who killed my husband."

He flinched and faltered back half a step as if she'd slapped him.

She hung her head. Such words wouldn't make anything better. A lone bluebelle wavered in the patchy grass by her knees, its bloom shriveled. Lifeless but not dead. How had it outlasted summer and early fall?

"I come back to camp." As if she had any choice. A sigh

rattled through her as she reached for the cradleboard and smacked away a spider which had dared crawl up the grain.

He motioned the other men away. "I…we were concerned about you."

She rolled her eyes. "About your prisoner?"

"You're not a prisoner."

"Hah." Cradle propped against her knee, she shoved the rags toward the bottom and wiggled the half-woken Little Star into the fur wrappings. A faint streak of blood smeared from her palm to the child's cheek. She gasped. How could she have pressed the rock that hard?

"What is that?" Ramsey leaned over. "You're hurt?"

"No. It's nothing." She yanked the lacing tight, securing Little Star in place.

"It's not nothing." He reached for her hand.

She jerked away and stood.

His frown deepened. "Here." He dug his handkerchief from his pocket and dribbled water on it from his canteen, then extended it toward her.

She scowled at the offering. Couldn't he leave her alone? The red cotton hung between them.

His mouth firmed into a thin line. "Take it, or I'll march you to the doctor's office."

With a sharp exhale, she snatched the handkerchief and wrapped it around her palm. The scent of him drifted up from the cloth. Sweat, lye soap, and a touch of another more pleasant odor—shaving soap, perhaps. A vague memory flickered.

"I'm sorry those people bothered you today, Tomopuikatukatu." His voice had lost its hard edge.

She shoved her arms through the leather straps of the cradleboard. "They didn't." But the tremor in the words betrayed her.

His gaze searched her face. "I don't believe that."

What did he see there? She jutted out her chin and huffed

up the bank, her loose-fitting moccasins sinking in the mud until she gained dry ground and grass. Caked, heavy-things. Useless. She stopped and flung them off her feet, then picked them up by the heels.

Ramsey caught up to her. "Angelina could cut those down to size for you."

"No. I do it myself." She tromped on, barefoot, over stony ground patched with a scattering of grass and sagebrush, side-stepping the prickly pear.

"You're not trusted with a knife yet."

Little did he know what was strapped to her calf. "Rather go barefoot." Rather not need any help at all.

A wagon sat up ahead near the corral, unhitched for now. The scoundrel of a newspaper man lounged against the feedbox on the back.

Her stomach knotted. She pivoted toward Ramsey. "You promised to make them stay away." Her Spanish slipped into broken English. "Let them come in my tent. Don't even ask. I have no say. No home. No nothing. Only Little Star."

Brown eyes, crinkled at the corners from too much sun, penetrated hers. "I give you my word, I'll talk to the colonel. No one enters—"

"Keep them out. All of them. He wants to take me to the city. Everywhere, white folk stare at me and Little Star. Find my family? Hah. You allow? We not reach Fort Worth."

Garret latched onto her shoulder. "What is that supposed to mean?

She narrowed her eyes and pursed her lips, but the spit would not come. "I take his horses, his water, slip away in the night. You warn him? You no better—"

"Tomopuikatukatu, I won't let him take you."

"You stop him?"

His hand dropped away. He set his jaw. "I won't let him take you. I'll convince the colonel. I'll keep the families away from you. Until your real one shows up."

"What if—"

"No. Your family will get to see you, take you back with them. It won't be as bad as you think."

Her heart clenched. "What if it is?"

~

What if no one came to claim Tomopuikatukatu as kin? The thought still rattled through Garret's brain an hour later as he sat across from the colonel's desk in a chair a couple of inches shy of comfort. "Sir, I need to talk with you about Tomopuikatukatu—"

"Miss Logan." Colonel Thorson dabbed his mouth with a napkin. The usual paperwork had been shoved to the side. Scraps of beefsteak and candied carrots remained on his plate. "The young woman needs to get it in her head that her Comanche days are behind her."

Miss Maggie Logan. The name didn't quite fit her.

Thorson stabbed a chunk of beefsteak. "My wife's not convinced Miss Logan is in the right state of mind to be caring for an infant."

"Sir, that baby is her life. She'd do anything to protect her child. We cannot take Little Star from her."

Leaning back, Thorson secured his coffee cup in his weathered hands. "Help yourself." The colonel nodded to the tin pot and empty cup at the edge of the desk.

Garret gripped his chair arms. Couldn't the man take his mind off his dinner for a moment? "No, thank you, sir. As I was saying, the baby means the world to her. I think—"

"You seem to be able to work magic with her, Captain." Thorson sipped deeply and set his tin cup down. "Does that mean you've got her under your spell? Or is it the other way around?"

Garret's cheeks warmed. "No spell, sir. Just decency."

"We'll see." The colonel's mouth curved upward as he sliced another bite of beef. "But you're not doing her any favors by letting her continue to play Indian."

"Play Indian, sir?"

"Dress in buckskin. Refuse to answer to her Christian name. My wife and the other ladies have tried to be civil to her, but she declines every invite. Won't even let them give the baby decent clothes." He dropped both forearms to the desk, eating utensils in hand. "She needs to reintegrate into settler society, or she'll become an outcast who doesn't fit in anywhere. That's the reality, Captain."

Garret leveled his gaze at Thorson. "Maybe she needs reality in bite-size pieces. I'm sure when her family comes—"

"I hope so, Captain. For her sake. I heard tell of a captive rescued over in New Mexico territory. Supports herself by touring the country giving lectures and showing off the blue tattoo the Mohaves scrawled across her face."

No kind of life for Eyes-Like-Sky and her baby.

Thorson loosened the bottom buttons on his frock coat. "Meanwhile, Mr. Wheeler of the Fort Worth paper has offered to take her back with him and help her find her family."

Brow furrowed, Garret reached for the coffeepot. "Sir, she's under our protection. Wheeler's no philanthropist. His job is to sell newspapers. Tomopuikatukatu's story on the front page would help with that."

"Miss Logan, Captain. Her name is Miss Logan, and what if having her on the front page helped her family find her?"

"If I may speak freely, sir?" He clunked his cup on the desk. "The man has a picture of her. A sketch artist could copy it for the paper. He doesn't need her in person." Words tumbled out a rifle shot beyond prudence. "What if she were your daughter, sir?"

"Excuse me?"

Garret winced but plunged ahead. "Colonel, we have no idea what Miss Logan has been through. If she were your daughter, wouldn't you want someone to look after her interests?"

A bugle blew, calling the enlisted men to dinner.

Thorson frowned. "My daughter is back in Virginia. I wouldn't have her anywhere near this God-forsaken country." He tore a hunk of bread from the soft loaf. "But for the sake of whose ever daughter Miss Logan is, I'll leave her reintegration into society in your hands, Captain, until we find her family. We'll see if she ends up on the soapbox showing off all her tattoos."

In his hands? Garret hung his head. Convince Tomopuikatukatu to acclimate to society? Perfect way to become her number one enemy, as if he wasn't already.

Butter dripped from Thorson's knife. "On a different matter, Ramsey, any day now, I expect news of who won the presidential election. We need to be prepared."

Garret sipped his coffee. The whole country had been holding its breath for years. It didn't matter who won. There'd be trouble either way.

Thorson pinched the bread between his thumb and forefinger as if he'd strangle it. "If Lincoln wins, there's no telling what some of these hotheaded Texans will do. Too many of them already blame their Indian troubles on us. Want to turn everything over to those renegade Texas Rangers."

"You figure we might have an insurrection on our hands?"

"We need to be ready for all contingencies. News will reach the towns before it reaches us. Maybe Lincoln won't win. He wasn't even on the ballot in the Southern states. But God help us if he does."

CHAPTER 9

Voices drifted past Garret's quarters, men on their way to either the preaching behind the mess hall or to the rumored card game in the enlisted men's barracks.

Garret slipped his arm into the sling and picked up his Bible from the small table by his bedside, not about to miss the circuit rider who had shown up yesterday and who would leave day after tomorrow. An actual preacher. Not an opportunity to be wasted. Tucking his Bible under the sling for a moment, he smoothed his hair and donned his Hardee hat before he walked out the door.

His footsteps faltered as he left his porch and cleared his grove. The Sibley stood in full view. Dare he ask Eyes-Like-Sky to the service? Likely as not, she'd say no. But maybe the tenor of her response would give him an inkling of who she prayed to when she sat outside, eyes closed, face turned to the sky. Or if she prayed at all.

Smoke curled out the top of the tent as he approached. A soft hum drifted out of the flap, which hung by one string.

Before he had a chance to knock, a muffled squeal cut through the melody. Metal rattled. A clunk.

"What's wrong?" He jerked the flap loose and stuck his head inside.

Eyes-Like-Sky whammed an iron skillet against the ground a couple of feet from the buffalo robe where Little Star lay on her belly. The baby's limbs jerked, but the child didn't wake.

"Shhhh." Eyes-Like-Sky narrowed her eyes at him and jabbed her finger toward the door.

He backed up and waited.

With a shuffling sound and a *swoosh*, Eyes-Like-Sky used the back of the cradleboard to bat something curled and black away from the tent.

He knelt to investigate.

"Don't." She dropped the cradleboard inside the doorway and stepped out.

He glanced again. A scorpion, its tail matted against its flattened body. One pincher dangled at an odd angle. "Thank God, you saw it and killed it." He stood and scuffed it away from them with his boot.

She rubbed her hands over her arms and shivered.

Unexpected tenderness swelled in his chest. His hand flexed around the spine of his Bible as he squelched the instinct to touch her shoulder.

Her brow furrowed. "Why are you here?" She stuttered through the English words.

"There's a preacher tonight. You're welcome to come listen."

"I told the women no."

"I'm not with the women."

"No. I stay here." Her gaze fell to the Bible at his side. "What's that?"

He lifted the leather-bound book with its worn pages. A gift from his mother, from her childhood. "A Bible."

An unreadable expression flickered across Eyes-Like-Sky's face. She half reached, but her hand faltered in midair.

He held out the book. "You know what a Bible is?"

"I'm not stupid." She hugged her ribs.

"I—I didn't mean you were. I don't know how long you were with the Comanche. Would you like to see it?"

She shook her head and turned.

He nudged the old book's soft cowhide against her fringed sleeve. "You're welcome to look."

She stared at the cracked brown leather.

He pushed it into her hands. Wagered she wouldn't throw it or rip it.

Her fingers trembled over the cover. As she opened the inside, she caressed the pages, her gaze traveling over the words.

"You can read?" He gaped at her.

Wide, wet eyes looked up at him. "Not anymore."

Lost in the sea of blue, he swallowed. "I could teach you."

"No." She shut the Bible and shoved it toward him. "You destroy my life. My home. My husband. Your fault. No gifts from you. Nothing."

He'd only wanted to help. Words spilled from his mouth. "Your husband raided the settlements. Men and women died."

"My husband was a warrior." With the sparking of her temper, her dribble of English switched to a flow of Spanish. "Defended his people from invaders. He was at war—"

"Does that include rape?"

"Dancing Eagle didn't—"

"Women were raped during the raids this fall. Just like every other Comanche attack on the—"

"No. Not my husband. He swore to me. Promised never to do that." Tears choked her words, even as her fists clenched at her sides. "He would not. Did not. Not his men. Two hundred warriors rode out. They divided, small parties striking different areas. I don't know what others did. But Dancing Eagle had no part of it." She scuffed her foot against the ground, kicking dirt in his direction before she pivoted on her heel and stormed into her tent.

He blew out a breath. Why in the devil hadn't he kept his mouth shut? He banged the Bible against his forehead.

The flap flew open. She flung the deer hide into the sand, the hide he'd purchased for her from an Apache scout and she'd scraped all afternoon. "I want nothing from you." And if that wasn't enough, she stomped out and kicked it farther away. Her glare sliced through him. "Don't look at me. Don't draw my picture. I saw you, last three days. No more. Ever."

Not draw her? That would be hard enough. If only he could stop thinking about her.

CHAPTER 10

Eyes-Like-Sky paced in front of her tent, her forearm securing Little Star to her hip. Sand and clay, wet from the morning's rain clung, to the bottom of her moccasins. How long would the soldiers hold her in this camp?

Crowded, stinky, suffocating place. Nothing but soldiers and their bugles and loud voices, too often rude, the English tongue more discernable to her ear with each passing week.

She'd tried to venture out an hour ago, but the stupid guard who watched her Sibley like a hound had said no, not without an escort. Last thing she wanted.

The skies had cleared. Overhead, a hawk circled, then drifted toward the canyons and beyond with its wings spread. Free to go where it chose. Unlike her.

New idea. She could head for the outhouses. Dare the guard to follow. Sneak off as she had before—

Footsteps behind her.

She pivoted and jumped.

Ramsey. How had she not noticed his approach?

"Didn't mean to scare you." He stepped over a puddle.

His arm no longer in a sling, he held it close it to his body at an angle as if still sheltering it. Twice in the last two weeks, he'd stopped by her tent to apologize. Both times, she'd stayed inside, flap tied fast and palms pressed against her ears until he'd gone away.

"Good afternoon, Miss Tomopuikatukatu."

Eyes-Like-Sky nodded toward the prairie east of camp, searching for the English words. "Lead your men to victory this morning? Or was the enemy too tough?" Across the muddy field, cloth bodies and heads had wobbled on posts, spilling their life blood of straw, victims of repeated saber charges at full gallop.

"Cavalry practice. Got to keep the men sharp." He tipped his hat. "I sat along the side lines and gave orders. I'm not back to full duty yet." He patted his arm.

"Sharp? Like knife?" She smirked. "I think straw heads won."

His mouth quirked to the side. "I noticed you pacing. Thought you might like to go on a walk."

"I can wait." She turned away from him.

"Now or later, doesn't matter. I'll escort you when you're ready."

"Never be ready." She stomped off.

Secured to Eye-Like-Sky's hip, Little Star waved her arms in reaction to the sudden movement, as if saying, "Giddy up. Giddy up."

Ramsey followed. Strode passed, pivoted in front of her, and halted. "We need to talk."

She dodged. "No."

He latched onto her sleeve. "I'm sorry about the other day."

"Don't touch me." She jerked her arm away.

Across the grounds, a laundress stood up from her tub, washboard in hand, and stared at them.

"Please listen, Tomopuikatukatu." Garret's sandy-brown

hair dipped over his forehead as he blocked her path. "I was wrong. I didn't know your husband—"

"Right about that." Spanish blurted from her mouth as she stepped forward and jabbed her finger against his shell jacket. "Rangers scalp women. Soldiers do too. Does that mean you do same? A soldier shoots a child. You guilty of that too? Just because you're a soldier?"

He glanced at her finger, then met her glare. His frown reached his eyes, where golden specks floated in a sea of brown. "No. A man should be judged for his own actions. Not his people's." His Adam's apple bobbed. "I'll not speak against your husband anymore."

"Words. You believe my husband guilty." Her gaze scoured his stubble-darkened face for the answer.

"You know him. I don't. If he was a man of honor who loved you as you say, then he kept his word."

She blinked at him, deciphering the sentence.

Little Star blew a bubble of drool and reached toward the man in front of her.

The corners of his mouth edged upward. "May I give her something?"

"No."

He pulled a cracker out of his pocket but kept it low.

But Little Star didn't miss it. Her fingers widened in anticipation.

"I said no." Eyes-Like-Sky pivoted and marched toward the outhouses.

"What about your walk?"

"Not with you. I wait."

"We heard from your uncle."

She stuttered to a stop, her feet like stones as she turned toward him. "My uncle?"

He stood his ground, waiting for her. "A letter came this morning."

Her tongue stuck to the roof of her mouth as she retraced her steps. "What uncle? His name?"

"Walk with me. Outside of camp. I'll tell you."

"You tell me now."

"No." He set his jaw. "You're dying to get out of camp. The way you paced all afternoon, I'm surprised there's not a ditch in front of your tent."

"You watched?"

Was there a touch of red beneath his tanned face? "Anyone who stepped outdoors today and was half awake couldn't help but notice you."

She rolled her eyes. "Tell me about my uncle."

He pointed to the front, more like a wide opening of a corral than an official entrance, except wider with two gates and a tall arch, better at holding people in than keeping them out. "A walk. Just stay within sight of me. We don't have to talk the whole time."

"You need to talk. Not me." She tightened her grip on Little Star and tromped off for the gate, ignoring the whispers of soldiers who had nothing better to do than stop their work on the corral and gawk at her.

Outside the camp and its assorted hovels, her steps quickened. Mud, sand, beaten-down grasses. New shoots springing up, waiting for their life to be syphoned by the next norther.

Another hawk overhead. Eyes-Like-Sky inhaled. Fresh air still sweet from the morning shower filled her lungs. Sage tendrils brushed against her leggings. She'd head down to the river. Wander beneath the hackberry and myrtle trees. Gather berries. If she were with her people, she'd make pemmican.

Late fall. Dancing Eagle would never see another. Her steps slowed. She'd face the coming winter alone. For the rest of her life. Both of her arms slid around Little Star, and she lowered her head to kiss the baby's silky hair.

Why had God allowed her to lose everything, almost everything, again? God loved her. He was a personal God, not just an all-powerful creator beyond the stars. He'd sent His Son for her. The truth had permeated her childhood and embedded itself in her heart. But where was that love now? As cold and distant as the stars.

She shivered and tugged Little Star's fur wrap past the baby's ears.

"You need a jacket?" Ramsey caught up to her.

"Yes. You go get."

He snorted. "Not hardly. You can have mine." He slipped his arm halfway out of his sleeve.

"No. I want nothing from you but the letter. And what it said. Who my uncle is."

He straightened his jacket. "Mr. Robert LeBeau."

The name. She'd heard it before. No face came to mind.

Fine lines formed at the corners of Ramsey's eyes. "Do you remember him? He's your mother's brother."

Her mother. A dull ache formed behind her eyes. She turned from Ramsey and tightened her hold on the child bound to her chest. "LeBeau?" *Think of the man, not Mother.*

"Yes. The letter says he owns a plantation in East Texas. From what I hear, that part of the country is beautiful. Lots of hardwoods, real plants, not a spot of sand in sight."

A shadow of memory. A large white house with a wrap-around porch.

Ramsey studied her. "He's coming to take you home."

"Home?" Her belly tightened. "My home is there." She jutted her finger to the northwest. "How many times I tell you?"

His brow furrowed. "I know you see it like that now, Eyes-Like-Sky." Her name in English on his lips, gently spoken. "But your uncle and his family are overjoyed. They feared you'd died. They'll take you in. Make you part of their family. You'll see."

"I have no choice?"

He blew out a breath. "You need to give it a chance. He'll be your guardian. The colonel won't tell him no. This camp is temporary. Not a real home."

Her heart thudded in her ears. A man she couldn't remember would control her life. As if she were a child. And Little Star?

"No more talk." She shoved past him and hiked toward the river, her legs wobbly. She had to plot an escape.

With the late-November sun barely warm enough to stave off a chill, Garret's gaze followed Eyes-Like-Sky as she trudged through the hip-high grass and shrubs. Hadn't the girl ever heard of using a path? The tension in his shoulders eased. He hadn't won her forgiveness. But she'd conversed with him and conceded to walk with him. Well, not exactly walked with him, more like tolerated his presence when given no choice.

He paused at the top of the small bluff. Wind rippled through his linen shirt. Teeth gritted, he bent his left elbow, stiff as wood from weeks of little movement, and fumbled with his jacket buttons.

Eyes-Like-Sky wove her way past a scattering of scrub oaks and sank down in front of the hackberry tree. Several yards beyond her, a cormorant perched on a fallen tree trunk. The battered wood stretched half way across the river, its branches engulfing the far bank in a tangled maze. The bird's narrow head and bill tipped toward the murky water in search of dinner.

A muffled sob. Eyes-Like-Sky's shoulders didn't shake, but the sound had drifted up from where she sat cross-legged by a gnarled root, cradling the baby on her lap.

Seven years with the Comanche. Garret patted the letter in

his jacket pocket. According to LeBeau, a Comanche raiding party had attacked a small wagon train, killing Eyes-Like-Sky's father, mother, and two brothers. A sister, age ten, had been taken along with fourteen-year-old Maggie Logan.

Maggie no more. What had happened in those years that made her cling to the people who had massacred her family? Where was the sister?

Garret should have asked. But Eyes-Like-Sky's face had paled at the mention of her uncle and her mother. A quiver had laced her voice. He'd said enough for today.

CHAPTER 11

Garret turned up the wick on the lantern by his bedside. The rice-bag carpet crinkled beneath his boots as he shifted his attention back to his belongings strewn across his Mexican blanket. He tucked an extra shirt and a pair of socks into his saddlebag. With two days on horseback to Fort Belknap and a week on the Butterfield stage to St. Louis—a dirty, rough ride all the way—he wasn't about to take anything valuable.

Besides, he should save room in case he brought back a gift. Something practical to help assimilate Eyes-Like-Sky into civilized society. Maybe a Bible of her own. She'd shown interest. It could give her an incentive to relearn to read. Or maybe something simple like a hair comb or ribbon.

Eyes-Like-Sky might be gone by the time he returned.

The reality rolled through him. Her uncle would arrive while he was on furlough. Likely as not, he'd have her in East Texas before Garret made it back to Camp Cooper. Garret wouldn't have to worry about her anymore. Her family would look after her.

Provided they could put up with her attitude.

He blew out a breath. Tall order. He should be here, but the colonel had turned him down flat when he'd asked to postpone his trip.

"You'll be my eyes and ears," the colonel had added. "Let me know the temperament of the country now that Lincoln's been elected. And it wouldn't hurt you to take your mind off the Comanche princess for a while."

Take his mind off Eyes-Like-Sky. Where had that comment come from? The colonel's wife must have fed him a load of nonsense. With a hard shove, he wedged his writing set into the bag next to his shaving kit.

"Are you sure you don't need an escort?" Charlie called from the outer room. "I'd be happy to oblige. A whole month in a decent-size city. Real food, brandy, a theatre... making the acquaintances of young, unattached women."

"It's not going to be as glamorous as you think." Garret lapped the saddlebags over his shoulder. "Two weeks at most in St. Louis by the time I'm done with all of the travel." He stepped through the beaded curtain. "A couple days with my father is usually more than enough. And then there's Lily—"

"Ahh, I could help you with the fair damsel, if you're not enamored with her charms." Standing beside the grime-ribbed tub and dressed only his long johns, Charlie rubbed a towel over his freshly washed hair.

"Depending on how the trip goes, I might come back and say you're welcome to her." Garret slipped his haversack off its hook. "What I really want to talk to you about is Eyes-Like-Sky."

"*Damsel*'s not the word that comes to mind in the case of your warrior woman."

"She's not *my* anything. I'm asking you to try to keep her out of trouble while I'm gone."

"That girl's your peck of trouble, not mine." Charlie

moseyed over to the small mirror as he added shaving soap to his tin mug.

"The woman needs someone to look after her, Charlie."

"And you think you're the man?" Charlie smirked.

"I think you're a pain in my backside."

Charlie dipped his boar-bristle brush into the soap and stirred. "I reckon I can make sure no one burns her clothes again or tries to kidnap the baby, as long as you promise to bring me back a jug of brandy and couple cans of oysters."

"The oysters are no problem, but transporting a jug back in one piece on that washed-out gully of a road?"

"I have no pity for you, mister. I spent the last three weeks in the saddle." Charlie lathered his face. "And I couldn't get an invite to a decent meal anywhere along the frontier."

"Not even at the larger homesteads?"

"Not hardly. The whole blasted lot blame us for their Indian troubles. And some fools still accuse us of helping those abolitionist devils who burned Dallas this summer." Charlie drew the blade in a steady swipe to his chin. "I'm tired of being called a Lincolnite because I wear a blue uniform. I'd be happy to spit on good ole Abe's boot."

Garret pressed his lips shut. He'd wasted too many hours arguing politics with Charlie. "I thought we'd agreed to disagree on that."

"All right, I've had my say for tonight. What about you and me go over to Doc's office and have ourselves a game of cards after supper?"

"That'd suit me fine." Garret closed the flap on his haversack. "But I've got an errand to finish first."

Charlie raised his eyebrows. "Don't tell me. Something to do with Miss Tomopuikatukatu?"

"I have no intention of telling you." He grabbed his jacket from the hook and winced as he worked his left arm into the sleeve. All these weeks, and his arm still only had the flexibility of green wood. "See you at the card game."

Eyes-Like-Sky squatted by the Sibley stove stirring the flour, salt, and water in an earthen bowl. Finally, they'd given her the means to cook her own meals. No more mealy bread and sawdust gravy. A pan of hackberry paste sat on the dirt beside her. She'd spread it on the finished flat bread. If she could get a hold of some nuts and dried antelope meat, she could make pemmican. Store it away in pouches for their escape.

Crinkling her nose at the smell, she dipped her fingers into a small jar and gathered a pinch of lard.

Footsteps crunched outside of her door. The canvas rattled. It was him. No one else knocked like that.

Her hand stilled.

"Tomopuikatukatu?" Ramsey tapped the canvas again.

She set the bowl on a gum blanket and wiped her fingers on a rag. Maybe he'd go away if she kept quiet. And miss her first chance at a conversation in three days? Besides, this wasn't a man to take silence as an answer. Best go see what he wanted before he managed to wake Little Star.

Ramsey stepped back as she came out of the opening. A rolled hide tucked beneath his arm, this time he'd readied himself before showing up at her door. Clean-shaven, jacket buttoned, and hat in place. A wave of rich brown hair dipped over his forehead.

"Want something?" She crossed her arms. "I'm busy. Work to do."

Across the parade ground, a bugle rang out the evening song, "To the Colors."

"I wanted to return this." Ramsey slipped the roll from

beneath his left arm. A piece of rope held it tight. "It's not doing any good sitting around my quarters."

The gift she'd thrown at his feet a couple weeks before. Enough to make a gown for Little Star and an extra blouse for herself. Her fingers twitched.

Ramsey shrugged. "I'm sure one of the scout's wives could make something out of it if you don't need it."

"No. I not let it go to waste." She took the hide and dropped it into the tent behind her. "Anything else? Work to do."

"I could take you for a walk? Might be your last chance until your uncle gets here."

"Why last chance?" She rubbed her nose with the backside of her floured hands.

Brown eyes looked dead center into hers. "I'm leaving in the morning."

"What do you mean?"

"I'm traveling to Missouri to see my family. I'll be gone four weeks."

Why should she care? But her heart thudded. She'd be more alone than ever.

She'd have to face her uncle on her own.

He removed his hat and tapped it against his thigh. "You'll probably be gone by the time I return."

"Maybe, maybe not." And maybe not where he thought she'd be going.

He cocked his eyebrows. "If you have any trouble while I'm gone, talk with Lieutenant Fuller. He's agreed to help."

She bit her lip. Fancy rider, fancy dresser, but Fuller could care less what happened to her and Little Star.

"Wait." She ducked into the tent.

"Excuse me?"

Her knees hit the ground as she slipped her arms through the cradleboard straps. This could be her last opportunity to see more of the surrounding area before she ran away.

His eyes widened as she emerged through the flap. A trace of a smile flitted across his lips. He wanted to go on a walk with her. Why? It was more than surface kindness. Guilt? Pity? Or something else? Her stomach knotted.

He let her set the pace as they walked. A wave of his hand at the sentries assured their exit through the gate. The dough in her bowl would stiffen, but that didn't matter. This was her chance to breathe.

Beyond the river and across the open prairie, the western sky blazed. Muted orange flowed toward the earth. Streaks of golden light shot towards the heavens and called to her across the darkening blue.

Her tribe was somewhere out there. Would they welcome her if she made it back? What had become of Owl Woman? Eyes-Like-Sky shivered.

"We can't stay out long. It'll be dark soon." Ramsey strode along beside her. "You could step on a snake or tarantula."

"I be fine. My people walk in the dark. Hear the rattlers." She didn't have time for pleasantries. It'd be dark soon. She needed to assess possible routes. The trees by the river would provide good cover. But what was the best way beyond that? "I walk ahead. You stay?"

"No." He touched a fingertip to her sleeve. "Too dangerous."

For her? Or was the danger that she might run off? Not even a mention of how the Comanche weren't her people. "I look after myself."

He glanced at the riverbank ahead and then back at the fort. "I'll tell you what. Leave the baby with me. Then, you can go on a little ways."

"I not leave Little Star."

He quirked his mouth to the side. "Then I'm walking with you. I don't want to have to find you in the dark."

She skewered him with her gaze. How had she come to the point of allowing the man who had killed her husband anywhere near her child? The man responsible for hollowing her insides out until she felt like an empty gourd. But this man would not hurt a baby. "If she cries, you yell for me."

"Hurry back. I don't care how well you hear snakes. We're going in after sunset."

Shoulders stiff, she settled the cradle against a rock and jabbed a finger in Ramsey's direction. "You take good care."

She hurried off as quickly as she could weave her way along the path and down the riverbank.

Frogs croaked closer to the water. Dusk fell heavy here. Tree branches obscured the remaining traces of light, but that was all right. If she escaped, it'd be at night. In three weeks, the moon would be full. That'd be her window. She'd wait for her uncle. Meet him, and then she'd decide.

A couple river bends later, a tiny wail echoed across the plain. Eyes-Like-Sky retraced her steps, quickening her pace, and scurried up the bank. *Hold on, baby girl.*

Up ahead, Ramsey knelt beside the rock, fumbling with the cradle.

Whimpers carried on the breeze.

"I'm coming, baby girl." Sky slowed and picked her way through a tangle of grass.

Ramsey lifted Little Star into his arms, his deep voice light, musical as he prattled to the child, the words indiscernible at this distance.

A half-hearted whimper answered.

The way Ramsey hoisted Little Star above him slowed Eyes-Like-Sky's step. His hands gripped her sides, holding her like a little flying bird. She giggled, and he returned the smile. This man would make a good father someday.

Goosebumps shimmied up Sky's arms. Good thing he was leaving. Before she had any more stupid thoughts.

~

Stars sparkled in the growing dark as Garret escorted Eyes-Like-Sky back to her tent. The ends of her dark, thick hair dipped to her collarbone, longer now than when she'd sheared it off in jagged edges after the battle. He winced and shoved away the image of her hands covered in her husband's blood.

Little Star watched him over her mother's shoulder, wide-eyed and chubby-cheeked.

He might not see either of them again.

Eyes-Like-Sky paused at the entrance to the Sibley and lifted her chin. Their gazes met. Lanterns and oil lamps glowed from the windows of the men's quarters. Murmurs carried from open doorways.

The long fringes of Eyes-Like-Sky's sleeve rustled as she touched the small leather pouch which swung below her collarbone. She never seemed to be without it. What treasure did it contain? "You leave tomorrow?"

"Yes." Too soon. Shouldn't even be going. He stuffed his right hand in his pocket. "There was something else in your uncle's letter I'd like to ask about."

She shifted Little Star to her other shoulder. "What?"

Settling the cradleboard against the canvas, he swallowed. "I'm wondering about your sister. Your uncle said she was taken captive with you."

She stiffened. "No concern of yours."

"Your uncle will be very concerned."

"My sister is dead." Her voice scratched the air between them.

His gaze traveled over her flat expression and deerskin garments to the buffalo robe beyond the open tent flap. "You'd say the same thing even if she were alive."

Eyes-Like-Sky jostled Little Star, lightly bouncing the child in her arms. "Maybe so. But she's dead."

"Your uncle will want to know the details."

She narrowed her eyes at him. "My sister, Morning Fawn, was adopted. Loved. Well-cared-for. But one hard winter got sick. Died."

Well-cared-for by some of the same people who'd butchered her family? He'd heard stories of younger captives being treated royally. Taken in by Comanche families who'd lost a child or didn't have their own. But was the girl really dead? He'd take her word for now. "I'm sorry for your loss."

"Long time ago."

He dug the toe of his boot in the sand. "What about you? How were you treated?"

Her glare could have skewered him.

Should have kept his mouth shut. He slipped his hat from his head. "Pardon me. You don't have to answer."

A dog barked in the distance.

"I tell you." Her free hand curled into a fist. "I was a slave to an angry man. His wife not any better. Many scars." She waved her hand over her body. "My sister snuck food. Gave it to me. But the man, Old Wolf, left the village. Took his wife and me. Never saw my sister anymore."

Garret's gaze skimmed over the small scar close to her hairline, then dropped to another mark on her neck before moving on to her hands. The dim lighting hid the rough pinkish marks from his eyes, not from his memory. How many more did she carry? How many deeper than flesh? His brow furrowed. "I'm sorry that man hurt you."

She jutted her chin. "Don't need your pity. I take care of myself. I stood up one day. Hit his wife with a bone. Almost killed her." Her voice sinew-hard, matter-of-fact, as she cuddled her child close. "No more beatings."

From the wife. What about Old Wolf? Nothing he could ask.

Her chest rose and fell hard as if she'd just finished the fight. Fire lit her eyes.

Words fell off his tongue. "I admire your courage and strength." Had he really just paid her a compliment? How stupid.

Her expression hardened. She stepped toward him, not in the soft, getting-closer-to-talk manner, but in the I'm-getting-ready-to-put-you-in-your-place way. "Dancing Eagle rescued me. Bought me. Set me free. Asked me to be his wife. He was like morning sun at end of dark night. And you—"

Garret sucked in a breath.

Killed him. Her eyes said it even though her mouth did not.

Little Star burst out with a small cry, wriggling her head against her mother's chest.

"I have to feed her. No more talk." Eyes-Like-Sky pivoted toward the tent opening.

This could not be goodbye. Garret dug into his pocket. "I have something for you, Tomopuikatukatu." His voice dipped on her name.

"I want nothing from you."

"Not from me. Dancing Eagle." What if she used it to run away? But he couldn't leave her with nothing. He held the neckerchief-covered metal out to her.

She gaped.

White linen slipped away to reveal a two-inch-wide gold armband.

"A man took them from the battlefield. Gave it to me later. He figured—"

She grabbed the band from his hand. The neckerchief fluttered to the ground. "Your coup. Like a scalp."

He flinched. "I didn't ask for it."

"But you kept it."

He tapped his hat to his leg. "What else was I to do?"

She rubbed her thumb across the engraved metal. "I never thought I see this again." Her voice faltered.

"I want you to have it. In case you need money of your own after you're off living with your uncle."

"I never sell it." Wet eyes sparkled up at him.

Did he see gratitude there? Sure looked like it. He cleared his throat. "I have a second armband. I'll...give it to you when I return."

"Why not now? I might be gone."

He exhaled. If he gave her both, she might be tempted to sell one and try to find her way back to Indian Territory. He had to give her a reason to stick around. "If you leave before I return, I'll travel to East Texas on my next furlough and bring it to you at your uncle's."

She glared at him. "Hundreds of miles?"

"It'll give me a chance to see how he's treating you." He shrugged. "It might take a while before I get that much leave. Six months or a year."

"You want to keep the gold for yourself."

"I'm a man of my word. I'll return the second band."

"We will see." Her voice trailed off to a whisper as she turned back to the tent. "Your word...worth as much as a handful of sand."

CHAPTER 12

Eyes-Like-Sky touched the green cotton dress which lay before her on the crate. Sturdy material, plain collar and undersleeves. A hand-me-down from Mrs. Clark, taken in to fit Eyes-Like-Sky's more slender proportions.

Angelina stepped closer. A few strands of black hair had slipped from the knot at the base of her neck and clung to her rounded face. "You could wear it just for today. For your first meeting with your uncle. Make a good impression."

Eyes-Like-Sky withdrew her hand. A memory played in her head. A swing hung from a tree. She'd spent hours in it, day after day, the breeze and the shade saving her chemise from being plastered to her skin. Angry, muffled voices had come from the fancy, paned windows. Sometimes her mother and LeBeau. Other times, LeBeau and her father or just the tight voices of her parents.

Her uncle had been a man to avoid. She turned to Angelina. "I don't care about impression."

Angelina's cactus-colored shawl sagged to her elbows. "I tell you, Maggie, Tomopuikatukatu, such thinking will not help you." She knelt beside Little Star on the buffalo robe and held out a bright-colored rag doll she'd made for the child. No hair, just a stuffed cloth body with arms and legs. "Your uncle came here to claim you and give you a home. Look at all of the trouble he's gone to. Those men he rode in with? The black one is his servant, but the other five are bodyguards. Three of them ex-Texas Rangers, to provide protection for you on the journey east."

"And Little Star." She threw back her shoulders. "She goes where I go."

"Yes, yes, Little Star" Angelina wiggled the doll toward the baby's open hands. "Your uncle has done so much. If you anger him and turn him away, who else is there? You can't live in a tent in the middle of two hundred men forever. Do you think I like the things that some of these texans call me? Or being treated like I am beneath them? No, but I have a home, and I make money. I send it to my family."

"I understand your words." Eyes-Like-Sky's gaze fell to the dress once more.

"Just the first day, señora, then return to your deerskin if you want. And keep quiet about your husband. Tell all that later."

One day, and then the next. Shedding her life, her people's ways, her ties to Dancing Eagle, one layer at a time. "No." Her voice shook. It'd never be for just one day.

The man coming to claim her would control her fate if she let him. She'd spied on him through a slit in her tent when he'd ridden in last night. The tight rein he'd kept on his horse, the way he'd barked orders at his men, the way the servant had jumped to anticipate his needs.

"Señora." Angelina slapped her hands to her knees. "You're too stubborn for your own good."

Little Star squeezed the doll in her small fists and gnawed on it, drool wetting the bright yellow and red.

Eyes-Like-Sky lifted her hands. "I'm sorry. No dress for me.

You want to put that on Little Star?" She waved toward the white lacey gown and bonnet Angelina had spread out on the robe. "I let you. And you can add a rag for her bottom."

Angelina sighed and turned toward the child, scooting the rag and washbowl closer.

Eyes-Like-Sky's stomach churned. Was she making a mistake? Risking hers and Little Star's future by not wearing the dress?

Wet rag in hand, Eyes-Like-Sky scrubbed the spot of curdled milk from her deerskin blouse. Still dressed in the Apache skirt, she'd only had time to make one garment from the deer hide Ramsey had given her.

Little Star had chosen the worst moment possible to spit up.

"Mmmmamama." The baby prattled as she pushed herself upon wobbly elbows and knees, teetered for a moment, then collapsed on her belly.

Eyes-Like-Sky threw down the rag and picked up her child, dusting sand off her soft cotton gown. She should not have agreed to change one stitch of Little Star's clothing.

"Miss Logan?" A deep voice boomed outside of her canvas.

"Come in." She retreated to the center of the tent and plopped Little Star down at her feet.

She held her breath.

A black felt slouch hat, so clean it must have been in one of those boxes on the back of the mules, poked through the flap. Dressed in a dark frock coat, Robert LeBeau tapped his silver-tipped walking stick on the ground and stretched up to his full height. Ice-blue eyes, a neatly trimmed mustache, and side-burns sprinkled with gray. A face just short of handsome, frozen in discontent.

She shivered.

Frowning, he slipped his hat from his head, his drawl more pronounced than any soldier's at the camp. "Marguerite?"

The foreign name rattled through her. "Maggie." *Eyes-Like-Sky.*

"Maggie? Yes, your parents called you that." His gaze scoured every inch of her before returning to her face. "You've changed. Grown." He walked half a circle around her. "You look so much like your mother, God rest her soul."

An image of a woman came back to her—soft voice, dark curls, a smile that lit her whole face. Mother. A pang shot through Eyes-Like-Sky's heart, followed by memories, flashes of blood, bodies, and war whoops. The meager bites of breakfast she'd been able to force down threatened to return to her throat.

Her uncle's breath came out in short puffs. "I never thought I'd lay eyes on Katie's daughter again. We thought you were dead."

"I survived." She swayed beneath the weight of the word, the reality.

He frowned. "What about Elizabeth, your sister?"

"No." She wrapped her arms around her midsection. "Lost her years ago. Got sick. Died." Would he believe the lie?

"I'm sorry to hear that." Coffee and alcohol wafted from his breath. "One more life taken by those devils."

"A Comanche family adopted her. Loved her."

He gaped at her. "What in the blazes are you talking about, girl? Are you touched in the head? The Comanche slaughtered your family." He swung his hand wide, his walking stick held out like a scepter.

She hung her head and bit her lip. "I know what they did. See it in my dreams."

"Then how dare you defend them?"

She dug her nails into her palms. Foolish to try to explain anything to this man.

He tapped his hat to his trouser leg and shook his head. “Never mind. You’re here now. We’ll have you home soon.”

Home? It would never be.

His gaze trailed over her once more and snagged. “What did they do to your hair?” He lifted his hand as if to touch her. “Couldn’t they find you decent clothing? You’ve been here two months, and they can’t get you a dress?”

She swallowed as she placed her palm against the soft doeskin that covered her chest. “My clothes.”

“You’re dressed like one of them.” He wrinkled his nose as if she stunk. “If I had any idea you’d been so neglected, I would have been here sooner. I’ve brought you proper clothing. That’s one of the reasons my arrival was delayed. I paid a dressmaker to rush the order. Had to guess at your measurements.” His voice echoed in her ears.

Little Sky’s face puckered, and she reached up with a whimper, latching onto her mother’s leggings.

Eyes-Like-Sky scooped the child up.

“That’s one of theirs.” The line across his forehead turned into a ridge. “They told me there was a baby.”

She wrapped her arms around Little Star. “My daughter.”

A crevice as deep as the Mississippi furrowed his brow. “Sired by a savage.” His voice dropped like a gavel. “I don’t blame you. You didn’t have a choice. If those blasted soldiers had done their jobs seven years ago instead of lolly-gagging around the fort...”

Her tongue stuck to the roof of her mouth. “Her father was my husband.”

“Husband?” He spit out the word. ”Her father was a murdering savage. I thank God he’s dead. If your pa had listened to me instead of dragging his family off into some God-forsaken wilderness... I opened my home to your family when your mama came begging after your father’s delicate sensibilities lost him his position at the bank. Found him a job as a cotton factor. But he was too hard-headed, too prideful—"

"My father was a good man." She clenched her fist. Every muscle in her turned sinew-hard. "My daughter's father, my husband, good man. Gave him my heart. No regrets."

Any trace of warmth dissipated in the ice-blue of his eyes. "Quiet." He rapped his walking stick against the ground.

Thud. Thud. The sound jarred her with each strike.

And as if that wasn't loud enough, he swung the end a third time against the side of the stove. "I'll not have you raise your voice to me, niece. I traveled four-hundred miles to come fetch you, most of it on stagecoach and horseback. Dirt, mud, wet, snakes. I will not stand here and listen to you defend those barbarians."

Little Star wailed.

LeBeau sucked in a deep breath and blew it out slowly before smoothing his forefinger and thumb across his mustache and over his chin. "I'll see you at dinner at the colonel's. My man will bring you the dress. Wear it. Angelina can alter it."

The sand crunched beneath his polished boots as he marched to the flap and exited. A path of toe and heel imprints remained in his wake.

Muffled voices came from outside. Raising her shirt, Eyes-Like-Sky shoved Little Star onto her breast to quiet her as she tromped across the buffalo robe and placed an ear to the canvas wall, heart pounding.

"Colonel, she's out of her blasted head. They've turned her wild. Defending those low-down, murdering devils..." Her uncle rumbled and sputtered. "Nothing but a pack of rabid dogs. I'd like nothing better than to put a bullet in every single one of them."

"I tried to warn you, LeBeau." The colonel's voice rattled. "You've got to give her time. Patience, civilization, a real home.

She'll come to her senses. They had her for seven years. It might take months or longer. I've heard stories—"

"So have I." LeBeau snorted. "Some lunatic girl over in Jacks County. A returned captive. Spends her days rocking on the porch, uncombed, unbathed, staring off into thin air, except every now and then, she runs off into the woods screaming. But I never dreamed, Marguerite—"

"Your niece isn't as bad off as that."

"Turns my stomach. Thank God, her mother didn't live to see this day. She looks like one of them. Smells like one of them. And clutching that half-breed baby—"

"Not the child's fault, LeBeau."

Eyes-Like-Sky shuddered.

"I know," he muttered. "I'll need your help to find the baby a home. And a wet nurse. My wife would never tolerate having a bastard child like that around, and neither would I. When I ride out of this camp with my niece, she's leaving every trace of Comanche behind."

Never. Her arms tightened around her child. No one was taking Little Star from her, ever.

CHAPTER 13

Garret slipped into the dimly lit library. The buzz of voices faded as he clicked the door shut behind him. A hazy glow emanated from a white-globed oil lamp on the small mahogany table at the center of the room. Shadows hung heavy across the thick carpet, book-filled shelves, and high-backed chairs. A heavy drape covered the bay window. He pushed it aside. Beyond the wraparound porch of the two-story brick Italianate mansion, lanterns lined the walkway, leading down through hedge and barren trees to the Mississippi. A world away from Camp Cooper. And Eyes-Like-Sky.

How was she fairing? The nine days since he left felt like a month.

His cravat scratched at his neck. It'd been over two years since he'd worn a formal suit. Since he'd worn anything but his uniform.

He exhaled, willing the tension to ebb from his shoulders. A few minutes of quiet. Solitude.

The door clicked. Light flooded in along with a trace of cigar smoke. His father's voice and Theodore Parker's laugh echoed from down the hall. Lily Stanwick stepped in, wine glass in hand, and closed the door. Trouble. Two slender blond ringlets framed her face above her magenta silk-satin dress. Draped across her white-gloved arms, her sheer stole fluttered behind her.

His gaze snagged on the sapphire necklace which dangled a couple of inches above the scooped neckline of her dress and her ample cleavage. He should have locked the door when he came in, but it was Parker's house, not his.

The lacy flounces of her skirt swished as she crossed the room. "I thought I might find you in here."

"Just resting for a few minutes before dinner." He pivoted back to the window. Best keep his eyes somewhere safe.

"Now, don't tell me a big, strong cavalryman like you is tired out from our little social gathering." She set the glass on the window sill and slipped her hand around the crook of his arm.

He stiffened. "I'm out of practice. No high-society dinners in Camp Cooper."

"We'll have to reacquaint you with civilized society, Captain." She swayed on his arm, allowing her bosom to brush against his sleeve. "I looked for you after your parents and the Parkers retired for the evening last night." She turned him toward her and traced her index finger along the buttons of his silk waistcoat. Pouty-lipped, she gazed up at him through half-closed hazel eyes. Her perfume filled his nostrils.

He took hold of her hand to still her incessant touch. "I was tired, and my arm was acting up."

"You could have been killed in that battle." She shuddered. "Thank goodness, you're an excellent marksman and put a bullet in that savage's chest."

He blew out a breath. "I'd rather not talk about it."

"If you insist." She pulled her fingers free of his and smoothed her hand over his sleeve, caressing his bicep. Her words curled around him. "But you're still my hero. Maybe I could massage your arm or place a warm compress over it. Make it feel better. You could show me the scar?"

"No." Last thing he needed to do was take his shirt off around her. During the summer of their courtship, he'd had no inclination to refuse her friendly overtures. Heated hours on the parlor sofa had filled their half-sleepless nights. They'd never consummated their passion, but they'd gone too far. He would not entangle himself again.

Her hand slipped beneath his frock coat, stroking his pocket watch fob. "Didn't you miss me?" She fluttered her lashes at him.

He squirmed beneath her touch. No. He pushed her hands away. "It's been two years, Lily."

"Two years and three months."

"We need to take things slow. Get reacquainted." Even that felt like too much of a commitment.

A regal smile spread across her face. "Getting reacquainted is exactly what I have in mind."

He stepped clear of her skirt folds which lapped against his trouser legs. "I mean in the daylight hours. Talking. Going on walks. Dinners. I want to keep things proper."

She arched an eyebrow. "Since when? I recall your enthusiasm for our late-night discussions." She tossed her head. "And suppose we became engaged? Then, it wouldn't be altogether improper."

He sidestepped to the table and turned up the wick on the lamp. "Let's take it one step at a time. Besides, I have three more years before my enlistment is up."

"Three years? Is there some new rule about officers not getting married?"

"You'd hate Texas. Snakes, tarantulas, sand, heat, and drought. Not to mention Comanche raiders. No place for a lady."

She tugged on the lapels of his frock coat and gazed up at him with sharp eyes. "Is there someone else?"

"No." As soon as the word left his mouth, blue eyes and dark wavy hair flashed across his brain. Stupid. Impossible. Best get that idea right out of his head. She'd likely be gone by the time he returned. Besides, she hated him. And had every right to.

"No one. But I never bound you to me, Lily. When I left for Texas, I gave you permission—"

"I haven't been sitting around gathering dust if that's what you're worried about, Captain." Lily smirked. "But before you turn all Puritan on me, I want to show you what you're missing." She stretched up on tiptoes, drew his head down, and pressed warm, wet lips to his.

Heat coursed through his veins. Two years since he'd kissed or held a girl. His lips moved against hers. It'd be so easy to—

He broke off the kiss.

She pulled away. "It appears you haven't forgotten everything." A self-satisfied smile glistened across her lips.

He scrubbed his hand over his jaw. "I meant everything I said about wait—"

"Surely, something could be done." She twirled the end of her feather-light stole around her finger and batted her lashes. "Your father could speak to someone. He has contacts in Washington. Maybe he could get you transferred to a decent post like St. Louis. A good place to settle down with a wife."

Garret's eyes narrowed. "I don't need my father's help. The U.S. Army isn't under his jurisdiction." His hands clenched. "Don't you dare suggest any such notion to him. If and when I'm ready to marry, I'll let you know." His dress boots clomped across the carpet as he left the room.

Halfway through dinner, Garret sat clenching and unclenching his hand beneath the table. The oyster stew had been perfect, but it'd slid down his throat with little notice, followed by portions of his peas, squash, potatoes, and beef roast.

He was getting himself worked up over nothing. His father had no control over his military post or career. Thank God there was some place where regulations and protocols were adhered to regardless of wealth, class, and backroom deals. He'd gotten into West Point without his father's help and against his father's will. But would the congressman have even considered his application to the academy if his last name had been Smith from some pig farm instead of Ramsey of Ramsey Industries? No matter. Once he walked onto that campus, everything had been based on merit or the lack thereof.

Across from him, Lily's fingers curled around Theodore Parker II's arm. She prattled on to him, lavishing her charm on the fellow who seemed to hang on her every smile. The poor man probably didn't have a clue she was doing it for spite. With his cream-colored complexion, large, soft hands, and rounded belly, had the man ever done a day's worth of physical labor in his life?

On Garret's right, his mother paused in her conversation with the plump Mrs. Parker and frowned at Lily.

"Garret, my boy." His father's voice boomed from the end of the table. "Tell Mr. Parker about that warrior you killed in hand-to-hand combat in the Battle of Mule Creek."

Garret laid down his fork. Might have known his father couldn't leave it to the simple telling last night to the family.

Mr. Parker swallowed his brandy. "Yes, please, Captain Ramsey. You boys in blue are doing our country a real service." His balding head reflected the shimmering chandelier light.

Garret exhaled. "It wasn't exactly hand to hand. We were on

horseback. He looked like some sort of chief." Funny, he'd never asked Eyes-Like-Sky if that were the case. "He was very brave. An excellent fighter." Sweat broke out on the back of his neck.

"The warrior put an arrow in Garret's arm, sliced clear through to the bone." Father plopped his forearms on the table, his black frock coat, tailored to fit snug across his broad chest, pressed against the table edge. More muscular than most of his class, his father had shoveled coal as a young boy and tended horses before he'd risen in the world. Saved every scrap he had and invested, then reinvested his gains. Bought a warehouse. Then a shipping company and an iron mill. Now he couldn't understand why his now oldest son didn't want to share the miniature empire he'd built.

"Maxwell, such words at the table." His mother scolded. "There are ladies present."

Mrs. Parker fluttered a hand to her throat, draping her thick fingers over her emerald necklace. "You poor boy."

"I, for one, am fine with hearing the details." Lily traced her fingernail along the curled design of the tablecloth.

"Did you whip the whole tribe?" Mr. Parker leaned forward.

"Mostly. A few got away." Garret stirred the remains of his peas.

"It's about time they give the U.S. Cavalry free reign." His father's eyes sparked above his neatly trimmed beard. "Those generals up at West Point and Washington need to stop their pacification of the savages and clear them out of Texas."

"It's not that simple, sir."

"Van Dorn had it right in 1858. Your first battle. That man didn't let a line in the sand stop him. His commander told him to pursue Comanches, and that's what he did. Crossed the Red River. Didn't wait to send a note back asking for permission. That's how a man fights a war. Same as running a business. Takes the initiative. He and Sul Ross, with Garret as a lieutenant, struck the rascals at Wichita Village. Two hundred cavalrymen and friendly Indians against more than four hundred Comanche, Chief Buffalo Hump among them. Those savages didn't know what hit them."

Garret cleared his throat and laid down his fork. "Those Comanches and Wichitas had just signed a peace treaty with a nearby fort the day before. They were celebrating. Figured the U.S. Army could keep their word for a few days."

His father clenched his knife handle, upending the blade perpendicular to the table. "Peace treaty, my foot. Those redskins just wanted free food and to lull that backwoods commander into thinking they wanted peace. They would have struck in middle of the night, caught those soldiers in their beds a week or two later, or traveled back into Texas and murdered farmers and ranchers."

"Van Dorn didn't have a clue about the treaty until afterwards." Garret worked the knot of his cravat free.

"Providence, then. The man did his job. He should receive a medal for saving settlers' lives and restoring order."

Garret's dinner threaten to return to his throat. The major should have been brought up on charges for ordering his men to fire into tipis. "Some hero. The Texas frontier has been paying the price ever since with revenge raids."

His father pounded the table with his fist, jarring the crystal. "The problem is that Van Dorn didn't finish the job. From what I've read in the papers, the War Department either needs to get a man with some guts or help Texas fund another five hundred Rangers. Take care of those savages."

Garret tossed his napkin onto his almost-empty plate. "Excuse me, sir. This isn't fit dinner talk for the ladies." His chair scraped the floor as he stood.

Was it any wonder he spent his life avoiding his father?

~

The next evening, Garret stood with his hands clasped behind his back and lips pressed shut. The lamp on the rent table blazed at full wick. His father paced in front of him. No use interrupting the tirade. Any comment could add an hour. The acrid smell of cigar smoke hung like a haze over their heads.

The floor creaked beneath his father's tromping. "What did you do to spoil things with Lily? The lady adores you, came all this way to see you, and now she's fawning over young Cyrus Parker? Can't you do anything right?" He jabbed the cigar in Garret's direction. "You had three months with her before you shipped off to Texas. We all expected an engagement."

Garret frowned. "I wasn't ready to marry."

"Well, you'd better get yourself ready. A lady like her won't be on the bride market forever. She could have had half a dozen fellows these past two years, but she has her eye set on you."

Probably has had a half dozen fellows. Garret clasped his hands tighter. The thick band of the family ring cut into the flesh of his finger—an emerald set in a circle of black onyx, the only thing of value his grandfather had passed onto his son. When he'd come of age, his father had handed it down to him. A gift or a chain?

"With her father's connections to the railroads, we'd have an unending market for our iron, clear across the country and beyond." Father's watch chain jingled against his waistcoat as he slung his arms about. "Those new furnaces I bought down by the Monongahela are blasting full force. Between that and the new steamboat, I'm a bit strapped. But this country is posed for war, and I'm going to be ready."

"War? You're betting on a war?"

Father drew a long puff on the cigar. "A smart man knows

what way the wind's blowing before the storm hits. I didn't vote for Lincoln, but he's the man who'll bring it."

Garret shoved his hands into his pockets. "Lincoln's not interested in starting a war. His goal is to hold this country together."

"I'm not going to debate politics with my twenty-six-year-old son who's had his nose stuck in Texas for the last two years." He hooked his thumbs beneath his suspenders. "This country's going to war, and Ramsey Industries is ready to help supply the country's needs. And you, son, as soon as you finish your cavalry stint, will join me at the helm. Right where you belong. As a matter of fact, if I get enough government contracts, I could work on getting you transferred. Tell them I need you as my military liaison—"

"Keep your hands off my military career." Garret's jaw clenched.

"Career?" Father spit out the word. "You're a good marksman and horseman. I taught you. But riding around in the desert, shooting Indians, and then whining about it? That's no career. A man's got to set his shoulder—"

"You interfere, and I'll never set my shoulder to any enterprise you've touched for the rest of my life."

"Don't you threaten me, son." Father scowled. "I've driven myself full steam ahead for decades to make a life for this family. And you have no appreciation for it. Spoiled. I'm the head of this family, and you will respect me."

"I show you respect." His hands curled into fists at his sides. "But I'm my own man. Not your servant boy."

"If you were my servant, I would have fired you a long time ago."

"Too bad you can't fire your son."

"Don't think I wouldn't."

Garret yanked the ring off his finger and slung it on the table. "Go ahead. Do it."

The slamming of the door echoed behind him after he marched out the front entrance. Thunder rumbled overhead, and sprinkles splattered against him as he strode past the gate and all the way to the river.

Stars twinkled through the light fog off the river as Garret returned through the Parkers' back gate. The sprinkles had turned to a downpour, but by this late hour, every cloud had evaporated, leaving the sky clear. He stomped at the bottom of the porch steps. Mud oozed from the sides of his dress boots. His hair had begun to dry, but his frock coat and trousers still hung heavy and damp on his limbs. No matter, getting away from his father was worth a drenching.

His mother stepped out onto the porch as he reached the top step.

He smiled. Might have known she'd wait up for him.

Her face brightened as she handed him a dry coat. "Have a good walk?"

He kissed the top of her head. "I've had better." He shrugged off his wet garment, tossed it on a bench beneath the porch roof, and stuck his arms through the sleeves of the dry wool coat.

Mother tugged her fur-lined cloak close to her throat. "So tell me about your meeting with your father."

"I'm surprised you couldn't hear him all the way in the parlor."

She winced. "Lucetta Parker entertained us on the piano, and with both her and her mother singing, and the closed door, we managed to stay blissfully ignorant."

Garret paced. "Where should I begin? He claimed I disrespected him when I walked out of the dinner, but believe me, walking out was more respectful than what I felt like saying.

And then, there was his reminder that he expects me to resign from the cavalry when my five-year enlistment is up and join him in the company. Finally, he reiterated how Lily would make a fine wife."

Mother patted his coat sleeve and drew him to the rail. "Your father loves you. Even though you might not think so. But sometimes his advice is misguided."

His arm throbbed. "Advice? Orders."

"He gets a little too used to commanding sometimes. It's part of his nature." She curled her fingers around the crook of his elbow. "But marriage is nothing to be rushed into. Don't marry until you find the woman you want to spend the rest of your life with. Don't let your father dictate this personal area of your life."

Don't let my father dictate any area of my life. "I have no intention of marrying Lily."

His mother scanned his face in the shimmer of the moon. "Then make sure you behave yourself toward her."

His cheeks heated. Not a topic he planned to discuss. He shifted his gaze to the tree line. Muffled voices crept up from the river. A boat passing? Dampness settled around them.

Dark hair, blue eyes came to mind. He should have found a way to delay his trip a week. That would have given him time to maybe meet Eyes-Like-Sky's uncle. How could he have left her fate in the hands of someone she didn't even remember?

His mother touched his knuckle. "Where is your ring?"

He flexed his fingers. "I gave it back."

"You did what?" She gaped. "And he accepted it?"

"I don't know. I didn't wait around."

"I'll get it back for you, and you will wear it." Two deep lines settled between her eyebrows. "Regardless of how badly you and your father disagree, we're family. We can't let words take that away from us."

He's the one who wants another son. Probably wishes it was me who died in the river instead of Max Jr. Garret clenched his jaw shut. He would not break her heart with such words.

"He loves you." As if she'd read his mind, her voice softened to a plea. "I'll retrieve the ring, and you will wear it."

For her sake. Yes. With a shaky exhale, he nodded. Fifteen years ago, he'd been thrown clear of the steamboat accident when the boiler blew. Max was the better swimmer. Max should have survived. But somehow, he hadn't, and Garret had washed ashore half conscious. Not his fault. He couldn't have saved his brother. Yet guilt still weighed his heart down like lead. And not just his brother, but the woman he'd shot in the Battle of Wichita Falls. His bullet. His fault. Her blood on his hands and in his dreams.

He wouldn't fail Eyes-Like-Sky.

A foghorn, lonesome, distant, moaned in the night air.

He cleared his throat. "I'm returning to Texas earlier than planned."

"Why? Because of your father or Lily?" Her voice trembled. "How much earlier?"

"Day after tomorrow. Day after that at the latest."

She gripped the porch rail and squeezed her eyes shut. "We were going to spend Christmas together."

"I don't think Father and I could make it together in the same house until Christmas. Nor Lily, either, for that matter." He ran his hand over his hair. *Dear Lord, don't let Mother start crying.* "But that's not the main reason. I'm worried about a captive back at the fort."

"What kind of captive?"

"A girl. Taken by Comanches seven years ago. She has a baby. I...I killed her Indian husband in battle." His swallow stuck in his throat.

"I'm sure you had no choice." She squeezed his arm.

"It was his life or mine. He was the warrior who gave me the arrow wound."

"Garret..." Her voice firmed. "You have nothing to feel guilty about."

He stared off into the night. "Not guilt. Responsibility. She's a widow with a baby to care for."

"Doesn't she have family of some kind?"

"We found an uncle from East Texas. He's probably there right now." Could be gone already. With Eyes-Like-Sky. The Sibley, empty.

Lines deepening across her brow, his mother planted herself in front of him. Her gaze searched his face. "I thought I heard something in your voice."

What? He swallowed back the word. Best not to ask a question he didn't want to know the answer to. He leveled his tone flat. "There was nothing in my voice, Mother."

She raised an eyebrow.

He shrugged and jammed his hands into his coat pockets. "I just believe I need to head back. I'm not sure how it will go with her uncle. She hasn't taken kindly to integrating into civilized society. Someone should smooth the way and make certain he has her best interest in mind."

She crossed her arms. "Have you sketched her yet?"

"Excuse me?" He gaped at her. "I've done over a hundred drawings in Texas. Cacti, mesas, sunsets, even Apache."

"Have you drawn her?"

He blew out a breath. "She's a curiosity. A white girl who turned Indian. What's it matter?"

"Have you ever sketched Lily?"

He didn't answer.

She squeezed his hand. "I rest my case."

"You're wrong, Mother."

CHAPTER 14

The sun shimmered onto Eyes-Like-Sky's face as she untied the rope at the well. A light breeze rippled through her hair, mild enough to leave the sand on the ground and not in her eyes. Perfect weather, but she wasn't ready to run away, not yet. She had enough pemmican and water for several days, but there was the matter of how to steal a horse and sneak out unobserved. Every time she stepped out of her tent, someone was watching.

She dragged the wooden bucket over. A small black spider scurried along the knee-high well wall. With a thud, she squished it and ground it into the stone. If only all of her problems were so easily solved. She rolled her shoulders beneath the weight of the cradleboard and lowered the bucket into the cool, dark below.

At the corral, her uncle squatted inspecting a roan mare. He slid his hand along the forearm to the fetlock and lifted the hoof. More than a half-dozen men hovered near him, watching. LeBeau's buying spree had turned into a contest of who could wrangle up the best mount for him to purchase for his stable back home.

Fine with her. Anything that delayed his departure and the moment he'd try to take her with him.

"Señora, you should make friends with the man." Angelina stepped up to the well. A wide-mouthed jug rested against the curve of her generous hip. "Ten days, you have this standoff. You refusing to wear the dress, him not allowing you to have dinner with him. Not good."

"Suit me fine if I never eat with him."

"Señora, you win more bees with honey than vinegar." Angelina wagged a finger at her. "This man is to be your guardian. He will control your life for now."

"If I were a young man of twenty-one summers, he'd leave me be."

"Maybe. Probably not. But you a young lady on your own. And with him and the colonel and most everyone else thinking —" Her words skidded to an abrupt halt.

"That I'm out of my mind?" Eyes-Like-Sky finished the sentence. "But you know better."

"What I think doesn't matter. They hardly see me. I'm the Mexican servant, nothing more." She swatted at a fly. "But you listen to what I tell you. Put on the dress. Go to dinner tonight. Try to get along with your uncle."

The dress wouldn't be enough. He'd said every shred of Comanche had to go. Her fingers wrapped around the small pouch secure beneath the neckline of her blouse. She would not humble herself to that man.

Squirming in the cradleboard, Little Star burst out with a jumble of "mummummum."

Eyes-Like-Sky's throat constricted. She glanced beyond the camp buildings to the canyon. An ocean of prairie and canyons lay between here and where her tribe had planned to winter. More than a week's ride, not counting the time consumed by trying to hide her tracks. And the battle had likely shaken all of their plans. What if she ran into hostile warriors on her way there?

Angelina moseyed behind her and cooed to the baby. “My sweet angel girl. How are you today, baby cakes?”

Eyes-Like-Sky shuddered. It wasn’t just her life she’d be risking. It’d be Little Star’s as well. What if she complied with everything short of allowing LeBeau to take Little Star from her? Could she stomach such a hollowed-out life? “I wear the dress, you think my uncle change his mind? Not try to take Little Star away?”

Angelina gasped. “What makes you think—?” Her jug rattled against the wall as she moved into view beside Eyes-Like-Sky. “I reckon you must have heard he’s looking for a wet nurse.” Eyes averted, she dried her hands on her apron, wadding the cotton in her grip. “He’s worried about an infant making the long journey. Believes it’s best to leave her here for now, for her own...safety. Just until next year, when she’s a little older.”

A year? As if a year were nothing. But it was a lie. Angelina couldn’t even meet her gaze. LeBeau had no intention of letting her fetch her baby, ever.

Angelina mopped her forehead with a handkerchief. “Mrs. Thorson has volunteered to supervise the wet nurse and the baby’s care until then. The colonel hasn’t quite agreed yet, but he will. So you don’t have to worry.”

“Don’t worry?” She spit the words out. “They’re planning to steal my baby.”

“No, señora.” The older woman’s hand clamped down on hers. “Just for a year, I tell you. Not more. Maybe if you wear the dress and appease your uncle? Maybe less.”

Eyes-Like-Sky jerked her hand free.

With a deep frown, Angelina leaned in and whispered, “I probably shouldn’t, but I tell you this one more thing. I heard Señor LeBeau talking to the doctor about laudanum.”

"What's that?" She gripped the cradleboard straps so hard that the leather bit into her shoulders.

"Makes you sleepy. Takes away pain. Señor LeBeau asked for some to give you for when you have to leave Little Star. To help the heartache and settle you down for the trip. If you act too upset, they'll give it to you before then, to ease your nerves." She glanced toward the corral and scooted back a step. "You mustn't tell 'em I told."

As if taking her child wasn't enough, the man wanted to poison her. Turn her mind to sop. She drove her nails into her palms. At least when a Comanche attacked, he came at you with his arrow or knife, not some insidious smile under the cloak of kinship and civilization. Her legs wobbled as she retrieved the bucket from the depths and sloshed water into her own pitcher. "Thank you. I'll wear the dress." Wear it and gain their trust. She could smile too.

~

Bell-shaped sleeves scratched against Eyes-Like-Sky's arms that evening as she pulled the blue silk dress over a petticoat and some new contraption called a crinoline. Weeds. Enough weight to mire a person in the mud. She shuddered. Not her clothes. Not her life. But she'd endure it a few days. The cost of freedom.

From the mess hall, a dinner bell clanged. A whoop echoed from the direction of the enlisted men's barracks.

Angelina shuffled between her and the stove, bending to smooth the layers of ruffles. The woman had already spent hours taking in the waist and shoulders to make the dress fit. "But what about underneath?"

Eyes-Like-Sky lifted the hems to reveal doeskin leggings. "I am Comanche." She shoved her bare feet into her fur-lined moccasins.

Angelina muttered and scooped up the squirming Little Star from the buffalo robe.

Eyes-Like-Sky tensed. What if all of this was a ploy to get her away from Little Star long enough for them to steal her?

"I've decided to take her with me to dinner." She tossed her hair out of her eyes.

"That will not go over well with your uncle." Angelina bounced the baby on her hip. "I'm happy to sit here with her until you return."

"My uncle should be pleased. I agreed to wear this fluff." She flicked the lace trim. "This dress wouldn't last two days on the trail." She pressed Dancing Eagle's gold bands, hidden beneath the silk, tightening them against her upper arms, lest they slip.

The morning of Garret's departure, he'd rattled the tent flap, then stuck the second neckerchief-wrapped band in her hand. He'd looked at her as though she were one of his men who'd disobeyed an order. "I want you to know you can trust me. But you sell this, and I'll be coming after you."

"I never sell what belonged to my husband."

"Good." He'd jabbed his hat on his head. "And I'll still be coming by your uncle's someday to check on you."

"No need." She'd jutted her chin, but the words had fallen against his back as he'd marched off for the corral.

Little Star jabbered in Angelina's arms, shaking Eyes-Like-Sky from her thoughts.

"Señor LeBeau brought a second dress for traveling, green wool. More sturdy." Angelina walked over and grabbed a clump of blue netting from a crate. "You could wear a snood. I have a pretty lace one."

"I could wear a headband." She tugged her child from Angelina's worn hands. "My child goes with me."

Angelina's brow furrowed. "Very well. I'll hold her while you eat."

Glasses clinked amongst the lamplight. Stiff as the wood beneath her, Eyes-Like-Sky shifted on her seat. The hard oak bit into her back and hips like a slab of rock. When was the last time she'd sat at a table to eat? A lifetime ago.

Venison, rice, canned tomatoes, and dried peppers in porcelain dishes lay before her on a white table cloth. How did anyone keep anything white in this country?

In a rocker by the stone fireplace, Angelina hummed to the almost-sleeping Little Star, the baby's tiny fingers curled over the edge of a downy blanket. The back-and-forth creak of the rocker beat a steady rhythm beneath the hum of conversation.

Eyes downcast, Eyes-Like-Sky scooped a spoonful of rice. The granules stuck to the roof of her dry mouth, and their flavor faded on her tongue. Too much bad company for a decent appetite. But she worked her way through the bite. She'd need every ounce of strength she could muster on the open prairie.

Mrs. Thorson sipped her tea, prim and proper with her collar buttoned to her throat and her greying hair coiled at the base of her neck. "You look lovely tonight, Miss Logan."

"Yes, she does." LeBeau's lips curved upward fbetween his distinctive side whiskers. "Thankfully, Marguerite has come to her senses."

Don't count on it. Eyes-Like-Sky picked up one of her forks. Why were there two? She stabbed her steak overhanded and dug in with a knife.

Amusement flickered across Mrs. Thorson's face. "My goodness, no, dear. Not that way."

Eyes-Like-Sky glared at her, half tempted to gnaw on a chunk of meat in front of the woman. Instead, she readjusted her hold on her fork and watched how the colonel sliced his meat.

"I'm sure Miss Maggie would put us all to shame if we were lost in the desert." Colonel Thorson nodded toward her.

A scowl settled on LeBeau's face. "Thankfully, she doesn't have to worry about that anymore." He lifted his wine glass, his features lightening. "Colonel, have I told you about Marguerite's mother, my sister, Katie? Lovely young woman. Sweetest laugh. And what a voice. Beaus from all around the county would come calling on Miss Katie LeBeau." He drained the liquid to the dregs. "She could have had her pick of any of them." His expression hardened. The goblet clunked as he set it down. "And she fell for some two-bit teacher who didn't own a stich of land. Full of dreams but too good to dirty his hands with slave money. His family owned a plantation south of Nashville, but he turned his back on it all when he came of age. Wouldn't pick it up again, even for Katie's sake. Foolish girl. I don't aim to allow my niece to follow in her footsteps of clinging to empty dreams. Marguerite has a new life waiting for her in Colorado County TX. Once my wife, Julia, finishes with her, I wager a year from now, she'll be such a refined young lady you won't recognize her."

Beneath the table, Eyes-Like-Sky strangled her napkin. Why couldn't the Comanches have attacked LeBeau and wiped him from the earth? She would never go with this man. She'd rather die than give up Little Star and be dragged away by him. Her lips trembled as she squelched the avalanche of words that threatened, allowing only a few to escape. "My father was a good man."

~

Eyes-Like-Sky had been searching for a man for three days. The right kind. One with a little bit of authority but not too much, and not too smart. One who didn't work too hard, and most of all, one who couldn't keep his eyes off her. She'd heard enough of the soldiers' muttered comments to know what they thought of her morals. No lady would willingly give herself to a Comanche. Therefore, she wasn't a lady or even close.

From her position at the well, she studied the men at the corral. The corporal with the coarse auburn hair. Stubble in dire need of a razor. He was the man. Worked his jaw more than his muscles, and the way he strutted around and bossed the privates? More cocky and sure of himself than any rooster. His gaze drifted toward her across the yard.

She stiffened beneath his leer and tugged the wool shawl tighter around the leaf-thin silk and up to her chin. But that was no way to catch a man. With a groan, she willed her fingers to loosen their hold. The dark wool slipped to the edges of her shoulders. Jaw clenched, she met his stare across the barren yard.

He stretched up tall, threw an arm over the rail, and barked an order to a private by the manure pile.

A bitter taste crept into her throat. She turned away and pressed a palm to the cool stone wall. Was she really going to do this?

There had to be some other way to get a horse. But time was running out. The weather had cleared, and for the last two days, LeBeau's men had sat outside the saddlery cleaning and repairing their gear, preparing for the trail. Already, she'd started digging into her store of food, afraid to eat anything delivered to her tent. No telling when LeBeau would have the doctor slip something into one of her meals.

If only Ramsey would come back. Maybe he could do something. But his lieutenant friend said the captain wasn't expected for almost two more weeks. Might as well be never.

If Ramsey had cared anything about her welfare, he would not have left. But what could she expect? Guilt only carried a man so far. He'd given her the gold band. Probably considered his debt paid. His kindness had been nothing more.

Dear Lord, help me. She scooped water out of the bucket with her hand and swallowed, shivering as cold drips ran down her chin. God had allowed Dancing Eagle to die. Let her whole world be torn from her. Again. She could not count on Him to rescue her now.

~

The wide brim of Eyes-Like-Sky's straw hat fluttered with a gust of wind as she approached the corral. Specks of sand scraped her cheeks and caught on her lashes. As the breeze settled, she slipped the hat from her head and tousled her collar-length hair. Failure wasn't an option.

At the other end of the horse pen, the auburn-haired corporal's boisterous voice faltered, his curry comb halting in mid-rotation on a mare's back. The three men gathered near him turned, all eyes on her.

Her footsteps wavered. She could head back to the Sibley. No. She pressed her hand to her arm, rubbing her finger over the gold band beneath her sleeve, and stepped up to the corral. The odors of leather, horse, and manure filled her nostrils.

A pinto gelding drifted over to the weathered rail. Eyes-Like-Sky rubbed her hand along the animal's brown muzzle. Large soft eyes greeted her attention, followed by a nicker. Pretty animal. Dancing Eagle had owned one like it. Maybe this had been his, stolen in the battle.

"Look what we have here." The corporal strutted over, smacking the dust from his gauntlets.

Her lip threatened to curl. "Afternoon, Corporal." She fanned herself with her hat even though goosebumps dotted her arms.

"Afternoon to you, Miss Logan." He edged his cap farther back on his head. "And here I was doubting you could speak in a civilized tongue."

"I have been learning." She retrieved a handkerchief from her pocket and dabbed it along her brow.

"I bet you have." He chuckled and leaned an elbow across the top rail.

She trailed the handkerchief down her neck to her bare collarbone. "And watching you."

His eyes bugged. "You have?"

"Yes. You remind me of my husband." She let her gaze roam over him, nice and slow so he couldn't miss it. "Not in looks, but strength. He was the finest warrior of our village. Makes me think I should get to know you better."

A carnivorous smile spread across his face, and he puffed out his chest. "Is that so, Miss Logan? Maybe I should come calling. Drop by your Sibley some evening."

She laughed. "You want my uncle to string you up? He doesn't want me to keep company with some soldier. No. It'd be better..." She ran her fingers through her hair. "If we met somewhere. After dark, after my baby goes to sleep."

Fox-eyed, he rubbed his thumb and forefinger across his scruffy mustache. "I could sneak into your tent."

"No. Colonel has it watched. I'm thinking someplace private. The supply building? Or maybe back of the corral?"

"And how would you get there?" He hitched his pants.

"I'll find a way." She fluttered her eyelashes. "You bring some liquor? I got used to it back in the village—you know, from the Mexican traders. Haven't had a good drink in many moons." She licked her lips.

"Poor girl." His throat rumbled, and he leaned in, panting.

"I'll see what I can do. Tomorrow night. I could arrange to be in charge of guarding the storehouse."

The putrid smell of sweat and unwashed body took her breath away. She inhaled through her mouth and forced another honey-sweet smile. "Midnight tomorrow. At the storehouse. Don't tell any of your buddies. Or you won't ever see me again."

"I won't tell a soul." He grinned and dropped his gaze to her bosom and below.

"Till tomorrow night, Corporal?" She waved the handkerchief at him and stepped back.

"Call me Jenkins. Ray Jenkins. Tomorrow night, you can just call me Ray."

Past the saddlery, the blacksmith shop and beyond, she held her head high. Slow, deliberate steps, all the way to her Sibley, fighting the urge to run. Squelching a screech, she slipped inside and yanked the flap tight behind her. Little Star awaited, snuggled in a bundle of rabbit fur. Still lost in nap time, her breath a steady rhythm.

Nausea rolled through Eyes-Like-Sky. She dropped to her knees and retched in a bucket. The smell of that man. The thought of him touching her.

Memory trembled through her. Old Wolf—her master until Dancing Eagle had rescued her. The stink of bear grease, the rolls of fat. There'd been others, too, when she'd first been captured and belonged to no one in particular. She retched again. Sweat soaked her chemise. The knife sheath strapped beneath her petticoat poked against her leg. Ray Jenkins would not have his way with her.

CHAPTER 15

Eyes-Like-Sky's knife snagged on the rough canvas. Working around the bundle of fur and buckskin which secured Little Star to her chest, she pulled the blade free and jabbed downward, sawing a two-foot slit into the back side of the Sibley. Heart pounding, she lifted the newly cut flap. Failure was not an option.

With skirt hem secured to her waist, she crawled out. Her meager belongings, doeskin blouse and skirt, *par fleche* pouches of pemmican, a flint, and a canteen, were wrapped in a petticoat tied on her back. She tugged the buffalo robe through the slit and slid it over her shoulders, good camouflage and warmth.

Pebbles bit into her palms as she glanced heavenward. Stars. Only a tiny sliver of a moon. Good. Less lighting. The enlisted men's barracks loomed to her right and cast a dark, imposing shadow. On the left, beyond the quartermaster's lodgings, lay the stone storage building with its picket roof.

From the other side of camp, a dog howled, echoed by a coyote from the distant hills. What else lay out there? It didn't matter. She'd face it.

Little Star sniffled and sighed, asleep for now.

Dear God, let her sleep. Eyes-Like-Sky's gaze darted back to the sky. *Dear Jesus...* It'd been years since she'd used the name of the one she'd given her heart to as a child. *Please watch over us. Keep us safe.* If only God, if only Jesus, would listen and answer. But the stars twinkled back, distant and cold. She crawled on, weaving her way through the dark.

At the back door of the storehouse, she dropped the robe and stood, flexing her aching knees. She tucked the petticoat bundle in the folds of the robe.

The latch rattled. In a flurry, she loosened her dress hem from her waist. Silk cascaded over her sand-covered leggings. Before she could catch her breath, the door creaked open. Mouth dry, she stepped into the dark, battle-ready.

An onslaught of smells assaulted her—smoked meat, spices, dried peppers, a nutty smell—maybe rice—along with old wood and leather. The door shut, and darkness closed in.

"Been waiting for ya, Miss Morgan." Jenkins's hot, brandy-laden breath struck her neck.

She stiffened, rigid as a fence post.

A callused hand, as gentle as tree bark, clamped on her arm.

Let go of me. The words boiled through her, but she gritted her teeth and coughed them back.

Little Star murmured.

"What's that?" He jerked her around to face him. "You brought the baby?"

Act. You can do it. It's not really you. Do it, or lose Little Star. She willed the hard knot of her muscles to loosen. "Couldn't leave her in the tent alone. Didn't want to have to hurry." Her voice flowed cool and detached. "You light us a candle. Find us a couple of cups. I'll lay her down by the door. Won't even know she's here."

"I don't need a light." He pulled Eyes-Like-Sky closer.

Little Star's cocoon bumped between them.

"What the—" He muttered and let go.

"We've got time, Ray. Light a candle. So we can see each other." She smoothed her hand over his wool jacket, trailing her fingers to his shoulder. "You want to see, don't you?"

"I reckon. But I don't have all night. I'm expected back at the corral."

One less guard to worry about. "I'll make it worth your while." She slid her hand down his arm and stepped back.

"You'd better." He stumbled against something as he made his way to the interior. Wood scraped against wood.

Fumbling in the dark, she nestled Little Star between the wall and a crate, adding a quick kiss to her daughter's nose. As she stood, her bell sleeve caught on a nail, ripping the silk and scraping her skin. No matter—another few minutes, and she'd never wear the ridiculous garment again. She slid her fingers into a slit in her skirt and touched the knife sheath she'd secured to her waist with a leather strip. If all went well, she wouldn't need it.

A dim glow awakened behind her. She tugged the neckline of the blue silk down to give him a good eyeful of cleavage. The more distractions, the better.

The floor creaked beneath her moccasins as she wove her way past barrels and sacks. Like goblin hands in the slither of the night, strings of peppers, spices, and sausages swung from the rafters.

Jenkins stood by a rough table, jacket off, shirt sleeves rolled to his elbows, and suspenders drooping past his waist. An eager glint in his eyes. "Come here, beautiful. Have a drink." He thudded a tin cup on the table and poured from an earthen jug. His tangle of auburn hair had been combed and plastered with some concoction to make it lay flat over his receding hair line.

"Don't mind if I do." She stepped toward him. Would the jug be enough to knock him out? A hammer lay on a nearby crate, bent nail still in its claw. A shiver ran down her spine. "So, Ray, tell me about yourself." She smiled.

"Eager to get to know a girl like you, sweetheart." He smacked his lips and handed her the cup with a wide, foxlike grin.

Her pulse throbbed in her temple.

The candle stub flickered on the table. A glob of wax teetered over the yawning gap and trickled down to the tin below.

Jenkins swallowed deep from the jug.

She strained a sip of the amber liquid through her lips. "How'd you come to be a soldier?"

"Gumption and brains." He clunked the jug down and swiped his forearm across his mouth. "My pap brought us over from the Old Country when I was a boy. The man died in a factory. My step-mam expected me to stay around and provide for their young'uns. No life for me. Let her find herself another man. I ran off and enlisted." He threw his shoulders back. "Learned my way around a corral. Know more about the animals and a gun than any of these school boy officers." He leaned in. "But we didn't come here to talk about me, girlie."

He clamped a hand around her waist and took her cup with the other, sloshing liquid on her skirt. "What about a kiss?"

The smell of his sweat and brandy mingled with the odor of cheap hair tonic. His thick lips loomed close.

She lodged her elbows between their bodies, pressing her palms to his chest and batting her lashes. "Turn around, solider boy, and count to ten. I've got a big surprise for you." Her voice honey-sweet, she stroked her thumbs back and forth over the muscles beneath his shirt.

"I got what I want right here, darling." He pulled her hard against him, forcing her elbows up. His mouth came down on hers as he shoved her against a shoulder-high stack of crates.

The stack teetered but held steady against the wall.

Rough, uneven boards dug into her back as he pawed her. At the filthy taste of him, panic welled in her throat. Old Wolf. The others before, when she'd first been captured. Screams echoed in her head, blood. Smoke filled her nostrils. Scorching heat. She was by the fire again, that first night after the attack. Total, soul-deep shame. Humiliation.

No. The silent scream ricocheted within. Never again. She chomped his tongue and shoved him with all of her might.

A mangled yelp.

As he stumbled back, she squirmed free.

He latched onto her hair and jabbed a hand to her throat.

Gasping, she drove her knee into his groin.

He doubled over.

Without thought, she grabbed the hammer from the crate and struck with a sickening clunk on his skull.

He crumpled to the ground.

She dropped to her knees, panting. Dear God, what had she done? The hammer slipped from her hand. Why couldn't he have listened and turned around? She'd only intended to strike him with the jug. But he'd come after her like that. What if he was dead?

The coppery taste of blood lingered on her tongue. She spat out every trace of him, but the trembling wouldn't stop. From her lips to her legs, she quaked.

Blood slithered from his wound, matting his hair. *Please don't let him be dead*. She bent down, placing an ear to his lips. Warmth, air, breath. Thank God.

A dog barked in the yard. What if others had heard?

She needed his clothes. Springing to life, she yanked off her dress and dove for his buttons. His blasted cavalry boots reached his knees, but she yanked and pulled until one and then the other slipped clear of his feet. Next came his trousers. Worse than skinning a buffalo. After she'd worked them free, she stuffed her legs into the light-blue wool.

Sweat coated her bare back as she rolled him over, tugging his shirt from one arm and then the next. She wiggled the garment over her head and grabbed his discarded jacket. And now Corporal Jenkins would be returning to the corral.

~

Jenkins's boots rubbed against Eyes-Like-Sky's heels, the hard leather scraping her skin raw despite the strips of silk she'd wrapped around her feet. But it couldn't be helped. A hand's length shorter than Jenkins, she needed the extra height they provided.

Making full use of the supplies in the storehouse, she'd replaced the petticoat bundle with a proper knapsack on her back filled to the brim, giving her extra girth beneath Jenkins's shell jacket. Wrapped in her cocoon, Little Star snuggled behind a rubber blanket and robe, belly full of new milk. Hopefully, anyone looking would assume Jenkins had decided to bring a blanket to keep him warm on guard duty. His rifle hung from her shoulder along with a canteen.

She headed for the far side of the corral with long strides, traveling behind the barracks, blacksmith shop, and other buildings.

A solitary soldier hurried away from a tree, pulling his pants up. No wonder this place stank.

A fire glowed near the gate. She headed left through a patch of mesquite and hackberry trees, tripping on a root and catching herself on a barren branch. Its spikey barb punctured her palm.

Movement at the tack shed. Her grip tightened on the knife handle hidden beneath the robe. There was no going back now. If they caught her, at the very least, they'd throw her in the stockade and take Little Star from her forever.

A soldier scrambled up and threw the barrel of his rifle against his shoulder. "Sorry, Corporal. Resting my feet."

Head down, she growled a curse and stomped past, steering clear of the shed, then swinging back in closer so that it lay between her and the man. Brush crumpled beneath her boots. Prickly pear snagged at her trousers.

A horse whinnied on her right. She edged nearer to the corral, feeling for the rail. A clump of horses shifted, indistinguishable from each other in the dark. Another whinny and a nicker. Her hand landed on a stretch of worn rail, warped like driftwood. She slowed her step to an amble. A secluded spot with a loose rail or two—that's what she needed, and she needed to take her time. Let the fellow by the shed settle back down for his nap. And the other guard? A pin prick of light glowed on the far side of the corral, toward the back of the saddlery. The private must be having a smoke. Let him. Tomorrow, if all went well, both would be in the stocks or strung over a barrel for neglecting their duty.

With soundless steps as Dancing Eagle had taught her years ago, she discarded her gear in a pile by a hackberry tree, her hands free except for a rope. Little Star slept against her chest in the cocoon. The rope hung knotted and looped over Eyes-Like-Sky's fingers, a makeshift bridle and reins.

All was quiet except for an occasional snort and nicker and the low hum of Eyes-Like-Sky's song. She didn't know the words, but she'd heard Dancing Eagle hum it to his horses to calm them.

At the thought of her late husband, she raised her hand to the pouch with his hair—only, there wasn't any pouch. She froze and frantically fingered her neck. She must have lost it in the scuffle with Jenkins. Her breath caught in her throat. There wasn't time to go back.

The babe on chest snuffled in her sleep. Eyes-Like-Sky had to get moving. She had the armbands. They would have to do.

No more light on the other end of the corral, and no movement from the side near the shed. These privates knew their corporal was unlikely to come check on them or throw them in the stockade for napping on duty. She'd picked her man well.

Bracing herself, she stood and slipped her palms beneath a loose rail and lifted. It creaked and budged. The horses nearby stirred. She continued to hum as she stepped backward one step at a time, her heels sinking into the sand until she'd shifted the rail outward enough for a horse to pass through. Kneeling with her load, she lowered the wood to the ground. Only seven more to go, four from each side of the post.

Her muscles ached and as she lifted each rail, careful not to bump the sleeping babe. Sweat plastered Jenkins's shirt to her back. The smell of the man permeated his clothes and invaded her nostrils. Tobacco, brandy, horse, his unwashed body.

She nestled number eight against the other, then crept into the corral, bridle in hand. She took slow, quiet, deliberate steps to reassure the horses.

A tail swished at her. She felt along another's back and another's. Dancing Eagle's tune buzzed across her lips as she held out her palm for eager noses to smell. She needed to pick the right one before they started drifting out the opening. Her wobbly boot landed in soft squish. The odor wafted up to her. No time to worry about that.

Her hand contacted strong withers and a firm back. She rubbed the animal's muzzle. "Hey, beauty. My sweet girl. Good girl." She dug in her pocket for the chunk of sugar she'd secured from a storage bin.

The animal's warm, wet tongue scoured her palm for every trace.

"I'll name you Raven." Speaking in Comanche now, she slipped her hands beneath the horse's jaw and lifted its nose to hers. She blew her breath into the animal, then stared into the dark flickers of its eyes. "Raven." She dipped her forehead to the animal's muzzle, then slipped the bridle over its head and led Raven out through the new opening.

Like slow syrup, a handful of other horses drifted out with them. It'd lead to discovery sooner than later. But what could she do? She didn't have time to fix the rails. Besides, maybe they'd be so busy rounding up horses, it'd take a while for them to discover Jenkins and realize she was missing.

She grabbed her gear and threw a blanket over the mare, thankful the moon was but a sliver sinking on the opposite horizon as she walked the horse toward the river. An owl hooted as they climbed down the slope to the water and reached a small grove of scrub oak. Fingers interwoven in Raven's mane, she shifted Little Star's cocoon to the side and pulled herself onto the horse's back. Lying low over the animal's neck, she nudged her toward the unknown.

CHAPTER 16

Garret slowed his chestnut mare, Ginger, to a trot and unbuttoned the collar of his dust-coated jacket. The too-warm December sun left his throat parched. He'd hardly taken the time to eat, let alone sleep after the stagecoach had reached Fort Belknap, not about to add another eight or ten hours between him and Camp Cooper. After a week of travel, he'd need a bath and a shave before he checked in on Eyes-Like-Sky. Provided her uncle hadn't left with her yet. His shoulders tensed.

Garret had been over it in his head a hundred times. If he was too late, he'd find an excuse to ride after them. Too bad he'd given her both armbands before he left for St. Louis. Otherwise, he could have used that as an excuse.

No, he'd take her extra supplies. Pay for them himself, act as though they were from the army. He still had ten days of leave. He had to see her one more time. Make sure she was all right. She'd filled his head for days. Foolish. Setting himself up for misery. Pining after a woman who'd never see him as anything but the man who ruined her life.

But he would look after her, all the same. If she was still at

Cooper, he'd volunteer to travel with her and LeBeau, at least as far as Fort Worth. No doubt the man could use an extra hand for protection.

Overhead, a falcon circled, its majestic, fine-tuned wings catching currents of wind that never came close to scratching the earth. A prairie dog squealed and dove into its hole.

Garret's horse shifted beneath him as they crested the ridge. Camp lay ahead, looking more like a scruffy, two-street town than a fort. Wide open for an attack with only their firepower and numbers as a deterrent.

Southeast of camp, a squad of men tore at the dirt with shovels. A new well or another latrine? An officer on horseback looked his way and waved. Garret waved back. The man spurred his horse toward him.

"Garret? What the devil are you doing back so early for?" Charlie neared. "You heard about Miss Logan?"

Goosebumps shivered across his skin. "What about her? Something happened?" He closed the distance between them.

"She ran off."

The words dropped through him like stones. "She what?"

"Night before yesterday. Spooked the horses out of the corral. Attacked Corporal Jenkins with a hammer. The man's in the infirmary half out of his head."

"A hammer? Why? What did Jenkins do?" He scrubbed a hand over his jaw.

"They found him knocked out cold in the storehouse dressed in his underclothes. No telling what happened between them before he was knocked out."

Garret strangled his saddle horn. "Nothing happened. At least not on her part."

"I don't know. Jenkins is only talking gibberish. But one of the other guards says Jenkins was bragging Eyes-Like-Sky had been swayed by his manly charms."

Garret scowled. "That man has the charm of a bullfrog."

"That may be, but she attacked him, stole his clothes and rifle, and ran off with at least one horse. They're still rounding up the strays." Charlie leaned forward in the saddle. "It was planned, not some spur-of-the-moment incident like, 'the man asked for one too many kisses, so I'll whap him in the head and run away so I won't get in trouble for crushing his skull.'"

Garret narrowed his eyes. "Don't talk about her like that."

"If you say so." Charlie cocked his eyebrows. "She asked about you a few days before she did it. Wanted to know when you'd be back. Looked disappointed when I told her it'd be another couple weeks."

He swallowed. She'd asked for him. And he hadn't been there to help her. "Did something happen between her and her uncle?"

"LeBeau and the colonel figure she's out of her mind. But from what you've said about her, my guess is, it's the baby. LeBeau had no intention of taking the baby back to East Texas. Found an Apache wet nurse to help Mrs. Thorson care for the child. He tried to keep it quiet. Everyone was ordered not to say anything to Eyes-Like-Sky about it. Didn't want to panic her. But she must have gotten word. She ran off two days before they were scheduled to leave."

Garret glared at his friend. *You were supposed to be looking after her*. "No one in their right mind would think she'd put up with having her baby taken from her."

"There wasn't anything I could do about it, Garret. Colonel's orders. Besides, LeBeau is her—"

"Well, I'm going to do something about it." Garret's gaze scoured the corral in the distance. "Did they send out a search party?"

"LeBeau's five hired men, a squad of cavalry led by Lieutenant Andrews, and a couple Apache scouts."

"Did they take Kuruk?"

"Nope, couldn't be found. Either he was out hunting or

holed up drinking. They took Bucking Horse and Half Moon instead."

"They're not half as good at tracking as Kuruk." Garret set his jaw. "Here's what I want you to do. Round up supplies for me and two fresh horses. Then, meet me—"

"You can't go after her. Not alone. And you know the colonel would have my rear if I went with you. They'll find her—"

"I can. And I will."

"But the colonel—"

"I'm still on leave. Got ten days left. I'm not asking you to come and risk court martial. You get me the supplies and the horses and meet me on the other side of the Brazos, down by the grove. I'm going to ride over to the Apache encampment and find Kuruk. If anyone can find her, he can."

"If you can find him."

"I'll find him one way or the other."

Garret snapped his reins and headed for the east side of camp. No sense announcing his presence by riding through the gate. He should have been here. Should never have left. And now Eyes-Like-Sky was out there somewhere with Little Star. Did she have any clue how to find her people? Her village had been a seven-day ride. But the tribe would have moved far away after the battle. And what if she came across warriors from another village or tribe during her journey?

He swung off his mount and tethered the chestnut behind the quarters he shared with Charlie. Hardee hat pulled low over his eyes, he quickstepped between the buildings and crossed the parade grounds to the Sibley. A quick glance for any clues, and he'd be on his way. He ducked inside.

The meager possessions the women of the camp had donated lay scattered about on the crates and the hard-packed dirt. The cradleboard stood alongside a yawning rip in the rear of the tent. No trace of the buffalo robe or doeskin clothing. He'd be looking for a single rider in a robe. Little Star would be on her chest, just as she had been the day of the battle. He winced.

The canvas rustled, and light poured in.

Garret pivoted toward the opening.

A dandy in a fine wool suit and a polished cane stooped in and stood. A high brow and slicked-back dark hair streaked with gray offset piercing blue eyes in a face as welcoming as wormwood. Her uncle, no doubt. No one else within a hundred miles would put on such airs. "What are you doing in here? Who are you?"

"Captain Ramsey." Garret straightened and threw back his shoulders. "I'm investigating what Eyes-Like-Sky left behind."

LeBeau snorted. "Ramsey? Aren't you the fellow—"

"I'm the one who was looking after your niece before you arrived."

"Fine job you did. I come here and find her still wearing those filthy Comanche garments. If you had worked on reintegrating her—"

"You're the one who tried to take her baby away." Garret's hand curled into a fist at his side. "I don't care what you think of me, but I'm the man who is going to find your niece."

LeBeau tugged down his waistcoat and brushed his hand over the striped silk. "Don't bother. I've sent my five men and two of the finest Apache guides. They'll bring her back."

Garret moved his dust-covered boots toe to toe with shiny leather. "I'm going to find her. If they already have her, I reckon I'll find all of them." He pushed by the worthless popinjay and hurried out before he said something he'd regret.

CHAPTER 17

Tiny ice particles pelted Garret's face and clung to his lashes beneath the turned-down rim of his Hardee hat. The norther had rolled in with amazing speed, heavy, dark clouds overtaking the sun in a couple of hours. The heat of their first two days on the trail dissipated. Temperatures dipped below freezing.

"We need shelter," Kuruk yelled above the roar of the wind. A coyote-fur hat protected his head and ears above his matted buffalo robe, but the sleet tore at his weathered cheeks and ungloved hands.

"No." Garret dug his boots into his stirrups and nudged his brown-and-white pinto forward along the icy path. At his insistence, they'd ridden through the night, stopping only for short breaks. No cooking. They'd made do with dried meat and hardtack. And they'd steered clear of LeBeau's men and the posse when Kuruk found their trail. Garret would not sit around a camp fire and argue jurisdiction. He had a woman and a baby to find. On his terms. Whatever it took.

Moisture dripped from his nose. He nudged his neckerchief

up to cover the half-frozen tip and squinted at the ground a few feet in front of his animal, protecting his eyes as best he could.

With a packhorse linked to his saddle pommel, Kuruk goaded his mare until he was knee to knee with Garret. Shaggy robe to wool greatcoat, the man leaned over. "Girl's not dumb. She find shelter. We keep going? Might pass her. Lose trail. Never find her. Cave this way." He pointed and grabbed Garret's bridle.

Garret jerked his pinto to a halt. The wind howled between them. Eyes-Like-Sky and Little Star could be huddled under a tree freezing somewhere down the trail. Kuruk had picked up sign of a lone traveler going this way. Garret could only pray it was Eyes-Like-Sky. But the Indian was right. She was resourceful. Even if she didn't know this area well, she'd likely find shelter. And he and Kuruk might ride by her and never know it. Never find her. She could even be in the cave.

Turning his face from the wind, Kuruk stared at him through reddened eyes.

Garret nodded and followed after him, his horse's hooves crunching the ice-coated grass.

By the time they reached the shelter, they were on foot, tugging their horses behind them in three inches of sleet-covered snow. Kuruk had chosen well. A small crop of trees hovered near the opening slit in the rocks on the backside of a mesa. Sheltered from the worst of the wind, they tied their horses in the trees and cared for them before inching their way through the gap in the sandstone.

On their bellies, dragging their gear beside them, they wriggled toward the pitch black. Something small and furry squeaked and ran across Garret's outstretched hand. He stiffened. "You sure there's a cave?"

"Yes." Kuruk crawled forward and pushed up on his hands and knees. "Wait." He fumbled with a pouch.

A snap and sudden flicker of light. A Lucifer match stick,

not flint. He dropped a clump of pine needles on the ground and lit them, quickly adding a rag. The scent of pine muted the stink of the sulfur. The smoke wafted toward a small updraft somewhere above them.

Garret crawled in farther until he could rise to his knees. No girl and her baby. Empty.

The cave opened up to a height of four to five feet for the space of a small-sized room before it sloped to a sandstone floor. Shadows wavered on the dark walls as Kuruk added kindling to the fire from his knapsack.

A buzz—no, more of a rattle, like a maraca—vibrated. Garret pivoted toward a darkened corner to the right, hand on his holster.

Kuruk motioned for him to be still. A rattlesnake. With slow, deliberate movements, the Indian slipped his knife from its sheath and threw it. *Thump*. The blade wobbled just below the coiled creature's half-severed head.

"You think there's babies?" Garret wiped his coat sleeve across his runny nose as his gaze scoured the corner.

"Don't think so." Shedding his robe, Kuruk half stood and retrieved his knife. His cotton hunting shirt clung to his back above his buckskin leggings. "But keep an eye out for tarantulas."

"I'll send them your way." Garret stooped his way over to a flat spot by the wall. "Don't get too comfortable. Three or four hours at the most. Just until the worst of the storm passes. Then we're heading back out."

"Storm could last all night." Kuruk added a couple of small logs they'd dragged in to the fire. The damp wood sizzled and spit. A plume of gray smoke threatened to spread into the shelter. The Indian coughed and used his blanket to billow the fumes toward a pinprick of light on the other end of the ceiling.

Garret settled on the cold stone floor, using his knapsack as extra padding between him and the cave wall. He tugged off his stiff gauntlets and rubbed his hands together. Spiky tingles pricked his fingers. His boots and socks were next. He pressed his lips together as he wrestled the hardened leather and ice-crusted wool from his feet. His toes throbbed.

How much protection would Eyes-Like-Sky's moccasins afford her? And what about the baby? He winced and ran a hand over his damp hair.

"She knows more about prairie storms than you, soldier man." Kuruk eased against the rock and stretched his feet and gnarled hands toward the fire. "Us getting lost or frozen won't help none."

Garret frowned and reached into his rubber-lined haversack. His fingers snagged a piece of dried buffalo. Eat, sleep a couple of hours, and then head out. There would be no more stopping. "Tell me what happens if she runs across warriors from a different tribe or village."

"Better hope they see her as an Indian woman. Not some white invader. She a good-looker. Make a good slave or second wife. That if she's lucky. Bandits not treat her any better."

Garret's throat tightened. "And if she finds her own tribe? Will her husband's relatives take her in?"

Kuruk shrugged. "Me not Comanche, but from what I hear, best hope someone take a liking to her. Make her a slave or wife. Comanches aren't a charity. Men hunt. She needs a man."

Elbows resting on his knees, Garret pressed his palms to his eyes. That's what she was risking? Slavery or, at best, a forced marriage? She loved Comanche life that much? Was there someone else in the tribe who'd grabbed her fancy? No. Couldn't be, given the way she'd adored Dancing Eagle.

Little Star. That's why she'd run. She'd risk her life, suffer anything, for her baby. He had to come up with a way for her to keep Little Star and return with him.

He blinked his eyes open and blew out a haggard breath.

Kuruk glanced across the fire at him. "You going to take her as your woman?"

Garret's eyebrows shot up. "What are you talking about? Of course not."

"Just curious."

"I'm trying to protect her."

The Indian smirked. "Hmmm." He chuckled and gnawed on a hardtack cracker, working around the gap of his two missing front teeth.

"You have a wild imagination, Indian." Garret chomped down on a strip of meat.

"You think she throw down gun? Come back with you, no fight? Think she want to be found? Almost killed last man got too close."

"I'll figure it out when the time comes. You just find her. Remember there's ten dollars extra if you do."

He jutted his chin. "*When* find her. I go in first. Get her weapon. Save your hide."

"You'll do no such thing. I'm the only one who goes near her. You'll block her escape. If you touch one hair on her—"

A slow grin spread across Kuruk's wrinkled face. "Not your woman? Ha. Let me know. Kuruk could use a second wife."

Garret narrowed his eyes but held his tongue. He'd not allow himself to get sucked into this man's goading. Back at camp, Kuruk wouldn't have attempted such familiarity, but here? Well, Garret would not pull rank on a man whose help he needed.

Kuruk took a long sip from the smaller of the two canteens he had brought along. "Get her gun and her knife. Maybe she got two knives. Then tie her up, throw her over shoulder and on back of horse. She come then."

"There'd better not be anything in that canteen but water."

"Water. You want to see? Have drink." He extended the canteen toward Garret.

"You're supposed to ration that. It's got to last."

"You see snow? Melts. More water. Don't worry, soldier man. You pay me well. I'm best tracker. We find girl."

With all of this snow and ice covering the trail? A frown wove its way across Garret's brow. He leaned his head back against the stone and closed his eyes. *Dear Lord, You know where she is. Please watch over her and Little Star. Protect them, guard them in Your hand. Help us to find them. Show us where they are. Show her who You are. And give me the words, the way to protect her. Show me the way, and I will do it.*

What if it wasn't God's will for him to find her and bring her back? The question rattled in his head as drowsiness overtook his thoughts.

And somewhere in the netherland between waking and sleep a whisper...

It will cost you almost everything.

Eyes-Like-Sky squatted beneath a rock overhang and dipped her canteen in a pool of melting ice. Best take advantage of the moisture before the warming sun sucked every drop from the land. But the red mud and wet sand couldn't dry fast enough. The last thing she needed was a trail of hoof prints leading right to her.

Little Star squirmed against her chest. Time for a feeding. They could take a break in the shade of the rust-colored butte, behind the security of the junipers. She lowered her chin and kissed downy-soft hair, the skin beneath warm, too warm. Eyes-Like-Sky's heart thudded. It was probably just the wrappings.

She'd take the baby out, nurse her, and then see. Capping the canteen, she tugged the fur away from the baby and fumbled with the lacings.

A whimper and bloodshot, fever-bright eyes revealed the

truth—Little Star was sick. Eyes-Like-Sky rocked back on her heels as a heavy weight descended on her mind. If only she had the luxury of holing up somewhere for a few days. She scanned the maze of chiseled red canyons stretching to the west.

A distant rumble. Thunder? With blue sky overhead? Her glance fluttered to the east, the way she'd come. She froze. Riders. Faint images on the horizon moving in her direction. Not just one or two. A group.

She crouched behind the juniper. Could she outrun them? Jump on Raven and head for the canyon maze? A gamble, since she had no clue of which paths led out and which ended in front of vertical walls.

With a wiggle, Little Star worked her arms free and seized her mommy's hair.

"No. Shush." Eyes-Like-Sky grabbed her hair away from the tiny pinching fingers. How far would a baby's cry carry? And the footprints. She'd been sloppy.

A quick glance to the east showed more than a handful of riders, maybe a dozen, growing more distinct as they cut a path through buffalo grass. Not dressed in blue or hats, and they bore lances. A war or hunting party. At this distance, she had no clue as to what tribe. They maintained a steady, even speed, not scouring the ground for sign. Thank goodness for that.

A lullaby trembled on her lips as she waddled back a couple of feet and mashed the heel of her hand into the mud by the water, smearing her moccasin prints. Even if they weren't looking for her, they'd keep their eyes out for water.

On top of the mud, she added grass. Bent it over instead of breaking it off. Maybe they'd think an antelope or another animal had bedded here. Hopefully, they'd be so eager for water that their own footprints would mar the area before they took notice.

She edged onto a patch of grass and crawled into the shadow of the butte. Remaining unnoticed was more important than speed. If the party continued straight, her moving to the far side of the butte would be enough to keep her safe. But the path diverged here. Clay and broken patches of grass led past a stretch of white-capped red canyons, while another trail led northwest, weaving into the heart of the ridges.

The steady tread of hooves pounded in her brain. Feathers, bare chests. Comanche, Kiowa, Apache? No guarantee of decent treatment with any other than her own band or maybe her sister's.

Pressed against the rock, she slipped around the side to where Raven munched. A vertical slit gaped in the stone, wide enough for her to squeeze into with Little Star at her side, but too narrow for her to nurse and quiet the baby. Raven would never fit. She could spook the mare. And risk them seeing the animal? They'd go after such a prize and then look for its owner. Even if they didn't find her, she'd be on foot.

Little Star rubbed her eyes and nuzzled, emitting a low whine a noise that would become a beacon once the riders arrived. Eyes-Like-Sky scanned the white-topped canyons and the distance between her and them. No guarantee she'd make it without being spotted. But better to act than to wait like prey. She tightened Little Star's lacings. Nursing would have to wait.

Eyes-Like-Sky jerked Raven's stake from the ground, gripped the reins, and heaved herself on to the mare's back atop the robe. If she kept at a parallel angle to the butte, she might be able to make it to the first canyon without being spotted.

Shoving the ends of the buffalo fur and rubber blanket away with her ankles, she whipped the end of the rope against the animal's shoulders and bent low across the mare's neck. Raven sprang into action, past sagebrush, beard grass, and too much clay. Her hooves clomped the ground as they gathered speed.

Knees fastened to Raven's sides, Eyes-Like-Sky's lower legs curled around the downward slope of the animal's belly like wax fitting a mold. No stirrups. Thank God, Dancing Eagle had taken every spare moment to pass on his horsemanship skills to her.

Faster. They needed to go faster. The maze loomed. Claw-like arms of the first canyon reached toward her, leading to nothing more than a shallow half circle. No safety there.

Wind scratched at her face and raked through her hair. She narrowed her eyes and drove her knees against Raven's ribs, veering away from a boulder before swinging back toward a gap between the claw and the second bluff.

A whoop echoed behind her, joined by another. A chill swept over her. Dear God in heaven. She'd been sighted. Nothing mattered now except getting away and keeping Little Star alive.

Raven's churning legs propelled them deep into the shadows of the looming rock. Muscles taut, Eyes-Like-Sky dug her fingers into Raven's mane. They cleared a narrow crevice. Two pathways opened up with canyons all around—red lower walls, fading into whitish sandstone caps sprinkled with scrubs and sagebrush. She swung Raven to the right, and they thundered around another set of claw-like arms.

A bobcat sprang out of their path. Raven reared, but Eyes-Like-Sky clung.

Another narrow crevice. A branch tore at Eyes-Like-Sky's thigh. She squelched her scream and drove the mare through the maze. Sweat plastered her deerskin blouse to her back.

Beneath her, Raven panted hard, stumbled, and then recovered. Behind them in the vastness of the rock expanse, a yell bounced off the canyon walls, followed by words—Kiowa, maybe—indiscernible at this distance and followed by three whoops.

She whipped Raven around a curve. The path opened and widened to an ascending slope. Rocks and pebbles scattered beneath slipping hooves. Raven's leg buckled, tumbling mother, baby, and horse. Cradling the child on her chest, Eyes-Like-Sky jumped clear. Her right arm and side slammed into hard clay and pebbles. A foot away from a prickly pear. Shaken but secure in the cocoon, Little Star squalled. Raven pawed at the ground, regaining her feet and shaking herself.

Eyes-Like-Sky scrambled to her knees. Pain shot through her shoulder, her ankle, and more.

Raven whinnied. With labored breathing, the horse could not go on, not with them on her back. Eyes-Like-Sky whapped Raven on her hindquarters. "Get."

The horse took off, skidding on the incline.

A small slope slanted toward the intersection of two pock-marked walls. Halfway down, a sagging hole exposed the gnarled roots of a juniper. An animal's burrow?

It didn't matter. Eyes-Like-Sky's moccasins slid on the loose gravel as she scurried downward. Dropping to her knees, she clawed at the hole, widening the opening. If something bit her, so be it. *Dear God, don't let it be snakes. Don't let them find us.*

Horse hooves.

She jerked the knapsack off and tossed it into the dark, damp cavity. Wide enough for her and Little Star. It had to be. With her knife, she sliced the cocoon's lacings.

The baby gasped, sucked in a huge breath, and—

Eyes-Like-Sky yanked up her deerskin blouse and jabbed Little Star's open mouth to her breast before the baby mustered a scream. Feet first, she pushed her way into the burrow, shoving away root tentacles and curling into a ball. Dirt in her face and nose, she squirmed until her back pressed against clay and root, and she could see shards of light.

Pounding hooves. Voices.

Sniffling, precious child at her chest.

Dear God, let them go past. Please, help us.

Would He listen?

CHAPTER 18

Garret dismounted next to Kuruk. He didn't need the Indian to tell him. He could see it for himself. Hoof prints polka-dotted the dried mud by the shriveled watering hole, too many indentations to count.

"Maybe she didn't come this way." Garret scrubbed a hand over his jaw. "I know you picked up her trail a ways back, but—"

"She came this way." Kuruk rubbed a gummied clump of broken grass between his fingers. "Human dung. Comanche and Apache mothers stuff grass, leaves in cradleboards. Helps soak things up."

Garret blew out an uneasy breath. "Can you—can you tell how soon after she was here the horses came through? Maybe they were wild."

"Not wild." Kuruk fingered an imprint near where he squatted, his forearms drooped over his filth-covered leggings. "Indian riders. Not for sure what tribe."

"Could be LeBeau's men and the cavalry posse."

Kuruk sighed and reached for his canteen at his side. "No

horseshoes. Indian riders around the same time she was here. Yesterday afternoon, most likely. The mud's had time to dry."

Garret shifted his gaze to the expanse of red-walled canyons. Deep into the labyrinth, turkey buzzards circled beneath white puffs of clouds. His mouth went dry. The birds had nothing to do with Eyes-Like-Sky or Little Star. He wouldn't even consider it. "All right." He swiped his sleeve across his brow. "Lead on. We'll follow the trail."

Slipping his rifle sling onto his shoulder, Kuruk stretched up to a stand. "And if that leads to a hunting or war party?"

"I didn't come all this way to turn around." He should have never gone to St. Louis. "I'm not heading home without her and the baby."

"I signed on to track." The Indian fingered the tomahawk that swung from his belt. "But I'm Apache. Apache don't back down from a fight."

"Good. Hopefully, it won't come to that." He headed to his pinto. If she'd been taken captive, would they have enough time to find LeBeau's men and the cavalry squad before the war party vanished? Better not count on it.

Lead rope held tight, Kuruk walked in front of his horse, studying the ground for sign. They followed the trail of tracks around the side of the butte and into the canyon fortress, each sand-capped tower formidable in and of itself.

"Hard prints, far apart. Broken shrubs. They galloped through here." Kuruk swung onto his black stallion as they passed the pincher-claw rocks. "Chasing her."

Garret closed his eyes. The news worked its way through him like liquid lead. "A body could get lost in this maze. Maybe she lost them."

"Maybe." Kuruk shrugged and laid his rifle across his pommel.

The packhorse plodded along behind them as they wove

their way in and out of crevices. Squirrels, jackrabbits, and crow scattered in their wake.

A fluttering came from a slope to the left.

Garret swept his carbine from his lap, cocking it as he shifted toward the noise.

Two antelope fled, their hooves pelting the carpet of sagebrush puffs which layered the burnt-orange slope.

"Good eating." Kuruk lowered his rifle. "But we need keep silent."

Warriors looking down on them from a mesa right now? Garret unsnapped his holster flap. Best have his Colt revolver ready in addition to his carbine.

The sun bore down as they wove their way farther into the heart of the canyons. Another antelope, a hawk, no warriors. Broken trails of hoof prints where the pursuers divided. If they had to separate, they hadn't caught her. At least not in this part of the canyon. Kuruk chose one of the two paths.

Late afternoon, they headed down an incline to a shallow river.

Legs stiff, Garret swung down off his pinto. "I don't see any tracks here."

"None here. Horses need water. So do we." Kuruk dismounted in the shade of the only cottonwood they'd spotted in two days, its thick limbs offering relief despite its barren branches. "I pick up trail easy after rest."

"We can rest after dark. We'll fill the canteens. Let the horses drink and munch on the grass. Then head out." Garret took off his hat and ran his hand over his sweat-dampened hair. This place could freeze a man one day and fry him a couple of days later.

They staked their horses by the bubbling river, swollen with melted snow. Kuruk untied his worn neckerchief from his head and dipped it in the cool water. Garret knelt near him and washed his hands before scooping up a drink to soothe his parched tongue.

Perched on a nearby hackberry, a crow cawed and pecked at shriveled berries.

Kuruk stilled, tapped a finger to his cracked lips, and pointed at a spot a couple of feet down the bank.

A footprint in the damp mud at the water's edge. Medium-sized. A woman's?

Kuruk traced his finger across the indentation and another on the sand a few inches beyond the first. "Fresh," he whispered. "Might still be here." He slipped his blade from its sheath.

"Don't hurt her. You'll answer to me." Garret kept his voice low as he slid his hand to his holster and eased his palm around the butt of his Colt

"Might not be her. Be ready. And if it is her, get her gun and knife. Then worry about pretty talk."

Revolver in hand, Garret eased up to a stand.

A horse neighed.

Garret pivoted toward the sound. On the far side of their other two horses, the pinto shook her head. Her lead rope dangled from her bridle. The tethered end hung a couple of feet below her nose. It'd been cut. Garret's upper body tensed.

Kuruk grunted and dipped a knee, ready to spring.

Alongside the pinto's hind legs, human legs crouched, the person's torso hidden behind the horse.

Garret had to get ahold of the pinto before the intruder slipped across the mare's back and took off.

Above them, the crow cawed.

A hand latched onto the pinto's mane.

Garret charged.

Kuruk leapt into the creek, blade in hand, arms wide, blocking the thief's direct access to a frontal escape.

An arm followed by a leg, and then, Eyes-Like-Sky's full body swept into the saddle.

Garret sprang across the distance between them and latched onto the bridle.

"Let go." She jerked on the reins and dug her feet into the animal's sides.

The pinto reared, lifting Garret to his toes.

Fingers locked onto the bridle, Garret stepped clear of the pawing hooves. "I'm here to help."

A baby squalled from the pouch of matted fur bound on Eyes-Like-Sky's chest.

"Not going back." She rammed the stirrup against his wounded arm.

Pain shot through him, loosening his grip. He grabbed her leg. She struck at him, and he latched onto her arm, as well. Like wrestling with a wildcat. Gritting his teeth, he yanked with all his might. She toppled off the horse and fell on top of him as his backside smacked the ground.

Faster than two breaths, she scrambled up and pivoted toward him, knife drawn.

Reflex ignited. His revolver was in his hand and aimed in less than a thought.

She froze.

Sense caught up to him. He tilted the barrel toward the ground.

Kuruk latched onto the pinto's bridle and pulled the animal clear.

Easing his finger off the trigger and his thumb off the hammer, Garret scooted backward and up, regaining his footing. "I'm not here to hurt you, Eyes-Like-Sky. I'm here to help."

"Don't need your help." Was that a tremor in her growl? She stood before him with her hair tossed and tangled, face smudged, scratches on her cheeks, and a limp in her stance.

Every inch of her battered deerskin garments was covered in dust and mud, not to mention the squalling baby on her chest.

Not captured. Not dead or dying, nor was Little Star. A smile so deep he couldn't contain it spread across his face. He wasn't too late.

"What are you smiling at?" Deep-blue eyes pierced him. "I'm not coming back with you, Ramsey."

"You're alive and so is Little Star." He palmed his revolver and jabbed it in his holster. "And my name is Garret, by the way."

She shifted the knife. A vein bulged on the back of her hand. "Stay away. I'm not going back. Not going to let them take my baby."

"I won't let them take Little Star from you."

"I'm supposed to take your word for that? Rather take my chances with my husband's people."

He leveled his gaze into hers. "That baby has no business being out here on the open prairie in late December. You survived one norther. No telling when another might come up. And we saw the tracks of the war party."

She bit her lip. "I got away."

"This time. What about the next? My friend here tells me you'd be lucky if all they do is make you a slave or a second wife. And you think you'll have any say with them about whether they let you keep Little Star?"

"Maybe there won't be a next. Here, I have a chance. More than I have with my uncle." She spit the words out. Her blade glistened in the sunlight.

Horses re-staked, Kuruk edged closer to Eyes-Like-Sky.

"No." Garret pointed at him without taking his eyes from the girl. "Leave her be."

She glanced from the Indian to him and cradled her left hand under the pouch on her chest, jiggling the whimpering infant. "You say you want to help? Let me go."

"Take a look out there." He jabbed his finger toward the western canyon walls. "Do you even know where your band is? By now, they could be a hundred or even two hundred miles from the Pease River Valley. Maybe if you didn't have a baby, and it wasn't winter, you'd have a chance of making it there." His brow contracted. "And what happens if you do?"

"I could help Owl Woman." Her lips were firm, stubborn. "Dancing Eagle's mother. We could look after each other—"

"Last I heard, the Comanche don't allow women to hunt. Maybe they'd give you scraps. Maybe some relative or friend of Dancing Eagle who's had his eye on you..." His voice trailed off. "That's if you find them. Are you willing to risk your daughter's life on that possibility?"

Her chest rose and fell hard. "Let me go without a fight, Ramsey. Don't want to hurt you. But no one's taking my baby." Stormy blue eyes begged him.

Words tumbled out of his mouth. "I won't let them take her. I give you my word. I'll find a way. Whatever it takes, I'll do it. Come back with me."

She blinked. The knife wavered. "How you going to stop them, Ramsey? LeBeau is my guardian. You said so. Colonel said so too."

He threw his shoulders back. "I'll take responsibility for you and Little Star." What in the world was he doing?

Her hand dropped to her side. "What does that mean?"

He hardly even knew.

A crisp gust of wind swept across them, ruffling her hair.

"That...I'll take care of you and Little Star. Provide for you. Look after you."

She gaped at him. "You...you're asking me to be your woman? Take up with you?"

"No. Of course not. It wouldn't be like that." His face heated, and his collar scratched against his neck. Exactly what was he asking? He exhaled. "I don't have all of the answers, Eyes-Like-

Sky, but I give you my word. I'll not let them take Little Star. I'll do whatever it takes. Except dishonor you. If LeBeau would be satisfied with my offer to pay your room and board and find—"

"My uncle thinks he owns me." Her voice shook. "A new feather for his war bonnet."

His heart thudded as he fell into the depths of her blue eyes. He stepped toward her. "He doesn't own you. No one does. I'll get you and Little Star away from him. I'll find a way."

He held out his hand for her knife.

She struck her empty fist against her leg and groaned. But then her gaze locked onto his. Her hand opened. The knife dropped to the ground.

CHAPTER 19

Eyes-Like-Sky clamped her foot down on the blade. What in the world was she doing, taking this man at his word? "I don't know if I can trust you."

Garret stepped closer. Deep-brown eyes held hers firm. "Yes, you do." His strong voice, sure and steady, wove a net. To capture her or pull her from a precipice?

He was unshaven and wind burned, with dark circles underlining his eyes as if he hadn't slept. Dust, dirt, and mud coated his knee-high boots and uniform. He'd ridden hard to find her.

"Where did you come from? You weren't at the fort."

"Got back two days after you ran off." He held his hands toward her, palms open. "As soon as I heard what happened, I grabbed the best tracker and a couple of fresh horses. I'm sorry I wasn't there to help you deal with your uncle."

Her legs wavered. "Who sent you after me, Ramsey?"

He scrunched his brow as if she'd asked an absurd question. "No one. I avoided the colonel. I didn't want to be ordered to stay put. As for your uncle? I did my best to not punch him in the face."

She glanced over his shoulder. Off to the side, the Apache stood like a stone wall, horses in hand, behind him, the serpent-like river and a sea of canyon walls. Beyond lay more prairie. The unknown. Weariness leached her resolve.

What if he was God's answer to her prayer? What if the God of the universe had intervened to rescue her and Little Star? Goosebumps ran over her skin.

The warmth in Garret's eyes invited her to dive in. She slid her foot off the blade, kicking it to the side. "Better for you to plunge a knife in my chest than break your word and let them take my baby."

"I'm not going to let them take Little Star. I'm a man of my word." He shoved the knife farther away from her before he knelt and picked it up, eyes on her as if he had to be wary of being kicked. "But you're not going to get off that easy. I need a promise from you too."

"What kind of promise?"

He stuck the knife in his belt. "That you won't try to run away as long as I keep my word."

A sliver of a smile creased the face of the Apache scout as he returned his tomahawk to its sheath and rubbed the pinto's neck.

She hesitated.

Little Star's intermittent whimpering erupted into a full wail. Eyes-Like-Sky wrapped her arms around the cocoon. "She's sick." As soon as the words left her tongue, unexpected tears swelled in her eyes.

Garret's brow furrowed. "How sick? What's wrong with her?"

"Fever. Since yesterday." She swiped at her eyes and dropped to her knees, her finger pushing the fur away from the baby's face. "There's plants I could use as medicine, but I haven't been able to stop to look."

"How bad of a fever?" Garret knelt beside her.

The breath-stealing tension which had tightened around her chest like a tourniquet ever since her uncle had appeared slacked off two or three notches. She didn't have to do this alone.

"It's hard to know, between the heat of the day and the fur." It was her fault, exposing her baby to such harsh weather. "Little Star got too cold in the norther. She shivered for a long while even after I found shelter."

Cheeks much too rosy, Little Star sucked in a breath and puckered her tiny mouth as Eyes-Like-Sky freed her from the pouch.

Garret tipped his hat off his forehead. "Tell me what you need. I'll go find it."

She bit her lip. The image of him holding Little Star the night before he left for St. Louis flittered through her thoughts. "You won't know what to look for. You watch her." She shoved the squirming baby toward him.

"I don't know—" He fumbled as his hands closed around Little Star's sides.

Wide brown eyes set in a cupid face stared up at Garret.

"Hello, baby girl." He shifted her away from his throbbing left arm and tugged her gown hem to the tiny moccasin-covered feet. "Momma will be back soon."

Eyes-Like-Sky splashed into the river, moccasins in her hands. The water swirled around her knees as she waded to the other side and limped up the embankment, obviously tired and probably injured.

He needed to get her and the baby to shelter for the night. Let them rest. And take a look at why Eyes-Like-Sky was favoring her left leg and foot.

Little Star inhaled and blew out a whimper.

"Momma's getting you medicine. Be back soon." He laid her chest over his tense shoulder and patted her firm little back. Heat penetrated her clothing.

"Thought so." Kuruk loped up to him with a quiet grin.

"Thought so what?"

"She be your woman."

Garret frowned. "I want you to follow her. Make sure no warriors show up. And keep your comments and imaginings to yourself."

"Yes, Captain." He slipped his rifle sling over his shoulder and ambled toward the river. "You make a fine-looking papa."

Papa? He'd said he'd take responsibility for them, provide for them. How deep did that go?

The possibility wove its way through him like molasses. And what about Eyes-Like-Sky? Determined to stay Indian and still in love with her deceased husband. His offer to pay her room and board wouldn't be enough for LeBeau. The man's pride was as wide as Texas, and his lack of respect for Garret all too evident.

He could tell LeBeau he'd proposed and Eyes-Like-Sky had accepted. That they were engaged. Then they could postpone the supposed wedding until the man headed home. But what if LeBeau didn't take the bait? What if he insisted upon an actual wedding in his presence?

Garret dropped down to a full sit and scrubbed a hand over his face. Keeping his word could lead him all the way to the altar...to a blue-eyed mystery, as prickly and welcoming as a cactus. After two years of avoiding an engagement to Lily. His swallow stuck in his throat.

Little hands patted his back.

He hadn't even gotten to the matter of Eyes-Like-Sky attacking a soldier under questionable circumstances. Somehow, on top of everything else, he'd have to keep her out of the stockade.

An hour later, he knelt by a modest fire, holding a small kettle filled with water and sneezeweed stems. Cross-legged, Eyes-Like-Sky sat across from him nursing the infant, his blanket thrown over her shoulder for privacy. Little feet kicked out from under the dark-blue wool.

His gaze lingered on Eyes-Like-Sky's weary features. "When's the last time you ate?"

"I had some roots last night and a bit of pemmican." Smudges darkened her cheeks and neck, leftovers from the dirt hole she said she'd hidden in to escape the warriors.

He set the kettle on a rock close to the flames. Heat from the flickers cut through the chill which had started to descend. "As soon as Kuruk finds us decent shelter, I'll make you a real meal."

She wiped her runny nose with the back of her hand. "Don't worry about me, Ramsey. Just simmer the weeds for—"

"Garret." He handed her his slightly used handkerchief. "You need to call me Garret. We're partners now."

"Partners?"

"We're working together to take care of Little Star."

She dropped her gaze to the wiggling infant and snugged her arms tighter. "Why are you helping us?"

He shifted his weight to his other knee and stirred the mixture of squishy stems. "Because I don't want to lie awake at night wondering if you're safe or if something happened to you or Little Star because I didn't help when I could have."

She breathed a word. It almost sounded like *why*, but she rolled her lips together as if she'd thought better of it. Good. Not a question he wanted to answer for her or himself.

The fire crackled. A pair of green-tipped teals glided to a landing, breaking the smooth surface of the river. Cinnamon and green colored the male's head, and brown specked the female. With shiny green underwings, they wove their way along the current.

Eyes-Like-Sky drew Little Star from the blanket and lifted the infant to her shoulder to burp her. A crease formed between her eyebrows. "I'm wondering about Jenkins." Her whole upper body drooped. "Please tell me he didn't die."

He frowned. "He's alive, last I heard."

She exhaled. "Good." She moved the blanket and shifted the baby to the other breast.

"So are you going to tell me what happened between you and him?" Just the mention of it tightened the cords in his neck and shoulders.

"Nothing." She unfolded her legs and squirmed to her knees. "The stems are done. We need to cool the pot by the river. Then bathe Little Star in it."

"I'll take care of the pot." He latched onto the kettle handle with his gauntlet. "You finish feeding her."

He secured the pot with stones at the water's edge, close enough for the waves to lap around the bottom without tipping it over. She'd avoided his question. Should he ask again?

He unscrewed the lid on his canteen and poured the contents on the fire. "I'm sorry. We can't afford to have one longer than necessary. There might be somebody out there watching."

The fire hissed and spit.

"I'm warm enough. Got the blanket for her." She scooted back a couple of feet as he kicked sand onto the sputtering embers.

A trickle of gray smoke drifted heavenward.

He pulled off his gauntlets and settled down across from her. "Talk to me." He removed his hat and ran a hand over his hair. "I need to know what we're facing back at camp."

Damp eyes looked on his, then shifted to the floating teal. "I did terrible things to escape. They were going to take my baby. I couldn't let them. So I...got Jenkins to meet me after dark in the storage building. I only meant to knock him out with the whiskey jug."

He didn't want to imagine what kinds of insinuations and enticements it would take to lure a man like Jenkins from his post. "So what happened?" Elbows on his knees, he picked up the stirring stick and poked it into the pile of charred wood and ash.

She hung her head. Her cheeks flamed. "He tried to..."

His jaw clenched. *Tried*, he reminded himself. Didn't succeed. Were any of her bruises from that man? "And you used the hammer to protect yourself?"

"Yes." She visibly trembled. "No one is going to touch me against my will. Ever again."

The last two words, less than a whisper, cut through him. Again as in, this time? Or before when she'd been first taken by the Comanche? He swallowed back the question. Not his to ask.

He cleared his throat and fumbled for a clear train of thought. "I'll do everything I can to keep you out of the stockade. I'll tell them Jenkins took liberties and you defended yourself. And if he argues that you gave him the idea you'd welcome the...attention, I'll tell them you were desperate to protect your baby at all costs. That it drove you temporarily—"

"Insane?" Sad eyes studied him. "Won't be news to them. They already think it."

A dark wave of hair slipped over her forehead and onto her lashes. He bit his lip against the overwhelming urge to reach across the firepit and tuck the errant lock behind her ear.

CHAPTER 20

A fire sizzled in the mouth of the yawning cave that evening. With the setting of the sun, temperatures in the canyon had dropped. Eyes-Like-Sky cuddled Little Star close, both of them wrapped in Garret's dark wool blanket. He sat cross-legged on his rubber tarp, cleaning his carbine. In the opening, Kuruk dozed with head tipped back against a rolled-up pair of trousers. His rifle lay across his lap, with his palm covering the trigger.

Heat still emanated from Little Star's body. The baby had hardly nursed at all before falling into a restless sleep. Sneezeweed and the pulverized roots from the prickly ash hadn't broken the fever yet.

Garret had helped in every way he could. Garret. She shuddered against the soft spot that had worked its way into her heart. What was she doing here in a cave with the man who had shot her husband? Too close. Too much like a family. The breadth and length of their shelter was hardly more than the tepee she'd shared with Dancing Eagle—taken from her by the man who'd worked to protect her ever since. If only she could will herself into the past and never leave. As she drew her knees up and curled around Little Star, she slipped her hand beneath her sleeve to touch Dancing Eagle's hard, smooth armband.

Pain throbbed through her ankle and thigh. First, there'd been the branch which had torn into her leg during the chase and then the tumble from the horse. Blood, so thick from the cut that Garret had noticed, glued her leggings to the wound. The man was hard-headed as could be. She'd told him four or five times her leg was fine, only scratched, and that her ankle wasn't anything more than a bruise. Nothing he needed to take care of. She wasn't some society woman who had to be coddled. She must be out of her head to follow him back to the camp she'd risked her life to escape. But he was like an oak in a storm.

"Eyes-Like-Sky?" Garret's whisper broke the quiet.

She startled. Who knew how long he'd been sitting there studying them? A wave of rich brown hair strayed onto his brow. He'd washed his face and hair and probably his whole upper body on the riverbank this afternoon, but he'd gone around the bend to do it. As if she'd never seen a man's chest before. He'd offered her the opportunity to wash, as well. But she had no intention of letting him think she cared what she looked like. Besides, she had a sick baby to care for.

He shifted the reassembled carbine from his lap and leaned forward, elbow to knee. "I've been thinking. I believe you're right. My commitment to provide for you won't be enough to satisfy your uncle."

Shadows from the fire played over his face. Gold specks swam in his somber eyes.

"So what will you do?"

"We need to show him that you're no longer in his charge. That his rights and responsibilities toward you have been superseded by another's."

"What does that mean?" She uncurled and pushed up to a sit, careful not to disturb the sleeping baby. Her thigh throbbed.

"I believe..." He cleared his throat and ran his fingers over his hair. "We need to tell him we're betrothed." His voice dipped. "That I...proposed, and you accepted."

"You're suggesting we marry?" She gasped.

"Not necessarily. My idea is to convince him we're going to wed in the near future. We delay the ceremony. Make up an excuse. Hopefully, he'll leave it at that and go home."

Her mouth went dry. "What if he doesn't?"

He exhaled sharply and lay back on the tarp, gaze fixed on the rocky overhang above. "We might have to go through with a wedding. I don't know if it'd have to be permanent. We could petition the court for an annulment afterward."

Her heart thudded. Hadn't she accepted as much when she ran away from the fort? That the price of saving Little Star might be taking a husband she did not love. However, she'd thought the man would be a Comanche, not a soldier. And not the man who'd killed her husband.

An owl hooted beyond their little domain. And somewhere in the distance a wolf howled. For the first night in a week, she would not have to worry about being attacked by a pack of wolves.

A heavy sigh arose from the man across from her. He awaited a response.

She fumbled. "You said annulment? What does that mean?"

"That the court could maybe undo the marriage. A possibility. Not a guarantee."

Wedded for life? She stroked her baby's hair and let her gaze travel over the man. His dirty blue uniform with dingy gold shoulder straps clothed a lean, muscular form. She took in his firm, unshaven jaw. A fine-looking man who'd put himself at significant risk to come to her rescue. Motivated by guilt? Probably, but there was kindness about him and determination that went layers deeper than that. He deserved a woman who thought the sun rose and set with him. "I'd make a poor wife, Garret Ramsey. My heart belongs to one who is in the grave."

Sparks flew up from the fire as a log crumbled into embers.

Garret rolled over onto his side, head propped on his hand, and studied her once more. A frown crinkled his forehead. "You're grieving." His words were hardly more than a breath. "I would not make demands of you."

What burned in his eyes?

She glanced away. "Save yourself trouble. Help me escape. If I can't make it to my tribe, Mexico is closer. I could wait there until someone I recognize comes to trade—"

"Do you know how big Mexico is?"

She threw up a finger to shush him and pointed to the baby.

Kuruk's snore halted, and he shifted against the cave wall, muttering in his sleep, before his breathing returned to its slow, deep pattern.

Garret pushed up to a sit. "I have no intention of dropping you off in some squalor of a border town on the half chance someone from your tribe will come through. Besides, if I head off to Mexico, Colonel Thorson will declare me a deserter and send the entire company after me."

Little Star's arms twitched. Eyes-Like-Sky placed her hand on the child's chest to settle her.

Garret lowered his voice to a whisper. "Running off would be a last resort. Only after every other option had been exhausted. But we'd run to your people, not Mexico. And there's no way I'd let you and Little Star go alone."

Desert. Throw his career away for her. And travel to her tribe where she could not guarantee his safety. She couldn't, wouldn't allow him to do that. "I'll do as you say. Tell my uncle whatever you need to. If it helps to say we lay together in a cave, that I am your woman—"

"I wouldn't soil your reputation like that."

"I don't care what anyone at the fort thinks."

He arched his eyebrows. "The day might come when you do."

"Little Star means more to me than anything. Whatever it costs to keep her safe and with me, that's the price I'll pay."

The sun hovered in the west, casting long shadows. Astride the pinto, Eyes-Like-Sky gripped a fistful of blue wool in each hand. Better to hold onto Garret's shell jacket than to wrap her arms around the man. She'd switched from the packhorse to his pinto a couple miles back. It was his idea to ride double, a demonstration that she was with him and under his protection.

A few miles prior, Kuruk had struck off south, heading for his tepee past the Brazos.

During three long days of riding after a day of caring for Little Star in the cave, she'd done her best to avoid conversation with Garret beyond the necessities. She'd do his laundry, do his cooking, be his betrothed, or even his wife in name if needed, but she would not be his. She would not let him inside her heart.

In the distance, a dinner bell rang out across the prairie. Garret's hat brim bounced a couple of inches from her forehead as she peeked over his broad shoulders. Camp Cooper loomed ahead, scruffy as ever with its hodgepodge construction of stone, picket, and plastered mud. Her stomach knotted. What if his plan didn't work? She'd been foolish to let him talk her into returning, risking everything on this man's word and his ability to persuade LeBeau and Thorson.

Her throat constricted as if a noose had been cinched tight around her neck. The horror of the last weeks at the fort washed over her. Fear leaked past her lips. "There's no guarantee you can protect me, Ramsey. Can't we please turn around?" *Please*. What kind of word was that coming out of her mouth toward a soldier?

His gloved hand closed over hers on his side. "I won't let them take her or you."

His first intentional touch other than helping her onto his horse. A tinge of warmth, comfort, surged through her. Against her will, her hungry heart lapped it up. She tensed. No.

Stupid idea to ride on this man's horse or to be anywhere near him. "Whoa." She reached around him and grabbed for the reins.

He elbowed her hand away and pulled the horse up short. "What are you doing? The horse can only obey one driver."

"I want down." She swung off the pinto, jarring Little Star's cocoon on her back.

Garret's brow furrowed. "Because you're worried? Or because of my hand?"

"Because I don't want your help." She smacked stray strands of hair from her face. When her hair got long enough, she'd braid it. She wanted nothing to do with those bonnets the white women wore. Was this man going to try to turn her white?

Tension pinched his weary eyes as he stared down at her, his uniform filthy, just like her leggings and doeskins. He'd been nothing but good to her ever since he'd found her.

She exhaled. "I'm sorry. It's just...I hate needing help. Anyone's. This is not my world." She wavered her hand toward the fort. "And my uncle. You don't know what it was like while you were gone. And then there's Jenkins. What if they throw me in the guardhouse?"

"If they do, I'll make sure it's only temporary, and I'll care for Little Star." He leaned over and extended his hand toward her. "The best bet to keep you out of the guardhouse and to prevent your uncle from controlling your life is to show them you're with me, that you're my betrothed, not a wild Comanche who might attack or run off at any moment. We need to create a different image of you in their minds."

She stared at his hand.

Deep-brown eyes looked straight into her soul. "We need to get ready for battle. And we need to fight together."

She took his hand. "Just as long as you remember who I am."

"I know who you are. And I understand your fear." His firm, steady grip pulled her up onto the pinto.

"I'm not afraid." She settled behind him as he clicked the horse into movement again.

CHAPTER 21

Might as well have been a parade, the way the men spilled out of their barracks to gawk as Garret rode through the gate with Eyes-Like-Sky. She tensed behind him, her breath coming in short, hard puffs while the stares mounted.

Cheers and hoots rang out. "Yea, Captain Ramsey found her."

"Caught the Comanche savage."

"Wild woman."

The empty Sibley sagged in its corner by the parade ground. At the end of the lane, LeBeau stepped onto the colonel's porch and gaped. His cane and felt hat dangled from his hand.

Garret's jaw tightened. What he wouldn't give to punch that man in the face.

Two plain-clothes fellows lounging by the water trough scrambled to their feet. Hired hands back from their failed search?

Eyes-Like-Sky leaned forward, her warm breath brushing his ear and scattering his thoughts. "I don't feel safe at the

Sibley. What if they come in the middle of the night to take Little Star? I could sleep on the floor in your quarters."

In his quarters? Heat spread across his cheeks as his mind spun. He gripped the reins tighter. "Not a good idea. I'm not going to spoil your reputation like that."

"I told you, I don't care."

"I'll post guards at your tent. No one allowed in. Except me or the colonel."

"Garret—"

She'd asked for his help. His given name from her was more intoxicating than a swig of brandy. "If I don't feel you're secure for the night after I meet with the colonel, I'll move you to my quarters." He called to the best man in sight. "Corporal Miller."

Miller jumped to attention and hurried over.

Up ahead, the colonel stepped through his office door, pipe between his lips. Bareheaded, Mrs. Thorson and Mrs. Clark hurried out of the kitchen.

Let them look. Garret turned the pinto toward the Sibley.

Miller met them at the flap with a sharp salute. "Yes, sir, Captain Ramsey, sir."

"No one comes near this tent. You understand me? Not without a direct order from me or Colonel Thorson."

"Yes, sir." Miller clicked his boot heels.

Garret swung down. "The baby's sick. I'll send the doctor to take a look." He turned and reached up for Eyes-Like-Sky, the first time he'd dared venture such a move. His heart skipped a beat when she slipped her hand into his and dismounted.

The idea of marrying her had been working its way into him, warming him deep inside, yet plummeting his stomach to his boots. Idiotic. She didn't love him. Shrunk from his touch and his eyes. Only tolerated his help. Not the grounds for a good marriage.

But as her feet landed and he withdrew his hand, her

callused fingers latched onto his as if she dangled from a cliff and his grip offered her only hope.

"I won't let you down," he whispered. *Dear God, make it so.*

Boots crunched on the graveled parade ground—men coming over to gawk or congratulate him on his successful hunt.

She tugged her hand free. "This is yours." She lifted his blanket which hung loose around her in place of her lost buffalo robe.

"Yours now." He swallowed and tugged the blue wool over her shoulders, tucking it close to her neck, beneath the old scar on her chin. If he had his way, no one would hurt her again. Ever. "They're all watching," he whispered and brushed a stray strand of hair from her forehead.

Wide-eyed, she sucked in a breath like a doe about to bolt.

"We're putting on a show, remember?" He leaned closer.

She nodded. "Give me your neckerchief."

He raised his eyebrows but complied, unknotting the red sweat-stained cotton from his neck and handing it to her.

Thorson's adjutant hurried over. "Colonel says you're to report right away, Captain, sir."

"Bring her here." LeBeau strutted down the lane toward them, cane striking the ground with each step.

Gaze locked onto Garret's, Eyes-Like-Sky wrapped his neckerchief around her temples like a headband. Her hands appeared to tremble as she quickly tied it. "I can act too."

Only he wasn't acting.

"Marguerite." LeBeau neared.

She scooted closer to Garret and whispered, "I don't know anyone by that name."

"Go inside and stay there. I'll take care of him."

Baby on her back, she slipped into the tent, shutting the flap behind her.

Garret stepped between LeBeau and the Sibley. "She needs

her rest, sir." The term of respect tasted bitter on his tongue. "You can see her in the morning."

LeBeau stuck out his silk-covered chest, dressed more for an evening in a parlor than a sandy parade ground on the edge of nowhere. "Who are you to tell me what to do with my niece?"

"I'm the man who found her, sir." Garret threw his shoulders back "Saved her from being captured again or worse."

Finger tapping a beat on the top of the silver-handled cane, Lebeau scrutinized him. "For that, I'm grateful. You've done your duty. Better than my hired men. They crawled back in here yesterday with no clue of what had become of her. But that doesn't give you any right to be familiar with her or to try and order me around. Now, if you'll excuse me—"

"No, sir." One more 'sir' to this man and he'd puke. But he had to at least try to remain civil. "The baby's sick, and your niece is injured. I'm going to send the doctor to take a look before anyone else goes in."

"All the more reason why I should see her." He side-stepped Garret.

Miller flickered an uncertain gaze but snapped to attention in front of the entrance.

"Try to go past that soldier, sir, and I'll have you arrested." Garret patted his holster, then motioned for Private James to join Miller.

LeBeau bristled. If he'd been a cat, his hair would have spiked, and his back would have arched. "Don't you threaten me, Captain." He struck the ground. Pebbles scattered, and one thudded against Garret's boot. "Marguerite is under my jurisdiction, not yours. You'll answer to your colonel for this insubordination."

"We'll see about that." Garret clenched his jaw and grabbed the pinto's reins, tugging the packhorse behind him, too, as he marched for Thorson's office. Along the way, he handed the trail-weary animals off to a stable hand and ordered a trooper to fetch the doctor.

LeBeau stomped past and clamored up the two stone steps at headquarters.

Minutes later, Garret paused on the stoop to brush off his jacket and stomp his boots, bracing himself for battle.

Above him, LeBeau's rant sounded out the open window. "That captain of yours has a lot to answer for. Never in all of my born days have I been treated so poorly."

Garret swallowed back his glower. *Lord, help me to hold my temper. Help me protect Eyes-Like-Sky and Little Star.*

Throat tight, he entered Thorson's lamp-lit office.

LeBeau greeted him with an icy glare.

"Captain Ramsey." Thorson tossed a linen napkin over his half-eaten dinner.

Garret snapped to attention and saluted.

"At ease, Captain." The colonel shoved his plate aside, looking as if he'd swallowed a sour pickle. "Mr. LeBeau tells me you threatened to arrest him for trying to visit his niece. I assume you must have a good reason for treating our guest in such a bullish manner?"

"Sir." Garret removed his Hardee hat. "Little Star is sick, and Eyes—Miss Logan is worried about her baby, not to mention she, herself, is injured. I've asked the doctor to take a look at both."

"All the more reason why her guardian should be there." LeBeau lifted his whiskered chin.

"Some guardian. You attempted to take away her child." Garret spat out the words. "That's why she ran. Any sane mother would have done the same."

"You told her I was going to give the child up?" LeBeau scowled.

"I had no idea what your plans were until I rode into camp

and heard she'd run away. She already knew. Your presence would only aggravate her distress."

"If she doesn't wish to see me, it's because her mind has been poisoned. First, by the Comanche and now by you."

"Gentlemen." Thorson clomped his forearms on the desk. "This isn't a debate. We're here to have a civil discussion." He blew out a breath. "Captain Ramsey, I understand your concern for Miss Logan. I'll allow her a night of rest, under guard, before she meets with her uncle on the morrow. Afterward, I'll have her in this office to answer for her actions. A soldier spent five days in the infirmary due to her so-called desperate measures, and the man still isn't fit for duty."

"Marguerite isn't in her right mind, Colonel." LeBeau stepped forward. "She cannot be held responsible. It is imperative that I take her home as soon as possible. And the sooner I separate her from that half-breed infant, the better—"

"The baby is her life." Garret hooked his thumbs over his cartridge belt. "I've offered to look after Miss Logan, and she has accepted."

Thorson's eyebrows shot up. "What are you talking about, Ramsey?"

"She's twenty-one years old and capable of making her own decisions. She wishes to decline her uncle's generous offer of provision and guardianship." *Generous*? His lips snagged on the term. "I gave her my word I'd provide for her and protect her."

LeBeau sputtered. "So that's why you had her all cozied up to you on that horse and couldn't keep your hands off her? You've got another thought coming, mister, if you think I'm going to let some two-bit cavalry officer turn my niece into his mistress."

Garret narrowed his eyes at the man whose mustache looked like otter whiskers. "I have no intention of making her my mistress."

"You think I'm going to take your word for that? My niece

might fall prey to every man with muscles and a smile, but I recognize a scoundrel when I see one."

"LeBeau." Thorson thudded his coffee cup. "Captain Ramsey might be misguided, but he's an honorable man. He's the one who killed your niece's husband in battle, and he has felt responsible for her well-being ever since."

"Perhaps the captain has become too attached to my niece." LeBeau simmered like a bulldog on a chain. "Too involved to think clearly and realize the only real way to help Marguerite is to take her away from everything Comanche as soon as possible. She needs a chance to heal. If this man can't handle the guilt of pulling the trigger, then he shouldn't be a soldier."

"Lebeau—" Thorson stiffened.

Enough of this. Garret stepped off a cliff. "Miss Logan and I are in love." A lie. Or was it only a half lie?

Both men's jaws dropped. The tick-tock of the mantel clock punctuated their breathing. "Tattoo" sounded from a bugle on the parade ground.

The colonel blew out an exaggerated breath. "Son—"

"See there, Thorson. I was right. He wants to turn her into his mistress."

Garret swallowed, praying his voice would prove steadier than his wobbly knees. "I proposed to Eyes-Like-Sky. She accepted. We're betrothed."

LeBeau's hat toppled from his head. He snatched it in midair and crunched it against his leg.

The colonel's eyebrows shot up. "Now hold on a minute, Ramsey."

"Ramsey." LeBeau stalked up to him. "I knew it. You are nothing but a licentious fortune hunter—"

"Enough." Thorson banged his fist on the table. "LeBeau, you should thank your lucky stars that a fine young man like Ramsey here would even think about marrying your niece. He comes from one of the best families in Pittsburgh, probably the whole state of Pennsylvania." Thorson flattened his palms against the smooth wood surface. "But we're all getting ahead of ourselves here. We're done for the night. I'll see both of you back here at ten in the morning. Keep in mind that nothing I've heard here precludes her from suffering some consequences for her actions."

"Henry, you can't possibly be considering this captain's nonsense." LeBeau hooked his thumbs beneath the lapels of his dress coat.

"We'll discuss this in the morning, Robert." The colonel's tone clunked like a gavel.

After the door had closed behind the Machiavellian dandy, Thorson turned to Garret. "What in the devil are you thinking, son? You can't seriously consider marrying that girl. Did you get yourself into some indiscretion out there with her on the trail? 'Cause if that's the case, you don't owe her anything."

"No, sir." Garret bit his lip. Maybe he should let the colonel think that. Help seal his claim on her, but no, not yet. He wouldn't sully her reputation any more than she'd already done. "I gave her my word I wouldn't let anyone take her baby away, and that I'd protect and provide for her."

A dog barked in the yard among the distant voices of stragglers back from the mess hall. Cheers and chuckles. Men who were not in the process of turning their whole lives upside down.

Thorson stood and ran his hand through his wiry, gray-tinged hair. "What the devil, man? I understand you feel sorry for her and the baby. I know you believe it's your fault, even though it isn't. But throwing your life away? A girl like that might fit in here on the frontier, but in Pittsburgh society, and with your family? You have a life ahead of you decades beyond a couple years in the desert."

Garret opened his mouth, but the colonel held up his hand. "Not another word. Go back to your quarters, clean up, and get some rest. That's an order, Captain. Come talk to me in the morning when you have more sense. Get here at nine-thirty, before LeBeau. And don't go anywhere near that Sibley tonight."

~

As Garret crossed the parade ground, his gaze drifted to the Sibley. A trickle of smoke wove its way out of the stovepipe on the side of the canvas. She'd settled in safe for the evening. Miller and James stood at her door. He'd given the doctor word to fetch him if there was anything serious.

For the first time in four nights, he'd not sleep within sight of Eyes-Like-Sky. After he'd recovered from the extreme exhaustion of the first night, he'd lain awake half of the others beneath the open sky, watchful for any hint of danger and studying the sleeping beauty across the campfire. Baby sniffles and the smooth, even pattern of Eyes-Like-Sky's breathing had filled in the gaps between the crackles and pops of burning wood.

A few nights from now, she might be in his quarters, permanently. As his wife. His partner through life? His stomach flip-flopped as if he'd been thrown by his horse. Marriage or desertion with her and a life on the run, those were his options. Unless by some miracle her uncle could be supplicated with a betrothal.

Yet the colonel expected him to sleep?

Sweet smells of bacon, beans, and hot biscuits welcomed him as he stepped into his wall-tent. His stomach rumbled for immediate attention and pushed his plans of bathing first aside. He hung his cartridge belt on a peg, followed by his scabbard and carbine sling. But the tension in his shoulders didn't ease.

Charlie pushed through the beaded curtain which separated the sleep area from the main room. "Did you leave any dirt on the trail, or did you bring it all back as a keepsake?"

"I didn't want you to feel you'd missed out." The corners of Garret's mouth quirked up as he dipped his hands in the washbasin and scrubbed his face. "But if you prefer to not have half of our quarters coated with the beautiful soil of Texas, I suggest you order one of the boys to draw me a bath."

"Already done, my friend. He's busy boiling water as we speak." Charlie grabbed two covered plates from the stovetop and carried them to the table. "The kitchen was short on tea and crumpets, so you'll have to settle for ham and potatoes." He grinned and sat down, fork in hand. "Besides, I can't wait to hear how you rescued the lady in distress. Relations looked a bit friendly when you rode in."

"It only took her weathering a blizzard, almost getting captured by enemy warriors, and losing her horse and most of her supplies before she slowed down enough to get found and consider talking." Garret pulled up a chair and uncovered his plate.

"Is that how you won her over? I always knew you were a charmer. I reckon she begged to come back."

"Not her." Garret chewed his way through a couple of ham bites before he continued. "She attempted to steal my horse and gave me a good kick when I tried to stop her. It was all I could do to not get hoofed in the head, but in the end, I was able to disarm her long enough for her to listen."

"Was that all? Thank goodness, she didn't give you any trouble." Charlie's face lit with amusement. "And by the time you rode in here, she was like a tamed kitten? How did you manage that?"

Garret sucked down a heaping scoop of potatoes and then sawed into the ham. Charlie wouldn't understand. No one would. "I talked to her. Reasoned with her. But 'tame' is not in her vocabulary."

"I'd love to hear what you said to convince her to come back and surrender her baby."

Garret scraped at his peas, a delicacy in these parts, but tonight, they tasted like sawdust. "She's not giving up Little Star."

"Her uncle's not giving her a choice." Charlie pointed his fork like a baton.

"It's not his decision to make. I told her I wouldn't let him. I gave her my word I'd do whatever it took to protect her and the baby."

Charlie's eyebrows edged up. The light faded from his face. "You did what? And exactly what does that mean? Are you going to challenge him to a gunfight?"

"I reckon that would have been one way to take care of it." Garret grabbed the coffeepot from the stove and poured himself a cup before sitting back down to his meal. Best finish what he could before this conversation shriveled his appetite. "I told her I'd provide for her and the baby."

Charlie's eyes gleamed. "Are you going to take her as your woman?"

Garret blew out a breath and braced himself. "Nothing of the sort. We're betrothed."

"You're what? You've got to be kidding."

"I told LeBeau I'd proposed and she'd accepted. My hope is that he can be persuaded to accept the engagement and head on back to East Texas. Eyes-Like-Sky and I would just keep putting off the wedding indefinitely."

"And what if he doesn't head home?"

His heart thudded in his throat. "Then I reckon we'd have to go through with it."

"Marry her?" Charlie's voice crescendoed. "Are you crazy? That woman could stab you in your sleep. What about everyone back home expecting you to marry Lily? I mean, plenty of fellows take up with an Indian woman here and then head back home as though nothing ever happened—"

"I'm not doing that to Eyes-Like-Sky." Garret clunked down his fork and scooted back from the table. "I'm not bedding her unless I'm married to her. Even then, I might have one foot in the grave before she'd welcome attention from me."

Charlie gaped at him. "You'd throw away an alliance with a beautiful, well-bred woman who would welcome your embrace for a woman who's only interested in what you can do for her and her baby?"

"Eyes-Like-Sky isn't like that." But wasn't that exactly how it was? Garret scrubbed both hands over his face. "Lily doesn't know the first thing about love, and I don't love her."

"That's no reason for taking the first pretty but desperate woman who cries out for help. What about your family? Your father will explode like a steam engine."

"My father is not going to choose my wife."

"You're choosing Eyes-Like-Sky?"

Choosing? Not exactly the right word for it. Garret stood and paced the length of the room. "I'm keeping my promise. That's what I'm doing. I couldn't leave her out there in the middle of hundreds of miles of prairie and desert with the baby, in danger of being captured or worse. And if you're my friend, you'll help me."

"Help you place a noose around your neck?"

"Help me convince LeBeau that he should welcome me as his niece's betrothed. Maybe if he's convinced enough, he'll go home without the ceremony. Or if it does come to marriage, you could help me figure out if it has to be permanent. You studied law. Your father's a lawyer. I told Eyes-Like-Sky there could be the chance of an annulment."

Charlie tossed his napkin onto the floor. "It's draping a noose over your head and praying the trap door beneath your feet doesn't open."

Garret slipped a finger beneath his collar. Air. He needed air and sleep. Grabbing his jacket, he headed out the door and shuffled past the scruffy grove which shaded their quarters. Stars blinked down from the canopy of the evening sky. Across the parade ground stood the Sibley with its inner faint glow, guarded still.

She's only interested in what you can do for her and the baby. Was Charlie right? Did it make any difference to Eyes-Like-Sky who offered her help, whether it was him, or Charlie, or some nameless Comanche she hadn't met yet?

More importantly, what would God have him do?

CHAPTER 22

Garret awoke at sunrise, poured a couple of pots of hot water into the bath which he'd neglected in lieu of a good night's sleep, and scrubbed every inch of himself.

A new thought had bubbled to the surface between waking and sleeping. What if he could win Eyes-Like-Sky's affection? Not today, or even this month, maybe not this year. But eventually. Her grieving could not last forever. He was committed to providing a home for her and Little Star. A home with him in it. Maybe with time, his care for her could compensate for that terrible day when he'd taken so much from her. He prayed that it could be so.

He planned on going to see her before breakfast, but the colonel's orderly caught up to him before he'd made it halfway across the parade grounds. Ten minutes later, Garret shifted in a hardback seat in the colonel's office, pressing his sweaty palms against his trousers.

Thorson paced across the bare wood floor in front of him, uniform coat unbuttoned. "Son, why don't you send a telegram to your father? Get his advice before you make any life-changing commitments. I could dispatch a rider to Fort Belknap. Don't wager your future on the possibility of an annulment that may never come. There's a verse in Proverbs about the wisdom of a multitude of counselors."

"No, thank you, sir." His father was the last person he wanted advice from. Maybe his father had had a heart once when he'd fallen in love with Garret's mother, but it'd long since been replaced by a balance sheet. "I appreciate the offer. But this isn't my father's decision to make."

Thorson shook his head and leaned back against the edge of the desk. "If it's the baby you're concerned about, there are other options to consider."

Garret frowned and drew his feet away from the colonel's outstretched legs. "What do you mean, sir?"

"I don't know why I didn't think of it earlier." Eagerness lit the colonel's face. "You could pay someone to care for the baby. If you're concerned about the Apache carrying the child off, you could advertise, find a nanny. I believe my wife would agree to watch Little Star until you find suitable help. You said you were willing to provide for the child. I bet LeBeau could be persuaded to sign over legal guardianship to you." Thorson dusted his hands together. "Problem solved. You can fulfill your word to protect and provide for the child without ensnaring yourself to a troubled girl you barely know."

Troubled girl? That wasn't how he saw her. Did he want a way out? A chance to provide a home for Little Star without turning his life upside down? He leaned forward, elbows on knees, and blew out a breath.

Thorson grabbed his coffee cup and sipped. "I wager you could arrange something so the girl could come see her child once a year. Not that you'd mention it to LeBeau until everything is signed and done. And she could have the assurance you're taking the best possible care of her daughter. I bet she'd be relieved."

Garret's eyebrows popped up. *Relief* wasn't the word. *Fury* was more like it. Eyes-Like-Sky seeing her daughter once a year? Little Star being raised by a stranger? That wasn't the deal he'd made with her.

He cleared his throat. "I promised to look after Eyes-Like-Sky, as well. I gave my word I wouldn't let her child be taken from her."

"What about your own future? That girl should be thankful you saved her from getting captured by enemy warriors and that you're willing to give her baby a home. Besides, you aren't doing Miss Logan any favors by letting her stay Indian." Thorson clunked his cup on the desk. "LeBeau is offering her a new start in life. She doesn't know what she wants right now. Her family was murdered. She was kidnapped and likely ravished by her attackers. Most women don't even want to live after what those savages do to them. But somehow, she survived and eventually, became part of the tribe. That's how she lived. I've seen enough captives to know."

Garret winced. Thank God, she had survived the horror. He couldn't even imagine...

If only he could take her in his arms and make all of the hurt go away. Hurt he'd contributed to by killing her husband in front of her.

He exhaled. "I have no doubt you're right, sir, about her life before she met her husband. But LeBeau acting as though it never happened isn't going to solve anything. It happened. She'll never forget it, and as far as I'm concerned, taking away the most precious thing in this world to her, her daughter, will only do more damage."

Thorson pinched the bridge of his nose. "Maybe it doesn't have to be either-or, Ramsey. You take guardianship of the baby, find a nanny, and let Miss Logan go with her uncle for a couple of years. Give it some time, give her a chance to make a well-educated decision. Let her have a taste of normal life. LeBeau's not going to lock her up in the attic, you know. His dream is to give her everything he couldn't give his sister. I reckon the mother eloped with a penniless schoolteacher, instead of the young man her father had encouraged. Led to a life of poverty and eventually, to setting out across the frontier and being attacked by Comanches. LeBeau wants to give Miss Logan back her future." Thorson held out his palm. "Give her chance to settle into her new life, Ramsey. Let her make up her own mind after she's experienced her options."

Garret ran his hand over his hair. "LeBeau is the one robbing her of the freedom to choose, not me. He doesn't have to take away her child to give her a home and an education."

"You and I both know how well she'd be accepted in upper-class society with a half-Indian child. And her admission of marrying a Comanche of her own free will? She might as well have the plague."

Garret slumped back in his chair. Exactly how his father and Pittsburgh society would view her as well. But he'd willingly throw every scrap of their approval away if only he could have the assurance of Eyes-Like-Sky's eventual affection.

When had that happened? Discomfort rose in the pit of his stomach. When had he started to fall in love with her?

~

Garret's breath vaporized into thin puffs of frost as he lumbered toward the Sibley. By the enlisted men's barracks, a murder of crows clustered in the lone crabapple tree, pecking away at the shriveled fruit. A discarded cedar bough lay against the base of the trunk, the remains of the cook's make-shift Christmas decorations. Christmas. All those days on the trail searching for Eyes-Like-Sky, he'd plum forgotten the holiday.

A shiver ran through him. The morning was better suited

for a greatcoat than a shell jacket. Up ahead, smoke puffed out of the Sibley's stovepipe.

Should he mention the colonel's idea? Offer to take care of Little Star and stand aside while LeBeau whisked his niece away to East Texas for now? He could go see her when he got leave, take Little Star with him and whatever nameless wet nurse or nanny he happened to find. Maybe it'd only be six months instead of a year. Maybe by then, he could think of another way for Eyes-Like-Sky to have her daughter short of a wedding. What if he courted her and worked to win her before marriage, as it should be done?

Court her? Who was he kidding? If he let her be taken from this camp without her daughter, she would hate him, and she would never adjust to civilized society. If he agreed to the colonel's plan, he'd lose her. His heart sank like lead in his gut.

At the entrance to the tent, he waved the guard aside. He'd given his word he'd do whatever it took to keep Eyes-Like-Sky with her baby. That's what she wanted more than anything. Not a closet full of ball gowns, some fancy education at a finishing school, and a porch full of gentlemen callers. Hat in hand, he smoothed his freshly washed hair and straightened his jacket. He rapped his knuckles against the canvas. "Captain Ramsey coming in."

Seated on his wool blanket, she jerked a shawl across her chest to cover the nursing baby. She'd washed her face and hair, but filth still covered her skirt and leggings. Her wet doeskin blouse clung to her skin.

Why hadn't he considered that she'd have nothing else to change into?

Expectant blue eyes focused on him.

"Pardon me for barging in." He tapped his hat against his leg and shifted his gaze around the too-empty Sibley.

"What happened last night? I hoped you'd stop by." Face pinched, she scrambled to her feet, infant in tow. Her right foot wobbled before she gained her balance. "I'd have come looking for you, but I was afraid they'd arrest me if I left my tent."

"I'm sorry. The colonel ordered me to wait until today to see you."

"Why?" She tightened her arms around the squirming infant, securing her once again to her feeding beneath the shawl.

"A little fatherly concern. Nothing to worry about." He motioned to a crate for her to sit and pulled up another across from her, setting the half-filled washbasin and cloth on the ground.

A frown settled across her face as she shoved her half-empty plate aside and plopped down. "I stop worrying when LeBeau leaves without me. You talk to the doctor? He came by last night—"

"Yes, I did." His voice softened. "I was thankful to hear Little Star is on the mend and that he treated your injuries. He said the cut on your leg was no small matter. I'm sorry you didn't let me look after it days ago."

"Little Star was ill. No time to worry about my leg."

"If you want to be strong for your baby, you've got to look after yourself too." His lips edged upward despite the weight that dragged his shoulders down. "And that includes finishing your breakfast." He nodded toward the plate.

"How could I eat when they could come arrest me or try to take Little Star at any moment?" She shoved a piece of bacon into her mouth. Windburn from the days on the open prairie colored her cheeks. "Tell me what happened last night."

"I'm sorry I didn't send you a message." Garret crumpled his hat. "Last night didn't go well. The colonel and I had a second meeting this morning, and after I leave here, I'm scheduled to meet with your uncle again. LeBeau's an ornery man. I'm convinced nothing short of an actual wedding ceremony will settle matters."

Her frown deepened. A little foot poked beneath the shawl, pressing against her abdomen. "You'd have been better off if you'd never brought me back here, Garret Ramsey."

"No, I wouldn't, and neither would you."

A sigh rattled through her. "After the battle, I wanted you to pay with your life. Now...I would spare you from promising away your freedom if I could, if there was any other way." Moisture dampened her eyes.

He gulped. Who were the tears for? Best not fool himself into thinking they could possibly be for him. He leaned down, elbows on his knees. "You lost almost everything in the battle. You didn't start it, neither did I. But the least I can do is to make sure you don't lose your precious baby girl."

She lifted her chin. "I'll repay you."

"You don't owe me anything." He met her gaze. "Except the chance to earn your friendship." *And your affection*. Dare he hope for more?

Her voice faltered. "I couldn't deny you anything you ask."

"Not denying and willingly giving are two different things."

She pressed her lips together.

Couldn't deny him anything. Was he forcing her into this marriage? Didn't he owe it to her to at least mention the colonel's other option?

Brow furrowed, he glanced down at her free hand which rested by Little Star's feet. "May I?" He reached out.

She stared at his hand as if it were some creature to be wary of, then lifted hers, halting a couple of inches short of touching his.

He closed his fingers around her rough, callused hand. Strong. Narrow fingers which once might have flown over keys on a piano, now scarred from years of cleaning hides and digging roots. Warmth spread up his arm and across his cheeks. "I want to discuss my plans with you. And options. It needs to be your decision, as well."

She nodded. A lock of hair slipped over her eyes. No neckerchief in sight.

He cleared his throat. "I've asked my friend, Lieutenant Charlie Fuller, to act as my go-between and help me convince LeBeau to agree to the betrothal and marriage. Charlie's also studied law. He or one of his learned associates can advise the best avenue for pursuing an annulment...in the future. But I need to know if this is what you want." He dropped his gaze and brushed his thumb across her rough palm.

Beyond her limp hand, her arm muscles tensed like a bow string. "Associates? Advise? Avenue? Too many words."

His thumb stilled before he sent her bolting. "I just wanted you to know I'm looking into the possibility of an annulment. However, the colonel has suggested another option. It'd free us from the necessity of marrying, but there would be significant cost."

She paled. "What kind of cost?"

His tongue stuck to the roof of his mouth.

"What kind?" She tugged her hand from his.

His arm twitched at the loss of her touch, and he rubbed his palms against his wool trousers. "I believe they're too high, but I want you to be fully aware of all options. The colonel's idea was for me to assume guardianship of Little Star and allow LeBeau to take you back to East Texas temporarily—"

She gaped at him. "You would consider this?" Her voice shook. "Of course you would. It'd save you from being tied to me permanently. And I said I would spare you from that if I could."

Little Star lifted her head out of the quilt, milk dripping from her chin, and cranked her head toward him as if she'd just now noticed his presence. "Mumummum."

Two stares. Big, dark eyes combined with piercing blue ones to decimate any other consideration outside of the woman and baby before him. "I'll tell them it's out of the question."

Eyes-Like-Sky's shoulders slumped. "No, tell them we accept."

"You don't mean that."

"Yes, I do, as long as you agree to help smuggle me and Little Star out of camp the night before they're set to take me. Get me a horse and supplies. I'll head to Mexico. They won't expect that. You don't need to come with me. You'll be free—"

"No. Absolutely not." He slapped his knees. "I'm going to grab Charlie, meet with Lebeau, and fix our wedding date. I'll keep my word to you, and you are going to keep yours, Eyes-Like-Sky."

Her countenance brightened. A smile flickered across her lips.

Had he ever seen her smile before? Maybe at Little Star when she thought no one was looking. His breath quickened.

"What did I give my word about?" She bit her lip.

His eyebrows arched. "You know what you promised. That you won't run away."

"Very well." She curved her forearm around Little Star's belly and drew her back against her. "I won't run away. And I'll go along with whatever your friend says about an annulment."

Annulment wasn't exactly where his mind was going at the moment.

Hair damp, the baby found her thumb. Little Star's eyes danced at him.

Goosebumps rose on his skin. She was going to be his little girl. He was going to be a father, as well as a husband. He'd have a baby crawling around his quarters and a wife...where? In his bed? On his floor? In his home. A woman of unfathomable depths guarded by walls as impermeable as the sides of the red-rock canyons where he'd found her.

He leaned forward and wove his fingers together. His gaze darted to her tattered moccasins. "In regards to our marriage, Eyes-Like-Sky, I want you to know, I won't pressure you. And you don't owe me anything. I don't expect to exercise my husbandly rights in the bed chamber. I understand you're still grieving." His cheeks burned. "But we would live together in the same house as husband and wife." His whisper scraped his throat. "Is this acceptable to you?"

"Yes." Her voice trembled, and so did his heart.

He stood. One more thought pricked his lips. "I'd appreciate it greatly if you'd pray for our situation today. We have no guarantee of LeBeau's cooperation, and there's still the matter of Jenkins and the consequences."

Her blue eyes widened. She wobbled on her injured ankle as she stood. "Not sure my prayers would help." Her voice was barely a whisper.

"They would. I'm confident of it." He patted her shoulder, then pivoted away, not waiting for her to tense beneath his touch.

CHAPTER 23

Eyes-Like-Sky tugged the voluminous skirt and petticoats over doeskin leggings. It was no one's business what she wore under this carpet of a dress. Garret had sent the clothes asking that she wear them until her uncle left camp, a part of his ploy to convince the colonel and LeBeau she was a reasonable and reformed young lady capable of making prudent decisions. What did *prudent* even mean? She'd known the word once, but whatever it was, it probably didn't fit her.

She studied her reflection in a scrap of mirror Angelina had left for her. Wind-burned cheeks, skin tanned to a light brown, and wispy waves of untamable, dark hair shorn short the day she lost her husband. Three months later, it hung almost to the tops of her shoulders.

What did Garret Ramsey see when he looked at her? His eyes had shone earlier this morning as he'd held her hand and talked of their plans. The touch of his skin had pulled like a magnet, like rain to parched soil. For one insane moment, the urge to slip into the comfort of his arms had almost overwhelmed her. But she would not lose her head over this man. It was a temporary marriage of necessity, to a kind man who sought to alleviate his guilt, nothing else.

She wrapped her arms around herself. *Dear God, please don't let him expect too much of me, more than I can give*. And what if it wasn't temporary?

Her palms scuffed against the wool dress. Too tight, too itchy, and way too many buttons. Settler clothes hung heavy like wet rags and pricked like cactus needles. She rubbed her hands over the emerald-green sleeves, pressing her fingers against the edges of the golden armbands beneath the layers.

Dancing Eagle. If only she could be in his arms again and hear the caress of his low, quiet voice saying her name.

Their last day of summer together before he'd headed off on a retaliation raid, they'd lain in the soft grass by a stream beneath the shade of a cottonwood. Dancing Eagle's dark hair had mixed with hers as she'd rested her head in the crook of his shoulder and pressed her palm to his chest while dragonflies fluttered overhead. A lifetime ago. And here she was, hoping and praying to be allowed to marry the man who had killed him. Did caring for one man betray the other?

But what else was she to do? She'd already run away and risked her life and Little Star's. With hardly a grain of faith that the Creator of the universe would hear her words, she had prayed that the Lord would look after them and provide a way for them to be together. And He'd sent Garret.

Who was she to say no?

~

A cool breeze rippled across Garret's sweaty brow as he paused by the hitching post in front of the colonel's office. Shards of bright light seeped out from a meandering cloud concealing the distant sun. Down the row, Mrs. Clark sat on her porch with her sewing in her lap, creaking back and forth in her rocker. Despite the bonnet covering half her features, there was no doubt where her gaze was aimed. How much had she heard about his proposal to Eyes-Like-Sky? It didn't matter.

Gauntlets tucked in his cartridge belt next to his saber, he rubbed his thumb over the heavy gold ring on his finger. He usually kept the emerald-and-onyx monstrosity tucked away in a pair of stockings at the bottom of his trunk, lest it remind him of his father, but today was different. He needed every trapping of wealth he could muster.

Footsteps sounded behind him.

Dressed in his newly pressed uniform and carrying a leather satchel, Charlie stepped alongside and clamped a hand on his shoulder. "Ready?"

"No."

"All you have to do is keep quiet and let me do the talking in there. Today, you're my client. This is business. My aim is to sell LeBeau on your family name and connections in exchange for his paltry offering."

"What do you mean by paltry? I hope you're not referring to Eyes-Like-Sky."

"That's exactly why you need to hold your tongue." Charlie moved his thumb over the brass buttons on his own jacket as if double-checking the eagles for smudges. "If you go in there and say she's the finest maiden who ever lived, and mother of all virtue, the man is not going to marry her off to the first gentleman caller who comes along. We need to impress upon him how thankful he should be that you're willing to take her off his hands."

Garret inwardly groaned and pointed to the colonel's open window as they climbed the steps.

Charlie leaned in close enough for their hat brims to bump. "You'd be better off if I fail today."

"I'm counting on you to win." Garret flexed his fingers at his sides.

If this failed, his army career would be over. He and Eyes-Like-Sky would be headed for Mexico with the cavalry on their tail. Maybe that's what he should tell his father after the steam stopped coming out of his ears. After the man had gone hoarse from yelling and threatening. *See, Father, I have not failed you completely. I saved you from the mortification of having a deserter for a son.* A wry smile hardened his lips as he opened the door, leaving the mild sunshine for the confines of the stuffy office.

"Come in, gentleman, and have a seat." The colonel tapped his cigar against a tin lid on his desk.

LeBeau clamped his silver pocket watch shut and settled back in the padded chair, ankle across his knee. His slender fingers wrapped around a glass of brandy.

Thorson shuffled the papers on his desk and shoved them aside. "I'm only here to keep the peace. This discussion is between you gentlemen. I believe you have all been introduced, and I've informed Mr. LeBeau that Lieutenant Fuller is your representative, Ramsey."

LeBeau's face contorted into its usual wormwood expression, his glare measuring Garret and Charlie from head to toe.

Charlie took the middle chair and sat. After a couple of stiff pleasantries, he moved to the matter at hand. "As you have been informed, sir, Captain Ramsey has proposed to your niece, and she accepted. He is now seeking your permission to wed her."

Garret ground his teeth. Seeking LeBeau's permission? He was here to declare, not beg.

"As I told Ramsey and the colonel last night, my niece is incapable of making such a decision at this time."

"We've all seen ample evidence that Miss Logan is capable of making decisions." Charlie raised his eyebrows. "Thankfully, this time, she's making a wise one. As her guardian, you can verify her choice." Charlie leaned forward and slipped a piece of paper from the satchel, a list of the Ramsey family holdings drawn up this morning over breakfast. "Captain Ramsey comes from a prosperous, well-established family, the Ramseys of Pittsburgh."

LeBeau sneered at the offered paper. "Never heard of them. Probably some tradesman with a puffed-out chest."

"No, sir." Charlie straightened and lowered the page to his lap. "An industrialist. Owns two iron works and a munitions factory. He also oversees a shipping empire. If you need something shipped along the Ohio, Allegheny, or the Monongahela, he's your man. He's among the Pittsburg elite."

"King of the anthill, huh?" LeBeau retrieved his cigar from the tin and muttered. "New money. Dirty work. My niece comes from a landed family."

"Your niece dresses in buckskin, refuses to be called by her Christian name, and is ready to commit crimes in order to keep custody of her half-breed baby. Not to mention, she's eager to tell anyone who asks the proud paternal lineage of her child."

LeBeau chomped on his cigar. "Captain Ramsey is the one who has encouraged such nonsense on her part."

"Captain Ramsey is the only one who can halfway manage her. You should be grateful that a man of his credentials and standing is willing to take her off your hands and offer her a respectable position as his wife. I'm willing to bet there's not another man in the whole state of Texas who'd make you such an offer, other than some fellow with a lean-to for a house who needs another hand around his scrub farm."

LeBeau jerked his chin. "My niece will make a fine lady someday. Once I get her away from this dirt hole."

Garret drummed his fingers on his chair arm. "Your niece is a fine lady. And too good for—"

Charlie sliced him with a sideways glare, then turned back to LeBeau. "Your niece is hardheaded and contrary. If you take her to your plantation without her child, she'll fight you tooth and nail to get back here. She'll be in a locked room, not sitting in a parlor learning how to sip tea. If I were you, I'd accept Ramsey's offer before he recovers from Cupid's spell and withdraws his proposal."

"Captain Ramsey has tarnished my niece's virtue—"

"P-please." Charlie rolled his eyes as a smirk spread across his face. "Let us not delve into a discussion of the young widow's virtue. My friend here would be willing to challenge us both to fisticuffs if we go down that road. Captain Ramsey has been a perfect gentleman toward Miss Logan. The only matter left to settle is the amount of the dowry."

Garret pressed his lips together as Charlie's words grated through him.

"Dowry?" LeBeau half choked on a swig of brandy. "Ramsey's not getting a penny. That two-bit vulgarian has another thought coming if he thinks he can weasel his way into my pocket."

"Miss Logan is your niece, and you are her guardian. I'd think a young lady from such an upstanding family would be accompanied by a parcel of good bottom land, or at the very least, a trousseau of jewelry. After all, she might have to pay Sergeant Jenkins's medical expenses and provide for his further recovery."

LeBeau rammed his cane against the floor and stood. "Enough." He clunked his brandy snifter down on the desk. "My time is too valuable to be wheedled away by the likes of you two and an uncivilized girl who doesn't appreciate my generosity. Ramsey can have her. Providing he marries her by the end of the week in a proper wedding. I'm leaving camp on Monday morning. If they aren't man and wife by then, I'm taking her and leaving the baby, and I never want to hear from Ramsey again."

CHAPTER 24

Eyes-Like-Sky scooped Little Star off of Garret's blanket. "I'll take her with me."

"No, señora. The colonel said just you. I'm to watch the baby." Angelina held out her thick hands. "I take good care of her."

"I don't think so." Eyes-Like-Sky tightened her hold on the child and ducked out the flap before Angelina could protest.

Little Star dug her tiny fingers into the green wool and babbled as Eyes-Like-Sky tripped on the long flounce of the settler dress.

Strong hands grabbed her shoulders and steadied her.

She jerked her head up to two warm brown eyes.

"Careful." Garret smiled.

What did the smile mean? Had his meeting gone well? "What happened? The colonel sent for me. Angelina tried to make me leave Little Star with her—"

"It's all right to leave her for a little bit. They're done with trying to take her away from you." Voice strong and sure, his hands slid down her upper arms before he released her and took a step back.

She stilled. "My uncle said yes?"

Angelina popped her head out of the tent. "Señor, I'm glad you're here. I tried to explain to her—"

"You can watch Little Star. Make sure you stay here at the Sibley with her." Just like that, he slipped the baby from her arms and handed her off to Angelina.

And she let him? She narrowed her eyes at his audacity.

But he cupped his hand to her elbow. "We'll talk as we walk." His eyes gleamed.

Somehow, someway, her uncle had said yes. The realization rolled through her like a boulder. Opening or closing off the horizon?

He slowed his pace to a meandering stroll. "Your uncle is stubborn as a mule. And you'd think he was a king, the way he's so puffed up. But yes, thank God, Charlie presented the case well, and we had LeBeau's agreement by the time we walked out of there. The ceremony will be Saturday."

Her legs wobbled. She would become this man's wife. Little Star would be safe. Tears pricked her eyes. God had provided a way for her to be with her daughter. At what cost? Would she lose all hope of ever returning to the Comanche? "What's today?"

"Tuesday. The circuit rider will be here at the end of the week for his monthly sermon."

So soon? "We couldn't put it off? Maybe my uncle will leave—"

"Not an option. Your uncle said by Monday or no deal." His hand slipped around hers, fingers entwined, and hers complied like dry reeds to a basket, sending her stomach for a tumble.

Holding hands? Part of the show to convince anyone who was looking that they were in love? Or was this man taking it to heart?

"Mrs. Thorson has volunteered to handle all of the wedding details. I'm sure she'll throw together a party afterwards."

"Party?" She stopped walking. "We don't need anything fancy. Just you, me, and the preacher." Standing in front of all those people, men who'd gawked at her and whistled, ladies who'd looked down their noses at her? When she and Dancing Eagle had married—

Nothing would be like that. This was not the same. She pulled her hand free of his and rubbed her sleeves, scratchy wool over gold armbands.

Garret frowned. "The colonel and the ladies aren't going to let it be a quiet little affair. It's winter. Friday is New Year's. And Mrs. Thorson insists there's never been a wedding at this post. Besides, the celebration will show every person in this camp you are my wife and someone to be respected." He gripped his scabbard. "It wouldn't look good if the bride was in the stockade. If the colonel feels duty-bound to put you in there, he'll have to let you out by Saturday."

She tensed. "There's still that possibility?"

Clouds passed over the sun, dropping them into shadowed gray. A tumbleweed drifted across the parade grounds, ignored by the handful of troopers unloading a wagon in front of the storage building.

He blew out a breath. "Yes. That's why he wants to see you. To question you and discuss consequences."

She tightened her arms around herself. "I have no idea of what to say him. I'd rather face a charging buffalo."

"I'm sorry I can't come in there with you, but he wants to speak to you alone. But keep in mind, he's not the enemy, Eyes-Like-Sky. He's reasonable." Garret's brow furrowed. "Tell him how much Little Star means to you, and how desperate you were to protect her. And—" His glance flittered to the horizon. "If you have to, you can mention how you feared for your virtue when Jenkins wouldn't keep his distance in the storage house."

A bitter taste surged up her throat. She had invited Jenkins's 'friendliness,' deceived him into thinking she was interested in his attentions. She was guilty. Virtue? She'd lost that long ago against her will. Her head dipped. What would the man beside her think of her if he knew her whole past?

The Lord knew every bit of her past. Had He forgiven her?

Immersed in the stink of old cigar smoke, Eyes-Like-Sky stood before the bushy-eyebrowed colonel and spilled the fears and worries that had inspired her actions. With her fidgety hands clasped in front of her, her voice scraped her throat as she mentioned the eventual panic that had led to her grabbing the only thing she could reach to defend herself, the hammer.

She dug her nails into her palms as Thorson issued his verdict. When the man's hairy lip and chin had finally stopped moving, she clamped her mouth shut, lest her bountiful opinion spill forth, and pivoted on her heels.

On the rough-hewn porch, Garret jumped as she banged through the door. He halted in mid-pace. "What happened?"

"That man—"

"Shush." Garret nodded to the open window.

She bit her lip and stomped down the steps past two sentries.

Garret caught up to her and matched her pace, their heels crunching on the gravel. Two soldiers stood by the colonel's house chopping gnarled branches into logs. Off to the right and down the lane, Mrs. Clark sat on the porch eyeing them beneath her stiff bonnet.

A person could suffocate in this scruffy place.

Garret touched a hand to her elbow. "Did he sentence you to the stockade?"

"No." She bristled. "I wish that was all. I told him I'd to stay there with Little Star until the wedding instead. But he wouldn't listen." *Squish.* Her moccasin struck a pile of horse manure. The hem of the stupid dress managed to brush against it, as well.

A muffled screech whistled through her clenched teeth. She bent down, yanked the shoe off, and threw it.

A couple soldiers by the watering trough cackled.

She spun in their direction, ready to tell what she thought of their lazy hides. What she thought of the whole place.

Garret caught her arm and whispered. "Ignore them. Don't let them see it bothers you, and they'll leave you alone."

"They're going to see plenty. The colonel is going to make me burn my clothes in front of all of them." Her voice wavered.

His jaw dropped. "What?"

Someone moseyed by on a horse. "Afternoon, Captain."

Garret waved the man off and frowned. "Take a breath, and tell me exactly what the colonel said."

Her lip trembled. "He's taking my clothes. Everything Comanche, even the cradleboard. He's going to throw it in the fire for everyone to see. I have until sundown."

"I had no idea that's what he had in mind."

"He's as bad as my uncle—"

"Let's take a stroll. And finish this discussion in private." Without waiting for her answer, he tucked her hand beneath his elbow and walked her over to where her moccasin lay. He bent to pick it up. "We can clean it."

"Why bother? They're going to burn it. I can go barefoot." She leaned down and snatched off the other one, throwing it toward the enlisted men's barracks where a handful of soldiers sat cleaning their guns in the afternoon sun.

Garret's eyebrows arched, and he tossed the soiled moccasin alongside the other. "If you prefer, we can talk in your tent."

"No." She latched onto his arm. "I want to walk."

His hand slipped over hers, and they headed toward the gate.

Down the trail toward the Brazos River, she boiled in silence. Pebbles and clumps of dead grass poked the soles of her feet. She humbled herself in front of Thorson, even alluded to the horror of the past, and this is what it'd gotten her. Sliding sideways down the muddy embankment with Garret at her side, she made her way close to the water's edge near the hackberry tree. A scrawny squirrel skittered away. Slimy leavening of weeds, duck-down, bark, and other debris washed ashore by the river lay scattered about.

"So tell me," Garret said.

Eyes-Like-Sky's foot scraped against a gnarled root as she turned. "Thorson says I have to wear settler clothes. Even tried to tell me that I can't make new Comanche ones after he burns my old ones." She clenched her fists at her sides. "Why can't they leave me alone? Thorson, his wife, LeBeau. They're all the same. They want to tear out who I am. I will not let them. I will not be Marguerite or Maggie Logan, this woman that they think I should be. It is my life. Not theirs." She smacked a low-hanging branch out of her way. A cluster of dead leaves tumbled to the ground.

Garret blew out a breath. "I'm sorry the colonel's doing this." His brow furrowed. "I know it might be hard to believe, but he probably thinks he's being lenient and helping you."

"Helping me? He might as well rip my skin off."

The corners of his lips twinged, as if he might actually dare smile at her exaggeration. "Taking away your possessions doesn't change who you are. Mrs. Thorson burned the clothes you came here in, and you made more. You'll always be Eyes-Like-Sky to me. To the rest of the world, you're about to become Mrs. Garret Ramsey. None of that changes who you are on the inside."

The river burbled as it passed over stones close to shore.

Mrs. Garret Ramsey. She couldn't even imagine that person. It didn't sound like her. And he was wrong. All of it would change her. The only question was how much. "You have no idea what it's like, Garret Ramsey, to have your whole world taken from you. Twice."

"No, I don't." Garret pursed his lips. His eyes tightened, accentuating tiny creases at their corners.

She jabbed her hand to her hip. "What happens if I don't listen to the colonel's order? They'll throw me in the stockade for a few days. So what?"

"I doubt it'll be as easy as that. Thorson won't tolerate disobedience. Not good for discipline. My guess is, he'd send men to confiscate your belongings by force, then throw you in the stockade. And it might be for more than a few days."

She folded her arms across her chest and lifted her gaze to the sky. A hawk circled above the mesa wall in the distance. Free. Unlike her. Would she ever be free to return to Comancheria?

Garret stepped beside her. "Do as they ask. I'll get you more hides. You can make new moccasins or leggings and wear them around our quarters. Make a whole outfit if you like. My wife may do as she pleases in our home."

Our quarters. Our home. Our. The word shut her mouth. She would be sharing a household with this man. And a bed? Absolutely not. But their lives would intertwine even if their bodies did not. He would take care of her and Little Star. She'd cook his meals and wash his clothes, they'd sit by the fire together in the evenings, and she'd worry about him when he was away on a mission. Just as she had for Dancing Eagle.

Her throat tightened. No. This would not be the same. She would not let it be.

The ribbon-like river gurgled at their feet. Her toes squished in cold sand. She shivered. "Thank you. I know you're trying to help." She rubbed her hands over her sleeves.

"You're cold?"

"I'm fine."

"I don't think so." He untied his neckerchief and spread it on a smooth patch of sand beneath the filtered light of bare branches, then held out his hand to her. "Have a seat."

"Sitting won't make me warmer." She didn't need some cloth to sit on. The dirt was good enough for her and this useless dress, but she swept the skirt folds beneath her and sat on the red checkered cloth because he'd offered it. "We could head back."

He perched on a root across from her. The muddy water lapped to within inches of his almost-shiny boots. "Do you really want to hurry back there?"

"No. But I don't want Angelina to forget whose baby she has."

A strong breeze whipped her hair in her face and almost toppled his hat. He slipped it off his head and set it on the root.

"Looks crumpled." She ran her fingers through her hair.

He glanced at the indented blue wool. "Rough meetings today with Thorson and LeBeau."

"You'll find me more hides?" She smoothed her hand over her skirt. The cut on her thigh burned beneath its bandage. Seven days ago, she'd been on the run with no horse and little food. This man had rescued her.

"Yes, but for now, I want to see your feet."

"My feet?"

"Yep. Scoot them out here." He shifted his leg over and tugged on his knee-high cavalry boot. "I'm not going to have you walking barefoot back to camp in winter."

"I'm not wearing your boots." She stretched her legs from beneath the folds. "My feet are fine." The wrapping around her ankle wobbled loose in defiance of her words.

"Not my boots. My socks." He yanked the first boot off, tossing it in the withered grass, and started on the other.

"Perfect way to wear holes in your socks."

"Perfect way to keep my betrothed's feet warm." Sure, steady eyes drank her in.

Betrothed. Her throat tightened.

"Here." He dropped the first sock on her lap. "Let me know if you need help putting it on."

"I can do it." She curled her lower leg closer to the covering of her skirt and wiggled the sock over her toes. Her armbands pinched her muscles. "I have a favor to ask."

"Only one?" His eyes twinkled as he laid the second sock on her skirt.

A twinge of nerves cramped her stomach. "Only one very important one for now." She pushed up her cumbersome bell sleeves and retrieved the armbands. "Please, hold these for me until after the wedding. I'm afraid they might search me and find them." She rose to her knees, despite the pain that shot up from her thigh and ankle. He needed to see how important this was. "Please, these mean more to me than anything else except for Little Star. They're the only possession I have left from Dancing Eagle."

A shadow passed over his face, sapping the brightness from his eyes as he stared at the gold in her hands. Resentment? Jealousy? Questions too deep for her frayed heart to tackle.

"I'll hide them for you." He reached out his hand.

CHAPTER 25

Garret had lain in bed long after he woke up. Now he stood by the small square of a travel mirror, taking his time drawing the straight blade over his taut cheek. Today was the day. He could feel it in his stomach and in every muscle. By suppertime, he'd be a married man, and tonight, he'd share his quarters with Eyes-Like-Sky and Little Star. And every night after that.

Ouch. Blood dribbled from the fresh cut on his chin. Taking this woman and forsaking all others. His hand shook as he pressed a towel against the wound. Till death do them part.

Did he love her? If he'd had nothing to do with killing her husband and if he'd never given his word, if this wasn't the only way to keep mother and baby together, would he still want to marry her? Was this the woman he wanted to have and hold and love for the rest of his life?

She didn't love him. Would she, could she grow to love him? Would she ever willingly share his bed in the way a man needed? He must have been in some dreamland Tuesday when he'd woken up thinking it possible. How could he ever live up to her image of the man who'd worn the armbands?

He lowered the blade and gripped the sudsy washbasin with both hands, bending his head. Wedding jitters. That's all it was. Or maybe it was God trying to tell him he was making the biggest mistake of his life?

His throat tightened. He needed air, fresh air. A ride, along the river, far out of sight of this camp and everything in it. To give himself a chance to clear his head.

Voices carried from outside, followed by a crunch and a pop of wood—boards being torn one from another. Charlie had ordered a detail of men to rip their porch apart. The wood was destined to become pickets around the bottom half of Charlie's new wall tent. Later today, he'd help Charlie move his bed out, leaving only the single bed in a half-empty room, and Garret knew exactly where he'd be sleeping tonight—the floor.

Should he build a second bed, or would that enshrine the separation between him and his wife? Wife. He'd be a husband and a father.

He'd stood beside her at the fire Tuesday when the whole regiment had watched the burning of her belongings. Silent and tense as a pulley rope about to break, she had endured it, squirming beneath his touch when he'd attempted to take her hand. And she'd shrugged off every mention of it since. Shutting him out of her hurt and grief.

"The men needed to see she's been duly punished." That's what the colonel had said to him in private later. "I did it to benefit her, as well. Help civilize her. But don't worry. Jenkins has his own consequences. I demoted him to private."

Garret ground his shaving brush against the bottom of the soap-filled cup. Jenkins had better pray the colonel never put him under Garret's command.

Boots clomped in the front room. Charlie pushed through the beaded curtain. "Hey, lazy bones, you plan on making it outside the door today? Or are you going to have your wedding in here?"

"I wanted to take my time this morning. I've hardly had a chance to breathe the last three days."

"The colonel wanted to make sure your men could still ride and hold a carbine after your extended leave and gallivanting around the prairie." Charlie hung his hat on a hook and grinned.

Garret rolled his eyes and lathered his cheek. "I reckon three days of drilling set them straight." And kept him from having a spare moment to visit with his fiancée.

Charlie flipped open his trunk lid and began packing the clothes from his shelf. "Did you write your father?"

"No. Haven't had time." Garret drew his razor down across his lower cheek.

"Likely story." Charlie smirked. He yanked his blanket off his bed. His pillow tumbled to the floor. "Maybe if you work it right, you can avoid telling him for a few months. By the time he hears about it, you could be in the middle of the annulment proceedings. He might be so eager to help you extricate yourself, he'll assist with the financial settlement for her."

Annulment. Garret bent over and splashed water on his face, washing away the stray smudges of shaving soap. What kind of marriage would it be if he entered it with one foot out the door? He wouldn't do that to her. Or maybe that's exactly what she wanted.

Charlie ambled over. "How about I spike Miss Logan's drink tonight? Help you along a little with the Indian princess. It wouldn't help the annulment, but—"

"Absolutely not." Garret tossed his wet towel at Charlie's face.

Charlie dodged, grabbed it, and tossed it back. "If I were you, I'd enjoy husbandly *privileges*. When it comes to the annulment, you could try the insanity clause. At the time of the marriage, she was out of her mind from the atrocities she suffered at the hands of the Comanche. Didn't know what she was agreeing to, and of course, you were too blinded by love to know she was insane. Might work, with the right judge, and a few dollars."

Garret glared at him. "Don't you have a party to work on, and your new quarters to fix up? It's your job to make sure the men don't get too drunk tonight. Let me worry about my bride."

"Just trying to help." Charlie shrugged and returned to his trunk.

Enough of this. Garret grabbed his shell jacket and headed for the corral. "I'll be back," he called over his shoulder.

After saddling Ginger, he rode out of the gate, toward the river, and beyond, to the cover of the mesa. He continued for half an hour before he picked a grassy spot along the Brazos, hidden away behind some scrub cedar and bushes. A blue jay called from a nearby branch as he dismounted. He stretched out by the water, hands behind his head, and hat angled to keep the sun out of his eyes.

Hawks sailed overhead against the backdrop of floating clouds. A mild day for the fifth of January. Whether still in St. Louis or back in Pittsburgh by now, his parents had probably enjoyed a regal gala for New Year's with no clue his wedding would be this week. He could only pray that at least his mother would understand when she heard.

He closed his eyes and let his thoughts swirl. Blue eyes, dark, wavy hair, and strength and courage deeper than the roots of an oak. Nothing in his entire life had felt as wonderful as when Eyes-Like-Sky had dropped that knife and decided to trust him. Finding her there in the patchwork of prairies and canyons spanning millions of square miles had been utterly amazing. A miracle. What in the world made him think that anything in his life could possibly ever be right again without her at his side?

Lord, I give you my worry. Please take it from me. Help me to trust You. If I'm making a mistake, please stop me. Otherwise, please work in her heart, to be open to me. And help me be patient and be the husband she needs me to be.

Three hours later, he rode back into camp sweaty and thirsty but settled down. With only an hour to spare, he yanked off his jacket and shirt the moment he cleared the door to his quarters. A tub of water awaited in the middle of the front office room. Thank goodness. He poked his finger into the water. Lukewarm. That would do. And no Charlie anywhere about. Another blessing. He stripped and stepped into the tub, grabbing the scrub brush and soap as he did.

Suds splashed onto the floor as he hurried. Finished, he found a towel and roughed it over his hair before drying the rest of him. In the back room, he found clean drawers, then snatched his best uniform from the hanger and started with the trousers.

Footsteps. Charlie.

Garret tugged his undershirt from his trunk. "Told you I'd be back."

"I was worried." Not Charlie's voice.

Goosebumps prickled his skin.

The beads swayed.

Garret spun on his heel.

Eyes-Like-Sky stood in his bedchamber.

The undershirt fell from his hands.

Beautiful. Light-blue dress. Silk, trimmed in lace, as delicate as butterfly wings. The fabric shimmered just like her eyes.

"What's wrong?" His heart pounded as he snatched his shirt to the patch of hair and muscles in the center of his chest, right where her gaze had landed.

"They said you'd gone for a ride." The rice-bag carpet crinkled as she stepped closer. A grapevine-like wreath of dried flowers encircled her thick, dark waves. "I... I was afraid." Red rims underscored her puffy eyes.

His Adam's apple bobbed, along with his stomach. "I wouldn't run away on you."

"I wouldn't blame you." Her voice wavered. She was within a couple steps of him now, the flounce of her skirt inches from his bare feet. "If you've decided escape is the better option—"

"No." He could hardly think above the thumping of his heart. "I want to marry you. Want to, not obligated."

"You do?" Her brow furrowed even as her eyes brightened. "I promise I'll wash and cook for you. Do your sewing. And whatever you say about the annulment."

"It'd suit me just fine if I don't hear the word *annulment* again." Ever.

Her eyebrows shot upward. "Really?"

He glanced at the neckerchief which encircled her right wrist. Twisted and braided. His? To please him? Because she'd feared losing him? She didn't need to entice him. He was already under her spell.

"I want you to be yourself," he said. "Any show we put on is for the eyes outside our door. I don't want you to think you have to please me from sunup to sundown to make sure I don't walk out on you and Little Star. I'm committed to providing for you from here on out."

She blinked at him, lips parted.

He should shut his mouth, but words continued to flow. "My hope is...you'll give me a chance to court you someday."

Her complexion paled as she hugged her arms around herself. Like a doe about to spook.

His watch chimed. Half past the hour. Thirty more minutes before they pledged themselves before God and man.

"Just a wish. Not an obligation," he whispered.

Her gaze fell to the red raw scar that marred his upper left arm. "That's from the arrow?" She reached out her fingertip.

Warmth shot through him at her touch. "Don't." He grabbed her hand.

"I'm sorry. I didn't mean to hurt you."

Hurt wasn't the word for it. More like desert soil drinking in its first taste of water. It was all he could do to keep from taking her in his arms. He inhaled rosewater and citrus. Her hair or her skin?

She looked away. "I can't promise—"

His fingertip to her lips shushed her. "You go finish getting ready for the wedding." His voice dipped. "We'll work on the rest later."

She gave a brief nod.

As she crossed the threshold into the front room, he called after her. "You know I'll have to kiss you at the end of the ceremony." He rubbed the back of his neck. "For the benefit of the audience." The mere thought of it warmed him all over.

In the front room, her footsteps faltered.

He held his breath, half expecting a retort. But the door swished as she left.

CHAPTER 26

Kiss her?

That thought quivered Eyes-Like-Sky's stomach more than the two hundred men, dozen ladies, and her uncle standing in the parade ground. Probably the largest wedding this side of East Texas. No quiet words uttered in front of a preacher in some private room. What if news of this reached her tribe? They'd assume she'd been quick to shed Dancing Eagle's memory.

She'd probably never have a chance to set them straight. Garret had come back from his ride to marry her. Little Star would be safe. That's what mattered today. Then why did guilt press on her chest like a stone?

Towering clouds billowed overhead against an immense blue sky. The light wind threatened to turn into a sand-raising bluster, but for now, it barely scraped across her skin and rustled her dress.

Dressed in a crumpled suit, the circuit rider stood before them on the colonel's porch, his long, wiry hair pulled back with a tie. His voice boomed as he read from the Bible. Ephesians. Her mind tripped on the once-familiar word.

The man closed the aged book with its cracked leather cover.

Her breath caught as Garret took her hands in his, strong and firm, roughened from soldiering. His spotless shell jacket with its polished brass buttons looked as if it'd arrived on the supply wagon from San Antonio only yesterday. A crimson sash around his waist secured his scabbard with its silver-handled saber. A warrior in his own right. He'd dressed his finest for today, even smoothing back his thick brown hair.

But his world was not hers. According to Mrs. Thorson, this man came from a big city in Pennsylvania with tens of thousands of people. His family lived in a fancy mansion. Prim and proper. Nothing like the Texas frontier. Sweat broke out on the back of her neck. She looked away from his warm eyes. Surely, he must understand she couldn't survive in a place like that.

The preacher paused. His words had flittered over her head.

Garret cleared his throat. His sweat mixed with hers against her palm. "I, Garret Benjamin Ramsey, take this woman, Marguerite Laura Logan—"

Not her.

Garret's fingers squeezed her own. "Eyes-Like-Sky, to be my wife to have and to hold from this day forward, for better or for worse, for richer or poorer, in sickness and in health, to love and to cherish—"

To love and cherish. Would he? Did he?

"To be faithful to you until death do us part." A brief cloud flickered over his eyes.

Faithful. Until death. The rest of their lives. But did he really mean that? What would he do with her on his arm when he returned to the fancy parlors back East? Could she live with his regret?

"Miss Logan." The preacher repeated her name.

She glanced up.

The man's bushy eyebrows arched above his spectacles, his weathered face tense. "I, Miss Marguerite..."

"I, Eyes-Like-Sky..." She fumbled through her vows one phrase at a time, her tongue sluggish as if it were weighted with sand. "... to love and to cherish..." How would she ever do that? With a heart that was entombed?

"And to obey." She'd have to work on that.

"To be faithful." That she could do. In body. But what else did this promise mean?

"Till death do us part." Her chest tightened.

The preacher closed his Bible. "Do you have a ring?"

"Yes." Garret tugged a large jade ring from his little finger.

How had she not noticed it before? Did he really mean for her to wear it, or was this just for show?

He rubbed his thumb over a strip of linen on the back of the band and frowned, then glanced at her and slipped the heavy gold past her knuckle. "With this ring, I thee wed."

Sighs and murmurs spread through the crowd.

The porch creaked beneath the preacher's weight. "I now pronounce you man and wife. You may kiss the bride."

Garret sucked in a breath.

Her heart thudded. She would do this for his sake.

Cheers and hoots rang out from the audience.

He smoothed his fingertips across her cheek and touched her hair. His wide palm encompassed her jaw.

Too close. Her body tensed.

His breath smelled of mint. Deep-brown eyes gazed into hers before he dipped his head and brushed his lips to hers. A light, feather-like touch that lingered.

The crowd faded. Her cheeks warmed.

One breath, two breaths, three. And still his lips lingered against hers.

His hand slid to her side. He pulled her close—

She stiffened as if someone had dumped a bucket of water on her.

An almost imperceptible groan came from his throat. Kiss broken, his hand dropped. The crowd cheered, unaware a boundary had been erected.

"Stick by my side for the evening, and I'll get you through the socializing." Garret held out his elbow.

"I could go look after Little—" But the people were upon them before she could finish the sentence. She latched her hand around the crook of his arm.

Lieutenant Fuller slapped Garret on the back, whispered something in his ear, then kissed her hand as though she was royalty. The colonel followed, good-humored, wishing them the best, expecting her hand as if four days ago he hadn't burned almost everything of value to her in front of the entire regiment. She gritted her teeth as his lips touched her knuckles. Orders could be amended and rescinded. That's what Garret had said. Well, she would see.

As soon as the man turned his back, she rubbed her hand against her skirt. If there hadn't been a throng waiting to congratulate them, she would have scrubbed it in the sand on the ground. She tightened her hold on Garret's arm, nodding and smiling at the well-wishers and gawkers, keeping her free hand to herself when she could.

Last in line, her uncle strutted up, no smile in sight, no hand offered. "I expect you to write me, Captain. Keep me apprised of my niece's health and situation. I also expect you to take her with you when you leave the frontier and head home." His eyes almost gleamed.

"I don't anticipate that for several years, sir." Garret threw back his shoulders and clamped his hand over his saber hilt. "I've linked my future to the army."

LeBeau's lips slipped upward into a foxlike grin. "I reckon you've been too busy to keep abreast of the news. Three days from now, Texas is holding a vote for convention delegates. A convention that will order the likes of you and every other Northern troop off Texas soil."

Garret glared at the man half a minute before replying. "It'll never happen as long as Sam Houston is governor."

"Sam Houston's an old man." LeBeau tipped his hat and turned to her. "Marguerite, I hope you enjoy Pittsburgh society." His voice dripped with disdain.

She exhaled as he strode away. Pittsburgh. Troops being ordered out of Texas. "What's he talking about?"

Garret's smile dimmed. "He's trying to spoil our day. Don't let him get to you." He squeezed her hand on his arm. "A group of plantation owners over in East Texas are stirring up trouble. A bunch of politics. A subject for another day."

Half a dozen questions came to her mind, but his gaze drifted to the horizon beyond the fort. Lips pressed tight, he led her to the food table. If the rigid rise in Garret's shoulders was any indication, LeBeau's threat was far from idle.

~

Lanterns lit the parade grounds as the last glimmer of sunlight disappeared over the horizon. Moths and gnats hummed around the flickering orbs. Long tables of food with their checkered tablecloths had been picked over, but stragglers still hovered in hope of an end slice of ham or a piece of neck meat from the cow. Eyes-Like-Sky had never seen such a feast. Or had she? A memory clung to the shadows just out of reach.

When she had asked for some punch, Garret had said no. Someone had spiked it, he said. And she could believe it. The men laughed more, talked louder, and some even swayed. If the Comanche had a spy amongst the scouts and were nearby, now would be the perfect time for an attack.

Even Garret was smiling easier and had loosened the top two buttons of his uniform jacket. He'd insisted on tasting every drink she was offered. No longer satisfied with having her cling to his elbow, he'd encircled her shoulders with his arm, and he held her snug to his side, making her feel warm and safe. Just as long as he kept his hand where it was.

Music of fiddles, banjos, and harmonicas filled the air, the tunes vaguely familiar. Every woman danced except for her—jigs, squares, and circles, occasional couples' dances, and now and then, they'd form two rows, and a couple would twirl their way down the line and then latch onto each other and sashay through the clapping wall of dancers. They allowed some Apache from the scout camp to round out the number of females to sixteen. Some men resorted to dancing with each other, while others awaited their turn with a lady.

Garret squeezed her shoulder. "You all right? Would you like a piece of pie or a sip of my wine?"

"No, thank you." She shifted her empty plate from her lap to the ground. "I was thinking about Little Star."

"I'm sure Angelina has her tucked in tight in our quarters. She'll come get us if there's any problems."

Her glance flittered to officers' row. This would be so much more complicated than sharing a roof, walls, and a floor. She rubbed her hands over her arms. He would return the gold bands tomorrow. She didn't have to worry.

A shadow passed between them and the lantern light.

"Garret, my man." Lieutenant Fuller strode up, glass in hand. "Surely, you don't plan to keep the lady to yourself all evening and not set a foot on the dance floor? I'm your best man, after all. The least you can do is let me have a dance with the bride."

Garret dipped his mouth close to her ear. His cologne filled her nostrils. "What do you think, my lady?"

"I don't think so." She firmed her lip. "I don't know these dances."

"I could teach you." Garret folded his hand over hers. "All you'd have to do is follow my lead. We could try a slow one."

Charlie leaned in, liquor tainting his breath. "Not for you, Ramsey. Me. I could teach her."

"Dance. Dance. Let's see the bride dance." A handful of men standing by the hitching post started the chant.

Garret exhaled. "Now that they've picked this up, I doubt they'll leave us alone."

"Definitely not." Charlie grinned.

Not her music. No drums. No flutes. She hadn't danced since last fall. Beneath a red moon, she and Dancing Eagle had celebrated with the rest of the village around a huge bonfire that had lit the night sky. Buckskin, fringe, and beads, damp with sweat and faces painted, they had stomped and slid and twirled until early morning.

The little that she'd eaten churned in her stomach. She released her hold on Garret's jacket.

"Would you consider just one dance?" The word *please* didn't pass Garret's lips, but it was there.

She never wanted to dance again, yet she did. She wanted to dance and dance until every memory evaporated. "You said I could have a sip of your wine?" She nodded toward his half-empty glass.

"If you'd like. Thankfully, it's just wine, nothing extra."

"Bride dance. Bride dance." Three fellows, with arms linked, swayed by the food table. More eyes turned, the same eyes which had watched her belongings be thrown into the fire four days ago. Across the way, LeBeau sat with Mr. and Mrs. Thorson on the porch. They thought they'd civilized her, made her one of them. Well, they were mistaken.

She sipped long and slow, tempted to up-end the glass and

swallow it all. Her hands shook. "I'll show them who I am. That they have not won." She stood.

Garret rose to his feet. "What do you mean?"

"I'll show them how my people dance." She pushed the glass against his chest until his hand closed around it. "And then I will dance with you. And only you."

Chin jutted, she strode to the middle of the parade ground before Garret could object and her courage quelled. The clusters of people parted and made way, looking back to see if the groom would follow. The fiddles and other musical instruments fell silent.

As she reached the center, she closed her eyes and concentrated on the whispers of the past. The blood-red moon, the thundering drums, and the mournful melodies. She could keep the beat if she hummed it. Her feet picked up the rhythm. Tapping, stepping. She drew her skirts up a few inches off the ground and twirled, relishing the freedom. She would do this to honor Dancing Eagle, show the beauty that had been lost.

Someone plucked on a fiddle, a thump, thump, thump, like a drum. Another fiddler struck a melody that fit the motion, and a lone harmonica joined in.

Her feet moved faster. She kicked off the troublesome slippers that didn't quite fit. Stomp, stomp, stomp, slide. Tapping and stepping. Lifting and lowering. Pivoting and twirling. Her skirts caught on the breeze of her motion and billowed free.

This dance was not what she had done at the bonfire in the early fall but how she had danced with Dancing Eagle on the dew-damp grass beneath the stars with no eyes but theirs.

Pain cut through her thigh. She spun faster, faster. Blue uniforms and lanterns blended into a blurred menagerie. Her injured ankle wobbled. Down she went on her knees, hard, spreading her arms wide as if taking a bow. She lowered her head. Tears streamed down her cheeks. The nights of the blood-red moon and dew-damp grass were gone.

Silence. A murmur, then a clap, followed by others. Whistles.

She rose to her feet, biting her lip against the pain of her injuries, only a trickle compared to the searing ache in her heart. Smoothing her skirts, she lifted her chin and crossed the grounds to her only friend.

CHAPTER 27

Eyebrows arched, Garret scrubbed a hand over his face. He didn't know what to say. Beautiful. Breathtaking. Defiant. Definitely not cowering in the Sibley. And not really his, despite what the preacher had pronounced over them a couple hours ago. He inhaled into his hollow chest as she strode toward him.

Her perfect posture sagged. As she reached him, she wobbled. He grabbed her shoulder to steady her, angling himself to shield her from prying eyes.

Her eyes blazed, despite the tears dropping from her chin. She stretched up on tiptoe. Blue folds lapped against his legs as she lifted her mouth to his ear. "I wanted them to know they haven't civilized me, that I'm still Comanche."

"I think you made that very clear." He blew out a breath. His head swam with her aroma of soap, rosewater, and citrus.

"Encore. Encore." Voices from the crowd picked up the chant. Men waved hats in her direction.

"What does that mean?" She blinked up at him.

"Never mind." He steered her from the circle.

Moisture dripped from her nose. He pulled a handkerchief from his pocket and pressed it into her hand. "Here you go."

The touch of his hand to hers sparked a tingle down his arm. The driving need to touch her, to be close to her, surged through him, way beyond the influence of the bit of brandy he'd consumed in tasting her drinks.

Slowly, the music started again. The crowd shifted, closing into a circle. Once more, she and Garret stood outside the edge. But the murmurs and muffled hoots still drifted their way.

"That's what I call dancing." Charlie walked up and slapped him on the back. Brandy hung heavy on his breath. "The little lady should be on a stage."

Eyes-Like-Sky stiffened and scooted closer to Garret's side.

Garret sliced him with a glare. "The little lady is my wife. And my wife doesn't need to be on any stage."

"How about a quick dance with an admirer—"

"No, Lieutenant." Garret stepped toe to toe with the man. "She's not dancing with anyone but me."

"Excuse me." Charlie held up his palms and backed off. "Reckon I should keep my thoughts to myself."

"You've got that right."

"Sure never spoke up for Lily like that," Charlie muttered as he ambled off toward the food, his old limp evident after a few drinks.

Couldn't the man just keep his mouth shut?

"Who's Lily?" Wide blue eyes blinked up at him.

Garret winced. Not a conversation he wanted to have tonight. "A girl I courted for a while."

"What happened?" Eyes-Like-Sky wiped her nose. The tears had stopped.

He ran a hand over his hair. The fiddles had taken up "Aura Lee." He and Lily had danced to this song. Nothing he wanted to repeat. "She wasn't the girl I wanted to spend the rest of my life with. That's what happened."

Laughter rang out from an Apache girl being twirled around and around by a soldier, out of step with the music.

A young, hatless soldier ran up and handed him Eyes-Like-Sky's wreath. "Mrs. Ramsey lost this."

Garret took it and turned it over in his hand as the private marched off. A dried rose drooped from the hardened grape vine.

Eyes-Like-Sky fumbled with the handkerchief. "Are you upset with me?"

No. Yes. Never. A shaky breath rattled through him. He could drown in those eyes of hers. "You captivated everyone. Including me." His voice thickened. "I'll see you dancing in my dreams tonight. It's not an image I'll forget."

He settled the wreath on her brow and brushed a lock of hair from her eyes. "Only next time...I'd rather you saved the dancing for my eyes only."

She lowered her gaze and swiped her cheeks. "I promised I'd dance with you."

"Are you up for it?" He shouldn't hold her to it. Her limbs looked as steady as reeds. But he couldn't let go of the chance to have her in his arms.

"Yes." She lifted her chin. "I'm not going to let anyone here tonight think I don't appreciate you and all you've done for me."

Dance with him out of appreciation? Garret's face tightened all the way down to his jaw. Had he expected to earn her heart in one night or even by giving her his name? He took her hand.

"I don't know how—"

"Follow my lead. Relax. It's all right if you step on my feet. I've got boots." He led her into the circle of dancers, past Sargent Clark's stare and Mrs. Clark, whose smirk outshone the peacock feather drooping from her snood. "Don't worry about what everyone is thinking. You've already blinded them with your performance tonight. They won't see anything else."

Eyes-Like-Sky sucked a breath as Garret lifted her right hand in his left and placed his right hand on her shoulder blade. His ring hung heavy on her finger. She blushed beneath the open stares of the nearby soldiers. Had she failed in her act of defiance? Did they understand?

In the shadows of the swinging lanterns, her uncle's face had hardened like a gnarled knob on a tree. He stood and walked into the colonel's quarters, letting the door bang behind him. At least someone got the message. Thorson's heavy glare was visible from the parade ground despite the meager lighting. His wife hung on his arm whispering in his ear and looking her direction.

All of a sudden, Garret drew her hand to his lips and kissed her fingers.

She jumped. "What was that for?"

"To get your attention." He smiled down at her. "I need your focus right here if I'm going to save my toes.

"'Oh, Shenandoah,'" he called to the musicians.

The potbelly fiddler struck a note, followed by a gangly man on a harmonica. The banjo players rested.

"Slide your right foot between mine." Garret stepped out on his left foot as the mournful tune started. "Then left and right to the side. Now I step between your feet while you step out, two-three. Relax and follow me."

As if following were easy. He turned her in a circle as a tenor added his voice to the plucked notes. "'Oh, Shenandoah, I love your daughter. Away you rolling river...'"

Garret leaned in and whispered close to her ear. "I couldn't miss the chance to dance with the most captivating girl in Texas."

She bit her lip. "I'm guessing you've seen very little of Texas."

He winked. “I’m confident you outshine every maiden of the prairie.”

Warmth spread to her cheeks and down through her middle. Surely, the result of the wine or the exhilaration of her Comanche dance. Not his flirting. “Don’t do that.” She misstepped. Her slipper mashed the side of his foot.

He winced. From the injury or her retort? But he regained the rhythm and glided them across the hard-pebbled ground as if they were skimming the surface of a lake.

The song...a fur trader had fallen in love with the Indian chief’s daughter, got him drunk, and stole his daughter away. Had she wanted to go? Right, left, right. Left, right, left. The lantern lights swayed in the Texas breeze.

The memory of another night, long ago on the open prairie beneath a harvest moon, exploded open, cutting through the years. A half circle of three wagons. A fire blazing. Papa with his dusty frock coat and neatly trimmed beard dancing with Mama, ringlets of her dark hair slipping from her snood. They’d found a water hole that day and had stopped early. Water and a half day of rest, a reason to celebrate. Her brother, Jim, and his blond-haired girl, smiling and dancing. Momma was sure there’d be a wedding at the end of the trail. And the boy who held her hand and swung her to the music? David had been his name. A pang clutched her heart.

The Comanche aren’t within a hundred miles of here. Her father hadn’t known what rumor to believe, but he’d wanted to get the family settled into a homestead before winter. Along with two other wagons, he’d broken off from the main train and pushed ahead.

The day had been hot and the night cool, sweet smelling. Fireflies had dazzled beyond the circle of activity.

A war cry rent the air like a shattering of glass. The first arrow—

Eyes-Like-Sky screeched and pulled free of Garret’s hold.

She doubled over. Arrows, blood-curdling cries, tomahawks, flames filled her head. Her father, Jim, and David...dead. Chaos. If only her mother could have died right away. The blond girl ran but not fast enough. Maggie, herself, running, tripping on her dress hem, falling forward. A hand grabbed her by the hair, dragged her across the gravel, her knees scrapping. Threw her onto a horse. Across a man's knees. The stink of him! She couldn't breathe.

Later...pain, soul-shattering shame, and humiliation.

Garret's saber dragged the ground as he knelt beside her. Too many people. Too many. She was going to suffocate.

She shoved his hands away and pushed through the crowd. Once she gained space, she ran past the barracks, the corral, and out the gate. The rocks cut into her bare feet. She plunged onward, through the prickly grass and down the bank to the river.

CHAPTER 28

She had to make the memory stop. Wash it away with fear or pain. Anything to escape the nightmare. She plunged into the river, her fancy skirt and petticoats acting like a sponge. The snow melt and rain from the week before had swollen the flow. She'd go deep enough to immerse herself. The dark current surged around her. Goosebumps swept over her limbs.

Her father grabbed his rifle, but a yellow-and-red-painted warrior drove a spear into his chest before he even got a shot off. He stumbled backward and collapsed. Blood—

Eyes-Like-Sky inhaled and bobbed under the water, swimming toward the middle, driving away the image. The skirts clung to her legs and impeded her kicking, dragging her down. Her feet skidded against the bottom but wouldn't stick. Cold lacerated her energy. Her lungs burned. She clawed for the surface, fighting the liquid wall.

Her head broke free of the water. She gulped air, heart pounding.

Tentacles of cloth pulled her below again. The current drove her forward. No need to panic. Yet. She could make the surface. The shore was a different issue. She lunged for it, stretching out with all of her might.

A hand clamped onto her shoulder. She gasped. Water streamed past her lips before she snapped them shut. She couldn't get her breath. Air. She needed air. A strong arm locked around her and drew her hard against a man's chest. Garret? He jerked her to the surface and toward shore.

She sputtered. Hacking racked her body as his legs kicked beneath hers, propelling her to the shallow edge through a weed bed.

As her knees scraped the silt, Garret turned her toward him, his breathing haggard. "What the devil are you doing, Sky? Are you out of your mind?"

Dropping to her hands and knees, she coughed until her throat burned. "Trying to make the memory stop." She swiped a hand over her mouth and eyes.

"What are you talking about?" He dragged her onto the bank. Wet hair clung to his forehead.

Body shivering, teeth chattering, she struggled to her feet. How could she expect him to understand? He probably thought she was insane.

His strong hands gripped hers and pulled her to a full stand. "Don't you ever do that again. You hear me?" His voice rumbled like thunder. Emotion contorted his face. Anger? Worry?

"I...I wasn't trying to...to not live." She trembled. "Pain and danger block the memories."

He scowled, but his arms closed around her, holding her tight against his chest as if binding her to him forever.

A voice from the bank. Lieutenant Fuller's. "What happened? Are you both all right?"

Garret jabbed a finger at him. "Get some blankets and don't say a word to anyone."

Her arms hung at her sides. But her head sank against his solid, safe shoulder.

He groaned. "Did you do this because of the wedding?"

"No. No. The dance. I'd forgotten." She'd shoved the memory so deep she'd believed it lost. "My family and the rest. We were dancing...the night...of the attack."

They dragged her mother—

Eyes-Like-Sky latched onto the back of Garret's shirt and dug her fingers in until she felt the firmness of flesh beneath wet linen. Sobs rocked through her. They were all gone. Her mother. Her father. Her brothers. No one left but her sister. And no one here to hold her but this man. An anchor.

Garret squeezed his eyes shut and pressed his cheek to her hair. Dear God, what if he'd lost her? His hands trembled. How could he have not known how much he loved her? Soul deep.

If only there was something he could do for her, take away her hurt.

Footsteps crunched in the grass.

He raised his head. Charlie, with a heavy frown, dropped a blanket around him and held out another.

"Do you need help—"

Eyes-Like-Sky jerked at the sound.

"No." Garret grabbed the extra blanket. "Thank you. Keep everyone away from here."

Charlie nodded and limped back up the slope toward camp. A faint tune carried on the breeze.

Garret edged Eyes-Like-Sky to a seat on the grass and draped the heavy wool around her.

She sniffled and swiped her face with her soaked sleeve, smearing the wet.

"Allow me." He kicked his scabbard and belt away from the spot where he'd discarded them before he dove in to rescue her. Settling down beside her, he gently wiped her cheeks and nose with a blanket corner.

"It'll get dirty." Her teeth chattered.

"Doesn't matter." He finished and tucked the wool beneath her chin before securing her deep in his hold once more.

A new sob broke from her throat, and she burrowed against him. "My papa wanted to make a good home for us. Momma loved him so much. She'd have gone to the ends of the earth for him. Everyone said the Comanches weren't close. It was so sudden, the war cry, the attack. Then the arrows, tomahawks, spears. Those who came at us were more like demons than men. For a long time, I wished I had died with my family. Better to have been killed quickly than to be...used, discarded like a beaten rag."

Her words shook through him. He'd like nothing better than to take a knife to every one of those devils.

She jerked away from his hold, bent to the ground, and puked.

The smell stung his nostrils. He dug his wet handkerchief out of his pocket and handed it to her.

Her chest rose and fell as if she'd been running.

Dear Lord, what can I say to her? He should take her back to camp, carry her back if needed. Get her in some dry clothes, give her a cup of brandy, and tuck her in. Settle her down.

Instead, he rubbed his hand up and down her back as she wiped her mouth. "I'm sorry. So very sorry." Puny words, not enough to even bandage the hurt. "Precious girl. Beautiful girl."

"I'm not any of those things." She sank against his side, her voice as frail as a dandelion puff.

He tightened his arms around her. "That's where you're mistaken." He nuzzled his chin against the top of her head. "You're beautiful and strong. Captivating. Spunky. Stubborn.

Precious. And a hundred other things my brain is too befuddled to name at the moment. The horrible things that happened didn't take any of that away from you. My guess is that they made you more so."

Her only response was to settle deeper in his embrace. Like a part of his soul coming home.

An owl hooted. The river purred beside them, as if it were tame and not a life-threatening beast. A faint glow of light flickered over the hill, the distant parade ground lanterns casting a beacon onto the dark prairie.

"Little Star needs you, Sky. And so do I," he whispered. "I want you to promise me you won't take any more risks like you did tonight."

Her forehead pressed against his collarbone. "Sky?"

"May I call you that?" He held his breath, more than half expecting a no.

Sniffles. "I guess."

He kissed the top of her head, then caught himself. *Stupid. Don't push her.*

"You'll find me more buckskin as you promised?" she asked in a choked voice.

His hand on her back stopped in mid-rub. Buckskin? She still wanted to dress like them? "I don't understand. After everything the Comanches did, why do you want anything to do with them?"

She sat up and pushed halfway out of his arms. "Dancing Eagle had nothing to do with what happened seven years ago. He was from a different village. I didn't meet him until four years after the attack. I was a slave. We fell in love. He convinced Old Wolf to sell me to him for two ponies. Then he brought me to his village and made me his wife. I owe Dancing Eagle my life. He was nothing but good to me." She swiped the back of her hand across her cheeks and scooted from his side.

Dancing Eagle's name dropped like a wall between them.

He kept his hand firm to her elbow, not about to let go of every touch. He cleared his throat. "I can understand wearing deerskin would help you feel connected to Dancing Eagle and remind you of the good parts of your life with the Comanche. But wouldn't it rip open the wounds of the past?"

"Women who wear dresses like this are weak." She closed her fist around a handful of her silk skirt. Venom colored her words. "They can't defend themselves."

"You defended yourself."

"You weren't there."

"You survived."

"I survived because I became Comanche." New fire lit her eyes.

Garret scrubbed a hand over his face. Tonight was no time to argue. Words would not change her.

A coyote howled from across the prairie.

Eyes-Like-Sky swayed.

"I should take you back to camp and get you dry." Garret exhaled.

"You'll get me hides?"

He curled his fingers inward, resisting the urge to nudge her hair from her eyes. "I have a tanned antelope skin waiting for you back in our quarters. A wedding gift. With more to come. I wouldn't take away something that means so much to you, even if I don't fully understand."

"Thank you." Wet eyes gazed at him. Shivering, she tugged her blanket across her chest. "We should go back. Little Star might wake."

"I still need your promise you won't go taking risks like this again. No going in the river. No running off onto the prairie." He massaged her shoulder. "And I still need to keep you warm. Can't have you catching your death of cold." He drew her up to her feet and took her in his arms once more.

"I'm warm enough." Her teeth chattered. But she didn't attempt to move from his hold. "And I didn't try to hurt myself."

"I know you didn't." His voice thickened as his gaze dipped to hers. "But you put yourself in life-threatening danger, all the same. In situations like that, there aren't any guarantees. Little Star and I need you, so I want your word."

She eyed his arms. "You're a stubborn man."

His heart thudded in his chest. A definite mistake to turn her toward him. "When it comes to stubbornness, you've got me beat by a long run."

She heaved a sigh. "I promise."

His gaze dropped to her lips. He couldn't even swallow. So close. Right here in his arms.

She stiffened, as if she could read his thoughts. "And you promised to give me back Dancing Eagle's armbands after the wedding."

The mention chilled him like a splash of cold water. It was all he could do to not jerk his arms away. "Tomorrow." His voice flattened. "But for tonight, I'm going to carry you back to our quarters and get you dry."

"I don't need to be carried." She pushed out of his embrace, wobbling on her injured ankle. "I can walk."

He didn't listen.

CHAPTER 29

Eyes-Like-Sky lay awake among the crumpled covers, listening to the steady rhythm of Garret's breathing. He'd insisted she take the bed even though she told him she wanted nothing to do with the horsehair-stuffed mattress. A buffalo hide or a couple blankets stretched on the floor were fine with her. But Garret refused to sleep in a bed while his wife slept on the floor. No, he was sleeping on the ground, and she could either join him there or accept the bed. She'd chosen the bed.

And then he'd changed his mind about sleeping in the front room where their wet garments hung by the stove. Instead, he'd thrown his blankets on the rice-sack carpet between the bed and the bundle where Little Star snuggled.

Sunlight trickled in through their canvas roof. *Their* roof. Their dwelling was a large wall tent divided into two rooms, with chest-high picket planks around the outside to give the semblance of solid walls. She'd heard talk of his men building a cabin for them, but wood was hard to come by. Fine with her. She preferred solid walls about as much as she looked forward to being thrown into a pit.

So hard to believe that here she was, sharing her life with this man.

He'd been out of breath by the time they reached their quarters last night. But he didn't set her down until they reached the bedroom, and he'd given Angelina orders to help her out of her soaked clothing. As if she needed help. Then he'd ordered her to stay in bed this morning and rest, that an attendant would bring them their meals for the first couple of days. The man was probably afraid she didn't know how to cook settler food. Maybe he was right about that, but she'd learn. At one time, she had known. Her mother had taught her—

No. She dug her nails into her palms. A bead of sweat broke out on her brow.

Enough of the past. She'd concentrate on today. A shiver ran through her. She cringed at the memory of how she'd acted last night, the weakness she'd shown in breaking down like that. She'd humiliated herself. If only she'd ended the evening with the Comanche dance and retreated to her tent.

But the warmth of Garret's arms, the solid steadiness of his chest, as though she was safe there, as though he wouldn't let anything happen to her—the thought of it made her knees wobbly and heated her cheeks. She must have been half out of her head to let him hold her like that and for so long. Comfort and security— that is what he'd offered and what she'd briefly accepted. Like a brother and sister, or two friends. Nothing more.

But the scent of his cologne still filled her nostrils. Perhaps it'd rubbed off on her last night when he'd held her, or maybe it was on his pillow. She poked her nose into the linen cover. Another smell. His hair.

"Mammamma." Cheerful babble erupted from across the room.

Eyes-Like-Sky rolled over and rested her head in the deep

fluff of the feather pillow, too soft for a decent night's sleep. She peeked over her elbow.

Little Star pushed herself up to a sit, fingers jammed in her mouth. Wide-eyed, she surveyed her unfamiliar surroundings. Black ringlets curled over her forehead and ears as she stared at the man on the floor. Dropping her hands, she maneuvered over blanket ridges and crawled across the crinkly rice-bags to Garret's arm.

There, she plopped her bottom down and patted a hand to his long, rough fingers. The man stirred, rolling onto his back and cracking an eye open at the invader. His thick brown hair ruffled against the pillow.

Eyes-Like-Sky sank deeper into her own pillow, allowing her hair to fall over her forehead. Through the strands, she peeked over her elbow, the better to gauge this man's true feelings toward her daughter in his home.

Little Star dropped to her hands again. One palm followed by a knee and then another mashed into Garret's arm as she made her way to his face. A muffled "mmmph" was his only reaction until the drool hit his chin.

His eyes flew open, and he jerked.

Little Star startled. Her face crumpled, and her lips parted as if readying for a cry.

But a wide smile spread across Garret's face just in time.

Little Star blinked at him.

"Hey, little girl," he whispered in a sing-song voice and reached his other hand over to stroke her hair. "How are you today?"

The baby smiled and patted his stubble-covered cheek, rubbing her palm against the grain.

"Yes, I'm hairy. Can't help it."

She pulled at his lip.

"Sharp fingernail." He caught her hand and kissed it. "Little

Star gave me an owie." With a wink, he took her in both hands and lifted her high above his chest, careful to leave the trail of drool hanging over the neck of his undershirt instead of his face. His grin matched the baby's.

Eyes-Like-Sky closed her eyes against the threat of tears. She could have looked through a hundred men and not found one who'd have taken to her child like this. Bittersweet. Dancing Eagle would never see his little girl grow up. The thought sank her heart like a stone.

Garret lowered Little Star to his chest, then he shot her into the air again, gripped in his strong hands, his muscles taut within the sleeves of his undershirt.

The little girl squealed in delight as he did it again and again.

Garret's glance slid toward the bed.

Eyes-Like-Sky dove deep into her pillow.

He'd caught her watching. She had to get up, scurry into some bothersome dress, and get in the other room before he decided to come over and shine that smile on her, as though they really were a family.

"Good morning." He cleared his throat and sat up, setting Little Star down beside him.

"Mamamama," Little Star cried out.

Eyes-Like-Sky rolled out on the far side of the bed so fast her head spun. "Morning. I'll grab her in a minute." She snatched the green dress from the hook, ignoring the stifling corset, crinoline, and petticoats. Her gaze dropped to her left hand and froze.

No ring.

"No hurry." Garret's easy tone came from behind her. "Little Star and I are getting acquainted. One of the men should be by any time now with a big breakfast for us."

His ring. She hadn't taken it off. But it'd been loose. The

river. It must have come off in the river. She sank back down to a sit, dress on her lap. Gold, jade, onyx. Valuable. His. And she'd lost it.

~

Garret splashed water from the basin on his face. Sand and clay caked beneath his fingernails and under his collar. A day of working with the horses had left him dirty. He removed his suspenders, stripped to the waist, and dipped a rag into a pan of sudsy water. Best clean up while he could before Sky came in from the fire. She wasn't used to cooking on a stove yet.

Tomorrow, he'd head out on patrol. Tonight, he had no intention of letting Sky scurry off to do chores, or sequester herself away in the bedroom to sew by meager candlelight after she'd put Little Star to bed.

The trick was getting Sky to cooperate. Five days since the incident by the river, and his wife had avoided every hint of his affection. He managed a touch to her back or arm in passing and an occasional brush of his hand to hers as he shifted Little Star to her care, but more than that prickled her like a porcupine.

And then there was the matter of the ring. She showed no inclination to wear his ring. Yet every waking hour, Dancing Eagle's armbands hugged her forearms beneath her sleeves. He dipped the rag in the clean jug and rinsed off, sloshing water onto the dry sink. He would be patient. Give her time. It could take weeks or even months. What if it took longer?

The tent flap opened. He grabbed a towel.

Sky waltzed in, the baby on her hip and a kettle in her other hand. Beautiful. Despite the smudge on her nose. She'd wound his red neckerchief like a ribbon to hold her hair back. The neck of the green dress was unbuttoned below her collarbone, and she'd shoved the sleeves to her elbows. Her gaze roamed across his chest and arms.

"I'll grab a clean shirt." His cheeks heated. "Take a look at the package I left on the table for you."

"Dinner will be ready in a few minutes." She set the kettle on a trivet.

Behind the beaded curtain, he shoved his arms into a red cotton shirt, not exactly military issue, but fine for an evening at home. He ran a comb through his hair before returning to the front room.

"Babababa." Little Star swung all four limbs in unison while nodding her head toward the floor.

Brown paper lay at Sky's feet, and a rare smile lit her face. "Perfect. Thank you." She clutched a smooth deer hide to her chest. "I'll start on a pair of leggings tonight." She raised her moccasin-clad foot from beneath her skirt. "The beading for these can wait."

"You did a fine job with your moccasins." He stretched his suspenders over his shoulders. An untreated hide would have cost half as much, but he wanted to give her a gift, not saddle her with work

Little Star lifted her arms and arched her back, attempting to squirm her way out of her mother's hold.

Sky set her down amongst the paper. "I could make you a pair if you like. Pay you back for getting me the hides."

Last thing he wanted was for her to feel as though she owed him something. "Someday. As a *gift*." He emphasized the word. "After you've finished making all of your things."

Crinkle. Crack. Grin wide, Little Star slapped at the coarse paper—a rare commodity here on the frontier, but the baby's fun wouldn't spoil it too badly.

Sky half twirled as she laid the skin on a crate. "A letter

came for you today. Lieutenant Fuller said it was from your father." She dug an envelope from her pocket and extended it toward him. Dark locks that made a man want to run his fingers through them brushed her shoulders.

Envelope in hand, he drifted to the desk. With his back to her, he grabbed his knife, slit it open, and scanned the letter. His father expressed his disappointment with him for leaving St. Louis early. A wry smile spread across Garret's mouth. The man had no idea. St. Louis was only a speck compared to what he'd done since. He crumpled the paper, tempted to pitch it in the fire.

"What's wrong?" Sky set a pitcher on the oak table his men had hammered together as a wedding gift.

He pivoted. "Nothing."

"I don't think so." Her brow furrowed. "Is he upset about the wedding?"

"My father doesn't know about it yet." He strode over to the stove and opened the grate. "He's bothered I left our family gathering in St. Louis earlier than planned." The paper settled onto the ash-covered embers as he closed the door.

"You came back from leave early? That's why you were able to find me so quickly."

"Believe me, it didn't feel quick. Days of blistering sun and then a blizzard. Scratching through sand for any trace of a footprint."

Little Star pattered toward him on all fours, fastest crawler west of the Mississippi.

Sky set a bowl and a spoon at his place. "Why *did* you come back early?" Blue eyes ventured to gaze directly into his for the first time in days.

His pulse quickened.

Little Star latched onto his trouser leg and pulled herself up, wobbling against his leg. He bent down and scooped her into his arms before he returned his gaze to the one who turned his insides to liquid warmth. "I had to come rescue a certain girl. Thought she might be getting herself in trouble."

"You mean Little Star?"

"No." He chuckled. "Little Star's not the type to go getting herself in enough trouble that a man's got to travel across a couple of states to rescue her."

"Oh." Another blush. She rubbed her hands over her sleeves as she turned back to the table.

A nervous gesture, or was she thinking of what lay beneath the fabric? His throat tightened. He pressed his lips together to stop the question from spewing out.

"I'll never be able to pay you back for everything you've done for me." Her voice fumbled as she retrieved a ladle for the stew.

He pulled out a chair and sat down at the table with Little Star on his lap. "Knowing I was able to keep you and Little Star safe and together, that's more than enough."

She pointed to the plate as if he hadn't spoken. "This is your place over here. I figured I could eat in the back room and put Little Star to bed."

No surprise there. Same thing she'd done every night this week. But he swallowed back his irritation. "You know what Little Star told me?"

"Little Star?"

"Yep." The corners of his mouth quirked upward. "She said we need two place settings at the table, and she'd like to try a wee bit of your cooking."

As if to confirm, the baby closed her hand around a fold in the tablecloth.

Sky quirked her eyebrows. "And just when did she manage to say all of this?"

"Secret baby code. Only I understand it."

Sky pursed her lips as if unsure what to make of him. But

her mouth twitched. "I reckon we can all eat at the table if you two insist."

"We do." He winked. Maybe he should have Little Star ask about the ring. "After supper, I could read to both of you."

She plopped a bowl, spoon, and cup in front of him. "I'll have to nurse her and put her to bed."

"You could cover with a shawl. As you used to in the Sibley." He reached for the ladle. "I'm heading out in the morning on patrol. I'll be gone a week, maybe long—"

Little Star yanked on the tablecloth. His bowl careened near the edge.

Sky sprung from her chair, then grabbed the bowl and the child. "She's stronger than she looks." She settled the baby on her lap and returned the dish to its place.

"I'll say." He exhaled and served her a portion of stew. "Good thing you came to the rescue."

"You're still learning." She stuck a cracker in the baby's grabby hand. "But what were you saying about leaving? The colonel hasn't sent you on a mission in months. Why now?" She frowned.

He dished out his own portion and settled into his seat. "Thorson gave me light duty while my arm was healing. Now I've got to earn my keep."

"I don't think your arm's fully healed."

Sky didn't want him to go? Best news he'd heard since LeBeau left three days before. "Let me say grace, then we'll talk about it." He smiled as she bowed her head, then cleared his throat. "Thank you, Lord, for this food. For Your many blessings. For Sky and Little Star. And for keeping us all safe. In Jesus's name. Amen."

"Is there some kind of trouble? Comanches?" She swallowed a spoonful of stew, careful to keep the utensil out of Little Star's reach.

Maybe it was them she was concerned about, not him. "No trouble. Just a routine patrol."

She bit her lip and mashed a softened carrot for the baby. "You can't tell when a war party might strike. You might think they're a hundred miles away..." Her voice trailed off, and her spoon wavered.

That's what her family had believed. No wonder she was bothered. "I'll have my whole company with me, Sky. Experienced fighters, every one."

"Be careful. That's all. Being the best warrior is no guarantee." She swallowed another bite.

"I will." He rubbed his finger across the tablecloth, a poor substitute for the hand he longed to touch. "Maybe we'll have a chance to do a little hunting while we're out. I'll see if I can bring you back a hide."

"Only if it's safe. Don't take any risks for me."

I can't count how many risks I've taken for you. "I'll be careful."

They drifted into silence as they ate—chunks of well-done beef and underdone carrots and potatoes in a watery broth. But he gobbled it up without a word of correction. She had cooked it for him. That's what mattered.

A bugle echoed "Tattoo" across the camp. Lights out would follow close behind, signaling the safe end of the day. A dog howled. The animal's mournful sound lingered after the song had ended. His men would return to their quarters to finish up their card games or packing for the trip.

Garret reached for the wooden ladle and served himself a second helping.

Blue eyes frowned at him. "I've been thinking about what my uncle said at the wedding. About Federal troops being kicked out of Texas."

He scooped a spoonful of stew into his mouth. His jaw slowed as he stalled for time. "No need to worry yet. It might not amount to anything."

"I want to know. I'm not a child."

A sharp exhale whistled through his teeth as he picked up his napkin and wiped his mouth. "It's complicated. There's trouble all across the country." He rested his forearms on the table. "Several of the Southern states don't like the new president-elect. They have some fool notion they can leave the Union anytime they please."

"Not be part of America anymore? But why? What's so bad about the new chief?"

"Lots of different reasons, such as they don't want the Federal government to tell them what they can and cannot do. States' rights. But for the majority, it boils down to slavery. They're afraid the new president will ban slavery."

She dipped her bread into the stew and tore off a couple of crumbles for Little Star's eager hands. "Doesn't sound like a bad idea. I... know what it's like to be a slave." Her gaze fell to her lap.

"I'd vote for freeing them." Garret chewed his lip. "But as it is, I'm afraid it could tear the country apart. Some folks are ready to let the South go. But my guess is, Lincoln isn't one of them."

"Lincoln?"

"The president-elect. Takes office in March."

"If my uncle and his planter friends have their way, Texas will leave the Union? What if they attack the fort?"

"I wouldn't be going anywhere if I thought there was danger of that, and the colonel wouldn't be sending me either. The vote a couple of days ago was to elect delegates to a convention at the end of the month, to vote on secession there. But I wouldn't be surprised if Governor Sam Houston puts a stop to it. He's mighty popular. And dead set against Texas leaving the Union."

She wiped Little Star's hands. "If they decide to kick us out, we could head west, or down to Mexico." Her voice lightened.

"Live off the land, hunt and trade, or we could start a ranch if you'd rather do that."

A momentary smile flittered across his lips. She saw herself with him beyond the fort, making a life together. But he laid down his spoon and steepled his fingers. "If the cavalry is ordered out of Texas, I'll have to fight if the colonel says fight, or march out if the colonel says march."

Sky glared at him. "What about me and Little Star? You said you'd protect us."

"I will."

"How are you going to do that if you leave?"

"I wouldn't leave without you. I'd take you two with me."

She gaped at him. "Leave Texas?" She pushed back from the table. "You promised you'd do whatever it took to keep us together. Including running off to Mexico if needed." Her gaze pierced him.

He ran his hand over his hair.

Little Star gave him a wide-eyed stare, too, as if she were adding in her disappointment.

"I've kept my word, Sky." He leaned toward her. "I've done what it took. Married you." *For better or worse, until death do us part.* How much more commitment could the woman want? "You and Little Star are safe and together. Your uncle's gone." He tapped his forefinger against the tablecloth. "But I also gave my word to the U.S. government. I can't let my country down."

"Your country. Not mine."

"I understand you feel that way right now."

Big, teary eyes accused him. "You promised you'd look after us."

"And I will." He swallowed hard. "Wherever we are. I pray Houston stamps out the succession fever and we can have another five years in Texas. I'd be happy to do so, if it would please you. But I wouldn't be much of a man if I turned my back on my country when she needed me most."

She stood, dumped her half-eaten stew back into the kettle, and clunked her bowl into the sink. "If you have to leave, you could find a place for Little Star and me to stay in Texas until you get back."

"Absolutely not." His fingers twitched inward to his palms. "I'll not have you someplace I can't protect you proper. I made a promise to you five days ago, and I aim to keep it—without breaking my oath as an officer."

With a roll of her eyes, she stomped toward the beaded curtain, baby on her hip.

There'd be no visiting by the lamplight this evening.

~

Eyes-Like-Sky lay awake. A shimmer of moonlight cast shadows across the canvas roof. The wind rippled against the taut covering. The smell of rain hung heavy in the air. Garret would need his rubber poncho in the morning.

She'd been too irritated with him to retrieve the deer hide. Just as well. She had no business cutting the leather until she was ready to concentrate and do it right. The man had another thought coming if he thought he could drag her off to Pennsylvania. Her uncle had sounded too gleeful for it to not be a real possibility. High-society folks. Swarms of people thicker than locusts. One building after another. Close enough to suffocate.

On the floor, Garret shifted in his covers. He wasn't asleep yet. His breathing was too quiet. She'd come to bed a whole hour before him. Hadn't bothered to speak another word to him since dinner.

The wool blanket scratched her skin, and the poufy pillow engulfed half of her face. How was a body supposed to sleep under such conditions?

Garret had given her his bed. Opened up his quarters to her and Little Star. She fingered the soft cotton of her chemise. It wasn't his fault she wasn't clothed in doeskin. He'd been nothing but kind since the day he'd brought her to this fort. And he hadn't asked about his ring.

The moonlight dimmed. Clouds. The rain might not wait for daybreak.

What if Garret left in the morning before she rose? In the dark, he'd gathered his supplies from his cedar chest at the foot of the bed. He'd packed his saddlebags with little concern about the noise. Probably wanted to wake her. Thank goodness, Little Star wasn't a light sleeper.

What if something happened to him? War parties. Raiders. Northers. There weren't any guarantees. The morning of the attack on her village, Dancing Eagle had snuggled close, draping his arm around her and Little Star as he slept until moments before the dogs barked and chaos broke loose. She'd awoken a few minutes before and closed her hand over his rough fingers with no idea it would be their last morning together.

Her stomach twinged. She rolled onto her side toward the edge of the mattress and propped her chin on her arm, squinting in Garret's direction, struggling to make out his shape in the dark.

His covers rustled. "Sky?"

Her heart pounded. "I'm not talking to you."

"God will watch over us. We need to trust Him."

The Lord had answered her prayer and sent Garret to rescue her. But could she trust Him to answer this prayer? She held her breath in the silence. *Dear Lord, he loves you. He knows much more about You than I do. Please take care of him, and bring him home safe.*

"I'll be back in a few days," Garret whispered. "I'll miss my little family."

Family? How had she ended up here, sending another warrior off? She couldn't bring Dancing Eagle back. All she could do was try to keep this man alive. "You come back to me and Little Star safe. You hear me, Garret Ramsey?"

"I hear you." The smile in his voice eased the tension in her shoulders and settled her stomach.

She rolled toward the wall and buried her head beneath the blanket. How had she ended up caring?

CHAPTER 30

Damp grass swiped against Sky's skirt as she made her way from the outhouses to the river. She shouldn't be here, in middle of the night, alone, without a word to anyone, but it was her only chance to search for the ring. The rain of the last two days had finally passed. She wouldn't go in the river, just search along the banks. Maybe the ring had washed ashore. Or she could have dropped it as she climbed out.

So much mud. She stopped and yanked her moccasins off, tossing them aside as she continued down the bank. Cold, wet earth squished between her toes. The full moon cast its muted light across the choppy surface of the water. She'd crawl along the bank, feel for the ring, venture into the shallows if needed, no further. Fueled by runoff, the river rushed like a raging serpent, even less tame than the evening of the wedding.

This time, she'd take off the dress. Her hands went around back to the buttons. Most inconvenient place ever. She'd leave on the chemise, tie it around her thighs to keep it from the mud and water as best she could.

Three buttons. Three more to go. Her arms strained. Maybe she'd shed her leggings too.

Snap. A footstep, then another. She jabbed her hand into the folds of her skirt to the pocket and clasped the handle of her knife.

A soldier crashed down the bank and jerked to a stop a few feet from her. "Evening, Mrs. Ramsey." No rifle. His revolver in his holster. But the sneer in his voice sent a chill through her. "Fixing to jump in the river again?"

The man outweighed her by at least fifty pounds, more muscle than fat. Scruffy whiskers adorned his cheeks. Huge, empty hands, open and ready to grab.

Her grip tightened on the knife hilt. Her dress hung loose around her shoulders. Thank God, she hadn't stooped to take off the leggings. "Just out for a walk. Headed back to camp now." She stepped away from the water.

He moved in front of her. "I don't think so. My friend Jenkins told me to pay my respects to you."

Her muscles tensed like taut sinew. Draw her knife or dart around him and run?

He lunged.

She dove to the side and stumbled in the slick grass as he crashed into the tree limbs.

With a wild swing to the right and left, he freed himself from the branches.

On her feet, she scrambled for the bank. Slid in the slimy damp. Her skirt tangled around her legs. Cotton ripped. Up again—

Bam. The man whammed into her from the side. They both went down. She kicked free, landing a solid heel in his gut. Knife in her hand, she clambered to her feet and spun toward him.

"Halt." A voice bellowed behind her.

Surrounded. She pivoted toward the new attacker.

Another soldier, charged to the top of the bank, revolver leveled at her attacker.

"The lady lured me out here." The ogre stumbled to stand. "Attacked me."

"I did no such thing." She threw the knife on the ground. "I—he attacked me. Said he was a friend of Jenkins."

"She's a liar." The brute swiped his sleeve across his mouth and stuck out his gut. "Started taking off her clothes."

Her mouth dropped. "No." She clenched her hands at her sides. "I came down here to find my husband's ring. The one he gave me for our wedding. I lost it the night— " Her voice trembled.

The soldier shifted his gaze between her and the ogre. "I saw you go to the outhouse, Mrs. Ramsey. Thought you were still there till I heard a ruckus down here."

"Told me to meet her down here, Carson. God's honest truth. Good thing you came along before she rammed me through with that knife." The scoundrel smacked his hands together. "She's nothing but a whore."

She cringed. What if they didn't believe her? What if they thought it was the same as Jenkins all over again?

Garret trotted his mare toward the corral. His company of eighty weary men followed, eager for beds instead of patches of poncho-covered ground. Forget the snakes and tarantulas. Tonight he'd sleep in his quarters and see Sky. Would she greet him at the door, or hardly roll over in bed? After twelve days on the trail, he was filthy. Maybe he'd have his orderly heat him up water for a real bath. Steaming-hot water to warm his bones after three days in soggy boots and mud-stiff clothes.

But his horse came first. Dismount, unbridle Ginger, and fill her feed sack after she'd gulped a bucket of water. Garret worked his way through the routine, his gaze toward officers' row. He strained for a glimpse of light behind his little grove.

Private Carson jogged up to him as he shucked his gauntlets and reached for a curry comb.

"Evening, sir. Good to have you back." Carson saluted, no welcome in his furrowed brow.

"How'd it go? You look after Mrs. Ramsey all right?" Garret held his breath.

"Went fine until a couple days ago." The young man shifted his weight and lowered his rifle butt to the ground. "She snuck down by the river."

"She did what?"

"Went to the outhouse middle of the night. I watched from the mess hall. Didn't want to get too close. Next thing I knew, I heard a ruckus toward the river. By the time I got there, she and Private Bradley were fighting—"

"Physically? He laid his hands on her?"

"Shoved her down. She got away from him and drew a knife. I had to threaten to shoot him."

Garret rocked back against a fence post. "Did that worthless dog *touch* my wife?" His hands petrified into hardened fists.

"No, sir." Carson jerked up straight. "I got there double-quick. Nothing like that happened. Bradley tried to make up some lie about Mrs. Ramsey inviting him down there. But she told me she was there to look for your ring. Said she lost it when she jumped in the river. The night..." His gaze trailed to the ground, along with his voice.

Garret tapped his forehead. She'd lost the ring. That's why she hadn't worn it.

Carson cleared his throat and straightened. "They drug her and Bradley in to see the colonel. But Henderson and I found two witnesses that overheard Bradley say he was going to pay her back for what happened with Jenkins. Plus, I'd witnessed him attack her."

"Where's that scum now?"

"Stockade. Colonel's going to have him bucked and gagged." Carson hooked his thumb over his belt by the brass eagle. "By the way, the colonel will be wanting to see you, sir."

"Bucking's not good enough." Garret clenched his jaw and tossed the curry comb to Carson. "Take care of my horse."

Shawl draped around her shoulders, Sky creaked back and forth in the rocking chair. The staccato rhythm filled the silence. Garret would walk in any minute now. His company had clomped through the gate as the bugler finished "lights out." An hour ago. More than enough time for him to hear of her misdeeds. Would he believe her? And even if he did, there was still the matter of the ring.

She should fix him something to eat. He'd be hungry. Food could settle more than a man's stomach. She hopped out of the chair, lit the lamp, and scooped a bowl full of beans out of the crock and into a pan. Beans and cornbread. That should do it. She placed the pan on the burner to warm it.

If he brought her a hide, she'd use it to make him a pair of moccasins instead of a blouse for herself. A pitiful start in making amends for the loss of the ring.

Footsteps. She smoothed her sweaty palms on the light-brown work dress Mrs. Thorson had donated until the green could be mended.

Garret entered through the flap. His saddlebags dropped to the floor. His frown was almost as deep as the day he'd found her in the canyon. "Are you all right?" He stood his carbine against the wall. It slipped. He grabbed it and righted it before crossing the floor to her, dirty boots still on his feet.

"I'm... fine. I wasn't hurt much."

He latched onto her shoulders. "How bad is not much? Did you see the doctor?" His hands slid down her sides and then her arms as if checking for wounds, stopping short of an embrace. Nothing like the night he'd rescued her from the river.

His fingers halted at the ridges of the armbands. He winced as if he'd been struck. His grip lightened.

She swallowed hard.

"Did he try to *touch* you, like—" His voice faltered, but his gaze scoured hers.

"No, he didn't try anything like Jenkins. Nothing like that." Her stomach lurched at the thought. "Didn't have a chance to. I ran, he knocked me down, I kicked him, and then your man Carson showed up."

His brow contorted. "What if Carson hadn't found you in time?"

"I would have stabbed that devil in the gut." She jutted out her chin, but her voice warbled.

"*If* he didn't get the knife away from you first. The man is twice your size. And a fighter."

"He wouldn't have gotten it away."

"You don't know that, Sky. You can't be sure." His hands dropped to his sides. "Just like the night you jumped in the river." He jabbed his finger at her. "You put yourself in danger."

She backed away. "You're angry at me? I was the one attacked."

"I'd like to wring that man's neck. And kick the pulp out of him." He spit out the words. "If he weren't already in the stockade and under the colonel's jurisdiction, that's exactly what I'd do."

"What's the colonel going to do?"

"Buck and gag him. Demote him. Send him to another post."

"Buck and gag?"

"Tie his wrists together and over his knees. Then run a pole under his knees and over his arms. They'll probably keep him like that from 'Reveille' to 'Retreat' at the end of the day. A man has to be carried to his quarters by the time he's done."

"Good. As long as he's away from here. As long as you know it's not my fault." She hugged her arms.

"I don't blame you for Bradley's actions. He's scum." He jerked off his jacket and tossed it on the table. "But you didn't listen to me. You promised you wouldn't go near the river again."

"I was looking for your ring, Garret. I lost it the night of our wedding."

He blew out a breath. "About which you never said a word to me."

"I was hoping to find it."

"In a river swollen with rain?"

"I wanted to try. I know it was valuable. The colonel said it belonged to your grand—"

"I don't care about the ring. You and Little Star mean more to me than any possession. But you broke your word. You disobeyed—"

"So I'm one of your men now? I'm supposed to hop when you snap your fingers?"

"You're supposed to keep your word."

"I thought we were partners." Her voice shook. "That's what you said back in the canyon—"

"When it comes to safety, you listen." His gaze bore into her. "You want to sit down and discuss everything else, we'll do that. But not when it comes to my protecting you and Little Star." He yanked his Hardee hat off his head, crumpling it in his grip. "And I *asked* you to give your word. I didn't order you. You gave it, and you broke it."

"You might as well buck and gag me too." Tears flooded her

eyes as she spat the words. Had she lost his trust? She hadn't meant to break her promise. Why couldn't he understand that? She shoved past him and stomped off to the bedroom. "I have nothing else to say to you."

The beaded curtain clattered behind her. In the dark, she scooped Little Star off her blanket and laid her in the bed beside her. The baby stirred, then settled. Sky buried her head in the pillow and cried.

Garret awoke to Little Star playing with his discarded suspender. She shook it with glee and rattled the metal hook against the floor.

Early daylight lit the canvas overhead. Pots and pans clanged in the front room. Sky. Still furious with him. He couldn't blame her. But he had to make her understand and listen. The possibility of that man or any other man hurting her—

And what if no one had shown up? Would she have dove into the river for the ring? He shuddered.

He'd waited an hour to come to bed, but still he could have sworn he heard her sniffling. Most miserable feeling ever. In the midst of all of his fussing, why couldn't he have stopped for a moment and told her the most important truth, that he loved her and that the possibility of someone hurting her cut him to the core?

Little Star dropped the suspender and plowed over the top of his legs. Black ringlets curled around her ears, and one dipped onto her forehead.

He rolled onto his back beneath the tangled blanket and picked the little girl up. "Good morning, angel."

She squealed and flashed a toothy grin.

"You miss me?" He smiled into her dark eyes and lowered her to his chest for a hug.

Sky stepped into the doorway, shrouded in strings of beads which hung from the cross pole. Stubborn. Beautiful. Displeased. Her sullen eyes drifted over him and the baby.

He exhaled and returned his gaze to Little Star. "I bet your mommy doesn't know she's still the most captivating lady in all of Texas."

Shoulder propped against a pole, Sky ground a bare toe back and forth against a rice bag as if squashing a bug.

He lowered the baby to the ground and sat up. The blanket fell to his waist. "I'm sorry about last night," he whispered. "I let my concern and temper get the better of me."

Her toe stilled.

"I don't want to argue with you, Sky. I just want to keep you safe."

Sky dropped her gaze to the floor. "I'm sorry about the ring. It was loose on my finger. I had no idea I'd lost it until the next morning." She clasped her hands in front of her. "I hoped I could find it."

He frowned. "I know it was an accident. In the spring, after the river's down, I can have my men look for it. If we find it, good. Otherwise, we'll get along without it."

"But it was your grandfather's."

His father would have a fit. "Yes, but I've been tempted to throw it in a couple rivers, myself." He chuckled and rubbed the knot at the back of his neck. "I gave it to you as a temporary measure until I could buy a ring for you." Every drop of merriment faded away. "Only, it'd be best if my father never learns you're the one who lost it."

"I couldn't let you take the blame."

"I've been his son for twenty-seven years. One more disappointment won't end the world."

"Sounds as if he's hard to please."

"Cut from the same cloth as your uncle. But I don't want to talk about him anymore today." He inhaled. "If you'll bring me my saddlebags, I'll show you the present I got Little Star. Please?"

Her expression lightened. "I reckon I could do that." She moseyed into the front room and returned with the weathered bags. She plopped them down near his knees.

He tugged the bags closer. "You could sit with us."

"I'll think about it." She stepped over to the bed and straightened the covers, the sheet followed by the quilt his mother had sewn as a girl.

Odors of horse and wood smoke wafted from the leather satchel. He inhaled and dug his hand inside.

Little Star hurried over and latched onto the flap, wiggling it up and down.

"Let's see what we have here, baby girl." He pulled out a doll, stuffed cloth with yarn stitches for eyes, nose, and mouth and a mop of red hair. A simple dress of dark blue. No feet, no hands.

Little Star squeezed her hands around the plump body and brushed her teeth against the head, as if looking for a good place to bite.

Sky hugged a pillow to her chest. "She used to have a doll. Buckskin, no hair, no clothes. A simple little thing. Owl Woman gave it to her. I haven't seen it since—"

The battle. He swallowed hard. What in the world could he say to that? "I'm sorry she lost it."

Layers deep of sorry. But sorry had its limits. If he could travel back to that day in early October, he wouldn't pursue the two riders who turned out to be three. He would let them go. But the past lay beyond his reach. And the woman he wanted to spend the rest of his life with stood in his bedroom and shared his name. All he had to do was win her heart. Challenge of the century.

Little Star smiled up to her mother and waved her new toy.

Eyes moist, Sky laid the pillow on the bed and knelt. "Come here, baby girl. Show me your doll, your *nuhitueta*."

Comanche word for *doll*?

The baby giggled and bit the cotton face.

"She'll probably chew the hair off in a couple of days." Sky eased down farther to sit cross-legged on the floor between the bed and his blanket.

"You can sew it back on." His gaze dropped to Sky's bare feet, her heel and the ball of her foot deeply callused. "Where's your moccasins?"

She tilted her head and fingered a fold in her brown skirt. "In the grass between the outhouse and the river, I hope. It was muddy, so I took them off on the way, and after everything happened, I didn't have a chance to retrieve them."

He drew his leg up and looped an arm around his knee. "I'll look for them after breakfast."

"You will?" Her gaze drifted up to his. "Thank you. And thank you for the doll."

"Can't have my wife going barefoot." He smiled. "I see you finished the leggings." He pointed to the hint of buckskin that showed beneath her skirt hem.

"Yes, I can work on your moccasins next."

"Finish up whatever you need first. Then work on mine." He shrugged. "I got you a present. You want to see it?"

"You don't need to give me presents."

"That's not what I asked." He tugged the saddlebag closer.

Little Star dropped to all fours and padded toward Sky, dolly in tow.

"What have you got, baby girl?" She reached for her daughter. "What did Gar—" She bit her lip.

He cleared his throat. "Garret?" What was he to be to this little girl? Captain Ramsey? Uncle Garret? He rubbed the back of his neck. He'd gladly lose a dozen rings if it meant being closer than that. Pa?

Sky squeezed her daughter to her chest. "Dancing Eagle will always be her father. I've vowed to teach her about him and keep his memory alive in her. I want her to know he was a brave warrior who loved us very much."

He pressed his lips together, half tempted to throw on his uniform and go volunteer for a six-month patrol in the desert.

CHAPTER 31

Briars and thistles ripped Eyes-Like-Sky's dress. Where was Dancing Eagle? He'd been missing so long she couldn't remember his face. She jerked and pulled at the thorny green tentacles with her bare hands. Something was behind her. Getting closer. Wolves. Their snarls and howls sent shivers through her. The vines fell away. She plunged ahead into the darkness. She had to find Dancing Eagle before it was too late. Smoke filled the air. Flames. Unbearable heat. Up ahead, beyond the tongues of fire, stood Dancing Eagle. Smoke obscured his face. She reached for him. The ground fell away—

A scream tore through her. She sprang up. Shaking, trembling. Her sweat-dampened chemise clung to her back.

On the floor, Garret raised up on his elbow. "Are you all right?"

Heart pounding, she gasped for breath. No words came.

Little Star stirred on her blanket.

No. *Please don't wake up.* "Could you..." she whispered and motioned with her palm down.

A small whimper arose from the baby.

Garret pivoted toward Little Star, stretched, and laid his hand gently on her back.

Another muffled sniffle, and the baby quieted.

Sky dropped her face into her hands. The dream had been so real. She drew her knees up to her chest and curled over them. Her heart pounded, its rhythm filling her ears.

At a gentle touch to her arm, she started and looked up into Garret's eyes. He was the only person alive who would look at her with such concern and care. He stood by the bed, dressed in his underclothes, his hair tousled from sleep.

"You're safe. It was just a dream." His voice wrapped around her like a layer of spun wool. If only she could curl up in it, lay her head against his shoulder, and snuggle deep in his arms, as she had by the river on their wedding night. No. Deeper than even that. Is this how the Lord loved her, except even more so? Why did she do such a poor job of letting either of them in?

A gentle hand rested on her back. "Would you like a drink of water?" Without waiting for her answer, he retrieved his canteen from a hook and brought it over. His glance fell to the rumpled beds as if he might consider sitting.

She reached for the canteen and scooted her foot close to the edge to occupy the empty spot.

As his fingers brushed against hers on the cloth-covered tin, a tingle spread up her arm. Did his breath hitch?

In a rush, she swallowed a sip, barely enough to coat her parched throat, and shoved it back toward him. "Thank you. I'm all right now. Sorry I woke you." Her voice wobbled, contradicting the wall of her words.

Across camp, a dog barked. Too much like the wolves of her dream. She shivered, praying Garret wouldn't notice.

He wavered there, canteen in hand. "If you need anything at all, let me know. Doesn't matter what time." His voice reached for her, strong, reassuring.

Don't go back to bed. Please sit. Hold me. She swallowed back the pleas before they could pass her lips. Instead, she laid down and rolled toward the wall. Her heart screaming for comfort, love, she hugged herself beneath the covers lest her wayward hands reach out to pull him to her. "Good night."

It was minutes before the rice bags crinkled and he moved back to his blankets. "Good night, Sky."

How could she shut him out like that? He deserved better. So did she. She curled into a ball on her side, but her knees pressed to her chest could not fill the emptiness in her heart. *Speak to him.* The thought throbbed in her head. *Give him something before he gives up on you.*

Her voice, small and faraway, scratched the dark. "Garret?"

"Yes?" The blankets rustled.

"Thank you."

"You're welcome."

"I've been thinking about what I said this morning about Dancing Eagle being Little Star's father."

Silence, then a slow exhale. "Maybe we should wait until morning to talk about this." A hint of an edge crept into his voice. She couldn't let him go on thinking she didn't appreciate everything he'd done.

This morning, he'd been dressed and out the door doing chores less than ten minutes after their conversation and hadn't returned until dinner. She hadn't intended to offend him, only wanted him to understand how important keeping Dancing Eagle's memory alive was to her.

Her throat constricted. "I want you to be Little Star's papa."

"You what?" He sat up or maybe even stood. She didn't turn to see.

"Little Star needs a man who'll care for her, guide her, and protect her, now that her father—" She swallowed hard and rubbed the quilt between her fingers. "I want her to call you

Papa because that's who you are." It was what she'd called her own father.

A sharp inhale. "Papa?" His voice softened to a reverent whisper. "Papa."

"Yes." The tightness in her chest eased. Her heart was no longer alone.

CHAPTER 32

The temperature had dropped thirty degrees since noon. A storm was coming. Dark, angry clouds continued to roll in from the northwest. Driven by the wind, sand blasted Garret's cheeks and neck. He gripped a nail between his teeth and one between his fingers as he hammered a rail across the top of the three-foot picket boards, encasing the canvas walls. His wall-tent quarters needed all the bolstering it could get in case the storm hit hard.

Two years of living in a tent. The colonel had talked of requisitioning enough wood or stone for each of his captains to have their own cabins, but with the constant threat of moving the fort to a more plentiful well, and the army's tortoise-paced chain of supply, reality had fallen short of promise. Best get everything secure before evening.

The last time a norther had come through, he'd been in a cave praying Sky and Little Star would survive until he found them. He'd had no clue he'd be a married man and a father a couple weeks later. God had turned his world upside down.

Last night, he'd shared his sketchbook, his most prized possession, with Sky. Opened a part of his secret self to her.

Warm and cozy by the table with her chair pulled up close to his. It'd taken him five weeks of marriage to be able to sit that close to her. As she studied his drawings, they'd drifted into talk, her asking about his past, his sharing his love of drawing, his father's disdain for it and demands that Garret join him in his business, and how he'd ended up a cavalry officer instead. The candlelight, her smile... He'd totally lost himself in her eyes...until she stood abruptly and said she was going on a walk. Alone. And when he'd followed her outside and asked what was wrong?

Her answer still rattled through his head. He was the problem. That's what she'd said. She'd enjoyed his company. And that was a problem? A man could live a thousand years and never fully figure out a woman. She'd gone to bed, lights out, without another word, and his bedroll had been scooted over at least a foot.

Then, today, she'd done her best to avoid him all morning, even though she'd made him his favorite breakfast. Afraid to talk to him because she might like it too much? In an odd way, it sounded like progress. Even a compliment.

By the time the bugler blared "Retreat," signaling the end of the official day, heavy droplets of sleet pelted Garret's dust-covered coat. He grabbed the water bucket by the door, broke its layer of ice, and tossed the pieces on the ground. Teeth gritted, he plunged his bare hands in and splashed frigid water on his face and neck. A shiver traveled all the way down his spine, but at least Sky wouldn't see him at his grimiest.

He inhaled as soon as he stepped inside. Beans, beef, and cornbread. Hot and ready to eat. Enough to send his stomach growling. Sky stood at the stove, a spoon in one hand and Little Star secured against her hip with the other. She'd tied strips of rabbit fur around the child's limbs for warmth. Lined booties covered the baby's feet.

Little Star smiled at him and babbled. She bent her head

and shoulders backward, as if ready for a head dive to the floor. Baby language for "put me down."

Sky glanced over her shoulder. A tentative smile lifted her lips. "You want to go to Papa?"

"Let me get these off." He shrugged out of his great coat and sat down on a crate to tug off his boots. A smile from both of his girls. What a way to start his evening. He prayed he could keep them warm and dry through the night.

"You might want to keep your coat on." Sky sat Little Star down.

"I'll be all right for now. After supper, I'll dust my coat off and wear it if I need it."

The baby chugged toward him on all fours, slowed momentarily by her extra layer of warmth.

"How's Papa's baby girl this evening?" He scooped her into his arms.

She patted his face, tender palms to bristly stubble.

He touched a finger to her tiny red nose. "I don't want her getting cold in the middle of the night. I think we should all sleep in here by the stove."

Sky paused at the table, bean pot in hand. "I can bundle her up in the bed with me."

Garret frowned at the roof. The canvas expanded and contracted with each blow of wind. "I've weathered storms before in these quarters and have woken up frosted a time or two. We need to haul blankets in here. I'll fix you up a cozy nest with Little Star, and mine will be separate." Separate or not, his heart beat thumped louder.

Sky pressed her lips together and finished setting the table.

Shimmering, twirling, peacock-blue silk—Sky's wedding dress. Drums thundered in Garret's head. He reached for his Comanche princess. She slipped into his arms, eyes full of stars, and her lips.... He lowered his mouth to hers—and woke. A crack of thunder boomed overhead. Grrrr. Not a dream he wanted to cut short.

Cool air struck his cheeks and neck. A bolt of lightning lit the shadows, followed by another rumble. Pellets of ice thumped the canvas. A thunderstorm in the middle of a blizzard. He rolled onto his side.

Sky. Her form was barely distinguishable from the blankets in the dim red glow of the stove burners. He stretched toward the stove and slowly maneuvered the door open a couple of inches. More light. Dark locks lay splayed across the pillow. With each breath, her back and shoulders rose and fell beneath the quilt.

The dream had felt so real—his wife in his arms.

Three feet separated them now. Too much. The crackling of the fire wove its magic, insulating them from the howl of the wind. He hadn't held his wife in his arms since the night by the river. A touch to her hand or arm now and then. Nothing more.

A married man could starve on such meager tidbits.

Longing pierced through him. He squeezed his eyes shut against it. He'd promised to give her time. But surely, it wouldn't hurt to touch her hair, for a moment. Leaning, he reached across the distance and skimmed his fingertips over the silky strands. His breath caught in his throat. Beautiful. Enchanting. He savored the softness as he stroked the dark waves with his knuckles, back and forth, as if strumming a harp. What would it be like when her hair had grown to her waist once more?

If only he could wipe the memory of the battle, the day she'd cut her hair, from his mind forever. He winced. But he would love her and take care of her for the rest of their lives.

And not just because of what had happened on the battlefield. If he'd first seen her across a crowded ballroom, Sky would have outshone every lady in the room.

Warmth flowed through him. His cold toes, the wind, all of it forgotten. He raised up on his elbow. His hand shifted from her hair to her shoulder, just a light touch across the fine wool of the shirt he'd loaned her for extra warmth. His fingers contracted. He didn't dare massage her muscles. It might spook her like a beautiful gazelle. Gazelle? She was more like a wild mare. He brushed his thumb across the back of her shoulders instead, across, down, and around, repeating the pattern, stroke after stroke.

Her breathing shifted, along with a slight tensing in her muscles. His thumb stilled. Had he woken her? It was all he could do to not draw her against him and wrap his arms around her. If only he could hold her like that all night long.

A haggard breath rattled through him. Best get himself back in his own pile of blankets before he overstepped. He tugged the quilt up to her neck. The rice-bag carpet crinkled beneath him as he shifted closer. With a feather-light kiss, he pressed his lips to her head, inhaling the sweet scent of her hair.

~

Sky stared in Garret's small shaving mirror. Her lightly tanned image reflected in the speckled glass. She fingered the ends of her shoulder-length hair. Last night, she'd awoken to Garret's touch and kiss. And she'd lain there. She could have scooted away or shoved his hand. Instead, she'd held her breath and tensed like a piece of hard wax, ready to melt at the first hint of flame. What would she have done if he hadn't moved away?

She drove her hands through her wavy locks. Four months.

Her husband who'd loved her, who'd rescued her from a life of misery and slavery, had only been dead for four months. And her fickle heart was ready to move on? No, just the part of her that needed to be held and comforted.

Dancing Eagle had died saving her. If she'd ridden faster, or not been so slow mounting her horse? They might have all gotten away alive. In a battle, every second counted. At first, she had blamed Garret. But she was as much to blame as he.

She picked up the knife from the washstand, tugged a lock of hair, and sawed through the strand. She sheared two inches of length off all the way around, one lock after the other. She would honor her Comanche husband.

CHAPTER 33

Sky's resolve dropped to the pit of her stomach when Garret walked into their quarters at the end of the day, cheeks rosy with cold and exertion. His eyes shone the moment their gazes met.

She edged her shoulders upward.

Gauntlets dirty and coat damp, he stomped on the woven mat and sat down on the crate to yank off his soaked boots. The ice and snow of the night had turned to slush by mid-afternoon.

Little Star banged a wooden spoon against a pan on the floor and laughed.

Garret smiled and hung his hat on a peg. Sweat dampened his hair line. "Is she helping with the cooking?"

"I think she wants to join the band." Sky's voice fell flat. "I'll fetch you a pair of dry socks. You should have sent for me to come help with the shoveling or the horses."

"I have a camp full of men to help. I wanted my wife and baby girl warm and dry."

His wife who'd cut her hair because he'd touched it. She

cringed as she picked a pair of wool stockings from his trunk. He deserved better treatment than that. Maybe he wouldn't notice. What was an inch or two, after all?

By the time she slipped through the beaded curtain, Little Star was on his lap, frowning at her hands.

"Baby girl doesn't like to be wet." He chuckled and kissed the top of Little Star's head.

A loving gesture of affection. Was that all his kiss to her own head had been last night? No, she recognized a midnight invitation when she received one. "I could get a change of clothes for you and hang yours by the stove to dry."

"That's okay. I can stand by the stove while you finish cooking." He looked up at her. "Did you do something different with your hair?"

Her throat tightened. "Just a slight trim. To smooth out the ends." Her gaze flitted away to the stove. She needed to distract him. "Dinner will be ready in a few minutes. Would you like some coffee?"

"Love some." But a frown had crept into his tone.

She tossed the socks at his feet and headed for the stove. "We're having stew. I found an edible rutabaga and a few carrots, threw them in with the venison." Her voice refused to hold steady.

A few soft words to the baby girl, and Garret set her down by the wooden spoon.

"Coffee's on the table. Help yourself." Sky lifted the lid and added pepper to the stew.

Thumbs hooked in his cartridge belt, he stepped up beside her at the stove.

She tensed. He wasn't going to leave it alone.

"What made you decide to cut it today? It was just beginning to grow out." With a light touch to her shoulder, he turned her to face him. "It looked more even before."

Her tongue stuck to the roof of her mouth. "I reckon I was

in a hurry. Maybe I'll have to smooth it out a little more tomorrow." The wooden spoon dangled in her hand.

"Why today?" He repeated the question as he scrutinized her face.

She could lie. Her gaze dipped to his boots. She wouldn't do that to him.

The stew bubbled. Heat from the burner baked her arm like rays from the sun.

His hand fell away. "You can't even look at me?" His voice shook.

Sky closed her eyes. "It—it's part of mourning. Part of the Comanche culture. Like I did when—"

"It was because I touched your hair?" Each staccato beat of a word sounded like a slap. Intended for him or her?

No. Her lips wouldn't form the words. She lifted her gaze.

"Tell me the truth." His fingers curled inward at his sides.

"I'm still in mourning."

"If I'd held your hand, would you have scrubbed your skin raw?"

Little Star whimpered.

He pivoted, picked up the baby, and kissed her downy head. "Sorry I raised my voice, baby girl." Then he set her back down and turned to Sky. "It won't happen again."

All the force of a yell funneled into a whisper.

The door clunked shut as he marched out of the tent, boots and coat in hand.

Sky threw the serving spoon into the pot. Stew splattered, and hot liquid stung her hand. No competition for the ache that engulfed her heart.

It was late by the time Garret returned. In the dark, he snatched up his bedroll and carried it into the front room. The faint smell of alcohol wafted from him. Sky rolled over in the bed and cried into her pillow.

The lively notes of "Reveille" echoed throughout the camp. Dampness hung in the air as Garret retrieved his clothes from the back of the chair in the front room of his tent. The gray of early morning seeped through the canvas barrier, and voices carried from the barracks. Garret twisted his back to work out a kink, then sat on a crate by the door. With effort, he wiggled his feet into his stiff socks. He hadn't slept well despite the two shots of brandy he'd consumed. Too busy letting his temper get the best of him over Sky's hair.

His jaw clenched. The problem was bigger than her hair. He'd never be good enough in Sky's eyes. Never live up to her exalted ideals of Dancing Eagle. Just as he could never measure up to his own deceased brother in his father's eyes. How could he compete with a dead man who could never disappoint or mess up again? Dancing Eagle could live on in rose-colored memory. Just like Max Ramsey, Jr.

No. Garret ground his teeth and grabbed his boot. He wouldn't harden his heart. Wouldn't build a wall, as he had with his father, numbing himself to all hope and potential for caring rather than risk the pain of failure. He would not do that to his marriage. God help him to not let it be so.

The beaded curtain chinked. Garret stiffened as Sky crept into the room with cat-like steps. Her multi-colored shawl hung loose over the wool shirt he'd loaned her. Doeskin leggings poked out beneath her knee-length chemise. Not exactly proper dress for a woman who didn't want a man's attention. If she couldn't stand his touch, she had no business wearing his shirt or anything else of his.

He pressed his lips together and shoved his foot into the boot.

"I'm sorry, Garret." Her plaintive tone broke the silence. She tugged the shawl across her chest as she stepped close, her bare feet barely missing the puddle left by his boots.

Dropping his gaze, he started on the other sock. "If you didn't want me touching you, you could have scooted away, or nudged my hand aside. Or whispered 'no.'"

She fumbled with the yarn fringe. "You're right. I should have. I'm sorry. I didn't mean to hurt—"

"Sorry doesn't fix it." He glared at her. The boot leather chafed his ankle as he shoved his foot in hard. "It's more than that. Maybe you're sorry you cut your hair, or that I noticed. But your feelings are your feelings. An apology doesn't change them. You wear his armbands day and night, yet you couldn't hold onto my ring more than a few hours."

She flinched. "You forgave me for that. You know I didn't mean to lose your ring. I tried to find it, and I wanted to try again—"

He groaned. "You're right. The ring has nothing to do with this. I shouldn't have brought it up." He drove his fingers through his hair. "I've got to go. I'm officer of the day."

"Let me grab you some bread and cheese to take with you for breakfast."

"I don't have time. I should be out there already." He tugged his second boot up to his knee and stood. "What I should have said a minute ago is that you have a right to your feelings. Your agreement to share my quarters and my name doesn't mean you're ready to share anything else." He grabbed his coat from the hook and stuffed his arms in the sleeves. "I don't intend to make that mistake again. That's why I think we need some distance from each other."

"What do you mean by 'distance'?" She sniffled as if she might start to cry.

Plink. Plink. Plink. Somewhere outside, water from the melt was striking metal.

"I'll be back for meals and to sleep." He shoved his hat on his head and reached for the tent flap. He had to get out of there before his stomach was tied in enough knots to ruin his appetite for the entire day.

CHAPTER 34

"Come on, baby girl." Sky tied the front of the rabbit-skin coat across Little Star's chest. "Let's go find your papa."

She'd never dreamed a man could be so stubborn. A whole week of Garret coming home only for meals and bedtime. Meals eaten at his desk, as though he couldn't stand to sit at the table with her, but he'd welcome Little Star to his lap and feed her bits from his plate. The first two days, Sky had moved his blankets back into the bedroom, but each night, he'd come in late and carry them to the front room without a word. In the end, she let them be.

Twice more, she'd tried to apologize, only to have him turn back to his reading or playing with Little Star. And when she'd persisted, he'd grabbed his coat and headed outside to some forgotten task. She'd hurt him. That much she understood. If only she could pick up the ends of her hair and glue them back on, she would. But that wouldn't fix this. He'd said as much. And what he really wanted, her heart free of prior entanglement, she couldn't offer.

"Bababbbaba." Little Star chattered as she patted her mommy's shoulder.

Sky tucked the tail ends of Garret's red shirt into the waistband of her skirt. Maybe that'd get his attention. His best shirt, not the one he'd loaned her the night of the storm. And she'd pilfered one of his neckerchiefs to wear as a headband. Not to mention, she'd shortened the green skirt a few inches, making the bottom of her leggings visible along with her moccasins. Let the colonel say what he might. She had to show Garret that he was important to her. That she'd missed him.

Little Star in tow, Sky marched out the door. Blue skies and mild temperatures pervaded the area, as if winter was nowhere to be found. The men at the commissary paused to stare as she headed past, but she tipped her chin and kept her gaze trained on two eagles circling overhead in the distance. Majestic birds. They mated for life. How quickly did they give their love to another if they lost their partner?

If Dancing Eagle could see her now, what would he think? Was he in heaven? She shuddered at the possibility that he wasn't and dug her fingernails into her palms to banish the thought.

Her gait carried her past the barracks and blacksmith shop. More gawkers. A few tipped their hats. One called to her that Captain Ramsey was in the corral.

Horses by the fence shifted as she neared. Blacks, grays, roans, paints—a beautiful assortment. Horse and manure scents wafted her way.

She found Garret close to the slapped-together shed. Eight weeks ago, in middle of the night, she'd crept behind it and stolen a horse with no thought of ever returning. Garret had certainly changed that. Now he would hardly speak to her.

His broad shoulders flexed beneath his jacket as he scrubbed a curry comb across the withers of a black beauty.

"Papappapa." Little Star bubbled and stretched.

Garret whipped around. His gaze traveled over them, lingering on the red shirt and leggings. A few days' worth of stubble darkened his cheeks, giving him the rugged look he'd possessed when he rescued her at the Caprock Canyons.

Sky stepped closer to the rail. "Little Star wanted to see her papa." Coward. Why couldn't she say she wanted to see him too? That she missed him.

He tossed the brush on the ground and smacked his gauntlets together. "Come here, baby girl."

Sky pressed her fingertips against the backs of his gloves as he took Little Star from her arms.

His pained gaze locked onto hers before he turned to Little Star and settled the child in his arms. "Your mama's got to learn to keep her hands to herself, doesn't she? And to not wear your papa's shirts without permission."

The nerve of the man. Sky rolled her eyes.

Little Star grinned at his sing-song tone, oblivious to the barbs.

Bare-headed, with his blond hair slicked back, Charlie stepped up to the other side of the black mare, his look incredulous. "Did I hear you say 'Papa'?"

Garret leveled his gaze at his friend. "Yes. This is my daughter." His tone was firm, as if he was ready for a challenge.

Sky could have thrown her arms around her husband in that moment. She had stood at the altar with the right man. Just too soon.

Charlie cocked his eyebrows. His gaze shifted between them. "If you say so." He shrugged. "Cute little girl." As he ambled off toward the shed, he shook his head.

Little Star patted her papa's chin. She knew who her papa was. Her father would only be a word and a story to the girl.

Sky looked heavenward. No eagle in sight.

Garret kissed Little Star's brow and glanced at Sky. "If you're hoping to start a row with the colonel over the leggings, you're probably out of luck. He's busy packing. Leaves on Friday."

She blinked at him. "The colonel's leaving? For good?"

"The army's giving him a two-month furlough, time enough for him and Mrs. Thorson to travel home to Virginia for a visit."

She bit her lip. "So it's got nothing to do with that secession vote you told me about a few weeks ago?"

Garret studied her for a moment, already having spoken more words to her in the last few minutes than he had in a week. He scuffed his boot against the dirt. "We got word a couple days ago. The vote happened last week. Sam Houston couldn't stop it. Secession passed."

"It did?" She shivered despite the warmth of the sun "Wh-what's going to happen to us?"

Garret's horse nickered. He dipped Little Star closer to the animal so she could rub her tiny hand over the mare's neck. A frown spread across his face. "We'll stay put until orders say otherwise. There's talk the regiment could be called to help fortify the arsenal at San Antonio or march off for New Mexico Territory. Or, as a last resort, head back east."

Sky's legs wobbled.

Garret turned to face her. "But whatever happens, I'll make sure you and baby girl are safe and taken care of. You don't have to worry."

Don't worry? Fortifying sounded like preparing for battle. Heading east didn't sound any better. The thought of a city filled with people tightened a band across her chest that threatened to cut off her air. She put her hand on the post. Would he really ask that of her? "You'd take us with you wherever you go?" She rubbed her hands over her arms.

"That's my plan." He glared at her hands. A muscle twitched in his jaw. "Unless you choose to do otherwise. I made a commitment to provide for you and protect you. I don't go back on my commitments."

The armbands. Did he think she'd touched them on purpose? She clasped her hands. "New Mexico Territory would suit me fine."

"Officials back in Washington aren't likely to give us a say in the matter." He shifted Little Star to her, careful to avoid any overt touch. "When I find out more, I'll let you know. Meanwhile, I've got work to do. I'll see you both at supper."

Dismissed. Some nerve. Shake her world, then turn back to his work. Had she gotten through to him at all? "You'd better not be late. I've decided to make a pie. My first one ever."

She pivoted and headed off, but not so quickly that she missed his sharp exhale. Or was it a belated chuckle?

~

Garret rested his arms on top of the rail and watched her retreat. A pie. He shook his head, but a shimmer of light peeked through his clouded heart. His shirt had never looked so fine. He should have told her so. But looking at the ends of her hair still hurt. Why did she have to tease him with affection and interest as she had just now, as though he was some lost puppy begging for a treat, when she'd come along later and slam the door on the hopes?

And her walking across camp with her moccasins and leggings showing? She had a rebellious streak a mile long.

Charlie ambled up beside him and draped his arms over the worn wood. "Getting pretty serious about your Comanche princess?"

"She *is* my wife." Garret nudged his hat off his forehead.

Charlie dug his flask out of his jacket pocket and unscrewed the lid. "My advice to you? Since you got yourself entangled with a temporary wife, against my counsel? Enjoy her while you can, before your father sucks you into his enterprises and gets you married off to Lily." He took a deep swig of the brandy. A dribble ran down his smooth chin.

Garret's stomach turned. "My father isn't in control of my life. And never will be. I have a wife, and her name isn't Lily."

Charlie cocked an eyebrow, his smile rueful as he raised the tin to his lips and swallowed again. "Don't count on it."

~

Enjoy your wife while you can. Charlie's words tumbled around in Garret's head as he watched the sun dip below the horizon. An afternoon ride to check the perimeter and beyond had been the perfect excuse to escape his friend's company. Charlie might let his own father dictate his nuptials, but Garret had no intention of doing so.

He wasn't about to let anyone take Sky or Little Star from him. His grip tightened on his reins. A breeze chilled through him. He needed to head back to camp and make up with his wife.

Half an hour later, he inhaled the aroma of dough and apples as he stepped into his quarters.

"Don't get your hopes up." Sky swiped leftover traces of flour from the table to her upturned apron gathered in her other hand, her tone conveying the unease of a schoolgirl asked to recite in front of the class. "I tried to make the crust with flour and water. At the last minute, I remembered something about butter or lard."

More flour on her than in the crust, most likely. White specks covered his red shirt, except for the sleeves she'd rolled to her elbows. Even the tip of her nose sported a spot. Two empty jars sat by the dry sink. The last of their canned apples, no doubt. But she'd done it for him.

He shrugged off his coat. "I bet it'll be the best pie I've tasted in months."

She quirked her eyebrows at him as if compliments were a rare commodity. With a quick flutter, she emptied the contents of her apron into the trash bucket. "It's probably the only pie you've eaten in months."

"That's why I know it'll taste good."

She eyed him for a minute, then chewed her lip. "I'm sorry about your shirt."

"A little dusty for the wear. But it looks good on you." The knotted muscles in the back of his neck began to loosen. It was home again, not just a place to lay his bedroll.

She blinked at him. A quick, delighted smile lit her face, enough to warm him through and through. But there he went again, amassing hope and expectations. Why couldn't he learn to let a smile be a smile and go about his business?

He tore his gaze away and walked to his desk while she grabbed the broom. The papers and books had been stacked off to the side to make room for his plate and cup. Time for that to change. He picked up his place setting and carried it to the table.

She danced a step or two as she whisked the straw broom across the floor.

My goodness, he'd better sit himself down before he got carried away. He pulled out his chair and settled onto the wood. He definitely needed the newspaper to read or something to keep his mind on track and his eyes off his wife's every move.

She'd made it obvious she missed his companionship. And just like that, hope was reborn. He could do it. He could win her. He had to be patient.

A whimper came from the bedroom.

"I'll get her." Sky propped her broom in the corner.

He inhaled. Apples, cinnamon, and venison. His stomach rumbled.

The beaded curtain shifted, and Sky plopped a sleepy-eyed girl in his lap.

"How's my baby girl?" He placed his chapped hands around her and smiled into her pouty face.

Sky set the coffeepot on the table and poured him a cup. Real coffee, dark and strong, just the way he liked it. She handed Little Star a cracker.

He traced his finger around the rim of the cup as steam curled above the black liquid.

Sky dug a gold armband out of her apron pocket and laid it on the table in front of him.

His eyebrows arched. "What are you doing?"

"I'm taking off one. For you." She hugged herself. "I'll—I'll keep the other for now."

He blinked up at her. "For me?" He swallowed hard. "Thank you." He ran his finger along the edge of the engraved gold, three eagles linked wingtip to wingtip. "But I was wrong the other day when I fussed at you about the ring and the bands. I want to apologize for my behavior this past week. I gave my word I'd be patient with you, and I've fallen short on that promise."

The pie bubbled in the stove, or was it the venison in the pot?

Sky's voice wobbled. "I'm sorry too. I didn't mean to hurt you."

The *tick-tock* of the clock on his desk punctuated the pause.

You didn't. It was nothing. The ego-saving lies stuck in his throat. Instead, he said, "It was a miserable week, being at odds with you."

Cracker crumbs from Little Star's chin dropped onto his lap as she gnawed on the treat. No one was going to take his girls from him, and no one was going to treat either of them as second best, not if he could help it.

Sky smiled. "It's good to have you home."

He fingered the band. "I think you should take this back for now." Was he insane? "I don't want you to take it off just because you think it'd please me or because you're worried about what will happen if we have to leave the fort."

"Thank you." She leaned down and threw her arms around him and Little Star, pressing her cheek to his hair.

His mouth dropped. A dipper full of affection for a parched heart. His free arm closed lightly around her as he fought the urge to tighten his hold and pull her close. Scents of citrus and soap wafted from her hair.

A deep inhale and she slipped free.

He pressed the band into Sky's hand. "When you're ready, you could make a little pouch, decorate it. A special place for treasures. You could keep it in my trunk or anywhere you like. No hurry." The last two words faltered.

Band clasped tight, she swiped a tear from her cheek. "I have something to ask you."

His world narrowed to the widths of her sky-blue irises. "What is it?"

She fidgeted with her apron. "I thought maybe you could teach me to read and write."

He shifted in his chair to face her. "I'd be happy to. I don't know why I didn't think of offering."

"You did once. And I refused." Crimson blossomed across her cheeks. "But now—I'm ready. You don't have to teach me. I mean more like, remind me. Help me practice. After seven years—"

"I'd love to." His knees bumped against her skirt as he rose to his feet. "Soon as dinner is over and Little Star's in bed. I bet you'll pick it back up in no time."

The smile that spread across her face lit his whole heart.

CHAPTER 35

The knock on their door came in the middle of the night near the end of February, almost two weeks later. Sky sat up in bed, but Garret whispered for her to stay put as he rose from his blankets on the floor and shoved his legs into his trousers, a now-familiar sight that she did not turn away from in the almost-dark.

Voices drifted from the front room. Garret and another man. Captain Carpenter, the infantry captain and temporary commander of Camp Cooper in Thorson's absence. A man who'd frowned the first time he saw her out on the parade ground in a doeskin skirt and leggings but in the end, had looked the other way.

Papers rustled on the desk. The maps? She'd get up and listen at the curtain if the blasted rice-bag carpet didn't crinkle so.

Footsteps shifted toward the door. The flap to the outside lifted and closed, and Garret stepped through the beads. He retrieved his shirt and jacket from the hooks and motioned for her to join him in the front room.

Chilled, she draped her shawl over her chemise and slid her feet in her moccasins.

Stove door open, Garret was busy stuffing dried grass on top of buffalo chips.

She handed him a match from the box. "What's going on?"

The odor of sulfur stung her nose as he struck the match. *Snap. Crackle.* Red threads of grass curled and disappeared. The chips caught flame.

Garret straightened and faced her, his eyes dark in the glow of the fire. "A contingent of armed Texans are headed our way. We don't know if they're coming to fight or work out a surrender."

"Whose surrender?"

"Ours." His voice scraped.

The word ricocheted through her.

Garret leveled his hands on her shoulders. "I've got to start my men working on building barricades and earthworks. I want you to gather all the supplies you can for our family."

Men were coming to attack them. Her pulse quickened. Just like that horrible morning by the Pease River. The gunfire, smoke, and dust, her and Dancing Eagle running to their horses…

"Are you all right?" Strong, steady hands squeezed her shoulders.

She blinked up at Garret. He could be killed. Her whole body trembled. She nodded, unable to trust her voice.

"Sky, it'll be okay. You and Little Star will be safe. I've asked Carpenter to grant you and Little Star permission to hide in the stone cabin if we're attacked. But I don't think they will—"

"What about you? I don't want anything to happen. I lost—Dancing Eagle. I couldn't bear losing you too."

He slipped his hand beneath her jaw and raised her gaze to his. "Nothing's going to happen to me. You pray and gather supplies.

Get a couple of packs together in case we have to leave in a hurry. Remember the 23rd Psalm I taught you, and the other Psalms? You keep repeating them to yourself whenever you start to worry."

She'd sent her man off on raids and to battle numerous times, and she, herself, had been caught in the middle of an enemy attack more than once. This weakness was nonsense. Except the man she'd sent off so many times had died in her arms. From a wound received in battle. Death came, and she wasn't able to stop it. And neither was he.

Her fingers ached to latch onto Garret's shirt. *Hold him. Touch him. Don't let him go.*

"Sky?" Garret brushed his thumb over her chin, his brow furrowed with concern.

She inhaled and blew her breath out slowly. *Dear Lord, Help us. Watch over us. Keep us safe.* She could, she would be strong. For her husband and her baby. And she would trust the Lord. "I'll be all right. I'll do whatever is needed. You take care of yourself." Her legs wobbled, but her voice held steady.

Garret dipped his head. Her breath caught. His lips brushed hers, and then he headed for the door.

It was well past dark by the time Garret returned to his quarters. A quarter-moon drifted toward the horizon. From sunrise to sunset, he and his men had manned shovels and axes, piling up sand and dirt around the outskirts of the camp and using every nonessential stick of wood, including the picket boards surrounding his tent, as pikes driven into the ground in front of the mounds.

In the hushed, semi-dark of his front room, Garret washed up quietly, gulped down a bowl of leftover supper, and slunk to the bedroom ready to drop into bed.

Sky sat up the moment he stepped through the curtain.

Light from the extra torches around camp filtered through the canvas to highlight her slender, shapely form and the way her chemise teetered at the edges of her shoulders...a sight to revive him even if he were half dead.

As if she felt his eyes, she reached for her shawl and draped it around her shoulders. "Tell me what's happening," she whispered.

He stepped close enough for his thigh to brush against her bedcovers. They'd have to keep their voices low for Little Star's sake. "We fortified every inch of the perimeter."

"Are they coming?" She gathered her blanket against her chest.

He rubbed his hand over his eyes. "The main force has joined the Texas home troops stationed at the remains of the old Indian agency a few miles from here. We don't know their plans." He leaned a hand to the headboard. "But they're not going to hurt women and children. And we have the best fighting force in all of Texas right here at this fort. Disciplined, battle-seasoned troops. You don't have anything to worry about. And as I said, they might be here to negotiate a surrender."

"And let us go off to New Mexico Territory?"

"That'd be a miracle I'm not counting on."

"Then where would we go?" Her voice wobbled.

"I don't have all of the answers, Sky. We'll be doing good if we have any choice."

Her shoulders sagged. But her gaze scrutinized his face. "You're tired and wore out. Did you eat?"

"Yes. Thank you for dinner." He tapped his thumb against the wood. It'd be heavenly to sink down on the mattress, a real bed, even if he didn't do anything but sleep. "I want you to keep praying." Yes, that's what he should be thinking about. "Would you like for me to pray with you now before I go to sleep?"

Big eyes stared up at him. Mouth pinched, she nodded, looking so very much like a little girl.

Trousers too dirty to even think of sitting on the bed, he reached out. "Hold my hand."

Her warm hand clasped in his, he inhaled and cleared his head. "Father, I thank You for Sky and Little Star, for You blessing me with the wife of my heart and a precious daughter. I pray for Your hedge of protection around us..." The quiet words wove their way into his inner being, muting the worry that lurked in the corners of his heart. Silently, he prayed it'd be so for Sky, as well.

As he finished, he bent to kiss her head. The intoxicating scent of her hair captured his senses. He needed to get himself on the floor before he stumbled on to her lips.

Pivoting away, he removed his dirty uniform in the dark and crawled beneath his blankets.

"Garret?" Her whisper crossed the distance between them.

"Yes?"

"Maybe I could sleep on the floor tonight?"

He blinked wide.

She fumbled with her shawl. Did it slip slightly from her shoulders? "I don't mean with you. Just close. We could put blankets in between. You'd have your side, and I'd have my side. It's just that—being way up here doesn't feel safe."

Mercy. He held his breath and rolled onto his back, struggling to rein in his thoughts.

Little Star sniffled in her sleep off to his right.

"If you don't think it's a good idea—"

"It's fine." *Excellent idea.* He sat up. "I don't want you being afraid. I'll help with the bedding."

Before he could stand, she was off the bed with an arm full of covers. She rolled the quilt and stuffed it in a row between them, saving the blanket for herself. Snuggling against her pillow, she lay facing him. "It's just—too many memories of the past." Her voice was small, uncertain.

He laid his hand atop the quilt. "I understand, my precious."

"I thought Little Star was your precious girl."

"She's my baby girl. You're my precious wife."

Sky burrowed deeper in her pillow.

His voice lilted. "You're also my favorite pupil, you know." He'd relished their evenings sitting side by side at the table, helping her sound out the words as they read from the Bible. Her eagerness extended beyond copying the letters he'd written on their small chalkboard to absorbing the truths in God's Word. It had become his favorite time of the day, and from the more than occasional smile on her face, hers too.

"I'm your only pupil," she said.

"I bet if I had a hundred, you'd be quicker and brighter than them all."

She moved her hand next to his on the quilt. "You're a good teacher."

I love you. Dare he come out and say it? What if something happened to him, and he never told her? Who knew what tomorrow would bring, or the weeks ahead?

This nation was teetering on the brink of war. If he were stationed somewhere permanently, he could try to keep them with him. But there were no guarantees. He could be wounded, taken prisoner, or worse. What would become of Sky and Little Star? He hadn't even written to his family about his marriage yet. He needed a will and a plan for their future. He couldn't leave them in Texas. Or anywhere in the South.

Sky had already made it perfectly clear how much she loathed the idea of going to Pennsylvania. And his father? He couldn't do that to her. But what if that was the only safe option?

His arm ached in the spot where Dancing Eagle's arrow had struck. He listened for her breathing in the dark. Was she asleep? "Sky?"

"Yes?" Quiet, warm.

He stroked the quilt with his thumb and swallowed. "I want you to know I love you. No matter what happens."

Silence. Then footsteps outside. Guards or pickets trudging to their posts.

"Nothing to worry about," he whispered. He was talking about his men, but would she interpret it to mean his love?

~

Twilight the next day dropped like a curtain over the camp. Throughout the grueling hours of uncertainty, soldiers had manned the fortifications without a shot being fired while white flags and messengers carried out the work of parley. Through the gaps between the buildings, Sky caught glimpses of the fortifications, an eyesore thrown up to repulse the enemy, and beyond that, campfires, horses, and clusters of men with guns. More than two hundred men who'd been in such a hurry to cross Texas and steal a fort, they hadn't bothered to obtain tents.

When Garret came to tell her the news, she met him outside by the well. She leaned against the stone as his words sank in. After tomorrow morning, the bugles would blow no more across the parade grounds.

"They're ordering us to march across Texas?" Sky blew out a breath after she repeated Garret's words back to him.

He gripped his saber hilt, his posture stiff, as if the future of the fort rested upon his stance. "Captain Carpenter doesn't believe we have any choice. If we fight them, there's a good chance we'd win the battle but ignite a war. Our orders are to avoid that if at all possible."

War.

The crinkles deepened around Garret's eyes. "So we're sacrificing the fort and our pride. The troops can keep their personal firearms, their horses, and any personal possessions they can fit into the limited number of wagons available. We'll head out tomorrow morning for Indianola."

"Indianola? I don't even know where that is."

"Over four hundred miles. All the way to the coast. The plan is to have steamboats carry the troops north." He squeezed her shoulder and attempted a half-hearted smile. "We'll be all right. You start packing, and I'll be in when I can to help."

Sky wrapped her arms across her front as he headed away. North. Civilization. Hordes of people. Some huge port like Boston or New York. No place she ever wanted to set foot in. Her chest tightened. Buildings and streets with no room to see the horizon or the stars. Folks like Colonel and Mrs. Thorson and Mrs. Clark who looked down on her and her half-Indian child and would try to strip away every trace of Comanche. She clenched her fists.

A six-mule wagon rattled past, headed for the infirmary. Two more waited outside the storehouse where soldiers passed each other with crate-laden arms. Not enough wagons for more than the necessities. Garret had promised to try and find her a horse.

Voices boomed across the parade grounds, last-minute orders. Tonight would be their final night in what had become their home.

Home? When had their quarters become that? Garret's intoxicating words from last night wrapped around her like a salve. He loved her. Yet how could those three simple words melt her like hot wax and make her want to flee at the same time?

Bugles blared from the other side of the barricades. Sky shivered.

Four hundred miles and a slow-moving wagon train. What if the Texans changed their minds about letting the Federal troops evacuate unhindered before they reached the coast?

CHAPTER 36

Sky lifted the canteen to Little Star's lips. The pinto at her side drank from the bucket provided by Garret's man. Mid-March and already the sun was hot. She'd given in and donned a hat—not a bonnet, but a wide-brimmed leather hat of a ranch hand. Three weeks into their journey, dust stirred up by their two hundred horses, fifty mules, and six wagons coated everything.

She stretched her stiff legs. the almost five months at Camp Cooper had softened her. Thank goodness, she had her leggings and doeskin skirt instead of an acre of cotton hanging from her hips and tangling her legs. A new cavalry company had joined them at Fort Chadbourne. They still stared at her. Probably figured Captain Ramsey had a half-Indian wife. But none dared disrespect her. Captain Carpenter's decision for the cavalry to proceed ahead of the infantry placed Garret as the ranking officer.

At San Antonio, the entire regiment had hoped for a reprieve, but the secessionists and Texas militia had kept them on the outskirts. Only the officers were allowed in for brief periods. The fine lines at the corners of Garret's eyes had deepened since his return from the city. Yet he'd said nothing about it in the two days since.

Around her now, men tethered their horses near patches of grass, and the drivers unhooked their teams. A day's ride southeast of San Antonio and closer to the coast, at least tonight's lodging offered a semblance of trees and a creek for water. She scanned the blue jackets. Garret wasn't in sight. Neither was Lieutenant Fuller.

She adjusted the shoulder strap on the cloth-lined leather pouch which secured Little Star and marched over to a young private gathering sticks in the brush. "Have you seen Captain Ramsey?"

"Not recently, ma'am." He straightened and nudged his forage cap off his forehead. "Last time I saw 'em, he and Lieutenant Fuller was taking a walk through them trees yonder down along the creek."

"Thank you." She handed Little Star a hardtack cracker and tromped through the brush to a cluster of scrub cedar.

Much better to take a walk with Garret than hang around the wagon. Mrs. Clark didn't need help with the fire. That woman could talk from sun-up to sundown if she gave her a chance, complaining one minute and gossiping the next. Instead, Garret could fill them a couple of plates from the officers' mess. Sky would happily cook his every meal, but she wasn't about to rub elbows with Mrs. Clark over a frying pan.

A toad leapt from Sky's path and landed in the cover of green blades. Spring. Beyond the cedar, Bluebonnet blossoms dotted the slope toward the creek. An occasional scarlet burst of Indian Paintbrush completed the tapestry beneath oaks whose infant leaves unfurled from buds. It'd been years since she'd seen such lush greenery. If only they could stay here. Permanently.

In front of her, voices carried on the breeze, not more than a buzz above the gurgle of the creek.

"You do this, Charlie, and you can never go back." Garret's raised voice.

She halted in midstep and, panther-like, lowered her foot to the ground.

"I've been thinking on it for two months. I can't fight against my own state. My own people."

"Virginia might not even secede."

"I got to get home while I still can. Before war breaks out."

"I can't believe you'd consider fighting against men you've served with and led."

Little Star opened her mouth. Sky broke another cracker in half and jabbed it into the baby's hand.

A squirrel chattered from a nearby oak.

"I pray that day doesn't come, but the other choice could place me across a battlefield from my family and neighbors." Charlie groaned and shook his head. "I've made up my mind. I'll stay and help you with the troops until we get to the cutoff for Houston. Then I'm taking off. Stagecoach. Train. Probably a lot safer than those steamers they're sticking you fellows on."

She moved around a tree and crept closer.

His back to her, Garret stood by a cottonwood, hat off, hand momentarily paused in his hair. Charlie leaned his shoulder against the trunk.

Garret said something low and shook his head.

Charlie scuffed his boot against a gnarled root. "We'll always be friends. No matter what. But I've got to do this." A trail of smoke trickled up from him. Cigar odor wafted on the breeze. "If you want me to take Sky with me, I will. Get her to Pennsylvania one way or the other. I swear."

Garret stuck his hands into his pockets. "We'll see."

Sky's cheeks puffed out with an unexploded scream. *We'll see*? Her legs started moving. No more quiet. A full stomp.

Garret and Charlie jerked toward her at the crunch of leaves.

"What do you mean, 'we'll see'?" She covered the distance with Little Star bouncing against her chest in the sling.

Garret sucked in a breath.

A flock of blackbirds scattered from the treetops.

Charlie's cigar wobbled, a full wince contorting his nose. "I'd better go check on the men back at camp. I'll save you some supper."

Sky scowled at him as he retreated. He could crawl all the way to Virginia as far as she cared.

Little Star reached grubby fingers toward Garret.

Sky pulled her out of the pouch and jostled her. "So when were you going to tell me this? I have no intention of going anywhere with Charlie. No intention of going to Pennsylvania or any place near your family. My place is with you."

His lips edged upward on that last note, but not enough to erase the sour expression that clouded his features. "I didn't want to worry you."

"Why would you even think of sending me away?" She swiped a droplet of spittle from her lips.

Little Star whimpered.

Hand clamped to his cartridge belt, Garret stepped toe to toe with her. "I want you with me, Sky." His gaze bored into hers, his eyes pinched as if in pain. "I want my wife and baby girl at my side. But there's something more important."

"What?" She swatted a fly from her face.

"Keeping the two of you safe. I heard news in San Antonio. Seven states including Texas have already formed the Confederate States of America and set up some puppet president. And there's rumors that some of the secessionists in Texas aren't happy about the agreement to allow Federal troops to keep their personal weapons and horses. A few hotheads are suggesting they take us prisoner as enemy soldiers. It's only a matter of time before someone acts."

"We might be on a steamer before they do." A steamer to New York City. Her mouth went dry.

He crumpled his hat in his grip. "The whole country's gone crazy. And now—" He waved his hand toward camp. "Charlie is going to join them. Throw away his military career. Betray his country." His head dropped.

"Then why would you even think of sending me with him?" Her voice quieted as she bobbed her knees up and down, bouncing Little Star.

"I wouldn't send you with him. I was being polite. The chaplain from Company H has booked private passage on an Indianola steamer headed for the Mississippi. A quicker, safer route. He's headed for Kentucky and would put you on a train bound for—"

"I don't know the man. Little Star and I belong with you wherever that might be."

"Sky, if a battle breaks out, there's no guarantee I can protect you. And if I'm taken prisoner, I'll have no control over what happens to you. The troop steamers are no guarantee of safety either. Chaplain Brown is a man of his word. He'll put you and Little Star on a train to Pittsburgh. Besides, his wife will be going along too. Give you some female companionship."

"I don't need female companionship." She plopped Little Star on the ground next to them and landed her palms against the solid wall of his chest with a thud. "You listen to me, Garret Ramsey. The thought of going anywhere near a city makes me sick to my stomach. I'd wither away there like some prairie flower in the desert. I can't do it. I won't do it. You didn't marry yourself a city girl. I'm willing to face the enemy with you, if needed." Her fingers curled inward against the blue wool.

Garret's hands closed over hers, his voice husky. "The thought of parting from you makes me heartsick. But we've got to consider what's best for Little Star."

No. It wasn't that simple. And who was he to know what

was best for her daughter? She raised her head to say it. But her breath caught. Rich brown eyes, depths she couldn't fathom, drank her in as if she were an oasis in the Llano Escatado, the driest stretch of bareness in all of Comancheria.

Determination filled his face. He took her in his arms. Her heartbeat skidded as his mouth lowered to hers. The world disappeared.

Her whole body trembled. She swayed against him. The kiss deepened, and his arms tightened.

She couldn't, shouldn't do this. But her hands slipped around his neck, and she wove her fingers through his hair. Her limbs wouldn't obey, and neither would her lips, which softened beneath his.

Dancing Eagle's armbands cut into her flesh beneath Garret's powerful hold. She stiffened. No. She pushed against Garret's chest, struggling to quell her panic.

Garret's arms slipped from her, and she stumbled back a step. Little Star tumbled onto his boots, thrown off kilter by her mother's sudden movement. Chest rising and falling hard, his gaze clinging to Sky, he knelt to pick up the baby. The glow in his eyes could have lit every fire in camp.

That was her answer. He probably had no clue he'd given it. Cooking and cleaning and companionship weren't enough. She had to give him a reason to keep her with him that he couldn't say no to. Before they reached Indianola.

~

With her back pressed against the wheel spokes, Sky sat on the far side of the wagon, away from the main thoroughfare of soldiers and campfires. Little Star suckled in the twilight. The thought of sleeping under the wagon with Garret tonight, as usual, was stifling. Too confined, too close. Sky had hardly eaten more than a few bites for supper. Nerves. Still rattled from this afternoon. One minute, Garret had been talking about shipping her off to Pennsylvania, and the next, he'd kissed as though she was the only woman in the world.

She rubbed her hands over her sleeves and closed her eyes. Remembering Dancing Eagle riding into the village, victorious, tall, and proud, taking her onto his saddle in front of everyone. They had been so in love. Three years with him weren't enough. And yet, here she was married again. To a man whose persistent affection had managed to weave itself into every nook and cranny in her walled heart.

Beyond camp with its scattered fires, circled wagons, and staked horses, buffalo grass swayed with the evening breeze. A wolf howled in the distance, barely discernible above the low voices of men complaining and laughing, worried about the future. Where she was headed, there'd be no wolves, no buffalo. Only prim, neat horizons framed by trees or marred by structures of brick and stone. She couldn't do it.

But what choice did she have? If she ran off now, Garret would come after her. Risk his life, just as he had before. Stubborn man.

She had to stay. Get Garret to keep her with him. The army wouldn't leave good fighting troops in New York or any big city. They'd station them on the outskirts, or in the country. Maybe they'd even send them back to Texas to fight. She'd come back with Garret—wash, cook, do whatever to stay with the regiment.

Sky flinched. Little Star's teeth scraped her as the baby drifted to sleep in mid-nurse.

She adjusted her blouse. The child's precious head weighed heavy against her arm. Little Star needed to be close to her papa who loved her, not in some mansion with a man just like LeBeau who'd hate them both. She had to make Garret understand.

Pebbles crunched, along with the *click-clack* of swaying metal.

Garret strode up with a Bible in one hand and an unlit lantern in the other. "You want to read out here tonight?" He settled down beside her against the wagon wheel.

She shrugged.

He smelled of wood smoke, horse, and bay rum. His hair was damp, newly washed. "I'm sorry about this afternoon."

She ran her fingers through her short-clipped hair. It only reached a couple inches below her chin. "Which part?"

Garret took his hat off and dangled it over his knees. "For not sharing my concerns with you earlier. I know you hate the notion of leaving Texas." He ran his thumb over his hat band. "In regards to the other part, it's difficult for a fellow to regret the best kiss of his life."

Her cheeks heated at the memory, then cooled. Of course, he'd had other kisses. Other women. Lily back in Pennsylvania who his father wanted him to marry. She'd better not forget it. And there might be other women, as well, wherever the army sent him. How faithful would a man be to a wife who wouldn't allow him into her bed? To a woman he'd married with the possibility of an annulment tucked away in his mind? A nice-looking man of good character, a fine soldier and officer, as well. Such a man would not go unnoticed.

He set his hat aside and exhaled. "We'll have our ranch someday, Sky. If that's what you want. I'll build us a home in Texas when things settle down." His voice drifted toward the wild, beyond their circle of wagons and horses. A carpet of stars dazzled above them.

She smoothed her hand over Little Star's hair. A home of their own. What would it be like to work the horses with him? To gaze out into the evening, looking forward to him coming in for supper?

His breath brushed her cheek. "Can I put my arm around you? You could lay your head on my shoulder."

She traced the beaded design on Little Star's doeskin dress. "If you promise to behave." Barely more than a whisper crossed her lips.

His voice dipped. "I promise. But behaving is getting harder and harder the closer we get to the coast."

She nodded, and his warm, steady arm came around her. She nestled her head against his neck. Safe. Secure. For the moment.

A soldier moseyed past, headed for the brush. Inside the wagon behind them, Mrs. Clark murmured to her children.

Dear God, what if they only had a few evenings left together? "Garret, I want to stay with you. Little Star and I are tougher than you think. Don't send us away, at least not until after the steamboat trip. Then, when you receive your next orders, we can decide."

A swallow worked its way down his throat. "We've got a week before we reach Indianola. We'll talk about it more. And pray about it. I'll see what other news I can get. The very thought of sending my beloved wife and baby girl away makes me sick. But in the end, I'll do what I believe is best for you both."

The baby stirred on her lap. Tiny feet poked against Garret's hip.

Sky slipped her fingers through buttons of his jacket and gripped the blue wool as if it were an anchor.

His lips brushed her hair. "I love you."

I love you too. The words swelled Sky's heart, begging to burst forth, even as tears for her lost love pricked her lashes.

CHAPTER 37

Garret removed his hat and faced the Gulf of Mexico. The morning sun shimmered on the water in blinding bursts as he strolled down the pier. He squinted at the steamers and frigates anchored in the bay. Closer to shore, a myriad of schooners floated by the docks. The army had contracted the *Coatzacolas* and two more steamers to carry the Federal troops north, but they were probably still chugging past the Florida Keys or stuck in Havana.

Waves crashed against the pilings. Salt pricked his lips. His gaze settled on the *Mary Lou*, due to depart tomorrow morning with Chaplain and Mrs. Brown as passengers. He scrubbed a hand over his face. Sky and Little Star should be on that boat. The thought made his insides feel gored out into an empty hull.

Boots thudded on the pier's weathered planks. Lieutenant Jeremy Braddock walked toward him, crimson sash around his waist and hand clamped on his saber hilt. His time as an adjutant to Colonel Robert E. Lee in San Antonio before transferring to Camp Colorado, Texas, had added a veneer of army polish to the man who'd given Garret a healthy competition for earning minor demerits at West Point. And the convergence in Green Lake of all Federal troops in Texas had given Garret a chance to reunite with his friend.

Garret straightened. "Any word from Major Nichols?"

Jeremy stroked his neatly trimmed dark-brown mustache and stepped closer, his deep Texas accent coloring his words. "The *Coatzacolas* won't arrive for another three or four days. But the morning after she steams into port, Nichols is going to have our men lined up on the pier ready to go. That turncoat Major Van Dorn is stirring up a hornet's nest."

Garret studied the Texan before him. Cut of a different cloth than Charlie. This man was willing to put his country before his state and his plantation-owning family. "I had more than my fair share of Van Dorn at the Battle of Wichita Village a couple years ago."

Jeremy nodded. "Word is that he's gathering troops. Has his cap set on taking our guns. It's not good enough that we've already agreed to turn over our horses. Never mind that we were his comrades-in-arms until a couple of months ago. Rumor has it that he begged the officials in Austin for permission to take us prisoner." Jeremy squished a beetle against the weathered plank with his boot. "Nichols isn't having any of it. Says it'll be over his dead body that any of our men are taken prisoner." His eyes twinkled. "I reckon he was talking about Van Dorn's body, not his own."

Garret exhaled. He wasn't about to let Sky and Little Star stay around to get caught up in this mess.

Kaboom! Muttered curses. Garret and Jeremy pivoted. Farther down the pier, busted wood and broken melons spewing chunks of red pulp lay at the feet of two workmen. The white worker shoved the black one. "That's coming out of your pay."

Jeremy winced and shifted his gaze to the *Mary Lou*. "Are you putting your wife and the baby on the steamboat?"

"They'll be leaving tomorrow." Garret gripped his cartridge belt and studied the man before him. "What about you? I reckon your fellow Texans won't take too kindly to you sticking with us."

A bitter chuckle rattled through Jeremy's throat. "My father has already spoken to his attorney. Written me out of his will. Nothing I wanted any part of, anyway. I'd rather be penniless than lift a bullet to protect slavery." He clamped his hand on Garret's shoulder. "From what I remember of our talks at the academy, your father is much like mine."

"Unfortunately." Garret glanced at the murky water lapping against the shore. Tangles of seaweed and shell scraps dotted the sand. Sky and Little Star in his father's household for weeks. If there was any other way… "If you'll excuse me, I've got some things to take care of before I head back to camp."

"I'll meet you at the stable and ride back with you. Best not travel alone. These secessionists have their blood up." Jeremy fingered his fine-tooled holster. Slight crow lines crinkled his tanned face at the corners of his eyes. "By the way, the exit plans are for officer ears only. Nichols is concerned we might have a few traitors in our midst. Plus, that first steamer isn't going to have room for everyone. He wants to look out for our boys."

No objections there. The land surrounding Green Lake had turned into the greatest mass of Federal troops on Texas soil since the Mexican War. No wonder the Texans were getting antsy. Garret bumped his fist to his friend's arm. "See you in an hour."

Seagulls clustered around a feeding trough vying for spilled grain as Garret left the pier and headed into the clapboard town.

Past the livery stable, he fingered the letter in his pocket as he made his way down the scraggly streets to the post office. Three full pages to his parents explaining how he'd come to be married without a word to them that should shatter his father's illusions that Garret was a man he could command and Lily's aspirations of an engagement. Almost an exact copy of what he'd sent from San Antonio, but with the whole country in turmoil, who knew if the first would reach its destination. It'd be better to mail a second letter to make sure. He'd transcribe a third copy before tomorrow morning and send it with Sky as insurance.

He prayed his mother would swoop in like a hen with chicks and protect Sky from whatever his father might throw at his new daughter-in-law. He would have asked as much if he could trust his father to keep his hands off mail addressed to his mother.

Nausea roiled his stomach. All week, Sky's clear blue eyes had pleaded with him, even when her lips had not. But he couldn't let emotion trump logic and common sense. He had to do what was best for her and the baby. Would Dancing Eagle have done any better if he were in his place?

Tonight would be their last night together. For how long? All week, he'd been hoping for another kiss. The memory filled him with liquid heat. And hunger for more.

He and Sky might not even be on speaking terms by tonight after she realized he was serious about putting her on that boat tomorrow.

~

Grasses swished against Sky's doeskin skirt and leggings as she walked with Garret through the field. Behind them, rows of white tents covered the hillsides like polka-dots. Green Lake lay ahead. Ticking away the hours, the late-afternoon sun streamed through wispy white clouds. Two pelicans with their wide, dark-tipped wings and long bills coasted overhead.

The steadiness of Garret's grip on her hand helped anchor her wobbly insides. He hadn't spoken it, but the firm set of his chin and deep frown said he'd made his decision. Tonight, Sky would have one last chance to change Garret's mind. She'd give him what he'd wanted since the day they'd married. And even if their physical union failed to persuade him, it would help insulate him against the wiles of any other woman who might come along.

"Not much farther." He squeezed her hand as they tromped by cotton fields. Dozens of slaves wove their way down furrowed rows. Planting time. At the mercy of their taskmasters.

Sky shuddered. Her back still bore the scars of the whip wielded by Old Wolf's wife.

Ash and pecan trees shaded the path. The green tint of a lake shimmered ahead. Handfuls of soldiers lounged on the shore, some fishing, some washing their clothes, others swimming in the chilly water. Garret tugged her away from the view and toward a cluster of pines.

A private guarded the entrance to the grove. He saluted and stepped aside.

Low-lying branches swayed as Garret moved into the center of the enclave. Dried pine needles covered the ground, limiting the grass to scattered tufts. Sky inhaled the sweet aroma. "How did you find this place?" Privacy with a thousand soldiers in the fields behind them.

He dropped her hand and squatted by a towering white pine. "I have more surprises." He pulled a large canvas sack from beneath a bough and fished out a woven blanket.

Her shoulders tensed. "What's that for?" He'd already insisted she leave the napping Little Star with the chaplain's wife. Maybe she wasn't the only one with a plan.

His look was undiscernible. "For picnicking and talking." He proceeded to spread the blanket with a jar of candied sweet potatoes, bread, dried fish, and cakes of dried nuts and berries.

She sat mute as he divided up the assortment between two plates and barely answered his small talk as they began to eat. Nibble was more like it. Nerves had swallowed her appetite, and Garret wasn't doing much better.

Two squirrels bounced from branch to branch, chasing each other. A pinecone tumbled to the ground.

Halfway through the meal, Garret heaved a sigh. "I spoke with Lieutenant Braddock in town today. The news isn't good. The potential of armed conflict before we make it onto the steamers is high."

Sky laid her fork down, unable to stomach another bite. "You don't have to tell me the details." She fingered the fringe on her skirt. "I know you believe you're doing what's best for us. But you're wrong. I'm tougher than you realize."

He exhaled and scooted his plate to the side. "You're the strongest, gutsiest woman I know, Sky." His gaze locked onto hers. "But we've got Little Star. I'm sure you'd protect her like a lioness, but you're not immune to bullets or to bad treatment from men. Men who'd like nothing better than to take me prisoner."

"I'm sure not having us around will make life easier for you."

His eyes narrowed. "Not having you around will make me down right miserable. Lonesome for the two most precious people in the world. But war is coming. And I need my wife and child where I know they'll be safe."

War. Hadn't she seen enough fighting? The whole country at war. Not just Comancheria or the Plains. And Garret in the middle of it all. She shivered.

A bugle blared. Distant voices rang out of men heading back to camp for supper after a day off from duty. Tomorrow evening would find her and Little Star far from everything they knew. Lonesome for the man who loved them.

"Sky..." Garret touched her arm.

She pushed his hand aside. "I don't want to talk about it further." She drew her knees to her chest and crossed her arms over them. What if something happened to him?

"Okay." He removed his hat and swiped his neckerchief over his forehead. "We won't talk about the decision, but I need to share some of the arrangements with you."

A cardinal flew onto a branch. A twig dangled from its beak. Life beginning afresh. Last spring, sshe and Dancing Eagle had welcomed their newborn baby into the world. A world that was no more.

"I have two gifts for you." Garret's words snapped her from the memory.

She hugged her knees tighter as he retrieved a bundle from the sack.

"I brought them in San Antonio and hid them in the supply wagon." He laid a brown-wrapper package against her leg.

She glanced at him. "If this package is part of the preparations for my departure, I don't want anything to do with it."

He cocked his eyebrows as if to say, "Really?"

With a sharp exhale, she scooted the bundle to her lap and untied the string. A peek inside revealed sturdy dark-blue cotton. A skirt and matching bodice.

"And there's a red cloak waiting for you back at camp. Don't misunderstand," he said. "I'm fine with the way you dress. But in the North, at least while you're traveling and until you get settled in, it'd be best if you blended in."

"Dress like everyone else?" Since the day she set foot in Camp Campbell, chunks of her Comanche life had been chiseled away. Erosion with no end in sight. She bit her lip. Garret didn't intend for it to be that way. He was only trying to protect her and Little Star.

"For now. Since I won't be with you. I don't want anyone to treat you and Little Star—" A muscle twitched in his jaw. "As though you're less than the finest young mother and daughter who ever boarded a train or walked down a sidewalk."

"Words and looks from strangers won't crush me. It's your family I'm worried about. I'd rather face renegade Texans."

"I believe you're tough enough to endure my father. For a couple of months, at least, until I can figure out something better."

Two months and two thousand miles from home. And no guarantees of what the future held. "Do your parents even know who I am?"

He massaged the back of his neck. "Yes, provided the letter I sent from San Antonio reaches them in time. I sent another today and a telegram to be certain."

Almost three months of marriage, and he hadn't written them until a week ago? Had he been uncertain about committing to the marriage? Leaving an opening for an annulment?

He picked up a silvery skink that had crept onto the blanket and tossed the reptile into the trees. "I didn't want to deal with my father's outrage before I had to. Didn't want to give him a chance to try to undo anything." He sighed. "But I'm confident my mother will look out for you."

"I don't need looking after."

"Having a good friend and a caring mother-in-law can't hurt."

"I don't know about that. She hasn't even met me yet."

"She has a good heart. And she'll adore Little Star."

Little Star. She had to do what was best for her daughter. *Their* daughter now.

Garret touched her sleeve. "I've got something else for you. Something you'll like better than the dress."

Reaching deep into the sack, he tugged a large skin free of the canvas and spread it over her lap. A buffalo robe. Soft and smooth on one side with a myriad of horse images mixed with triangles surrounding a multi-colored sun, and on the other side, fur. The finest specimen she'd ever seen.

A smile edged across her lips. She smoothed her palm over the tanned hide, tracing the images, then ran her fingers through the thick wool beneath. No telling how much he'd had to pay for this. Too much. "Beautiful."

He took her hand in his and brushed his callused fingers over her knuckles. "It's so you can think of home—Texas and the ranch we'll have some day. And it's so you know I'm not trying to make you into somebody you're not. While you're away, you'll have this at night to remind you, even if by day, you have to endure a world and a life that's not what you want."

"Thank you." She swallowed. This man loved her. Would that love last across distance and time?

Shadows filled their alcove. The sun was setting. Tomorrow everything would change.

His voice grew husky. "I'll miss you terribly, my precious girl." He tucked a stray wisp of hair behind her ear. His fingers lingered on her cheek, her jaw, then along her neck and collarbone before working their way across her shoulder in one long caress that sent butterflies down her middle.

Now it would come—her chance to give him what he wanted. Maybe it would change his mind. Maybe it wouldn't. But if she wished to be remembered as more than a charity case with a child, more than someone he'd entangled himself with out of guilt, she needed to prove to him that he had himself a wife. Her heart thudded.

She'd first made love with Dancing Eagle in a grove by a river. *Don't think about that*. It'd been the first time she'd given herself of her own free will.

Garret leaned closer, filling her nostrils with the scents of bay rum, soap, and horse. His clean-shaven cheek brushed against hers as he whispered, "I arranged for two of my men to guard the entrance to make sure no one interrupts our picnic. In case I had a chance to kiss my wife."

This man wanted so much more than a kiss. She turned her head away and studied his hand on her leg. Kissing was too personal. Better act before she lost her nerve. Her voice wobbled. "Make me your wife."

He half coughed, half chuckled. "Excuse me?"

"You heard me." She worked her fingers beneath her sleeve and clasped the gold armband. Like ripping skin, she tugged it off with a shudder. And flung it to the end of the blanket.

His jaw dropped.

She removed the second band. Not like ripping skin, more like peeling off a layer of her heart.

Garret's chest rose and fell hard, his voice thick. "There's nothing I'd like better in the whole world, but are you sure you're ready?"

Sweat broke out on her palms and the back of her neck. "Make me your wife." Her voice was barely a scratch above silence, like the click of chickadee feet against bark.

He slipped a trembling hand beneath her jaw. Her whole body quivered. He lifted her face to his.

She closed her eyes.

His lips brushed her cheek, then wove their way to her ear and her neck before returning to her mouth and overtaking her lips in a kiss that melted her to her core. He pulled the buffalo robe over them as he lowered her onto the blanket.

CHAPTER 38

Garret cuddled Sky close, snug in his arms. Her head rested on his shoulder and her hand on his chest. His heart still pounded. If only they could lie there forever. No parting on the morrow. Let the country settle itself and leave them alone.

Shimmers of pink and orange showed through the tops of the pines. Sunset. He inhaled the scent of Sky's hair and nuzzled his chin against her. Beautiful. So beautiful. And to have given herself to him on their last day together? More than he'd dared hope. Glorious beyond imagination. "I love you so much."

Silence.

Sky's shoulders jerked, and she rolled away.

A chill settled over the spot she'd vacated. He shifted onto his side and drew her back against him, his arm loped over her. "You all right?" he whispered.

She clasped her hand over his, holding on as tight as she had the night he'd pulled her from the river. "Yes."

But the hitch in her voice said otherwise.

He entwined his fingers with hers. Should he press further

for an answer, or let it be? Her body jerked again. A sniffle, followed by another. She was crying.

The realization cut through him like a knife. "What's wrong?" He scooted and rolled her onto her back.

Tears clung to her lashes and stained her cheeks. "Nothing's wrong." She turned her face and curled into a ball away from him.

"Did I hurt you?" His hand trembled. "I...I was gentle."

"You didn't do anything wrong. You were fine." A muffled sob. She rubbed her hands over her bare arms. Over the slight indents in the skin where the gold bands usually clung day and night.

The realization pelted him. He wasn't good enough. She didn't love him. He wasn't the one she wanted to be lying there with. He sat up. The buffalo robe slipped to his waist. "You said you were ready. I asked you. I didn't push you. I didn't force you. I would have waited if I knew you needed more time."

"I...I thought I'd be okay. You...we're...I'm leaving tomorrow. There wasn't time to wait. I...had to make sure you knew you had a wife. That you wouldn't forget me. I had to give you a reason to come rescue me and Little Star from your parents."

His breath hissed through his teeth as he grabbed his undershirt. "I would never forget about you. You didn't have to throw yourself at me to strengthen my memory." He jabbed his arms into the sleeves and reached for his trousers.

Another muffled sob. Like a blade slicing farther into his heart.

He had to get out of there. Trousers in hand, he stuffed his legs in and stood. Words echoed in his head. *You're not good enough*. His father's voice.

Strands of hair falling across her eyes, Sky sat up and clutched the robe tight around her. "I'm sorry." She gulped. "I was afraid of losing you."

What in the world had made him think she'd fallen in love

with him? He stretched his suspenders over his shoulders and snatched his uniform shirt and boots from the ground. His temper spilled into words. "Afraid of losing me or my protection and support?"

She flinched.

A bluebell crumpled beneath his foot as he pushed his way through the boughs.

Sky's hands shook as she worked to jam the button through its hole on her bodice. Early-morning light seeped in through the half-open doorway of the A-frame tent Garret had managed to acquire for them. Dampness from a heavy dew permeated the canvas and hung in the air.

Her stomach was a mess of nerves. Garret hadn't slept at her side last night. Hadn't slept at all from the haggard look on his face when he'd shown up at dawn to make sure they'd be packed and ready to go.

He'd walked her back from the grove last night three or four feet in front of her without a word.

How could the joining of bodies drive two people so far apart? But it wasn't the joining. It was the indelible tears.

She smoothed her sweaty palms down the front of her blue cotton bodice and skirt with its ripple-like layers trimmed with satin.

Little Star sat at her feet, a yellow wooden block clamped tight in her hand. Brow knitted in fierce concentration, the baby girl attempted to set the prize on top of a smaller green block. The intended tower toppled. Just like Sky's plans.

The baby whimpered but picked up the green block again.

Wagon wheels ground on the dirt path outside.

The flap opened wide, and Garret stepped in, hat in hand. His head bumped against the six-foot-high apex pole that stretched across the length of tent. "It's time to go. It'll take us an hour to get to the pier."

All business, he didn't wait for a response. His face chiseled into a frown, he reached for her luggage—a carpet bag, buffalo robe, and a red cloak.

She gathered the blocks into a knapsack and picked up Little Star. Poor little girl had no idea how much their lives were about to change.

An open wagon and a team of mules waited a few yards away by a tree stump. The middle-aged chaplain and his dainty wife occupied a seat bolted behind the first. No privacy. No chance to talk to Garret alone. He had seen to that by picking the couple up first.

"I'll help you up to your seat." He returned to the tent and grabbed his satchel, slinging the strap over his shoulder.

"You're coming too?" She blinked at him with a sliver of hope.

"No." He glared at her as if it was the stupidest question in the world. "I'm sending a few things back with you to store at my family home."

"Papapapapa." Little Star babbled and reached out with her tiny hands as he stomped past.

He stopped dead in his tracks and pivoted. His expression softened.

Sky shoved the baby into his arms. "You haven't said good morning to your daughter yet."

Wordlessly, he wrapped his arms around the child, her frilly petticoat draped over his forearm. The lines around his eyes and mouth deepened as he stroked her dark hair and kissed her head.

Sky swallowed. He loved Little Star. But did he still love her?

Little Star grinned a toothy smile. "Papapapa. See."

He swallowed hard and sniffed. "I'll say goodbye to her at the docks." He pushed her toward Sky. "I've got to drive."

"You could let somebody else drive." She jutted out her chin and clamped her arms to her sides. "It'll be your last chance to hold your daughter until who knows when."

His eyes narrowed at her.

Correcting him in front of a fellow officer wasn't a way to win favor. But she wasn't about to let him short change Little Star because of her.

At the wagon, Chaplain Brown spoke up. "I'd be happy to drive, Captain. Give you time to say goodbye to your family."

The tips of Garret's ears reddened. "Thank you for the offer, Chaplain. But I can have one of the men do it."

"Nonsense." The chaplain swung down from his seat, his hat slipping off his balding head. "I know my way around wagons and mules. I used to be a circuit rider."

Garret nodded.

Brown helped his wife down from the back and into the front. Garret lingered so long at the back of the wagon situating the luggage, one-handed, that the chaplain assisted Sky into her seat. Probably suited her husband just fine. One less touch.

Without passing Little Star, Garret used one hand to pull himself up and settled on the seat, careful to keep several inches between him and Sky, placing the satchel in the gap.

Brown flicked the reins, and the mules snapped into motion. Sky rocked backward with the jolt, then gripped the seat as they started out on the bumpy trail. A rabbit skittered across their path and into the tall grass on the side.

Little Star clapped her hands. Garret nestled her on his lap and stared straight ahead.

The wagon rattled past the camp and the hastily thrown-up fortifications and onto the open road toward Indianola. A lifetime ago, Sky's family had traveled down the Mississippi to the

Gulf of Mexico on their way to Texas, ready for adventure and a new life. If only they had known.

Sky pressed her calves against the seat edge to hold herself steady. Garret acted as though she had the plague. Would he ever forgive her? She hadn't intended to hurt him. But yesterday had felt like a betrayal to the man who had died defending her. Even now, her heart was a tangled knot.

Now and then, Brown turned his head to chat. Garret answered with a sparsity of words. She wanted nothing to do with it. She was heading north and east to a past she never wanted to see again. And the man who'd pried his way into her heart, making himself as necessary to her wellbeing as the sunrise, not only wasn't coming with her, but was hardly speaking to her.

If only she had the buffalo robe up front with her, she'd burrow deep in its comfort and hibernate from this day and all the ones to come until Garret rescued her and Little Sky from Pennsylvania. What if he didn't send for her? *Please God, don't let that be the case.* Her meager breakfast threatened to return to her mouth.

She pulled her knapsack onto her lap and retrieved the dolly Garret had given Little Star. "She might like to play with this."

Little Star latched onto it when Garret's hands didn't move. A squeal of delight burst from her tiny lips as she swung the toy, then wrapped her arms around it before gnawing on its head.

Garret cleared his throat, his voice quiet, matter-of-fact, a current beneath his daughter's steady jabber. "We have important details to go over."

Sky tucked a strand of hair behind her ear. "I'm listening."

"You're wearing the money belt I left for you?"

"Yes, under my skirt."

"Good. Be careful with it. I've given the chaplain money for your train fare once you reach St. Louis. But all other expenses, you're to take care of out of what I've given you. Brown can help you with figuring out how much to pay for things. I've also included a letter to my parents in the satchel, and a separate one for my mother. Give it to her out of sight of my father. I've asked her to handle the mailing and receiving of any letters between us. If you have anything to write to me." He rattled the last sentence off under his breath.

"You're my best friend in the whole world. I'm going to live with your family who I don't know." She whispered, turning her head from the two people sitting in front of them. "Of course, I'll write to you. As best as I can." More like the scratchings of a school child than the prose of an elegant lady.

"Best friend?" He cocked his eyebrows. "I've always wanted a pal I could write to."

"You're more than that. Much more." She fished in the pocket slit in her skirt for a hankie. One wouldn't be enough by the time this morning was done.

"I'm not trying to force words out of you. Especially ones you don't mean." He shot her an icy glare, then turned his attention back to Little Star. "Papa's little girl is going on a big adventure. Papa's going to miss her something terrible—"

His words faded into the background as Sky squeezed her eyes shut against tears. She would have her say. Out of earshot of these people, before she boarded the boat. *Dear Lord, please let him listen. Please open his heart to me.*

A swarm of seagulls squawked overhead as Garret walked down the gangplank. The last of the luggage was aboard the *Mary Lou*, and Chaplain and Mrs. Brown stood on the upper deck with its white railing amongst a hundred other passengers. He had minutes to say his goodbyes. Hands in his pockets and stomach in his boots, he lumbered toward Sky and Little Star.

Next to a bulging cotton bale, Sky stood stiff and straight in the blue dress and red cape, looking like a picture. Firm chin, slender nose, defiant eyes. Wisps of dark hair framing her features. Untouchable beauty. A prairie flower never intended for a vase. Little Star wobbled at her feet, clutching her mommy's skirt in one hand and a puff of cotton in the other. If only he had his sketchbook and pencil. And time. He'd draw a picture to immortalize what he was saying goodbye to and had never owned

Sky ran a finger beneath her sleeve cuff as if the material chaffed her skin. He didn't have to ask to know she'd rather be five hundred miles west of here and dressed in doeskin. But if food and safety weren't a concern, would she pick a ranch with him or a tipi amongst her old village with a Comanche warrior to come calling? Three months ago, she'd had a choice between imminent danger and losing her child, or him. No wonder he'd won out against such competitors. But her heart hadn't been on the table.

He clamped one hand on his saber, solid steel to steady him while the rest of his world threatened to topple. "I wrote my parents' address on a piece of paper in the satchel. You can hire a buggy at the Pittsburgh train station to take you there. If you're short on funds by then, someone at the house can pay the driver when you arrive."

She jutted her hand toward him as if he hadn't spoken. "May I borrow your knife?"

"What?" He cocked his eyebrows.

"I'm not going to cut myself or anyone else, if that's what you're worried about."

Two dock workers in sweat-stained shirts, muscles bulging, waddled by carrying a large crate between them.

Garret crinkled his brow, then flipped open the flap on his

leather sheath and handed her his Bowie knife. Maybe she'd hack off her skirt hem, shorten it.

Instead, she grabbed a lock of her hair and sliced off a couple of inches.

He flinched. Was she going to wreck her hair just as she'd done when he'd kissed her during the storm? "Is that for Dancing Eagle?" His voice hardened. "I don't know if you can cut enough of it to erase what we did last night."

Her cheeks blazed. "Sometimes you can be the most stubborn, hard-hearted man I ever met." Lock pressed between two fingers, she knelt, lifted a coil of Little Star's black hair, and sliced.

The little girl blinked up in wonder, then pointed at a pelican perched on the railing across the pier.

Sky stood and handed him the knife by the hilt, then removed a small sachet from around her neck, one she'd made weeks ago for dried petals. With trembling hands, she tugged the leather open and inserted the locks. "For you."

His swallow stuck in his throat as she pressed the sachet into his palm.

Coal smoke wafted on the ocean breeze. The *chug-chug-chug* of the steam engine revving to life and churning waves rumbled in his ears.

"Are you going to give me something of yours?" Sky's voice wobbled.

His heart. Only, she was afraid to come near it. Might as well have tossed it in the river with the ring. "I stuck something in the satchel. Feel free to give it to my mother when you've seen enough of it."

"Maybe I won't ever be finished with it." She jutted out her chin. Defiant.

Maybe if he told her to keep devoting herself to Dancing Eagle and worshiping the ground the man had stood on, perhaps then, she'd actually give her love to someone else.

Little Star toddled over and gripped his trouser leg.

"Come here, baby girl." His voice cracked as he scooped her into his arms. He pivoted away from Sky and hugged his daughter close, pressing his cheek to her hair. He inhaled, letting her baby scent flood his memory. How big would she be by the time he saw her again? Would she remember him?

Little Star patted his face, smoothing her petal-soft palms over his stubble. He swallowed and kissed her forehead. "May the Lord watch over you and bless you."

The steamboat whistle hissed like a fiery dragon before erupting in a lonesome bellow. His chest tightened. They only had a couple of minutes.

A late passenger thudded up the gangplank, carpet bag in hand. Waves lapped against the bow of the ship.

He returned Little Star to her mother's arms.

Sky latched onto his hand and held tight. "You're wrong, Garret."

"About what?" His pulse strummed beneath her fingers on his wrist.

"I love you." The words dropped between them.

"Like a friend?"

"More than that."

"I'm not convinced." His throat felt as raw as his heart.

Tears glistened in her eyes. "I can't help that I still have feelings for him. But that doesn't mean I don't love you."

Buried thoughts spilled onto his tongue. "There's a difference between having an abiding love tucked away in the corner of your heart for a departed spouse and weeping when we make love or chopping off your hair when I kiss you."

Her mouth crumpled.

A second whistle pierced the air. No more time. He loved her. Why couldn't he say it?

What if something happened, and he never saw her again?

He grabbed her by the arms, his hands sinking deep against

the blue cotton. No armbands. He rubbed his palms from her shoulders to her elbows.

"I'm not wearing them," she whispered, her gaze piercing his, her eyes the color of a lake at sunset on a clear day.

Little Star squirmed between them.

Easy enough to take the bands off for a few hours, until she was safely on the ship. Easy enough to wait to whack her hair off until he was out of sight. But his fingers refused to let go. He closed his eyes, fighting the urge to kiss her.

With her free hand, she latched onto his jacket front and pulled him close, melting his resistance. His arms tightened around her, and he kissed her hard and rough as if he would imprint his soul upon her.

Her lips moved beneath his, sparking a fire so deep, he broke the kiss and pushed her away.

Haggard breaths. He struggled for logic and reason. "If you discover we started—a child, write to me as soon as you know. Use a code word. Say you have a package for me." His stupid body hadn't learned anything since last night. And neither had his heart.

"Sir, time to go," a dock worker called behind him. "We've got to shove off." Water churned beneath the boat.

Tears trickled down Sky's heated cheeks, her lips swollen.

Garret took Sky by the elbow and steered her to the gangplank and up its creaking boards. At the rail, he leaned his mouth close to her ear. "Let me know when you're really ready to be *my* wife. And not just ready to be rescued."

CHAPTER 39

Rain pelted Sky's cloak as she walked down the lantern-lit pathway toward the cover of the wide, wrap-around porch with its massive columns. The Ramsey house loomed in front of her, three stories of unyielding brick. Candlelight glowed behind closed curtains, illuminating two rocking chairs. The heels of her stiff leather boots, which had created no end of blisters, clicked against the stone steps as she ascended. Little Star snuggled in her arms, asleep beneath the red wool.

Sky ignored the driver as he pushed past her and settled her bags in front of the oak door with its two narrow side-windows and archway over the entrance.

"Need me to knock, ma'am?" He tipped his stovepipe hat.

"No, thank you." She released the coins from her clenched hand into his, and he hurried down the steps.

She rubbed her covered fingers. Chaplain and Mrs. Brown had seen to the minutia of detail that Garret had forgotten or spared her from. Gloves, black leather boots, and a bonnet. Making her into someone she was not. And still so beneath what these people would expect in a daughter-in-law.

Her stomach tumbled as she rapped the brass knocker against its plate. *Dear Lord, help me.*

An older man in a frock coat and a fancy cravat opened the door. "May I help you, miss?" Light from an ornate chandelier flooded the entry behind him.

Too polite to be Maxwell Ramsey. "May I speak with Mrs. Ramsey?"

The man looked her up and down, his glance lingering on the bundle of a child clutched beneath her cloak. "May I ask who is calling?"

She blinked at him. How stupid of her to have not given this some thought. Eyes-Like-Sky? Mrs. Garret Ramsey? Not Miss Maggie Logan. What if they hadn't received Garret's letter? Her tongue tripped over the words. "Mrs. Garret Ramsey."

The man's eyebrows shot up halfway to his hair line.

"What did she say, James?" A young voice spoke from the hallway. A girl of maybe eleven or twelve with brown wavy hair down to her waist poked her head around the man. The younger sister Garret had mentioned?

Her eyes widened at the sight of Sky. "You're the captive?"

That's how Garret had described her to his family?

"And you said *Mrs. Garret* Ramsey?" The girl gaped as if she'd been told a horse could talk.

James frowned at the girl. "Now, Clara, you leave the announcing to—"

"Mama? Father?" Her feet pattered against the black marble floor until she reached the carpet and the mahogany doors on the right. She burst them open. "Garret has a wife."

A sour note banged from a piano, cutting off a melody Sky had not noticed until its absence.

"Clara." A woman's voice.

Then a man's deep boom. "Nonsense."

"But it's true." The girl jumped up and down in the parlor doorway. "The captive's here, and she says she's Garret's wife."

A crash. A dish or glass smashed to the floor, followed by a muffled screech.

Sky stuttered back a step. Garret hadn't told them. The baby in her arms squirmed, digging a knee into Sky's belly. She shifted Little Star's head to her shoulder and covered the child's face with her blanket.

Clara slipped farther into the room and shut the door, Trimmed voices sounded behind the mahogany, the man's gruff tone discernible through any wood.

"You best come in." James shuffled aside.

Sky glanced at her carpetbag and buffalo robe.

"I'll set them inside. Until we see—"

See what? Sky's swallow stuck in her throat.

A middle-age lady stepped into the hallway. Her green taffeta skirt swished against the marble tile. Fine lines marked her handsome face, but a gentleness showed through her eyes that her shock could not douse. A breath shuddered through her. "You're—Garret's—you and he are... And a baby?" She placed a hand to her heart.

"Rebecca, bring her here." The voice of the man behind the door snapped, like two fingers struck together, demanding instant action.

A crease deepened between Rebecca Ramsey's brows. "James, bring our guest's luggage in and tell Fanny to heat some soup." She gripped her handkerchief and opened the door wide.

Sky's legs wobbled as she followed.

Papered walls patterned with pale swirls and images of raspberry bramble flanked the interior of the parlor, a match for the lush carpet that absorbed Sky's damp shoe prints. Her gaze skittered across the furniture-filled room. Clara hovered at the piano, hands clasped behind her back.

A fine-looking lady in a shimmering magenta dress shifted her wide-hooped skirt away from a maid scooping up slivers of crystal. A nasty curl distorted the lady's lips, marring her fine features, as she narrowed her eyes at Sky. Her gracefully sculptured hair circled like layers of light honey atop her head.

"Who are you?" A broad-chested man rose from a leather chair and strode across the thick carpet toward Sky. Streaks of gray highlighted the hair at his temples and his waxed mustache. His frock coat clung to his muscular arms as he threw his shoulders back and pinned her with his fire-poker glare. "What is this nonsense about you being Garret's wife?"

"Maxwell." Mrs. Ramsey latched onto his arm. "Give the girl room to breathe and a chance to sit. Garret told us he was sending someone for us to look after."

"Garret said he was sending some charity case. Not a wife."

Sky's chest tightened.

"Garret doesn't have a wife." The blonde sniffed and looked down her nose as if Sky were something to be swept off the carpet. "She looks like a street urchin. Doesn't even know how to wipe her feet."

"She's our guest, Lily." Mrs. Ramsey stiffened. "We need to hear her out." She tugged on her husband's arm. "Maybe Garret forgot to mention—"

Lily. The woman Garret's father wanted him to marry? More like an aristocratic wench than a fine lady. This worthless, pampered city woman had another thought coming if she thought she had a right to Sky's husband.

"You can finish cleaning up later, Maria. Leave us." Maxwell Ramsey shook off his wife's hold and smoothed his hand over the front of his gray silk waistcoat. "And you, too, Clara."

"But Father, I have a right to know if Garret's married."

"You have a right to go to your room this instant. Or else..."

Clara flipped her hair over her shoulder and stomped out of the room, followed by the maid, who bobbed with a curtsy and clunked the shards into a dustbin as she scurried out.

Mr. Ramsey hooked his thumb around his golden watch fob

as the door clicked. "Forgot to mention he had a wife, Rebecca?" He scoffed. "Or afraid to tell us he'd gotten himself in trouble?"

"He didn't get himself in trouble." Sky's voice scraped her ears. She wouldn't stand by and let the man run down her husband. "Garret rescued me. He sent a letter explaining it. But I'm sure mail service has been a mess. I have a copy." She glanced around. "In my luggage."

"We'll have James bring in your things." Mrs. Ramsey motioned to one of two scarlet high-back chairs. "Have a seat, dear. You must be exhausted." She twisted the hankie in her fingers. "Garret mentioned you to me in St. Louis."

Lily huffed.

Mr. Ramsey turned to his wife. "He told you? And you didn't say anything?"

Mrs. Ramsey pressed her lips together and inhaled slowly, as if struggling for calm. "He didn't say anything about marrying. He only said he'd rescued a young woman from the Comanche, and that she had a baby. I told you that the other day when the telegram came."

"A telegram that said..." He marched over to a writing desk in the corner of the room and snatched up a piece of paper, reading as he strode back. "'All federal soldiers to evacuate Texas. Sending someone to you. Indian captive. Please take care of her and the child as you would me.'" He rattled the paper in the air. "Not one mention of a wife."

Lily jabbed her finger toward the baby. "So let me get this straight. Garret is or is not the father of that—that infant?" The word sounded dirty in her mouth.

Sky gritted her teeth. "This child's father was a Comanche war chief. My first husband. Whom I married of my own free will."

The room fell silent save the hard breaths of Mr. Ramsey

and the *tick-tock* of the mantel clock. All three people looked as if Sky had sprouted horns.

Sky's pulse throbbed in her head. If she'd had any sense, she would have jumped aboard the western-bound stage at St. Louis instead of continuing north. Little Star felt as heavy as a sack of flour, but Sky would let her arm break off before she'd set the child down in this room with these people.

"If you thought so highly of the Indian," Lily said, "why didn't you stay with him?" Her snotty tone grated like a saw against a wound.

"Because Garret killed him." Sky clenched her hands, grappling for a smidgen of control in the face of the most obnoxious woman she'd ever met.

Mrs. Ramsey paled.

Sky shuddered. "Not like murder. There was a battle..." Her thoughts stuttered beneath the memory. "Then he married me to keep my uncle from giving my baby away to a stranger. Garret volunteered to be her papa. He wanted to make amends..." Her voice trailed off. It was so much more than that. Wasn't it? He'd come to love her. Hadn't he?

"You poor dear." Mrs. Ramsey clasped her hands together across her middle. Tears sparkled in her eyes. "I know he felt terrible about what happened to your husband." Her shoulders sagged. "He was worried about you. That's why he left St. Louis early."

"Guilt," Max muttered and tugged down the ends of his waistcoat. "Like when he was eight years old and brought home a fox kit because he'd shot its mother." He stuck out his chest and returned to his chair. "Just like him to overdo. To offer marriage to ease his conscience, when money would have sufficed."

Sky gaped at him. "This has nothing to do with money."

"Of course, it does." Max stroked his mustache. "Tell me.

Was there an official wedding? Who officiated? A medicine man or chief?"

Lily flicked the folds of her skirts outward as she strode to her scarlet chair. "I'm sure it's not a real marriage."

Sky narrowed her eyes. "It was at the fort. First week of January. A circuit rider preacher said the words over us."

"How much?" Mr. Ramsey crossed his ankle over his knee and settled deeper in his chair.

"How much of what?" Sky's brow furrowed.

"Money. Enough for housing and schooling for your daughter. Somewhere out West. And a job for you as a store clerk or cook? A few fine dresses? I could start my attorneys working on the annulment tomorrow."

"Maxwell." Mrs. Ramsey's voice snapped like a ruler across a hand.

The audacity of this man. Sky dug her nails into her palms. "I don't want a penny from you. If I had my way, and if I didn't have my daughter's safety to worry about, I'd still be in Texas. At Garret's side. Ready to pick up a rifle if needed and fight beside him."

Raised eyebrows and wide-open lips around the room met her declaration. Then a snort and smirk from Lily. "Garret sent you away. He didn't want you with him."

Word barbs so dead center to the heart of doubt that it was as if the vixen could see through her flesh. "T-that's not true." Sky stumbled through her rebuttal. "He...he sent us away to keep us safe. He wanted to protect Little Star."

"Of course, he did." Mrs. Ramsey stepped beside Sky.

Lily's lips spread in a cold smile. "Maybe that's what he said. But if he wanted you with him, he would have found a way, even if you parted for a few days. He wouldn't have sent you here to roost. He and I have courted for five years, and I'm not about to allow some dalliance on his part stop me from becoming the real Mrs. Garret Ramsey."

Little Star broke into a wail and wiggled beneath the cloak.

Sky shushed her daughter and glared at Lily. "That name's already taken."

"What did you say?" Lily rose from her chair.

Little Star's dolly tumbled to the floor.

"Poor baby." Mrs. Ramsey picked up the toy. "We've talked enough tonight, Maxwell." She turned to her husband.

"I haven't seen any letter yet." Mr. Ramsey huffed.

"You'll have your letter." *You overbearing ogre. And may I never see your face again.* Sky scooted past her mother-in-law and headed for the door. The sooner she got out of this suffocating room, the better.

Mr. Ramsey rapped his knuckles on the arm of his chair. "And I have one more question. My attorneys will want to know if Garret consummated the marriage."

"Maxwell." Mrs. Ramsey's voice echoed off the walls.

Heat flooded Sky's face. If only she could tell him what he and his attorneys could do. She pivoted and marched out of the room, almost tripping over her bags. In the hallway, she yanked the bonnet from her head and threw her cloak half way off, leaving it hanging by the portion which lay beneath the whimpering Little Star. She'd had enough of being someone she wasn't.

Behind her, the mahogany door opened and closed. Heels clicked on the marble. Mrs. Ramsey. "I'm so sorry."

"I'm leaving." Sky's voice refused to hold steady. What she wouldn't give to be able to dig her nails into that blonde's face and get a handful of pale hair. "I won't stay where I'm not welcome." No matter that her purse was empty. She'd rather sleep in a ditch if it weren't for Little Star.

"Please don't go." A gentle hand clasped her shoulder. "I beg of you." Mrs. Ramsey stepped in front of her. Her lace hair net bobbed with the weight of her wavy brown hair. "I humbly apologize for my husband's and Miss Langston's rude behavior." She clasped her handkerchief. "Not that it's an excuse, but Miss Langston has indeed waited years, expecting to marry Garret. And then to find out that he's married someone else, without a word to her?"

How had Garret even for one minute considered marrying that woman?

"As for my husband? He's used to managing his family as he does his business. I can't control him, but I will not have Garret's wife—" Mrs. Ramsey's voice faltered on the word. "And the child he's pledged to care for turned away from this house."

Sky stood tall. If only her body would stop trembling. "I'm not asking for any handouts. Or money. I came because Garret told me to."

"Then stay. The baby needs a warm, comfortable bed. You'll be my guest."

"Guest?" Sky almost choked on the word.

Mrs. Ramsey flinched. "I can't speak for the rest of them, but I'm the lady of this house, and you two are my guests."

Little Star's whimper crescendoed into a cry, and she squirmed downward, tugging at Sky's bodice.

"The little darling's hungry." Mrs. Ramsey ventured a touch to the baby blanket. "What's her name?"

Sky gazed into eyes that echoed the deep brown of Garret's. And just like him, this woman made her an offer she could hardly refuse. "Little Star." Her arms, her feet, everything ached. "I reckon we could stay the night."

Mrs. Ramsey stroked the back of the baby's head. "Pretty name." She wrapped her arms around Sky's shoulders. "Fanny should have you a nice, hot bowl of soup by now. My given name is Rebecca. What's yours?"

The warmth in the motherly touch seeped into Sky's weary frame. The marble gave way to carpet, then wood as they walked down the hall. "Eyes-Like-Sky." She'd hold onto every scrap of Comanche she could muster in this foreign, hostile place.

Garret's telegram hadn't mentioned their marriage. Had called her a captive instead of his wife. And that was before her tears beneath the buffalo robe and his hurt and anger that seemed to go soul deep. She leaned into her mother-in-law's shoulder. All she had to do was make it through the soup, and then, behind a closed bedroom door, she could pour her hurt into a pillow.

How had she been foolish enough to hope in Garret's dream of a life together?

CHAPTER 40

Beneath the buffalo robe, Sky curled her arm around Garret's sketchbook and drew her knees close. She'd found the gift tucked in the satchel Garret had packed for her. Drawings of Texas landscapes and of her and Little Sky filled the rough-edged pages. Faint scents of cedar and bay rum still wafted from the book. She'd tucked the leather-bound treasure in bed with her last night, hungry for some tangible evidence that she had been more to him than a debt to be paid or a raw spot in his conscience.

Through the pale-blue curtains, filtered sunlight cast its glow on the cherry writing desk and wardrobe. The hum of a man and a woman's raised voices had penetrated the floorboards for more than an hour. Now silence pervaded below. Had Mrs. Ramsey defended her right to allow Sky to stay?

Sky kicked her heels against the wadded bed clothes and stared at the floral pattern on the overhead canopy and drapes. What she wouldn't give to be back in Garret's quarters at Camp Cooper. To watch him play with Little Star before dinner and see his grin. Then have her lesson with him sitting at the table after Little Star was snug in bed, the Bible and slate spread in front of them. And savor the warmth of him a couple inches from her, their forearms and hands touching on occasion as she listened to the quiet, steady sound of his voice.

Garret hadn't mentioned their marriage in the telegram to his family. Why? He'd sent it before the picnic when all was well between them. She should have glanced at the two letters he'd entrusted to her care, but she'd handed both to Rebecca last night before bed, without a peek.

If only he were here now to reassure her that everything would be fine and that he still loved her no matter what. Her fingers pressed in between the sketchbook and the place on her arm where the band used to rest. There was no reason to get out of bed. Ever.

But the prattle of Little Star on the rug pulling things out of the carpetbag one item at a time said differently.

A knock.

Sky swung her legs over the bedside to the floor and grabbed her shawl.

"Mrs. Ramsey?" Fanny, the maid she'd met last night, called through the door.

Mrs. Ramsey? She didn't feel like Mrs. Garret Ramsey. Mr. Maxwell and Lily were probably already applying their efforts to making it not so. "Come in." She picked up Little Star.

Fanny bustled in with a covered silver tray. Her thick black hair, a few shades darker than her skin, rested in a knot at the base of her neck, and a white apron covered her plaid dress. "Mrs. Ramsey thought you and the baby-child might like breakfast in bed this morning."

A diplomatic way of saying they weren't welcome at the table? Fine by her. If she ever saw Mr. Ramsey or Lily again, it'd be too soon. "Thank you." Sky eyed the bacon, bread, and eggs as Fanny settled the tray on the desk and removed the lid. "Very generous helpings."

"We've got to put some meat on your bones, Miss Eyes-Like-

Sky." Fanny dusted her hands on her apron. "You mind me calling you that, or do you prefer Mrs. Ramsey?"

"Eyes-Like-Sky suits me fine." Sky jiggled Little Star on her hip.

Fanny scooted the chair out from the desk. "Have a seat and enjoy your breakfast while I make the bed."

"I can take care of the bed. And I couldn't eat in front of you."

"You go ahead and enjoy your meal. I ate earlier." Fanny smoothed her hand over the colorful designs engraved on the hide side of the buffalo robe. "Mighty fine. You part Indian?"

"I lived with the Comanche for seven years." Sky sat at the desk and grabbed the edge of the plate as Little Star latched onto it and jerked it forward.

"Mommamamma." Little Star frowned and dug her hand into the scrambled eggs.

"That baby girl's hungry." Fanny clucked her tongue at the wadded bedsheets. "You ever need me to watch the little angel, you just let me know."

Sky nibbled on a piece of bacon. "It's not settled yet, whether I'll be staying."

"According to Mrs. Ramsey, you're staying until Mr. Garret comes to fetch you." Fanny tossed the pillows aside and straightened the sheets. "She also wants me to measure you."

"Measure me?"

"For a new wardrobe. She noticed you only had the one carpetbag and figured after living on the frontier, you could use some pretty new dresses."

Sky gaped at her. "I don't want her going to any trouble. I didn't come here for that. I have a dress for nice occasions and one for work. That's plenty."

"Honey, if she wants to pamper you, let her. She feels bad about how the rest of them treated you last night. She wants to help you build a trousseau. You being Garret's wife and all, and not having a mama of your own. Think of it as a wedding present."

"A wedding present?" Rebecca was celebrating their marriage? Sky slipped her bare feet into her moccasins beside the chair. The bottoms of her leggings showed beneath her chemise.

Fanny raised an eyebrow and smiled. "Mrs. Ramsey's looking at the cottage out back. She's thinking you might like the privacy of having a place of your own for you and the little girl."

Mr. Ramsey didn't want her in the main house. Just as well. "I appreciate her generosity, but as I said, I haven't settled on whether to stay." Sky swallowed a spoonful of eggs as Little Star scooped up another handful.

"And just where else would you go, with that baby-child?" Fanny fluffed the counterpane. "Don't let Mr. Ramsey scare you off. Or Miss Stanwick either."

Sky's voice firmed. "No one's going to scare me off."

"That cottage is mighty nice. Mrs. Ramsey's spinster cousin lived there for a while until she got married last year. Not as fancy as the main house."

"I don't need fancy." Just air to breathe, an uncluttered horizon, and— "Does Miss Stanwick live here?"

Fanny scrunched up her mouth as if she'd tasted something sour. "Not officially, but her pappy and mama are away in Europe, so she's staying here for a few months. Her father's Mr. Ramsey's partner." Fanny jabbed a hand to her hip. "Thinks she's Queen Victoria. I have to remind her now and then what's what. That I's a free woman, not a slave. She doesn't take kindly to it." She turned her attention to the buffalo robe at the foot of the bed. "I don't mean to worry you none, but Mr. Ramsey headed out this morning to visit his attorney's office. Once that man starts his interfering, not many can stand up to him. I figure you had your time of fighting with the Comanches. This is a whole different battle. But don't you worry. If the Lord's fighting for you, it don't matter what that man or anyone else is up to."

The promise sunk soul deep. The Lord was with her even here.

Garret wove his way past clusters of enlisted men. The deck rocked beneath his boots as the pilot geared the engine down. New York Harbor loomed ahead. After days of sullen silence, every soldier onboard seemed to have turned out in the open air, talking and cheering, eager to set foot on shore.

A flotilla of clippers, barges, and steamers lined the port. Workers hustled about unloading crates. Derricks swung the heavier merchandise from the holds to the shore. Beyond the docks stood an infinite maze of buildings—wood, brick, and stone. Less than three years ago, Garret had disembarked from this city as a green, naive West Point graduate. He'd had no idea how soldiering in the West would tarnish his soul with killings and compromises. Bury the good in him with so much filth, it'd take a pick axe or the sparkling eyes of Sky and Little Star to find a soft spot.

The salted breeze scoured his face as he held the rail. Thirteen days at sea. Miserable. In the grip of storm-tossed waters, he'd seen more of his thin mattress and bedside bucket than the seas. No Sky, no Little Star. He hadn't realized how the sounds of their breathing had become part of his night. And their smiles, though Sky's had been rare, the light of his days.

Seagulls drifted overhead. Their *caws* clipped the air until the steamboat whistle blasted a shrill toot. The birds scattered.

Jeremy stepped up beside him. His saber clanked against the railing. "Ready to set foot on dry land?"

"More than ready." Garret tipped his hat off his forehead

"Rumor has it that command is going to keep our whole regiment together. Maybe they'll give me a company alongside yours."

"About time you earned your keep, Braddock."

"You'd better watch I don't take over your company, Ramsey."

"That'll be the day." Amusement faded from Garret's voice. "Though I need you to look after my company for a bit if the colonel can spare you. I have to send a quick telegram as soon as we get the men off the boat and receive our orders."

Jeremey cocked his eyebrows. "To your wife?"

If only it could be directly to her, instead of through the bulwark of his father. "Yes. About as personal as announcing my arrival in a newspaper, considering my entire family will likely read it."

"Good luck." The corner of Jeremy's mouth quirked up in a wry smile. "Best do what you can. I don't imagine any of us will be seeing home anytime soon." His smile dissipated as his gaze drifted to the murky water below. "I wish I had a wife waiting for me." He slapped Garret on the shoulder and walked off.

Garret leaned his forearms on the metal rail. Having a wife and having one who wanted to be with you were two different things. Maybe it was better Sky and he were apart for a while. If he saw one of those armbands again, he'd be liable to throw it into the nearest body of water. And that buffalo robe? He'd wanted to give her a piece of her home, of her former life to carry with her into the strangeness of his family's world. Not remind her of nights with Dancing Eagle. Stupid mistake on his part. He never wanted to sleep beneath that thing again, but she'd likely cling to it with all of her might.

The boat eased into port amidst a final hurrah from the men. Smells of the city hung in the air as Garret made his way down the plank—coal smoke, fish, refuse—his nose numb to the stench of the hundreds of unwashed bodies of the Second Regiment soldiers who'd made the journey with him.

Two hours later, with his luggage and men secure and on their way to the train depot, Garret stepped into the telegraph office, a two-story stone building with several clerks at the massive front counter. One of the fellows in a billed hat hobbled over, and Garret handed him his message to send. *Arrived New York. Traveling Carlisle Barracks. Did wife and child arrive safely?*

He prayed they had. There was no guarantee she'd actually listened to him. For all he knew, she could have hopped a train west or taken off at the first sight of his father. He wouldn't half blame her.

"Three dollars, sir." The clerk squinted through his spectacles.

As Garret reached into his breast pocket and pulled out his billfold, a youth with his shirt sleeves rolled to his elbows burst through the door behind the counter.

The boy waved a piece of paper. "The Confederates attacked Fort Sumter in South Carolina."

A shiver ran through Garret. War. And he'd be right in the middle of it.

~

Hands clasped in front of her, Sky braced herself as she faced her enemy across the polished mahogany desk.

Maxwell Ramsey leaned back in his chair, toying with his silver pocket watch in one hand, his gaze fixed on her. "You see my treasures?" He nodded toward the miniature steamboat in a bottle which rested near the center edge of the desk, next to a telescope and a lump of iron ore entombed in a glass jar. "My past and my future. My son's future, as well. Shipping and iron smelting. And with his knowledge of the West, we'll take Ramsey Industries across the continent."

Did the man ever bother to ask what Garret wanted? She pressed her lips together. "You wished to speak to me?"

He clicked his watch lid shut. "I have a few questions for you."

No "good afternoon" or preliminary pleasantries. Just straight to the point. She'd managed to avoid him since the night of her arrival. Overwhelmed by Rebecca's generosity in updating the furnishings in the garden cottage, Sky had spent the last three days working to turn the two rooms into a home.

"Yes?" Sky stiffened. The word *sir* stuck on her tongue.

The hard flint of his eyes measured her. Her fingers twitched, eager to tuck a stray strand of hair behind her ear, but she held them firm. In response to his summons, she'd spent a quarter hour debating whether to wear a snood to hide the shortness of her hair and whether to wear the boots Rebecca had given her. In the end, she'd tied her hair back with ribbon and donned her moccasins.

He tucked his watch in his waistcoat pocket. "I need to know the name of the man who performed the wedding. Then I want a list of all your relatives you know of and their whereabouts."

"I lived with the Comanche seven years. I haven't kept in touch with any of them." Shadowed memories trembled through her, bits of places, names, and faces lost in the fog of her past.

Maxwell tapped his fingers on his padded chair arm. "My wife is dipping into our household purse to furnish you a place to stay and clothe you and that infant. I expect your full cooperation."

That infant? Sky bit her cheek to hold back the first brunt of her temper. She dug her nails into her palms. "Little Star is your son's adopted daughter."

"We'll see about that." His grimace slid upward into a slippery smile that didn't reach his eyes. "I deal in legal contracts here, not half-hearted promises made in the heat of the night."

Cheeks aflame, she narrowed her eyes at the man. "You don't even know your son." She pivoted on her heel, grabbed her skirts, and marched for the door.

"What I do know, Miss Sky Eyes"—his voice dripped with disdain— "is that my son likes to help lost puppies. Do you really want to trap a man whose only connection to you is guilt and a bit of infatuation?"

She didn't stop to answer. Just closed her hand on the knob and jerked the door open before she told her father-in-law what she really thought of him—that he was an overbearing bully whose heart was as hard as that chunk of iron ore on his desk, who thought money ruled the world.

Rebecca hurried toward Sky across the marble floor at twice her normal speed, her green-and-brown plaid skirt swishing across its hoop. Two pieces of paper dangled from her hand. "Garret made it safely to New York." Tears filled her eyes.

"Then what's wrong?" Sky closed the distance.

"War." Rebecca heaved a sigh and gripped Sky's hand. "We're at war."

~

Sky sat down at her small dining table. The buffalo robe lay across her lap, and the sketchbook rested on her pillow, reminders of Garret's care for her. A fire crackled in the fireplace. In the week since her arrival, this had become a warm, secure home, provided by Garret's mother. If only Garret were at her side—and their little cottage a couple thousand miles away.

Her fingers strangled the pen as she stared at the blank

page. A dictionary lay at her elbow. She wasn't about to send Garret a letter filled with misspellings.

What should she say to him? He'd been angry and closed off like a wall when they'd parted, except for that kiss which had shaken her to her toes. Yet his final words, "Let me know when you're ready to be my wife," still grated. The hardness had settled like salt after the warmth of his embrace had evaporated.

And now war. For how long? Her stomach clenched. *Dear God, please protect him. Bring him home to me. You've given us this marriage, so please help us save it. Help me follow You, Lord Jesus. You are with me though the earth shake and the heavens fall. You will uphold me in Your hand.* Her pen scraped across the page.

April 14th, 1861

Dearest Garret,

Dare she use the term of endearment?

I thank God you are safe. I hear you're on your way to Washington. Little Star and I are well. Your mother has been very kind. She's furnished the cottage on the back of the property for Little Star and me. A four-poster bed, wardrobe, and dressing table for the back room, and a dining table, sofa, rocking chair and cupboard for the front. I'd be happy cooking in the fireplace, but she has a full-size cook stove on order.

She would not mention the dresses. Surprise him instead.

Most of the time, your father and I pretend the other doesn't exist.

She wouldn't complain further. And she wouldn't waste her ink on Lily.

Little Star said "bye-bye" the other day. She can walk without holding on to anything now. I'm saddened to hear about Fort Sumter. I pray that the Lord will watch over you.

God had not intervened to save Dancing Eagle. Why should she expect—

No. She would not think like that. She dug her nails into her palms and closed her eyes. She whispered, "Dear Lord, help my unbelief." With a shudder, she picked up her pen.

Little Star and I miss you. Greatly. Come home when you can. I don't have a package for you. Sky.

Would he be relieved or saddened by the news? She'd thought she'd welcome her monthly, but somehow, its arrival brought her no joy. A child between them would have offered hope.

Garret stretched out on his bedroll, letter in hand. Shadows danced on the canvas walls at the whim of a flickering candle. A lukewarm cup of coffee sat at his elbow. Mere feet from his quarters, troops tromped down the lane which separated his camp from the War Department, whose upper windows glowed even at this late hour. Farther down the street, rowdy voices called out, men too full of liquor and liable to end up in the stockade before the night was out. In the warmth of early May, this city never slept.

Garret stared at the words on the page. His gaze lingered on *Dearest*, then swept over the rest. It wasn't quite a love letter. More like something one would write to a friend. He had to keep in mind that Sky had written it, knowing his mother might read it, or possibly even his father. How forthcoming could she be? But all of the logic in the world couldn't argue away the fact that he felt discarded, second best, not dear.

No package for him. Thank God, they had not started a child. He rolled onto his back, gripping the letter tight. But a child, one of their own together, part of his blood...maybe that would have bridged the wound between them and finally made her his.

Miss you. Greatly. Did she mean it? Of course, she did. She was stuck there with his father in the main house. Probably couldn't wait for him or someone else to come rescue her. He was wrong to let the bitterness take root. But knowing it and stopping it were two different things. *Dear God, help my attitude.*

He swallowed hard and undid his upper jacket buttons. Digging beneath his shirt collar, he tugged out the small leather pouch Sky had given him before she'd boarded the steamboat in Indianola. He squeezed the soft leather against his palm. What he wouldn't give to hold his wife close and know she wanted to be held by him.

CHAPTER 41

Sky stuffed the crumpled letter into her apron pocket and stepped out of the shade into the sweltering heat. Dogwoods in full leaf, blooms wilted, lined the crushed-rock pathways, along with trellises of morning glories and roses, dividing the different sections of the Ramsey garden.

What would it be like to stroll with Garret beneath the vines, inhaling the sweet aromas?

Little Star sat there now beneath the archway, dropping pebbles into a tin bucket. If only they could all three be together again as a family. Far from here.

With a frown, Sky put on her straw hat and tied it under her chin. Only three letters in three months, and the last one four weeks ago. Maybe Garret had written more, and the letters had gotten lost. Or perhaps Mr. Ramsey was intercepting their correspondence. Rebecca had left two weeks ago for Baltimore to help Garret's older sister who was about to give birth. With her gone, there was no telling what Mr. Ramsey might try.

Sky reached for Little Star's hand and grabbed the bucket handle in the other. "Come on, baby girl, let's pick some blackberries."

"Bebbies," Little Star chattered as they strolled down the path toward the berry plots.

Sky swatted a fly.

There could be half a dozen reasons she hadn't received more letters from Garret, or it could be Garret had little desire to write to her. His lack of warmth echoed in what he didn't say.

He described life in Washington and asked about Little Star. Sometimes he'd recommend a trail or creek for her to visit in the area. Brief, distant. Good letters for a friend or brother. Did he assume that's what she wanted? The word *love* seemed to have evaporated from his vocabulary. Her footsteps dragged along the path.

Once she and Little Star reached the rows of bushes, she settled the child in the middle of a patch of loose dirt and gave her a spoon. The buzz of cicadas filled the air. Harmless, but nasty-looking creatures.

Sky squatted and reached for a handful of plump berries.

Footsteps crunched on gravel. Lily...in delicate coral silk, wide hoops, and a bonnet plaited with ribbons and daisies. The exact opposite of a cicada. Beautiful on the surface, far from harmless, and on the inside, uglier than any insect that ever shed a skin.

Sky swiped her forearm across her sweaty brow and stood, feet planted.

Lily sashayed over. "Mercy, it sure is hot out here today." She touched her handkerchief to her neck. "Sky, could you be a dear and go fetch me my fan?"

The nerve of the woman. Sky fixed her with a glare that could freeze a furnace. "If you were on your death bed, I might consider it."

Lily smirked and slipped a folded pamphlet from her pocket. "I reckon you must have heard about my little visit to Washington, then."

Sky stiffened.

"Oh? You didn't? Well, Garret sends his regards." She batted her lashes and tossed her head as if she had an audience of a dozen gentleman callers. "You should have seen how handsome he looked in his new major's uniform. He was so busy. His regiment was getting ready to move out. We only had an afternoon to visit. Privately, that is. Then we had the dinner with his commanding officer."

Major. Private visit. Dinner.

Sky dug her nails into her glove-covered palms. Her pulse pounded in her temples. How sweet it'd be to wrap her hands around the tart's skinny white throat and throttle the woman. "Garret Ramsey is a married man." Her stupid voice shook.

Lily's lips curled up in a smile that would have fit any Jezebel. "From what I hear, Mr. Maxwell Ramsey's detectives haven't been able to locate a record of the union. It appears the marriage was never officially registered with the courthouse in the county where you had the ceremony." She unfolded the flag-covered pamphlet and fanned herself. "Maybe Garret wanted to give himself a way out. Or maybe it's just pure luck. A blessing from God."

You don't know the first thing about God, you lying tramp.

Sky ground her teeth and pressed her lips against the words that threatened to explode. She would not give this woman the satisfaction. She yanked Little Star away from a blackberry bush and swung the child to her hip. "I know what Garret intended. And a missing piece of paper won't come between me and him." Of course not. Dancing Eagle and her tears had already ripped a gaping hole neither knew how to reach across. She pivoted and marched toward the cottage. The tin bucket rattled to the ground.

"You keeping telling yourself that, Sky-pie. But he's been in Washington, a day's train ride away, and hasn't sent for you once."

"He didn't send for you either," Sky muttered under her

breath and kicked a clod of dirt out of her way. "At least I don't have to throw myself at him like some wench."

~

Sky burst into the main kitchen with Little Star on her hip. Why couldn't she stop the ridiculous trembling that gripped her?

Bunches of dried herbs hung from the ceiling. The aroma of chicken drifted from the roaster.

A hymn on her lips, Fanny glanced up from the work table. A bandana secured her hair away from her face as she massaged her fingers in a gooey glob of flour and lard. "What's wrong, Miss Sky?

"Did Lily go to Washington?"

Fanny straightened. "I reckon."

"You knew, and you didn't tell me?" Sky's shoulders sagged. Little Star wiggled, eager for the floor. Sky plopped her on the stone surface next to a basket of carrots.

"I'd only heard rumors, child." Fanny ground the palm of her hands into the dough. "I figured there was no use worrying you. Didn't know for sure until this morning."

"No use worrying me? If that woman even thinks of going near my husband again, I want to know about it. Please." Sky gripped the edge of the table. "And what's this about him being a major?"

Fanny kneaded the dough. "That was even news to Mr. Ramsey. Lily said the promotion came through the day before she arrived. She brought a letter from Garret for the family explaining it all. Of course, with Miss Rebecca gone, Mr. Ramsey hoarded it for himself." Fanny clicked her tongue. "I bet a letter will come for you any day now, Miss Sky."

Sky swatted at the air. "If Garret isn't too busy visiting."

Fanny arched her eyebrows. "If Mr. Garret loved Miss Stanwick, he'd have married her long ago, child."

"There's a difference between marrying and being tempted." Sky's cheeks heated at her own boldness.

Fanny frowned. "I don't believe Rebecca's boy would ever be unfaithful to his wife. No, siree." She plopped the dough on the tabletop and grabbed a rolling pin. "I can't speak as to what happened before he wed you, but he's a man of his word once he gives it."

A word could be mighty cold and empty if the heart wasn't in it. Tears stung her eyes as she scooped up Little Star. "But what if Garret isn't bound? Lily said something about Mr. Ramsey claiming our marriage wasn't registered at the courthouse. Would that, could that mean—?"

Her eyes warm and sure, Fanny's brow crinkled as she reached a floured hand to Sky's shoulder. "I don't know about all them fancy court rules, child. And I have no idea what Mr. Ramsey might dream up to cause trouble. But if Mr. Garret has his heart set on you, nothing Mr. Ramsey or the whole lot of them can do will change him."

~

Wrapped in the buffalo robe, Sky stood in the open doorway of the cottage, soaking in the cool night air. The sweet aroma of the rose-laden trellises saturated the moonlit porch, but her stomach refused to calm. Fanny was wrong. There was no guarantee Garret's heart belonged to Sky.

What should she say to Garret? Dare she confront him? She was the one who had mourned after they'd lain together.

What if she'd spoiled everything? He hadn't sent for her. Would he?

A mantel clock chimed over the fireplace. She latched the door and sat down at her table. Her pen scorched the paper.

Lily told me of her visit with you. How could you give one friendly word to such a Jezebel? You have a wife, if you feel like visiting. Have you forgotten how to write?

No. Perfect way to push him further away. She threw down the pen and wadded the page in her fist.

What right did she have to confront Garret? She squeezed her eyes shut against a memory. Gabriella. The Mexican slave girl Dancing Eagle had brought back from a raid to help Sky after Little Star was born. He gave his word the girl would be a servant not a second wife, although the latter was acceptable according to Comanche culture. He hardly even looked at the girl, but Sky had seen him go into the girl's tipi once. Probably nothing. But she'd never know. He'd died two days later.

She would not go through the same torture with Garret. If she found out he had anything to do with Lily, she and Little Star would be gone from this house, gone from this state, gone from his life.

Ridiculous. She slapped her hand on the table. All she had was Lily's word. The woman could create an entire affair out of one hello. She could not let this woman get to her.

I heard about your visit with Lily.

In the shade of a tree a couple of blocks from the War Department, Garret stared at the letter dated July 22nd. One sentence. *I heard about your visit with Lily.* What was he supposed to make of that? Nothing else on the entire page, except *Garret* had replaced *Dearest Garret*, and she'd signed it *Mrs. Garret Ramsey* instead of *Sky*. She'd used a whole sheet of paper, an envelope, and postage for one sentence. Was she yelling at him? Accusing him of something? Or did she even care?

His visit with Lily? He hadn't asked for it. Hadn't wanted it.

Had been surprised when Colonel Thorson told him he had a visitor. What in the devil had Lily said to Sky? Whatever it was, it was only enough to get one sentence out of his wife. But somehow, the statement felt like a noose.

Maybe Sky was jealous. The sweet taste caught him off-guard. No, if she cared enough to be jealous and with her fiery disposition, she'd fill a page with ranting and putting him in his place as if he'd done something wrong. Or maybe her one sentence was her version of an icy glare, worse than a heated rant?

He rubbed the back of his neck. His thumb brushed the bandage which covered the flesh wound he'd received ten days ago at Bull Run. Another inch to the right could have meant his life. It had been the sorriest excuse for a battle he'd ever seen. His regiment had held steady, but the thirty thousand raw Federal recruits had panicked when they'd been flanked. The greenhorns had fled the field in a mad race back to Washington. Anyone brave enough to hold ground had been ripe for capture or a bullet.

Dear Sky,

I hope you and Little Star are well. You didn't ask about how the battle of Bull Run went or my part in it...

He gave her a paragraph about the battle and a sentence about his wound before addressing her statement.

Miss Stanwick came to visit me of her own accord and initiative without my knowledge or permission. Once she was here, I felt obliged to give her a tour, and Colonel Thorson invited her to join us for dinner. I walked her to her rooms where she was staying with family friends, and that was the last I saw of her. I explained to her that in the future, it wouldn't be proper for her to call on me and that I wouldn't be available.

I haven't heard much from you lately...

Other words begged to be written. *I miss you and Little Star. I'm miserable over how we parted. I love you. You're the only woman I care about. The only woman I want.*

He touched the pen tip to the paper, then pulled it back. Did she care? Or was her heart still buried in a grave?

How was she holding up against his father with his mother away in Baltimore?

Lily had brought a letter from his father. Too bad his father couldn't fit his anger into one sentence instead of yelling across the entire page.

If he were certain he'd be in Washington for an extended period of time, he could send for Sky and Little Star. But he had no way of knowing whether he'd be here six months or ordered to ride for Richmond, Virginia, the capital of the Confederacy, in a month. And if Sky showed up with those armbands on, or pulled away when he tried to kiss her?

He'd been foolish to think his pledge to provide for and protect her could nullify all that divided them.

CHAPTER 42

Chilled air nipped at Sky's cheeks as she strode down the lane, returning from a walk past the wooded estates of the other Pittsburgh elite on Squirrel Hill beyond the outskirts of the city. Oblivious to the tide of gray which had swallowed the sun, Little Star pitter-patted ahead, crunching leaves underfoot. Summer had dragged into fall. Garret had sent one letter explaining his visit with Lily and then nothing. Camp Cooper and her days with Garret there seemed but a dream.

Of course, Lily didn't help. That Jezebel stopped by a couple of weeks ago taunting her with an envelope she claimed was from Garret. "Still hasn't sent for you yet, huh?"

The woman was worse than a headful of lice.

A raindrop splattered on Sky's cheek and then another. "Come on, baby girl." She scooped Little Star into her arms and ran. A chilly November wind rustled the branches overhead. She shivered as the sprinkling expanded to penny-size drops pelting every dry inch.

By the time Sky clomped onto her cottage porch, their outer garments clung to them like seaweed.

Little Star rubbed her eyes. "Wain. Wain."

"We'll get you dry." Sky grabbed the quilt from the back of the rocker beneath the roof. "Get you inside—"

The door was open an inch. She hadn't left it that way.

Bundling the quilt around Little Star, she nudged the door open. Perhaps Fanny had stopped by—

She stuttered to a stop on her threshold.

Maxwell Ramsey. In her cottage. Her home. He glanced up from the straight-back chair. His wool coat and hat lay on the table.

Her knees wobbled. "Is Garret all right?"

"As far as I know." He collapsed his steepled fingers and straightened. A half-smoked cigar dangled on the edge of one of her plates.

Was there no limits to this man's audacity? Water pooled from her skirt hem and onto the floor. "What are you doing here?"

Little Star peeked out of the quilt and pointed. "*Puniitu*."

Maxwell scowled. "Baby talk? Or is that some Indian word?"

Sky gently roughed the quilt over her daughter, drying her hair. "It means *look* or *see*."

"Just as I thought. Raising her to be a little Indian." His gaze fell to Little Star's moccasin-covered feet.

"Can I help you with something?" She swiped her wrist over her forehead. "I need to dry off and make dinner. If you'll excuse—"

Her gaze narrowed. Garret's sketchbook lay open on the table, half covered by Maxwell's hat, not beneath the extra pillow on the bed where she kept it. "How dare you go through my possessions!" She marched across the room. "That's mine."

"Garret has a fascination with you." He nodded toward the sketch of her.

Hands trembling, she snapped the book closed, snatched it up, and quick-stepped back to the threshold. "As I said, I have dinner to make. And this is my house." Her voice quivered on the word *my*. He could take it all away from her with the snap of his fingers.

A smile slithered across his face. "I have a proposition for you, Miss Logan. Or do you prefer Miss Sky?"

"I prefer Mrs. Garret Ramsey."

Little Star wiggled and threw her head sideways. "Wet go." She dropped her dolly onto the floor.

"Might as well let her play while we talk." He pulled a folded paper from his inner coat pocket.

"I don't have anything to discuss with you."

"Elizabeth Logan."

She startled. "My sister?" She lowered Little Star to the ground.

"Precisely. Your only living family." He tapped the papers against his knee. "The proficiency of my detectives should not be underestimated."

"What about my sister?" She hugged the quilt close, the sketchbook wrapped in a fold.

Ramsey stretched his legs out in front of him. "I have good word that your sister is alive and well with the Nokanis Comanche."

Yes, it rang true. Beth had been with the Nokanis last time she'd seen her. Beth was alive and safe. Thank goodness. "But you wouldn't waste your time and money to bring me news."

"No." His eyes glistened. "I'm willing to help you find her. I'll pay your way to Texas and hire a guide. What you do once you locate her is up to you. Stay with her tribe? Or head off to Mexico? Settle in Texas? I'll provide the funds." He puffed out his chest and laid the papers on the table. "All you have to do is sign these documents. They state the marriage was a sham. Hastily arranged to save the child from being taken from you."

Her head swam. Was that all it had been? Garret had loved her at some point. There in the middle, between the desperate beginning and hurtful ending. A soul-deep shiver ran through her. Return to the Comanches?

Ramsey's voice reeked of confidence. "My attorneys assure me that the annulment application should be successful, but we can always throw in the argument that you were beside yourself with grief at the time, not in your right mind."

"Dadadada." Little Star banged a wooden spoon against a pan.

Sky winced. The noise echoed into a throb behind her forehead.

"If you're afraid to risk the Comanche, you could travel to Texas and live on your own. Either way, you'll have the money."

As if money could fix everything. She rubbed her hands over her arms. "Whatever I do, it won't be because I'm afraid." Her voice didn't sound like her own. She had to get away from this snake-oil salesman.

"Think it over. You can have until December. A whole month." He stood and hitched his trousers. "If you care for Garret, you won't tie him to a hasty decision he made out of the kindness of his heart."

She glared at him. "You don't know the first thing about kindness, Mr. Ramsey." She marched over and scooped Little Star to her hip, clutching the quilt-covered sketchbook in her other hand. "And as long as this cottage is where I live, you're not welcome inside."

"I'll leave the papers for your perusal." He tipped his hat as he crossed the threshold. "I don't claim to be a benevolent benefactor, Miss Logan, just a man who is offering you what you claim to want."

Garret gripped the cushioned chair arms in the parlor of regimental headquarters to keep his hands from balling into fists. Thank goodness, his father had arrived after dinner. Sitting across the table from the man would have been too much. The late-November rain pelted the windows, offering no opportunity to move this discussion outdoors.

His father slapped the papers down on the end table, barely missing the lamp. "I'm offering Miss Logan everything she wants and paying a pretty penny for it. Just to clean up your mess."

Every hair on Garret's arms bristled. "Mrs. Garret Ramsey. If her name was still Miss Logan, you wouldn't be here."

Voices sounded beyond the parlor door. The requisitioned house a few blocks from the center of Washington hummed with activity from dawn to long after dusk. The parlor and Garret's own room offered them the only hope of privacy, and he had no desire to deal with his father in the sanctuary of his quarters.

His father scowled. "I'm taking time out of my busy schedule to save you from being unequally yoked for the rest of your years." He shoved his fingers through his smoothly combed hair. The gray at his temples had deepened in the last year. "You think I was never taken by a pretty face or comely figure in my bachelor days? But I waited until I found your mother. A fine lady suited for my path."

"Don't bring Mother into this." Garret stood and waved his hands at the papers. "She wouldn't support your plan. Probably doesn't know about it."

"My point was..." His father puffed out his chest. His silk waistcoat stretched against the movement. "That I married the right woman. The temporary Mrs. Garret Ramsey goes around in moccasins and buckskin leggings. Sleeps beneath a buffalo hide, and has her daughter babbling Comanche. Do you think I dreamed up this idea of her wanting to go back to Texas?"

The buffalo robe. Garret pivoted toward the fireplace with its tidy blaze cracking in the hearth. His stomach felt like lead. Of course, Sky wanted to return to Texas. He'd had to practically drag her from there. And now...the opportunity to find her sister? A sister she'd claimed was dead.

She'd had no choice but to marry him. Now she had a way out.

A match struck. Sulfur stung his nose. Cigar smoke wafted his way as his father stepped up beside him on the thin, paisley carpet. "You did your duty. You saved her child. If you care about her, you'll let her go."

CHAPTER 43

Sky moved her finger along the rough surface of the paper. Garret's skill with a pencil had captured her Comanche dance at their wedding party in fine detail and frozen the swirling folds of her blue dress in mid-motion, a moment locked in time. If only she could dance like that again. This time it would be for him. To please his heart and his eyes. The way he'd looked at her that night still brought heat to her cheeks.

Her shawl slipped from her shoulders as she turned the page to a sketch of her cuddling Little Star in her arms. She'd never seen Garret draw her except for the time in front of her Sibley tent, back when he was nothing more to her than the officer who had killed her husband and tried to make amends. But he had pages of drawings of her.

She flipped toward the end. Red Rock Canyon. He'd risked his life to come find her and Little Star. Not find —rescue.

Texas filled earlier pages. Palo Duro Canyon. Cacti. Prairie flowers interwoven with waving prairie grass. Garret captured the heart of the place. And her. The thought of going back there without him left a hollow spot all the way through her middle and to her knees.

She hugged the book and inhaled the sweet aroma of leather mingled with bay rum. How did it still smell of him after all these months?

The early December wind rattled the windows of her cottage. The rocking chair creaked as she drew her feet beneath her. Was Garret in this weather in a tent somewhere in Virginia? Or was he in a fancy parlor chatting with some general's daughter, contemplating how a simple signature could free him from the burden of his good deed? No. She'd been more to him than that. These drawings proved it.

Her glance fell to the papers on the table.

Texas and the unbounded prairie. Fresh air without a trace of coal smoke. The freedom to ride. Wind in her hair, sun on her face.

Her sister Beth. Morning Fawn. Ten at the time of their capture. Beth would slip her food...until Beth's new family moved to a different village. Better that way. Better for her sister to not see what she had become before Dancing Eagle rescued her. They'd seen each other a couple of times since then, on the trade route to Mexico.

Oh to be reunited.

If she left now, there'd be a hole in her heart and Little Star's life that the whole state of Texas couldn't fill. She couldn't sign the papers without knowing if there was still hope. Garret had loved her. Once. Surely, she had not lost her chance with him forever.

A few days later, Sky shivered as she opened the cottage door with Little Star underfoot. If Mr. Ramsey had come to gloat again, she'd slam the door in his face. According to him, Garret was eager to sign the papers, provided she agreed. Maybe it was a lie, but the uncertainty gnawed beneath her skin.

Rebecca Ramsey stood there, dressed in her green velvet traveling dress and cloak.

Sky gasped. "You're back?"

"Finally. Just arrived this morning." Her face lit up. "My goodness. What do we have here? This big girl can't be Little Star?"

The child darted behind Sky's skirt.

"Look what I found." Rebecca stepped aside. A wooden rocking horse, chestnut brown and the right size for a young child, sat on the stone stoop.

Little Star peeked out and squealed. "Horsey."

"Yes, go see." Sky nudged her forward.

Little Star toddled over, fingers in her mouth and eyes wide.

Rebecca knelt. "You want to help me take the horsey inside? He's looking for a big girl who wants to ride." She reached out her hand, and Little Star took hold.

Sky smiled as she stepped aside and watched Garret's mother position the horse and settle the child on top.

Click-clack, click-clack. Little Star galloped as Rebecca stepped over to Sky. "I'm sorry I've been gone so long."

"Your daughter and new grandbaby needed you." Sky shrugged. "We've been fine." Her tongue tripped over the last word.

"How have you really been?" Rebecca offered her hands in greeting.

The deep warmth in her tone, so much like a loving mother's, snapped Sky's heart open. Tears stung her eyes.

"Oh honey, come here." Rebecca opened her arms.

Rebecca's arms drew her like a magnet. She fell into them, and her body shook as a thundershower of tears burst forth.

"What has happened?" Rebecca patted Sky's back.

Words spilled forth. "I don't know if Garret loves me. He hardly writes." She sniffled. "We had a terrible falling out the day before we parted. He doesn't think I love him—" So much drainage filled her nose, she couldn't breathe. She grabbed her apron hem and blew.

Rebecca belatedly handed her a handkerchief.

Taking a step back and folding the dirty end of her apron into her waistband, Sky wiped her eyes and nose. "He—I was still grieving my late husband. It was too much, too soon. And now...Mr. Ramsey made me this offer to go back to Texas."

The furrow deepened on Rebecca's brow. "Mr. Ramsey told me about his proposition this morning. But no one is going to force you to do anything. I'll see to that."

"I can't decide without seeing Garret first. And the decision might not be up to me. Mr. Ramsey took the papers to him. He claims Garret is going to sign them."

"No one has signed anything yet." Rebecca smiled and pulled a telegram out of her pocket. "This arrived today." She handed the crisp paper to Sky. "I wanted to hear your thoughts before I showed this to you."

Sky rubbed her finger over the words. *Coming home on leave as soon as I finish one more mission. End of December at the latest. Keep Sky there until I arrive. Garret.*

He wanted to see her. To ask her to remain his wife? Or to say his farewells? Either way, she'd have a chance to persuade him. God had opened a door.

CHAPTER 44

Rain dripped from brim of Garret's Hardee hat and trickled in streaks down his rubberized poncho. A few drops managed to sneak beneath his collar and breach his undershirt. Miserable weather. Better suited for an evening by a warm hearth than plodding down the backside of the Blue Ridge Mountains after midnight. But General Thomas needed a map of the passes and trails leading into the Shenandoah Valley, and Colonel Thorson had volunteered Garret as the man for the job.

The hooves of his men's horses squished behind him as they sloshed their way along the path. A small company of cavalry, enough men to provide firepower if they came upon the enemy, but hopefully not enough to garner the attention of General Stonewall Jackson or his renegade commander, Turner Ashby.

General Thomas had promised him a month's leave at the completion of the mission. What if Sky left before he arrived home? Garret gripped his reins and kneed his roan gelding forward. She'd wait if she cared about him. But who was he kidding? His father had provided her the opportunity to be reunited with her only living family member. Every week she delayed heading west, the chances of finding her sister shrank. And since his parting from Sky, he'd given her every reason to hop on that train.

You don't win a battle by giving up. His father, of all people, had said that to him when he was a boy. But that's exactly what he'd done the last eight months. No more. He was going to get back to Pittsburgh, put his injured heart aside, and court his wife.

Mud splashed. Jeremy drew up alongside, the man's face a pale spot between his cap and his poncho. "Scout's back, sir. Found us a cave for the night on the south side of this ridge."

"What else did Baker say?"

Jeremy leaned forward in his saddle. "He spoke to a local Unionist. The lady said Ashby and his men passed through Front Royal yesterday."

"Twenty miles from here." Garret jerked his horse to a halt. "And what makes Baker certain this lady can be trusted?"

"He seemed pretty confident."

"And what if she was sweet-talking him and rode off the minute he left to report our presence to Ashby?"

Jeremy swiped rain from his eyes. "Baker's not one to be swayed by a pretty face, but there's no guarantee."

"Forget the cave." Garret straightened. "We're riding through the night."

"Yes, sir," came his cheerless but faithful reply. He drew his reins and headed back to alert the men.

A cough or a sneeze now and then intermingled with the plodding of horses as the double column wove its way along in the inky dark.

Halfway through the night, the rain stopped, and a quarter moon slid from behind the clouds. Garret nudged his horse to a trot. They'd find a good piece of woods and stop at daybreak.

The path headed into a clearing. A low-hanging fog

hovered over a field of cornstalk stubble, the wasted leavenings of a hasty harvest. In the distance, an owl hooted. The hair on Garret's arms bristled. An owl? It sounded more like a coyote. Like some Comanche signal right before—

"Whoa." He yanked on the reins. His men halted, two-thirds of them out of the woods and in the clearing. Silence.

Jeremy rode forward. "You thinking what I'm thinking?"

"Fall back to the trees, Lieut—"

A shot cracked the air. His friend jerked and crumpled forward.

A banshee Rebel yell tore through the night. Flashes exploded from the tree line ahead. *Boom. Boom. Boom.* Gunfire erupted from the front and from the mist-covered field.

"Return fire," Garret yelled, with a quick glance at his wounded friend. Retreat to the crowded trees where they could be surrounded, or do the unexpected? Less than a breath to decide. He turned his mount toward the field. "Charge!" They'd take a chance on breaking through the enemy line or be swallowed up.

With a sharp groan, Jeremy raised himself from his horse's neck and drew his weapon.

Garret dug his heels into his gelding and drove the animal forward, saber raised high. His men followed, fanning out behind him at a gallop, carbines blasting. The stink of sulfur stung his nose.

Enemy horsemen spilled from the tree line on Garret's flank where the first flash had originated. Ahead, dismounted Reb cavalry scrambled in the gun smoke-laden mist, racing to their horses.

Outrun the mounted and break through the rest before they reached their saddles. Simple plan. *Dear God, make it work.*

The first row of Rebs in the field fell away. One man dropped his rifle and threw himself out of Garret's way. A bullet grazed Garret's sleeve. He charged forward and swung his saber. Metal clashed against metal as the Reb struck with his gun barrel. Garret reared his horse and drove the hooves down onto the man's legs. The Reb fell by the wayside, and Garret charged onward, shoving his saber into its scabbard and grabbing his carbine. They could do it. They could break the line.

The riders from the trees closed the distance. Fire tore through Garret's thigh. He wobbled in the saddle. The world spun. He gripped his reins and carbine, firing into the scattered mass of men ahead. If he could only get clear. Get his men to safety. Tend to his wound later. He gritted his teeth and dug his heels into horse flesh. The animal thrashed forward. Garret leaned over the saddle horn and held on. His men followed.

Bullets whizzed. Fewer Rebs in front. Garret waved his men onward. Corporal Smith led the way through the barnyard ahead and beyond, to a road.

Garret's horse jolted, whinnied, and toppled toward the ground. Garret jumped. Pain spiked down his leg, up through his hip, and all the way to the bottom of his skull. The world darkened.

Sky ran through the back door with Little Star on her hip. Down the elegant hallway with its sculptured trim to the foyer, her pulse pounding in her head.

The servant girl had said, "A telegram about Mr. Garret. Hurry."

Mr. Ramsey stood in the entry way, his arms around his wife. "I offered to secure him a desk job at the War Department. He didn't listen, didn't want my help."

Rebecca clung to his lapels and buried her head against his neck. Her shoulders shook. "Hush. He wanted to serve his country."

Sky stuttered to a stop. Her legs jellied as she slipped Little Star to the ground. *No. Dear God, please, no.*

Red-faced, Maxwell looked up and glared at her. Flexing his hands at his sides, he stomped into his study and slammed the door without another word.

Rebecca wiped her nose. A piece of paper dangled from her fingers. "He's been wounded."

Sky stumbled forward and reached for the paper. She sank to her knees on the cold marble as she read the telegram aloud. "'Major Ramsey has fallen behind Confederate lines. Severely wounded. Taken prisoner. Not known if he will survive.'"

At her side, Rebecca dropped onto the velvet-covered bench. "Our dear boy." She clamped an embroidered handkerchief to her mouth and sobbed.

Sky dug her nails into her palms and squeezed her eyes shut. *Dear Lord, no.* She could not lose another. *Please, God.* She could not lose Garret.

Pale sunlight streaked through the porch window.

Little Star toddled over and patted her hair. "Mommy? Mommy okay?"

Sky gasped and wrapped her arms around the child, hugging her close. Tears streamed down, mixing with her baby's black curls.

"He's alive." Rebecca's voice wobbled. "The Lord will watch over our boy." She shuddered "But I hate to think of him among strangers, enemies. In pain and in need. With no one to—"

Sky lifted her head. "I will go." She could do something. Hope blazed through her as brilliant as the sun conquering a storm. "There's no telling how the Rebs will treat a wounded prisoner. I'll get through the lines and find him. I'll take care of him. No matter what it takes." He'd done no less for her. She released Little Star and latched onto Rebecca's hands.

Rebecca's lips trembled, her brown eyes full of love and

sorrow. She sniffled. "No, child. I'll not have you put yourself at risk."

Sky rose to her knees and tightened her grip on the dear woman's fingers. "I survived seven years with the Comanche. I can look after myself. I will find him. God will watch over me."

Rebecca gazed deep into her eyes. "What about your baby? You can't take her across Virginia beyond enemy lines."

Sky rocked back on her heels. Her hands fell to her lap. Little Star stood at eye-level and patted her wet cheek. She couldn't leave her.

Rebecca leaned forward. "I know you love Garret. But I would never ask you—"

"I have to go to him. I'll never forgive myself if I sit here in comfort and he doesn't make it home. Knowing I could have helped. We have no idea how severe his wounds are." *We don't even know if he's still alive.*

Rebecca fumbled with her handkerchief on her lap as her gaze drifted far off and then returned. "God bless you, child. I'll not stop you." She touched Sky's cheek. "I'll take care of Little Star. Guard and love her with all that I am. I give my word." Her tears had slowed. The heavy shadow across her face lightened. "She'll be here waiting for both of you. And I'll get Mr. Ramsey to arrange a pass for you through Federal lines."

The image of Dancing Eagle in her arms, his blood soaking her clothes, pierced through her. She'd lost her first husband. How could she not do everything in her power to save her second?

CHAPTER 45

Rough hands. A piece of canvas slid beneath him. Pain. So much pain. Fire consumed every nerve in Garret's leg. His parched tongue stuck to the roof of his mouth. Not enough strength to even open his eyes. What if he died here? He'd never see Sky or Little Star again. *God help me.*

He was plopped down on rough boards. A wagon bed? A deep groan escaped his lips. What felt like red-flaming pokers pierced his bones from his hip to his ankle. Other wrecked men were laid alongside of him. Was Jeremy one of them? Water. What he wouldn't give for a drink.

Darkness, slipping into the fuzzy world between real and not real. Nightmares.

Wheels jostled. His body cringed with each jar, his muscles barely unlocking before the next bump sent a new shock to his system. If only they'd take him out and lay him in the grass somewhere.

Many dreams later, a bright light blasted his eyes. A grizzly man stood over him, shirt-sleeves rolled to his elbows and apron soaked in blood. "Your leg needs to come off. Your knee's swollen to twice its size. Bullet went in a couple of inches above that."

"No." The word scraped Garret's raw throat. He grabbed for the man's hairy wrist. "Don't take my leg. Don't you dare." He couldn't be a soldier without his leg. Couldn't run a ranch. Couldn't hope to live up to Dancing Eagle. "No." He forced the word out belly deep.

The man placed a hand on his shoulder. "If infection sets in, it could kill you. Wouldn't be able to stop it."

"I said no."

Sky slowed her mare to a walk. The Confederate fortifications lay ahead, mounds of dirt piled chest high and studded with spiked stakes, pointed end up on either side of the Berryville Road. A cluster of men guarded the gate, but pickets lingered along the line to where it disappeared into the trees. No one was getting into Winchester without permission.

For two days of hard riding in Virginia and skirting around the Rebel fortifications in Centerville, dread had gnawed at her every step of the way. What if she was too late?

She nudged the hood of her red cloak off of her head and fluffed her hair beneath her black felt hat, then splayed her skirt folds across the back of the mare. The Rebel hordes ahead needed to know a woman approached, not an enemy soldier. A year ago, she'd fought to hold onto every stitch of Comanche clothing and custom she could. Now, all that mattered was finding Garret alive and helping him.

Two men stepped forward from the barricade, one a slender private. The breeze ruffled blond tufts of hair beneath his cap. The other had stripes on his shoulders. A corporal. Muscular, his girth was double that of his fellow soldier.

"Halt. Dismount." The corporal held his gun at an angle in front of his chest. "Who are you? What's your business here, ma'am?"

She drew rein and threw in every ounce of drawl she could muster as she slid down off her horse. "I'm from Texas, and I'm lookin' for my husband."

One of the soldiers behind the earthworks chuckled. "You're a long way from home ma'am."

"Well, so is my husband, but he's not originally from Texas."

"Good thing." The corporal spit a chaw of tobacco at his feet. "We don't have any Texas boys in the Stonewall Brigade."

"I'm sorry to say, he's from Pennsylvania, Corporal, and of course, had to do his duty and sign up with the other side."

The mare shifted and nickered, as if restless with all of these onlookers.

"A Northerner?" The corporal scowled. A drop of tobacco juice trickled onto his lip. "All those Texas boys, and you married a Northerner?"

A chilly breeze rippled between them. A flock of crows glided to a landing in a nearby field.

She nudged a stray strand of hair from her eyes and forced a smile. "He was my knight in shinin' armor. Rescued me from the Comanche."

One of the gawkers hollered, "Wonder if she has all of her scalp under that hat."

The man next to him elbowed him hard. "Ain't you got any manners?"

"So you see, gentleman, I really must find him. I hear tell some of your boys took him prisoner, and he's wounded."

The corporal narrowed his eyes. "You heard all of that in Texas?"

"No, sir. Pittsburgh." She patted the mare's neck. "He drug me off to Pennsylvania to wait on him, but when I heard what had happened—"

The corporal shifted his rifle. "I heard tell Colonel Ashby's men had a run in with Federal cavalry north of Front Royal."

"Yes." All of her airs faded. "Do you have the wounded prisoners here in Winchester? My husband's Major Garret Ramsey."

"I don't know the names. Only that there were a couple officers shot and captured. One of them didn't make it. The other's on the second floor of the courthouse and in bad shape."

Her legs wobbled. Garret had to be the one in the courthouse. "Please take me to him. I beg you."

"A Federal major's wife traipsing through our lines and our town, free to report back to those turkey buzzards in Washington? No, ma'am. General Jackson would have my neck in the stocks."

"Please. My husband's safety is all I care about. Blindfold me if you have to. I don't care. Just as long as I get to stay with my husband."

He leaned forward, using his rifle like a post. "Sorry, Mrs. Ramsey. Can't do it. If you want to come back tomorrow, maybe by then, I'll have a chance to ride in and speak with General Jackson. No guarantees on his answer."

Sky jutted out her chin. "I'm not leaving Winchester without seeing my husband." She crossed her arms. "And if you don't see fit to let me in yet, I reckon I'll sit here and wait until you all talk to your colonel or general or whoever it is who needs to give permission." With that, she pivoted on her heel, stomped over to her mare, yanked her rubberized blanket off the saddlehorn, and spread it on the ground.

By sunset, she was walking behind the corporal past rows of brick and clapboard houses. Two privates marched on either side of her, one leading her mare. The next street widened. Soldiers loitered on the corners, hands stuffed in their pockets, talking and smoking, a stray cough here and there. Ladies in wide hoopskirts and winter bonnets strolled down the brick sidewalks in groups of two or three or on the arm of a fellow in gray. A general store, a tobacco shop, a bank, and a dozen other buildings comprised the center of town.

More people than she'd seen anywhere outside of the Pittsburgh train station and her one-day stay in Washington on the way here. Enough to make her tense and draw her arms in close to her sides.

A brick church with high gables stood at the end of the block. Candle lights filled the windows, and organ music drifted into the street. Christmas Eve. She'd plumb forgotten it. Hadn't celebrated Christmas since before...the raid on her family. Would she by some miracle celebrate tonight at her husband's side?

Without Little Star. Her darling baby girl. An ache cramped her chest. *Dear God, keep her safe.* Sky shivered beneath her cloak.

A harness jingled. She scooted out of the way as a wagon bustled by. Up ahead stood a grand three-story building with wide white columns and three floors of balconies. A curved staircase led to the first floor. This was the most popular spot in town—if the number of people in the vicinity was any indication.

"Is that it?" She swallowed.

Corporal Husby turned around. "Taylor Hotel. Rumor has it General Jackson's expecting his wife on the stage tonight, so I reckon he'll be here." He jabbed his finger in her direction. His thumb poked out of a tear in his glove. "The general's not a man to be trifled with or moved by a woman's tears. Us boys call him 'Stonewall.' And if you think he's going to let you waltz out of Winchester, you've got another thought coming. He doesn't trust Yankees farther than he can throw them."

She flexed her fingers, palms sweaty. She couldn't worry about that now.

A tall man in a gray slouch hat stepped onto the porch. A long blue cape hung down to his boot tops.

The crowd parted. "Evening, General."

"Merry Christmas, General."

Husby's shoulders jerked. "That's him. You stay put." He nodded to the two privates. "Keep an eye on her."

The corporal hurried up the winding steps and snapped to attention, ramrod straight as he approached the fully bearded Jackson.

Sky pressed her lips together and shivered. *Please, Lord.*

Above the ornate railing of the first-floor balcony, Jackson stared down at her, his face set in a deep frown as Husby talked.

Had she come this far to leave it all up to the corporal? She gathered her skirts and started for the stairs.

"Ma'am? You can't do that." One of the privates reached for her arm.

She quickened her steps, her too-tight leather boots clunking against the boards.

"Mrs. Ramsey." Husby moved between her and Jackson. "I told you to wait."

Jackson straightened. "Let the lady speak, Corporal."

She curtsied deep, her hat almost tumbling from her head. "I beg your pardon, General. Please, sir, I must see my husband." Hands entwined, she dared glance up at his steel-blue eyes and stern mouth. "I don't care anything for this war. I don't mean you or your men any harm. I only want to look after my husband, Major Ramsey. Lock me up if need be. Put me in prison. As long as I'm with him." Her pulse pounded in her temple.

Jackson clasped his hands behind his back. "Who came with you, Mrs. Ramsey?"

"With me, sir? No one. I rode all the way—"

"On the Berryville Road? All the way from Washington City alone? I find that hard to fathom, ma'am. No lady would ride such a distance without an escort, at the very least. And it's that escort that worries me."

"I came alone. I swear. Sir, I'm a Texan. I can look after myself. I rode every mile from the Federal lines in Fairfax to Winchester on my own." She straightened. Failure wasn't an option. She'd beg if she had to. "I have my baby girl waiting for me back in Pennsylvania at my husband's family's estate. I left her to come look after him. It's Christmas Eve. I've never spent a Christmas with my husband. I have no guarantee he'll see another. Please, have mercy."

Jackson scrubbed a hand over his thick beard and gazed off toward the street. Snow flurries tumbled from the sky, clinging to the banisters, the men and horses below. Even the lamp posts didn't escape.

Sky's heart thudded. "Please, sir."

Jackson cleared his throat. "Only the Lord Almighty knows if any of us will be alive next Christmas, Mrs. Ramsey." He tugged on his plain uniform coat, void of brass and fancy trim. "Consider yourself a prisoner of the Confederate States of America until further notice."

On the second floor of the stone-columned brick courthouse, Sky stepped from a closet. The female servant who had just searched her handed Husby her pistol and knife. Off to the side, a blushing private set Sky's carpetbag, haversack, and buffalo robe on the floor in the dim hallway.

Husby coughed. "We'll have you a meal sent up, ma'am."

Sky nodded. Her stomach didn't feel like food.

Heavy steps sounded behind them. Keys clanked. She stepped out of the way of the burly sergeant. "Major's behind the door on the right. Only him in there now. We had another officer pass away the first day."

Voices came from the door on the left, the wood as thick as logs. A cluster of three faces shoved close and filled the small barred window. "It's the major's wife from Texas."

"I didn't know he was married."

"Comanche princess."

"Quiet down, boys." The sergeant rapped his knuckles against their door, then nodded to her. "We keep the enlisted men separate from the officers."

One face remained at the window. More of a boy than a man. "Sorry, Mrs. Ramsey. I remember you from Camp Cooper. Give the major our regards. And let him know the Rebs didn't get Lieutenant Braddock. Tell him not to give up. And if you could send a word to my mother—"

"Lady's not delivering any messages, soldier." The sergeant shoved a chaw of tobacco into his cheek. "Given herself up to be prisoner, just like you."

The rest of the conversation faded as she turned to the door on the right. She fumbled with her hands. "Sergeant, can you tell me how the major's doing?"

"Feverish. Doctor gave him morphine for the pain. If he's lucky, he'll sleep through the night. Leg's infected. An orderly will show up after midnight to check on him. Doc will be by in the morning." He opened the door. "Not locked yet. No danger of the major going anywhere. But I've orders to turn the lock behind you, missus." His shoulders sagged.

She sucked in a breath as she stepped across the threshold. Garret was so still lying there on the cot. A single lamp with a turned-down wick illuminated the sparsely furnished room. A washstand, a stool, a couple buckets, and a small stove. Nothing else. A medicinal smell, iodine or maybe bromine, stung her nose.

Her heart quavered as she crossed the shadowed floor.

Garret...his face pale against the pillow and his hair rumpled and damp with sweat. A murmur, more of a groan than a word, crossed his lips. His forehead crinkled, and he squeezed his eyes tight as if in pain.

She dropped to her knees, her hand to his arm. Sky pressed a kiss to his stubbled yet too-warm cheek. Tears stung her eyes. She was here. He was alive. Thank God! The tight band of tension which had encompassed her whole upper body since the telegram arrived five days ago loosened.

From the street below, voices of carolers echoed through the bar-covered window, carrying the tune of "God Rest Ye Merry Gentleman."

Swiping her tears, Sky leaned down farther and nestled her head against his shoulder, sharing his damp pillow, and draped her arm over him. Her hair brushed against his cheek. "I'm here, my love."

"Mmmm." He murmured from far away.

She spread her palm on his chest, relishing the steady rhythm of his heart. Tomorrow, she'd change his nightshirt to the clean one his mother had sent. Feed him. Bathe him. Take care of his dressings. Show this man her love. And pray they would have a life time together.

In the distance, church bells clanged. Midnight. Christmas. Home. The Lord had given this to her. His grace was so amazing.

CHAPTER 46

Warm pressure on his hand. The scent of orange blossoms. Sparkling sunlight shimmering on water. Sky in his arms. Dancing in her blue dress, her smile lighting his soul.

A clank. Metal. Bromide. Sweat. The dream faded. The hospital, or was it a prison cell? Reality. The hand in his. The orange blossoms. If only he could fade back into the dream. A steady roar of pain encompassed his leg. Did he still have a leg?

A hand, soft but firm. Solid. The balm of touch. He opened his eyes. Piercing blue irises. His breath caught in his throat. Rosy cheeks. Waves of dark hair cascaded beneath a black felt hat, past the tops of her shoulders, and onto her red cloak. Sky? He blinked again. Couldn't be. A dream. A figment of the morphine they'd given him. But his heart thundered like a drummer.

She kissed the back of his hand. "It's so good to see you. I've missed you so much."

Her voice, so real. He squeezed his eyes shut and shook his head. Couldn't be. He opened them again and fell into her gaze. "You're really here? How?" A tremor slurred his words.

Her face glowed. "You don't know me at all, Garret Ramsey, if you think I'd sit up there in Pittsburgh safe and sound while you're wounded and in need of care."

A half laugh croaked out of his throat. His gaze drifted to the brick walls, the high window, then back to her. "You're really here? Winchester? Prison?"

"Yes." Tears glistened on her cheeks. She smiled, the widest, biggest smile he'd ever seen.

The truth knocked the air out of him. He shivered. She'd come to Virginia to find him. "You're not on your way to Texas?"

She arched her eyebrows and gave him a look that said he should know better. "Why would I be there when my husband needs me here?"

Husband. "Because it's your home. Where you want to be."

She leaned closer and smoothed her cool fingers over his forehead, her touch like sparkling rays of sun. "Where I want to be is right here with you. Texas will wait until we can go there together as a family."

Together. Family. Her here with him. Everything he could dream of. Tears dampened his eyes. He would not cry. "You're not going to sign the papers?"

"If your father dares show me those papers again, I'll rip them into pieces and throw them in the fire."

Goosebumps spread across his arms. "I...thought I loved you before. Back in Texas." He swallowed hard. His mouth was so dry. "I was wrong. I'd only scratched the surface." The room spun.

Sky stood, bent over, and brushed her lips to his. "I love you. And I don't want Texas without you."

"Be here when I wake up." He squeezed her hand, his eyelids heavy.

"Drink first." She slipped her hand behind his head and raised him slightly, then pressed the rim of a tin cup to his lips. "You get some rest. I'm not leaving your side."

Cool, sweet water. So good. His eyes barely open. His voice only a whisper. "Kiss me once more." *Please God, don't let this be a dream.*

Hands red and chapped with lye, Sky hung up Garret's meager laundry on a piece of rope she'd strung across the end of the room. Strips of bandages dangled alongside his undershirt, uniform, and drawers. The now-putrid wash water sat against the wall in a wooden tub. If it weren't for the blasted bars on the window, she'd heft it and toss it onto the street below. As it was, she'd have to wait for the orderly to haul it away.

Drying her hands on a rag, she added a couple of pieces of coal to the fiery belly of the small stove, then set the shovel in the bucket. Sprinkles of the black dust flittered onto her skirt hem. If she wasn't here, who would keep the fire going?

Voices muffled by wood and walls drifted into the cell—Garret's men imprisoned on the other side of the hall, talking and singing carols.

Garret shifted restlessly on the cot. Poor darling. All day, he'd wrestled with tortured sleep. Though he'd only been half aware of the goings-on, she had managed to bathe him, give him a clean undershirt, and watch the orderly change the dressing on his wound. She'd held Garret still as the man tugged off slough- and blood-caked bandages. She'd studied the way he applied honey to the ravaged flesh and stuffed moist lint in the gap left by the incision. Then he spread morphine powder on the wound and wrapped the bandage. Tomorrow she'd do it.

Her shawl slipped off her shoulders as she returned to his bedside and sat in the cane rocking chair, a luxury in this barren cell. Courtesy of Mrs. General Jackson, along with extra bedding and another cot.

Garret's fingers moved nervously across his blanket. Sky rubbed his arm. Heat poured through his sleeve. She gnawed her lip. If only she was back in Texas, free to gather the herbs the Comanche had used for treating fevers. A deep frown settled over her as she lifted the cloth from his forehead, dipped it in the basin, and wrung it out before replacing it.

Dear Lord, please quiet his fever and heal his body. Remove every trace of infection from him—

God had allowed Dancing Eagle to die. No, she would not dwell on that now. Down on her knees, she finished her prayer. That the Lord of the universe would intervene this time. If it be His will. Such hard words to acknowledge, harder to accept.

A tune came to mind, "Shenandoah's Daughter." Their wedding song.

Evening shadows danced on the brick as the lamp light flickered. The rocker creaked against the cold floor.

Voice low, she sang. "'Oh, Shenandoah, I love your daughter. Away, you rolling river.'"

Garret turned his head toward her. His eyes fluttered open. "Sky?"

"Yes." She sat forward and clasped her hand around his.

"You're still here?" He smiled, his eyes bright with fever.

"I told you I would be."

"I was afraid I'd dreamed you up." He lifted his fingers toward her, his nails short and broken. "Let me see."

She bent closer.

He touched her cheek. A look of wonder spread across his face, as if he'd discovered a butterfly. "Beautiful." He rubbed a strand of her hair between his fingertips. "Your hair is longer."

The tremble in his hand pierced her heart. Tears threatened, but she swallowed them back. She would not even hint at crying. "It's been eight months since we parted in Indianola, and I've been growing it out for you."

His brow furrowed. "Where's our baby girl?"

She wilted.

"What's wrong?" He tried to raise up, got as far as his shoulders off the cot before he groaned and dropped back down. "Where's Little Star?"

She tugged the blanket up to his collarbone. "I had to leave her with your mother. Couldn't risk putting her in danger." Her stomach twinged, threatening to upset her dinner. "I know your mother will take good care of her, but the darling won't understand why Mommy's not there." The weight of it crushed her. But now wasn't the time to trouble Garret with her convoluted emotions. "She'll be fine. Doted on by your mother. You need me more right now."

"I'm so sorry." He shuddered. "As soon as I'm a little better, you can head home—"

She kissed his palm. "We'll leave here together if I have any say so."

"That'd suit me fine." He licked his parched lips. "But I don't want to keep you from your...*our* daughter."

She flinched. "I can't exactly walk out of here. In order to get into Winchester and see you, I agreed to be their prisoner. They're worried I might share secrets with the Federal high command. Not that I've paid attention to anything but you."

"You're a prisoner too? Sky, I never would have asked you to—"

She touched a finger to his lips. "My choice. I demanded I be allowed to see you. I sat down at the picket line and refused to move. Threatened to sneak in. I wasn't about to take no for an answer. Not when the man I love needed me."

A smile lit his face. "You...are...the most amazing woman... I've ever met."

If only she could crawl in bed with him, snuggle close, and

never let go. "I'm thankful you think so." She brushed her fingertips against his jaw. His cheeks were so red. She bit her lip. "Is my prince charming ready for dinner? The orderly brought some broth. I've been keeping it warm on the stove in the corner."

"Not hungry." He turned his head on his pillow and nuzzled against her palm.

She'd been here a night and a day, and he'd had nothing but water. "Major Ramsey, how are you supposed to dance with your wife if you don't eat?"

His smile evaporated. "You haven't told me. About my leg."

Garret squeezed his eyes shut, afraid he'd see the truth in Sky's expression. His leg throbbed. Shooting pains sliced through him like a Johnny Reb saber on a regular basis, but none of that meant he still had a leg. He'd heard of phantom pains. The stench of his wounds stung his nostrils.

What if Sky was here because she felt sorry for him? Felt as though she owed him for rescuing Little Star from her uncle? He clutched his covers. No. It was more than that. The way her eyes shone had nothing to do with debt or pity.

He reached for her hand, ended up with her wrist instead. Held on for dear life. As if she was his anchor. "Tell me, please."

"They saved your leg. But they had to take a couple inches of bone out. An excision. That's what the doctor called it. Experimental. Your one leg will be a little shorter than the other, but you can have special shoes made. You've got another thought coming if you think I'm going to let you skip out on dancing with me."

"They didn't amputate?" Tension ebbed from his upper

body. *Praise God*. He and Sky would have their ranch. He'd take her riding.

His sandpaper tongue stuck to the roof of his mouth. He needed water.

As if she could read his mind, she slipped her hand beneath his sweaty head and lifted him enough to touch his lips to the rim of the tin cup. Cool. Refreshing. He drank deeply. Why was he so hot? And weak? Infection. He didn't need to be told. Now, all he had to do was live. "I'm so sorry I didn't write you more, Sky. And even the letters I did send, I couldn't be certain they'd reach you. I was stubborn. Wrong—"

"The manner in which we parted is my fault. My heart was lost in winter." She eased him back onto the pillow. "But now, spring has come." Her gaze unfurled like a field of Texas bluebonnets coming into bloom at last.

"Hold me, please," he whispered. They'd had so little time together. He had to recover. "Tell me about Little Star. She must have grown a bunch. And tell me what kind of house you want me to build you after the war."

Leaning from her chair, Sky laid her head on his pillow and rested her chin against his shoulder. She wrapped her arm over his chest. "Little Star is such a big girl now. She can almost run, and you should hear her talk..."

His eyes drifted closed.

~

The days blurred, a series of teeth-chattering chills, sweat-drenched sheets with his nightshirt clinging to his skin like a clammy hand, and restlessness. Memories of battles and nightmares interspersed with his blue-eyed angel. His tongue swollen, his throat parched. His leg on fire. Utter exhaustion. The firm, faithful pressure of Sky's hand became his only tether to the here and now.

CHAPTER 47

Mid-February

Garret stirred in the gray of dawn, clear-headed and free from the fog of heavy medication. His ears strained to catch the sweet rhythm of Sky's breathing. She stirred on her cot adjacent to his. The buffalo robe covered them both.

Mourning doves cooed outside the barred window. Down below, the streets were still quiet except for an occasional clomp of hooves on the pavement and the rattle of a wagon. Cool air chilled his nostrils. The stove fire must have gone out in the night.

Teeth gritted, he gripped his wounded leg and rolled onto his side. Over a month of fever had taken its toll. It'd left him weak as a baby when it'd broken at last. Two weeks ago, he couldn't lift his head. Yesterday, he'd sat up for an hour.

Sweat broke out on his brow as he adjusted his knee to rest atop his other thigh. He took a moment to recover, then slipped his other arm beneath his pillow and let his eyes drink their fill of his beautiful wife.

She was turned toward him, lips parted. A wave of dark hair dipped across her forehead. If he had paper, he'd sketch her. Jackson was sending him farther South, maybe all the way to Richmond. Any day now, he'd be loaded onto a wagon. How was he going to say goodbye to her?

Sky's blue eyes fluttered open. A smile spread across her face as she stretched and rolled closer, tugging the robe to her shoulders.

"Good morning," he whispered.

"My, you're looking as though you're feeling better today." She curled her hand around his forearm at the edge of his bunched pillow.

"Only because I've got the best nurse a man could ask for." He stroked her cheek, then her hair, memorizing the feel of her skin beneath his fingertips. Smooth as rose petals. The caress wove its way into his tone, as well. "When this war is over, I want to wake up to you by my side every morning for the rest of our lives."

"When the war is over?" She pressed her lips together and pushed up on her elbow. "It's over for you as soon as we can figure out a way to get you out of prison and sent home. Your leg—" She stopped herself in mid-sentence. Her expression fell.

"It's all right to talk about my leg." He exhaled. "I know there's no guarantee the bone will grow and close the gap. But I believe you're right about what you said, that my leg will heal. I'll walk again. Ride again. That's my hope."

"Ride and walk on our ranch in Texas." She sat all the way up now. "And until then—"

"Until then." He hadn't intended to ignite the kindling of her concern. "Sooner or later, the officials will strike a bargain. I'll be swapped in a prisoner exchange for some Confederate major. Then, after my leg has healed—"

"Your leg could take a long time to recover." She hopped off the cot.

"I'd like nothing better than to be traded next week and have months with you and Little Star before I have to go back to my men."

"No. Don't you dare think of putting yourself in harm's way again." Her voice trembled, and she swung her arms wide. "I don't know why we're talking about this right now. You're in a Reb prison. Bed-ridden. Just beginning to recover."

"I'd be a poor excuse for a soldier if I gave up. I have no intention of being an invalid forever." He pushed halfway up on his elbow and stifled a groan. A cramp contorted his muscle from his knee up through his hip. What he wouldn't give to be able to stand and talk to her face to face. "My country and my men need me."

Her mouth opened. He braced himself for a dose of reality that he was in no shape to be of help to anyone.

Instead, her shoulders slumped. "I'm not asking you to give up your duty. Just to be safe and not away from us."

He eased his head back to his pillow. "When I return to the cavalry, you and Little Star can come with me as long as the regiment is still stationed in Washington or in winter quarters. Who knows? We might be assigned there indefinitely. They might keep me behind a desk. That's what my father has pushed for all along."

"But that's not what you want."

What I want is you in my arms. He swallowed back the notion before it reached his lips. "I don't want my father running my life. I'm a decent officer, and the army needs all of the help they can get before these Rebs destroy the Union permanently."

"You're a fine officer." She jutted her chin. "I have no doubt you're the best in the regiment." She flipped the fold of her skirt. "But you still haven't told me why we're talking about this today."

She plopped down on the cot, her one leg tucked in toward the other, her chemise revealing more cleavage than he'd seen since he'd lain with her by the lake last March. She tugged the robe around her shoulders, leaving her low neckline unencumbered. His thoughts scattered.

"Because..." He cleared his throat and redirected his gaze. "When they allowed you to go downstairs yesterday to do laundry, the doctor had a talk with me. Told me they plan to move me in a few days."

"To a different building?"

"To Centerville at the very least, and probably on to a prison in Richmond."

She gaped at him. "How can they do that? You've finally started regaining a little strength, and they want to stick you in the back of a wagon or train and have you out in all kinds of weather?"

He held up his hand and whispered, "My guess is that they're either getting ready for a troop movement or they're afraid the Federals might take the city."

"But what about me? I'd go with you."

"I'm sorry but no." That's exactly what he'd negotiated with the doctor. Pleaded for her release.

"What do you mean no?" She crossed her arms.

He steeled himself for another battle. "The doctor knows about Little Star. He's petitioning Jackson to allow you to be escorted out of town blind-folded and driven to Centerville where you can be exchanged across the lines into Federal territory."

Her eyes flashed. "You told him. You asked for this?"

"I don't want you to go. I'd love for you to stay. This room will feel like a dungeon when you're gone, but it'd be selfish of me to keep you away from Little Star any longer. She's been without you for over seven weeks. She needs her mommy."

"Next to the last thing in the world I wanted to do was leave her."

"I know." His voice softened. "You sacrificed to come here. Please allow me to sacrifice in sending you home." He shivered. Fine words, but how could he bear to part with her? "In the end, it's Jackson's decision, not ours."

"No place will be home until you, Little Star, and I are all together."

Her admission blew him away. His gaze met hers. The intensity there caught him off guard. "Any place with you and Little Star sounds like the perfect home to me. You just have to go ahead of me, and I'll be there as soon as I can."

"I don't want to leave you." Her whisper wrapped around his heart.

He lost himself in her blue irises. "If I had my wish, I'd ride out of here with you." Heat stirred within him. "We've got a day or even a few days to treasure our time together."

From the street below, a wagon clacked, and a newspaper boy began hawking his wares. "Morning paper. Read all about it." His voice carried.

The first rays of morning sun penetrated the dull window pane. Garret nudged his left shoulder backward. "Will you help me roll over?"

"Maybe." She stuck out her lip but moved closer, leaning over him. Her chemise brushed his nightshirt as she reached and supported his shoulder, easing him onto the cot. The wooden frame creaked beneath them.

Solid canvas. He pressed his molars together, waiting for the pain to ebb.

Her knee wobbled against his side as she retreated. "I should get dressed and get you some breakfast."

"I'd rather you keep me warm. We've got a little while

before the orderly comes by." He tugged on her sleeve. Desire thickened his voice. "You could lay your head on my shoulder. We could cuddle a bit."

Hovering on the edge of the two cots, she blinked at him, not quite on one or the other.

He held his breath. He'd waited ages to hold his wife. Didn't know if he was strong enough for more than snuggling. His heart pounded. A prisoner exchange could take weeks or months. There were no guarantees. He slipped a hand to her waist.

Cheeks flushed, she shifted toward him and gently lowered her upper body down, diagonal across his chest.

He wrapped his arms around her, savoring the feel of her. The comfort of her presence soaked layers beneath his skin. He brushed his lips against her hair, inhaling her scent. "I love you so much," he whispered. "You are the love of my life."

She wove her lips across his collarbone and his jaw. "You are my beloved. And I am yours."

His pain. The brick cell. The war. All faded as he lost himself in caresses.

CHAPTER 48

Late April

Sky paced beneath the vine-covered archway. The intoxicating scent of morning glories blended with the dogwoods whose boughs overhung the pebbled path. Bees hummed. Spring in full bloom, and Garret would be here any minute. Excitement sizzled through her. God had been so good to them. He was so much more than the distant creator of the stars. He was as near as her very breath, and His love outshone the sun.

She smoothed her hands down the front of her royal-blue dress, the same color as the one she'd worn to her wedding.

Little Star stepped in front of her, but it was Dancing Eagle's eyes staring up at her. "Papa coming?"

Sky gulped. "Soon, baby girl." She rubbed her arms out of habit, bare beneath her sleeves. No bands. She'd tucked them away in a velvet pouch and placed them in the bottom of her wardrobe. Memories not to be forgotten or neglected. But one could not live in the past. She'd teach her daughter to love and admire both men.

She smoothed a hand over Little Star's dark waves that fell against the collar of her forest-green dress.

If they'd ridden with Mr. and Mrs. Ramsey to the train station to meet Garret, she could have been in his arms at this moment. For about five seconds. Then everyone else would have swarmed in to hug and greet him. Instead, Garret and she had decided she'd wait for him here in the garden. They'd say their hellos with no eyes and ears but Little Star's.

Her heart pounded at the very thought. Ten weeks since they'd parted in Winchester.

"Berbies." Little Star pointed at a flock of robins on the lawn and ran ahead, clutching her dolly in the crook of her arm.

The orange-chested birds turned their heads right and left listening for earthworms beneath the surface. But at the patter of the small moccasined feet, the whole flock took flight. "All gone." Little Star put out her lip.

A carriage door closed. Or was it just her imagination? Would a sound like that really carry out back to the garden from the front of the mansion?

"Why don't you look for a butterfly?" She stepped toward Little Star. Anything to distract the both of them.

A door closed. Footsteps. Slow, deliberate. Every other one followed by a scrape.

She looked up.

Garret. Tall and straight in his dress uniform coat, crimson sash, and sky-blue trousers. Brass epaulettes with gold fringe topped his shoulders. She'd never seen him in the full major regalia. Cane in hand, he halted and removed his Hardee hat. A wave of smoothed-back brown hair dipped to his forehead, and a close-trimmed beard shadowed his jaw line, his face thin and cheekbones more prominent than usual.

Not a bare-chested warrior in buckskin leggings atop a painted mare. But no less a warrior. A man of great courage and strength who'd give his last breath to protect her and Little Star.

A man who'd embedded himself in her heart so deeply that her love for him was as dear as her very breath.

Her knees teetered.

Little Star squealed and ran her way, dolly flopping against her leg. "Mommy. Soljer."

Sky squeezed her hand. "It's Papa."

"Papa's leg funny."

"His leg has a big booboo. We need to help him get better."

Garret's smile crinkled his eyes. "And who do we have here?" He moved toward them, step, step, and scrape. His saber thumped against his right thigh.

Little Star darted behind Sky's skirt and peeked out. "Wittle Sta."

He chuckled. "Can't be. Little Star is a baby. What I see here is a big girl."

"Me is big girl."

"So I see." He pressed his lips together and slowly knelt on one knee. Pain pinched his eyes but could not diminish his glow as he offered his hand to the child. "How old are you now?"

She held out her dolly to him.

He stared and stuttered. "T-the one I gave her. She still has it?" His gaze flew up to Sky's. "I thought my mother would have given her two or three fancy dolls by now."

"She did. But Little Star prefers the one from her papa."

His eyes glistened as he scooped the child in his arms. "Papa loves you so much, baby girl."

She threw her arms around his neck and squeezed. "You stay?"

He kissed her head. "Yes. And when I have to leave, I'll take Mommy and Little Star with me on an adventure."

"Wenture?" She drew back and stuck her finger in her mouth. "You play dolly with Wittle Sta?"

Sky ran her fingertips through the thick waves atop Garret's head, anxious for his embrace.

He grinned up at her, then winked at Little Star. "Papa's got to say hello to Mommy. Don't want her feeling left out."

"Poor Mommy." She scooted off his lap and stared up. "It's okay, Mommy." She patted Sky's skirt.

Atremble, Sky offered her husband her hand, helping him stand. His saber bumped the ground.

The moment he gained his footing, his hands went to her waist, and he took her in his arms, sending her heart skipping. "Saved the best for last," he whispered against her hair. "Prettiest, sweetest, gutsiest lady in all of Texas and Pennsylvania and everywhere in between."

She tightened her arms around him. "I've missed you so much." She buried her head against his shoulder, shifting her cheekbone away from the brass epaulette, and inhaled bay rum and soap with a twinge of coal smoke from the train. Tears wet her lashes. "Thank God, you are home safe."

He nuzzled his cheek against her hair. "I've been counting the days. Hoping and praying headquarters would push a swap through to get me back here to my girls."

"They could have been holding out for the King of England as long as it took them. But you're here now."

Garret slipped his hand beneath her jaw and tipped her face toward his. "My love." His voice was barely a breath as he lowered his lips to hers and overtook her mouth in a kiss that shook her to her toes and filled her limbs and tummy with liquid warmth. By the time their lips parted, it was him steadying her.

Little Star swung on her skirt. "Mommy love Papa."

"Mommy does indeed love Papa." Eyes closed, Sky didn't stir as Garret dipped his forehead to hers. Heaven on earth, in Garret's arms, with their daughter at their side. Safe. Home.

His chest rose and fell hard against hers, his breath as shaky as she felt. "I told my parents we'd have dinner with them this evening. But before that, I'm yours and Little Star's, and afterwards, when we tuck the baby girl in bed... then, I can't wait to have you all to myself."

She met his gaze. "I'm all yours."

His smile was better than a Texas starlit night.

"Look." Little Star shoved a daffodil toward them. "Come see." She pointed toward the garden.

"How about we see the cottage first? And the presents I brought you and Mommy?"

"Presents?" Little Star's eyes widened.

"There's a small sack just outside the back door. See if you can bring it to us."

"Me do it. Me do it." She skipped down the stone path toward the main house.

Garret chuckled, but his expression turned serious as he released Sky from his hold. "I hope you're all right with dining with my parents and sister tonight. They're desperate to visit."

"I'll manage." She slipped her hand around the crook of his elbow. "Your mother's overjoyed to have you home. And your father's backed off a bit since I returned from Winchester. Gave up on the annulment. Instead, he wants to hire a tutor to show me how to be a proper lady."

He scoffed. "My father needs a tutor to show him how to mind his own business."

The crumb of worry that Garret might agree she needed polishing evaporated. "I told him that in so many words."

"You're my lady, and I love you exactly the way you are." He turned her toward him. "I've informed my father I won't be attending any events, social or family, without you at my side as my wife."

"That'll be a conundrum for him, especially since, according to Fanny, he previously informed his acquaintances I was a refugee from Texas you took pity on."

Garret's brow crinkled. "I'm sorry for the way he's treated you."

"Not your fault." She shrugged. "Besides, high society's opinion doesn't matter to me. You're what I care about."

"Still, I'm sorry." He brushed his fingers to her cheek. "And I've informed him you and I will be staying in the cottage while I'm here, Mrs. Garret Ramsey."

The late-afternoon sun poured through the leaves.

She smiled. "It'd suit me fine if we hibernated there for a month."

"I'll see what I can arrange." He winked.

"Here." Little Star dragged a canvas sack behind her. "Need help."

Garret slipped the sack string over his shoulder. "Thank you. Now why don't you and Mommy show me our home?"

~

An hour later, Garret settled back in a red velvet parlor chair with his injured leg resting on a stool and Sky tucked in beside him, her skirts across his lap.

On the floor, Little Star played with a spinning top he'd picked up for her in Washington City as he'd passed through.

Fresh baked bread, butter, and cheese filled his belly. His second cup of good, dark coffee sat on the end table next to the chair arm. So much better than the scant rations in Richmond's Libby Prison. Thank goodness, Sky had been spared the misery of that place. The Frederick County Courthouse in Winchester was a haven compared to what had followed. After his release, he'd spent five days in Washington City recovering before boarding the train for Pittsburgh.

Sky nuzzled her head against his neck and slipped her arm inside his open uniform coat, the warmth of her penetrating through the layers of cloth. "I'm a little worried about the gold." Her voice lilted.

"Excuse me?" He cocked his eyebrows without stirring his head from the cushioned chair back, too lost in bliss to move.

"This gold." She flicked the fringe of his epaulette with her finger. "Seems to say you're mighty important. That the army will want you back sooner than later."

He snuggled her closer. "We've got months. I don't expect the doctors to approve my return to the field before the end of summer. And if they stick me in some office for a while, you and Little Star will come with me."

How could he ever bear to part with his precious little family when duty called? But what kind of man would he be if he deserted his men for the comforts of home, after he regained his health? Defending the Union against the evils of secession and slavery required sacrifice.

"Thank you." Sky's whisper interrupted his thoughts.

"For what?"

"For not giving up on me. For giving me spring."

"Oh, lady." He tipped her face to his. "Just when I think I couldn't possibly love you any more than I already do, you show me a new sunrise that takes my breath away."

Her eyes twinkled. "I've got a surprise for you."

"What kind of a surprise?"

She placed his hand on her abdomen. "That kind of a surprise."

He stilled for a moment. "You...you're not saying what I think you're saying?" A possibility burst through him like a firecracker.

She pressed his hand hard against her skirt and nodded.

A grin broke out across his face as he sat forward, catching Sky before she spilled from his lap. "You're...we're...?"

"Yes." Her eyes sparkled. "That last day in the courthouse."

He drew her to him. "You've made me the happiest man in

the world." Her lips warm and welcoming, he poured his joy into his kiss.

Little Star patted his leg. "Me want up."

He grinned and reached for her. "Of course, you do."

"Be careful of your leg."

"She'll be fine." He settled her between him and the side of the chair, then wrapped both wife and daughter in his arms. His heart was filled to overflowing. God had blessed him beyond imagination.

THE END

Did you enjoy this book? We hope so!

Would you take a quick minute to leave a review where you purchased the book?

It doesn't have to be long. Just a sentence or two telling what you liked about the story!

ABOUT THE AUTHOR

Originally from Tennessee and the Shenandoah Valley, **Sherry Shindelar** is a romantic at heart and loves to take her readers into the past. She is an avid student of the Civil War and the Old West. Her latest novel is set in 1860 Texas. When she is not busy writing, she is an English professor working to pass on her love of writing to her students. Sherry is an award winning writer: 2020 ACFW First Impressions winner, 2021 and 2023 ACFW Genesis semi-finalist, 2021 Maggie finalist, and 2022 Crown finalist. She currently resides in Minnesota with her husband of thirty-nine years. She has three grown children and three grandchildren. Visit her website and subscribe to her monthly newsletter at sherryshindelar.com

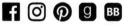

AUTHOR'S NOTE

This novel was loosely inspired by Cynthia Ann Parker's life, the most famous captive of nineteenth-century America. Twenty years ago, I read her story, and I have been haunted by her broken heart ever since.

Captured at age nine during an attack on her family's Texas fort in 1836, Cynthia Ann lived with the Comanche for twenty-four years before being recaptured by the U.S. Calvary and Texas Rangers in 1860 on the eve of the Civil War. She was taken from her tribe along with her infant daughter, Prairie Flower, never to see her beloved husband and two sons again. Historical sources disagree about whether her husband died in that battle, as I have portrayed with my fictional Dancing Eagle, or survived for a couple more years.

Cynthia Ann never fully re-acclimated to settler society, and she made numerous attempts to run away from her bewildered relatives. Her daughter died of pneumonia in 1864. Cynthia died of a broken heart a few years later, never having seen her husband or sons again. Her son Quanah Parker went on to become one of the most famous Comanche chiefs who ever lived.

Texas Forsaken reimagines a happier ending for a young woman similar to Cynthia Ann. Eyes-Like-Sky is not Cynthia Ann, but she, like Cynthia, is a woman caught between cultures.

Eyes-Like-Sky has only been with the Comanche seven years instead of twenty-four, and she only has one child. I used Olive Oatman's life experiences for further research. Olive spent five years with the Indians, most of it with the Mohave, before she was recaptured. Margot Mifflin describes Olive's life in *The Blue Tattoo*.

In case you're wondering, Cynthia Ann really had an uncle. As a matter of fact, she had two, but thankfully, they were nothing like LeBeau. One of them, James Parker, spent years searching for family members who were kidnapped in the attack on Parker's Fort. He recaptured Cynthia Ann's cousin, Rachel Plummer, after two years, and one of Rachel's sons seven years after the attack, along with a young man believed to be Cynthia's brother, John. Rachel never fully adjusted to the return, even though she was poorly treated by her captors, and John, according to many accounts, ran back to the Comanche. James gave up on finding Cynthia Ann.

When Cynthia Ann was recaptured, she went to live with her uncle Isaac Parker, and he and the other relatives, thankfully, welcomed Prairie Flower. However, they could not comprehend Cynthia Ann's passionate desire to return to the Comanche.

Overall, I love captive stories. If you do, too, here are some books from my research into the lives of real live captives: *Empire of the Summer Moon* by S.C. Gwyenne, *Narrative of my Captivity Among the Sioux Indians* by Fanny Kelly, *Indian Captive: The Story of Mary Jemison* by Lois Lenske, and as mentioned above, *The Blue Tattoo*.

I also love Civil War dairies and letters, but I'll save that discussion for another time, another book.

More truth in fiction (spoiler alert—wait until you've read all of *Texas Forsaken* before reading this next paragraph): Eyes-Like-Sky's travel behind enemy lines to nurse Garret back to health is based on a real-life incident after the Battle of First Manassas. Fanny Ricketts crossed into enemy-held territory and put Confederate officers in their place in order to reach her husband, Major James Ricketts, who had been shot four times and was being held prisoner in a house-hospital near the battlefield. Fanny stayed by his side until he was moved to prison in Richmond. Not one to be put off, Fanny traveled with him and lived in the prison with him for four months until he was exchanged north. Check out my Voices of the Past blog for more information on Fanny, Cynthia Ann, and Quanah: https://sherryshindelar.com/?page_id=604.

Several historical figures are mentioned in my story, including Sam Houston (Governor of Texas until he was removed from office for refusing to support secession) and Sul Ross (Texas Ranger, Confederate soldier, and eventually, governor). My character Captain Rick Jamison is inspired by Ross, and General Stonewall Jackson makes a cameo appearance. Colonel Thorson is loosely inspired by General George H. Thomas, who commanded Camp Cooper until November 1860. Thomas was from Virginia like Robert E. Lee, who served at Camp Cooper before Thomas, but Thomas sided with the nation instead of his home state when the Civil War started. Some of his relatives never forgave him for that decision, but the "Rock of Chickamauga" made major contributions to the overall Union victory. All other characters are fictional.

In my story, I wanted to show a man of honor who once he gave his word, kept it no matter the cost. Garret is that man. I wanted to write a story of forgiveness and redemption, a story of determination and perseverance, a story of second chances. That is Eyes-Like-Sky and Garret's story.

I want to thank my editor, Denise Weimer, for her belief in

my writing and for making this book happen. I also deeply appreciate my writing critique partners, Erma Ullrey, John Tipper, Jack Cunningham, Shannon Dunlap, Dave Parks (posthumously), Patti Shene, and Kathy McKinsey, who have faithfully given me feedback on my story week after week, chapter after chapter, helping my writing to be the best it can be. I'm grateful to my other writing friends (Mary Pat Johns, Gwen Gage, Sarah Hanks, Jamie Ogle, and Kristine Delano) as well, for their encouragement and input.

In addition, I'd like to thank the Panhandle-Plains Historical Museum for their help with my research.

To my husband, who has always encouraged and supported me in pursuing my dreams, and to my mother, who knew I could do it.

And to you, my reader, I greatly appreciate you reading my story.

I'd love to connect with you:

Newsletter: https://sherryshindelar.com/follow/

Website: https://sherryshindelar.com/

Don't miss the next book in the Lone Star Redemption Series!

Texas Divided

Chapter 1

Late November 1863
Colorado County, Eastern Texas

Morning Fawn "Beth Logan" did not want to be here. She sucked in a breath and blew it out hard. Despite the chill in the air, sweat dampened her palms. All around her, families, mostly mothers and their children, stopped to greet each other as they headed into the double doors of the weathered church. Black and deep purple, the colors of mourning and half-mourning, reigned amongst their apparel. Too many deaths from this war, but these were not her people, and it was not her war.

A few elms and scattered oak trees dotted the pebbled yard. Above their heads, the bell clanged in its wooden tower. Empty of welcome for her, the sound scraped her nerves.

She looked up, placing a hand to her straw hat to keep it from falling off. Aunt Judith LeBeau had wanted her to wear a proper bonnet, just as she'd wanted her to wear a hoop beneath her dress. Morning Fawn had silently placed the straw hat on her head, tied the ribbons under her chin, and walked out to the waiting four-seat landau with her skirt flat against a single petticoat and chemise.

On the way to church, Cousin Thea had prattled on and on about her visit to Robson's castle the day before. Who cared about a limestone monstrosity in the middle of the prairie where all the folks who considered themselves high society could go to put on airs? Morning Fawn had escaped the stuffy carriage as soon as they arrived at the church.

"Beth, hurry along." Aunt Judith adjusted her fox stole across her shoulders as she turned toward the clapboard building. Her broad-rimmed bonnet with lace trim did little to hide her displeasure. "We're going to be late."

"Never mind her." Cousin Thea smoothed her flounced wool skirt after its crunch through the narrow carriage door. "If Beth wants to stay out here with the servants and the drivers, let her."

"She'll do no such thing." Aunt Judith extended her gloved hand. Morning Fawn grimaced and stepped to her aunt's side, avoiding her clasp. The woman's touch was as far from comfort as a prickly pear.

Nothing like Morning Fawn's *pia*, her adopted Comanche mother. Would she ever see her again? For nine years, Morning Fawn had lived with the Comanche only to be ripped from her home and family by two-bit ruffians her uncle had hired to kidnap her. *Rescued*. That's what they called it. Destroying her life was more like it.

Thea tossed her head with a familiar scowl marring her otherwise pale, smooth complexion. Ringlets of auburn hair jiggled beneath her high-brim bonnet. "Cousin Beth has the manners of a fishmonger," she muttered and waved to the middle-aged man at the hitching post. "Mr. Henry?"

Mr. Henry handed his reins to his slave and tipped his stovepipe hat, revealing graying temples and a receding hairline. "Good morning, Miss LeBeau, Mrs. Lebeau...Miss Logan."

Morning Fawn turned away as Thea curled an arm around the portly man's bulging sleeve. Let her cousin set her cap at a man twice her age. There was no light in their eyes when they looked at each other. Nothing like the glow between Morning Fawn's sister, Eyes-Like-Sky, and Dancing Eagle. That was love, regardless of her sister's marriage to a soldier after Dancing Eagle's death. A love she, herself, had never known.

Thea gushed as Mr. Henry guided her past. "Thank goodness, there's still a few men around these parts to look after us women folk."

Any man worth his snuff was out fighting. Not that Morning Fawn agreed with these Texans and their Confederacy, but if there was fighting to be done, a man did it. He didn't hide behind his servants and his acres of cotton. And he didn't ruin someone's life for three hundred dollars, like the blue-eyed, dark-haired weasel warrior who had helped kidnap her from the Comanche and thwarted her best escape attempt. She clenched her hands.

"Please try to behave yourself," her aunt whispered at her side.

"Don't I always?"

"Most certainly not. We're going to Cedar Crest plantation after church. Mrs. Brown has invited us for tea and dinner." Worry lines across her brow and at the corners of her mouth deepened. "Try not to slurp your tea, and if you're not for sure which fork to use, follow my lead. A young lady is judged by her manners."

Morning Fawn rolled her eyes. "In East Texas, women are judged by nothing that matters." She jutted out her chin. "I can ride faster and hunt better than any woman in this county."

"You're not on the frontier anymore. Hunting won't—"

"I wish I was."

"Excuse me, young lady." Judith bit off her words. "You interrupted me. I was about to say that hunting won't get you a husband. That you need—"

"Last thing I need." Beth gathered her bothersome skirt and marched ahead, sidestepping two little boys playing jacks in the middle of the pathway.

She wanted nothing to do with citified men. Three years ago, Two Feathers had been her intended. She'd collapsed in the village circle when his fellow warriors had returned from a raid with only his shield and spear. Besides, she'd had more than her share of lectures from her aunt on proper behavior. Better to sit in church and hear the preacher than to listen to another dose of her aunt's disapproval.

Despite the wool stockings, her rock-hard leather shoes pinched her feet, rubbing her big toe raw. She was going to find a way to go hunting, kill a deer, and make her a pair of moccasins and leggings. She'd learned to pick the lock on her door. It was just a matter of getting access to a shotgun.

But it'd be simpler to persuade Mr. Sam Dauber, the new captain in charge of the cotton depot in Alleyton, to take her hunting. She'd seen the way he looked at her, and the way her uncle's jaw had clenched when she'd flirted openly with the man at dinner the other night. There was more than one way to show her uncle he couldn't control her.

Flirting was one thing. Finding a way to use Dauber's resources for an escape was another. Seventeen months since her kidnapping, and she'd failed to make it back to her Nokoni Comanche home. Even if she found a way to return, it would never be the same. She wasn't the same. What if she didn't belong anymore?

Head down, as though buffeting a wind, she clomped up the wooden steps and past an elderly gentleman at the door. The whispers and stares of the congregants, muted now compared to the roar they had been months earlier, trailed behind her.

"'Amazing grace, how sweet the sound...'" played from the piano as Morning Fawn walked down the aisle, past the pews of families of storekeepers, tradesmen, and overseers. Only a couple able-bodied men under fifty sat among them. She slowed near the front row of padded seats where the planter-class families sat and entered the LeBeau pew. As if one needed a special pew or four stuffy walls to worship the creator. It was show, all show, except for the way the preacher's eyes lit up when he spoke, and a few of the voices from the back which usually sang out with gusto.

"'Amazing grace...'" It had been her settler mother's favorite song. How did she know that? She couldn't remember her mother's face aside from the portrait in LeBeau's library, but she recalled the song. Her throat tightened as she shuffled to the far end of the pew. She would not think of her mother.

Face frozen in a scold, Aunt Judith pulled in alongside her, taking a seat almost a foot away. Cousin Thea, Mr. Henry, and Aunt Clarey followed close by, leaving Morning Fawn hemmed in between them and the wall on the other side of her. Stupid mistake to bolt ahead and be the first one in. Her heartbeat thrummed in her head.

Dressed in a dark suit and a white cravat, the slender preacher with spectacles stepped up to the pulpit. The music stopped. Thank God. Hungry for air, Beth trained her eyes ahead and swished her fan. Couldn't they open a window in this place?

The preacher's voice rose and fell as he read a few verses. *God help me.* Did He listen? Did He care? A portly woman whose girth dominated the piano bench struck the chords of a hymn on the ivory keys.

The congregation stood. Beth followed suit, gripping the back of the pew in front of her. Then came "Amazing Grace." The first time had only been the prelude. They'd sing all the verses this time. "'I once was lost...'"

A snippet of memory. Her mother brushing her hair. Morning Fawn squeezed her eyes shut and tried to swallow, but the acid stuck in her throat. Her mother. *Oh, Lord...*

The spells, which had started shortly after she'd come to the Comanche and often struck at night, had dissipated after a couple of years. Shortness of breath, shivers, waking dreams. Her Comanche pia had wrapped Morning Fawn in her arms and held her until the terrors faded. However, they'd returned full force since her arrival at the LeBeau plantation, the last home her family had stayed at before they'd headed for the Texas frontier and their deaths—except now, there was no one to hold her.

"'I once was blind, but now I see...'" She had to think of something else. The bronze and golden leaves of the pecan and cottonwood trees along the creek on the way here. Had she finished pealing the apples in the basket this morning on the back porch? How many apples were there? But when she started to count them in her head, they turned red, red like blood. The brown reed basket turned red too.

The song finished, and the congregation sat. She did not. Her aunt nudged her arm with a knuckle, nodding toward the pew.

Sweat beaded on Morning Fawn's temples. Sitting with her mama by the campfire, the last calm moment before the night exploded with nerve-piercing howls, warriors charging, and shrieks. Blood red. The fire and screams. The neighing of horses. Too many horses. She mumbled, "I need to be excused" and squeezed out past half a dozen legs, trampling a shoe in the process.

Mr. Henry jumped to his feet to make room. Heads turned.

Morning Fawn kept going. Couldn't she go to the privy without causing a commotion? But the privy wasn't what she was aiming for. Out the door and down the steps, she willed her legs to take one step at a time until she'd made it around the front to the side of the church, away from the curious eyes of the drivers by the hitching posts.

Her head pounded. She had to get away. From the past. From everything.

Stumbling on a root, she bent down and yanked the deplorable shoes off of her feet. Ahead, Mr. Franklin's chestnut Thoroughbred horse nibbled on grass, no owner in sight. She'd heard rumors it could beat any horse in the county.

A thought sizzled through her. Freedom. She broke into a run, her skirt flapping against her legs. Pebbles dug into her stocking feet. No walls. No people. Escape. She yanked the lead rope from the rail and grabbed the reins.

The horse snorted as Morning Fawn latched on to the pommel, stuck a foot in the stirrup, and heaved herself onto the saddle.

"Miss Logan—" A man came around the corner.

Morning Fawn snapped the reins and pressed her calves to the horse's side. The chestnut quickened from a trot to a lope past the weathered fence and down the hill. Horse hoofs tore through dried grass and onto the packed dirt road.

Wind whipped the hat from her head, and her hair unfurled as they galloped past stubby brown picked-over fields, empty of cotton. The blood red faded, along with the screams.

Someone yelled behind her in the distance.

No. She would not, could not stop. She'd never get free. If they caught her, they'd lock her up.

When she'd first arrived at her uncle's plantation, they'd promised to let her eat once she took off her buckskin garments. She'd gone hungry instead. When they'd finally offered food, she should have suspected something. Instead, she'd gobbled down the dinner and promptly fell into a deep sleep, drugged. Her Comanche clothes were gone when she awoke, along with everything she owned.

She'd been livid. If she'd had her knife, she would have sliced LeBeau. Instead, he'd had his men carry her to the attic, throw her on a mattress, and lock the door on their way out. She'd spent a month there. And he'd threatened to send her to an asylum if she tried to run away again or refused to listen to their lessons on how to be civilized. Her uncle wanted a porcelain doll, not a niece with a mind of her own.

The stink of manure assaulted her nose as she rode past a hog farm.

The horse's muscles churned beneath Morning Fawn. She tightened her grip on the reins, digging her nails into her palms.

A slave boy, fishing pole across his shoulder, jumped out of her way as she swerved her mount around a corner. Trees. She needed the cover of trees. A jerk of reins, and her mount left the road, pounding down the hill toward the creek. Scatterings of cottonwood, pecan, and mesquite populated the banks.

They plunged through the gurgling water and up the other side. She dodged a limb and bent down over the horse's withers, her nose inches from the tousled mane. It didn't matter where she was going. Anywhere was better than here. After her third failed attempt, she'd played it safe too long, waiting for a perfect plan. No more.

Want more?

If you love historical romance, check out the other Wild Heart books!

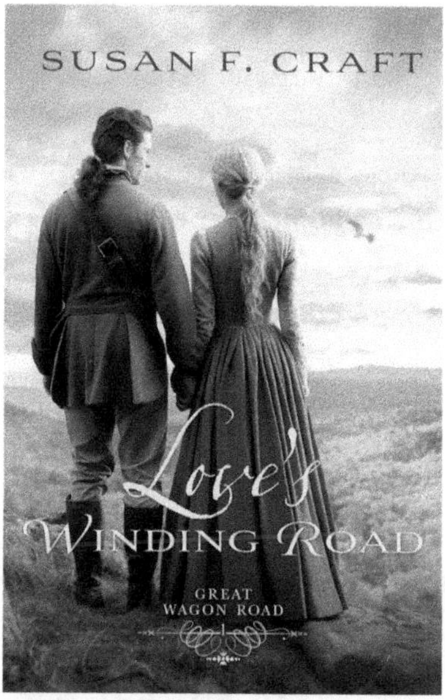

Love's Winding Road by Susan F. Craft

They were forced into this marriage of convenience, but there's more at stake than their hearts on this wagon train through the mountain wilderness.

When Rose Jackson and her Irish immigrant family join a wagon train headed for a new life in South Carolina, the last thing she expects is to fall for the half-Cherokee wagon scout along the way. But their journey takes a life-changing turn when Rose is kidnapped by Indians. Daniel comes to her rescue, but the effects mean their lives will be forever intertwined.

Daniel prides himself on his self-control—inner and outer—but can't seem to get a handle on either when Rose is near. Now his life is bound to hers when the consequences of her rescue force them to marry. Now it's even more critical he maintain that self-control to keep her safe.

When tragedy strikes at the heart of their strained marriage, they leave for Daniel's home in the Blue Ridge Mountains. As they face the perils of the journey, Rose can't help but wonder why her new husband guards his heart so strongly. Why does he resist his obvious attraction for her? And what life awaits them at the end of love's winding road?